BEEN THERE?
DONE THAT?
NO WAY!

WELCOME TO TOMORROW, A REALM OF INFINITE POSSIBILITIES, WHERE—

- ▲ A boy and his dino have fun on a killing spree
- ▲ *Software* means falling in love with an icon
- ▲ Lonesome cowboys ride the English moors
- ▲ Piracy is the First Protocol of interstellar contact
- ▲ The Moon sprouts repulsive new life forms
- ▲ Emotions are put on—and taken off—like clothes
- ▲ Killer melons attack in a bio-tech war
- ▲ The written word is not only obsolete but forbidden
- ▲ A doctor gets the opportunity to kill Death itself

THE FUTURE IS BACK
in the

Year's Best SF 3

Edited by David G. Hartwell

Year's Best SF
Year's Best SF 2
Year's Best SF 3

Published by HarperPrism

Year's Best SF 3

EDITED BY

David G. Hartwell

HarperPrism

A Division of HarperCollinsPublishers

RP

HarperPrism
A Division of HarperCollins*Publishers*
10 East 53rd Street, New York, NY 10022-5299

These are works of fiction. The characters, incidents, and
dialogues are products of the authors' imagination and are not to
be construed as real. Any resemblance to actual events or
persons, living or dead, is entirely coincidental.

Individual story copyrights appear on page 449–50.
Copyright © 1998 by David G. Hartwell

For information address HarperCollins Publishers, Inc.,
10 East 53rd Street, New York, NY 10022-5299

ISBN 0-06-105901-3

Cover illustration © 1998 by Chris Moore

First printing: June 1998

Printed in the United States of America

Visit HarperPrism on the World Wide Web at
http://www.harperprism.com

❖ 10 9 8 7 6 5 4 3 2 1

To Everett Bleiler and T. E. Dikty, who invented Year's Best volumes in SF; and

To Judith Merril, who died in 1997 and who showed what really could be accomplished in a Year's Best with a strong and coherent aesthetic; and

To Peter Henry Cramer Hartwell, who was born October 17, 1997, just because.

Acknowledgments

The existence of *Locus* and *Tangents* makes doing an annual anthology easier and I thank them both for their devotion to considering the short fiction published each year in the SF field. I am grateful to the publishers of the SF magazines for continuing the uphill battle to stay in business and publish fiction in 1997.

Table of Contents

Introduction

First, my annual clarification: this selection of science fiction stories represents the best that was published during the year 1997. In my opinion I could perhaps have filled two more volumes this size and then claimed to have nearly all of the best—though not all the best novellas.

Second, the general criteria: this book is full of science fiction—every story in the book is clearly that and not something else. I personally have a high regard for horror, fantasy, speculative fiction, and slipstream and postmodern literature. But here, I chose science fiction. It is the intention of this year's best series to focus entirely on science fiction, and to provide readers who are looking especially for science fiction an annual home base.

And now for 1997.

All the trends mentioned in last year's introduction continued in 1997: the magazines continued to lose circulation but still publish the lion's share of the best stories in the SF field; original anthologies remained mediocre, with honorable exceptions that gathered stories often better than all but the best magazine stories. I'll discuss some of them below. And the best stories were most often short, novelettes or shorts according to Hugo or Nebula Award rules (just plain short stories according to the standards of non-genre literature). 1997 was not a great year for novellas.

SF Age emerged as a leader among the magazines for high quality science fiction, though *Asimov's* and *Fantasy & Science Fiction* and *Interzone* continued strong. It was a particularly good year for *Asimov's,* and there were a number of talented new writers in *Interzone.* There were some consolidations in the publishing industry, some cutbacks in paperbacks, but they were offset by an extraordinary increase in the number of trade paperback titles. 1997 was the year of the trade paperback in SF, with Del Rey alone issuing fifty or more titles of its extensive fantasy and SF backlist in trade paperback.

I have several hot tips for readers. You may well have missed three of the best (maybe three of the four year's best—the only other leading contender is Linaweaver & Kramer's *Free Space,* which was reviewed widely and attracted many Nebula story nominations) original science fiction anthologies of the year: *Decalog 5, New Worlds,* and *Future Histories.* All of these books appeared unexpectedly and without advance warning and I only saw them at first by accident. They helped make it a particularly good year for anthologies in general.

Decalog 5 is the fifth in a series and is suddenly distinguished (after four previous volumes that were not— the first two were filled with unmemorable *Dr. Who* stories!). This one, however, has originals by Stephen Baxter, Dominic Green, Ian Watson, and others, all set in the far future. A good book in any year. Editor David Garnett's latest *New Worlds* appeared as a trade paperback original from White Wolf with no fanfare and is in my opinion the best original anthology of the year, including new stories by William Gibson, Michael Moorcock, Brian Aldiss, Kim Newman, Ian Watson, and many others—some SF, some speculative fiction, as you would expect. If there is such a thing as good old fashioned *New Worlds* at its best, this it it. Editor Stephen McClelland's *Future Histories* is a trade paperback published in the UK (only?) by Horizon House and Nokia, full of original stories by such writers as Nancy Kress, Gregory Benford, Pat Cadigan, Stephen Baxter, Pat Murphy, Brian Stableford (and interviews with Sterling, Bear, Gibson, Stephenson, Vernor Vinge, Alexander Besher, and others). The theme is "Twenty Tomorrows for Communications"—a corporate anthology, by golly, but done extremely well.

There was the usual, sad to say, glut of mediocre original anthologies, many with one or two good stories, but most a bit below the acceptable level for the professional magazines. The same level maintained for the semiprofessional magazines in 1997, though the good story balance there was a higher percentage than in the anthologies.

On the whole, it was another year in which there were in the end more than fifty, perhaps a hundred, really good SF stories published, certainly enough to fill several Year's Best volumes, providing me with a rich diversity of selection for this one.

Comments on thematic trends in the literature I have saved for the notes to the stories, that follow immediately. Let's get to them now.

—David G. Hartwell

Petting Zoo

GENE WOLFE

Gene Wolfe's body of work over the years is a challenge and a delight to serious readers of science fiction. This year, as in the past, there were several fine Wolfe stories to choose from for this volume, but this one, published in a paperback original anthology of lightweight pieces on the theme, *Return of the Dinosaurs,* seemed to me just the thing to lead off a Year's Best volume, in a year when dinosaurs on film and TV are in vogue. There has been a fair amount of disagreement in recent years as to what makes a good SF story and in what way such characteristics as plot and action, character or idea ought or ought not to be central to the enterprise of science fiction story-telling. In my opinion, each good story implicitly makes its own statement and influences the argument it its own favor. And so the literature evolves. This is a cracking good story with subtle, and some quite clear, implications. But never mind that for now; read this slick, fast piece for fun and surprises and then stop and think afterward: what might it mean if the dinosaurs came back as Barney?

Roderick looked up at the sky. It was indeed blue, but almost cloudless. The air was hot and smelled of dust.

"Here, children . . ." The teaching cyborg was pointedly not addressing him. "—Tyranosaurus Rex. Rex was created by an inadequately socialized boy who employed six Build-a-Critter kits . . ."

Sixteen.

"—which he duped on his father's Copystuff. With that quantity of GroQik . . ."

It had taken a day over two weeks, two truckloads of pigs that he had charged to Mother's account, and various other things that had become vague. For the last week, he had let Rex go out at night to see what he could find, and people would—people were bound to—notice the missing cattle soon. Had probably noticed them already.

Rex had looked out through the barn window while he was mooring his airbike and said, "I'm tired of hiding all day."

And he himself had said . . .

"Let's go for a ride." One of the little girls had raised her hand.

From the other side of the token barrier that confined him, Rex himself spoke for the first time, saying, "You will, kid. She's not quite through yet." His voice was a sort of growling tenor now, clearly forced upward as high as he could make it so as to seem less threatening. Roderick pushed on his suit's A-C and shivered a little.

It had been cool, that day. Cool, with a little breeze he had fought the whole way over, keeping his airbike below the treetops and following groundtrucks when he could, pulled along by their wake.

Cold in the barn, then—cold and dusty—dust motes dancing in the sunbeams that stabbed between its old, bent, and battered aluminum panels.

Rex had crouched as he had before, but he was bigger now, bigger than ever, and his smooth reptilian skin had felt like glass, like ice under which oiled muscles stirred like snakes. He had fallen, and Rex had picked him up in the arms that looked so tiny on Rex but were bigger and stronger than a big man's arms, saying, "That's what these are for," and set him on Rex's shoulders with his legs—*his* legs—trying to wrap around Rex's thick, throbbing neck . . .

He had opened the big doors from inside, gone out almost crawling, and stood up.

It had not been the height. He had been higher on his airbike almost every day. It had not been his swift, swaying progress above the treetops—treetops arrayed in red, gold, and green so that it seemed that he followed Rex's floating head over a lawn deep in fallen leaves.

It had been—

He shrugged the thought away. There were no adequate words. Power? You bought it at a drugstore, a shiny little disk that would run your house-bot for three or four more years, or your drill forever. Mastery? It was what people had held over dogs while private ownership had still been legal.

Dogs had four fangs in front, and that was it, fangs so small they did not even look dangerous. Rex had a mouthful, every one as long as Roderick's arm, in a mouth that could have chewed up an aircar.

No, it had not been the height. He had ridden over woods—this wood among them—often. Had ridden higher than this, yet heard the rustling of the leaves below him, the sound of a brook, an invisible brook of air. It had been the noise.

That was not right either, but it was closer than the

others. It had been the snapping of the limbs and the crashing of the trees falling, or at least that had been a lot of it—the sound of their progress, the shattering, splintering wood. In part, at least, it had been the noise.

"He did a great deal of damage," the teaching cyborg was saying, as her female attendant nodded confirmation. "Much worse, he terrified literally hundreds of persons. . . ."

Sitting on Rex's shoulders, he had been able to talk almost directly into Rex's ear. "Roar."

And Rex had roared to shake the earth.

"Keep on roaring."

And Rex had.

The red and white cattle Rex ate sometimes, so short-legged they could scarcely move, had run away slowly only because they were too fat to run any faster, and one had gotten stepped on. People had run too, and Rex had kicked over a little pre-fab shed for the fun of it, and a tractor-bot. He'd waded hip-deep through the swamp without even slowing down and had forded the river. There were fewer building restrictions on the north side of the river, and the people there had really run.

Had run except for one old man with a bushy mustache, who had only stood and stared pop-eyed, too old to run, Roderick thought, or maybe too scared. He had looked down at the old man and waved; and their eyes had met, and suddenly—just as if the top of the old man's head had popped up so he could look around inside it—he had known what the old man was thinking.

Not guessed, known.

And the old man had been thinking that when he had been Roderick's age he had wanted to do exactly what Roderick was doing now. He had never been able to, and had never thought anybody would be. But somebody was. That kid up there in the polka-dot shirt was. So he, the old man, had been wrong about the whole world all his life. It was much more wonderful, this old world, than he, the old man, had ever supposed. So maybe there was hope after all. Some kind of a hope anyhow, in a world where things like this could go on, on a Monday right here in Libertyberg.

Before the old man could draw his breath to cheer, he had been gone, and there had been woods and cornfields. (Roderick's suit A-C shuddered and quit.) And after lots of corn, some kind of a big factory. Rex had stepped on its fence which sputtered and shot sparks without doing anything much, and then the aircar had started diving at them.

It had been red and fast, and Roderick remembered it as clearly as if he had seen it yesterday. It would dive, trying to hit Rex's head, and then the override would say, *My gosh, that's a great big dinosaur! You're trying to crash us into a great big dinosaur, you jerk!* The override would pull the aircar up and miss, and then it would give it back to the driver, and he would try the same thing all over.

Roderick had followed it with his eyes, especially after Rex started snapping at it, and the sky had been a wonderful cool blue with little white surgical-ball clouds strolling around in it. He had never seen a better sky—and he never would, because skies did not get any better than that one. After a while he had spotted the channel copter flying around up there and taking his picture to run on everybody's threedeevid, and had made faces at it.

Another child, a scrubbed little girl with long, straight privileged-looking yellow hair had her hand up. "Did he kill a whole lot of people?"

The teaching cyborg interrupted her own lecture. "Certainly not, since there were no people in North America during the Upper Cretaceous. Human evolution did not begin—"

"This one." The scrubbed little girl pointed to Rex. "Did he?"

Rex shook his head.

"That was not the point at issue," the teaching cyborg explained. "Disruption is disrupting, and he and his maker disrupted. He disrupted, I should say, and his maker still more, since Rex would not have been in existence to disrupt had he not been made in violation of societal standards. No one of sensitivity would have done what he did. Someone of sensitivity would have realized at once that their construction of a large dinosaur, however muted in coloration—"

Rex interrupted her. "I'm purple. It's just that it's gotten sort of dull lookin' now that I'm older. Looky here." He bent and slapped at his water trough with his disproportionately small hands. Dust ran from his hide in dark streaks, leaving it a faded mulberry.

"You are not purple," the teaching cyborg admonished Rex, "and you should not say you are. I would describe that shade as a mauve." She spoke to her female attendant. "Do you think that they would mind very much if I were to start over? I've lost my place, I fear."

"You mustn't interrupt her," the female attendant cautioned the little girl. "Early-Tertiary-in-the-Upper-Eocene-was-the-Moeritherium-the-size-of-a-tuber-but-more-like-a-hippopotamus."

"Yum," Rex mumbled. "Yum-yum!"

A small boy waved his hand wildly. "What do you feed him?"

"Tofu, mostly. It's good for him." The teaching cyborg looked at Rex as she spoke, clearly displeased at his thriving upon tofu. "He eats an airtruckload of it every day. Also a great deal of soy protein and bean curd."

"I'd like to eat the hippos," Rex told the small boy. "We go right past them every time I take you kids for ride, and wow! Do they ever look yummy!"

"He's only joking," the teaching cyborg told the children. She caught her female attendant's left arm and held it up to see her watch. "I have a great deal more to tell you, children, but I'll have to do it while we're taking our ride, or we'll fall behind schedule."

She and her female attendant opened the gate to Rex's

compound and went in, preceded, accompanied, and followed by small girls and boys. While most of the children gathered around him, stroking his rough thick hide with tentative fingers, the teaching cyborg and her female attendant wrestled a stepladder and a very large howdah of white pentastyrene Wickedwicker from behind Rex's sleeping shed. For five minutes or more they struggled to hook the howdah over his shoulders and fasten the Velcro cinch, obstructed by the well-intended assistance of four little boys.

Roderick joined them, lifted the howdah into place, and released and refastened the cinch—getting it tight enough that the howdah could not slip to one side.

"Thank you," the female attendant said. "Haven't I seen you here before?"

Roderick shook his head. "It's the first time I've ever come."

"Well, a lot of men do. I mean it's always just one man all by himself, but there's almost always one."

"He used to lie down so that we could put it on him," the teaching cyborg said severely, "and lie down again so that the children didn't have to use the ladder. Now he just sits."

"I'm too fat," Rex muttered. "It's all that good tofu I get."

One by one, the children climbed the ladder. The teaching cyborg's female attendant was standing beside it to catch each if he or she fell, cautioning each to grasp the railings, and urging each to belt himself or herself in once he or she had chosen a seat. The teaching cyborg and her female attendant boarded last of all. The teaching cyborg resumed her lecture, and Rex stood up with a groan and began yet again the slow walk around the zoo that he took a dozen times a day.

It had been a fall day, Roderick reminded himself, a fall day bright and clear, a more beautiful day than days ever were now. A stiff, bright wind had been blowing right through all the sunshine. He had worn jeans, a Peoria White Sox cap, and a polka-dot shirt. He had kept his airbike low where the wind wasn't quite so strong, had climbed on Rex's shoulders, and watched as Rex had taken down the bar that held the big doors shut. . . .

"Now," the teaching cyborg said, "are there any additional questions?" Roderick looked up just in time to see the corner of the white Wickedwicker howdah vanish behind Rex's sleeping shed.

"Yes." He raised his hand. "What became of the boy?"

"The government assumed responsibility for his nurturing and upbringing," the teaching cyborg explained. "He received sensitivity training and reeducation in societal values and has become a responsible citizen."

When the teaching cyborg, her female attendant, and all the children had gone, Rex said, "You know, I always wondered what happened to you."

Roderick mopped his perspiring forehead. "You knew who I was all the time, huh?"

"Sure."

There was a silence. Far away, as if from another time or another world, children spoke in excited voices and a lion roared. "Nothing happened to me," Roderick said; it was clearly necessary to say something. "I grew up, that's all."

"Those reeducation machines, they really burn it into you. That's what I heard."

"No, I grew up. That's all."

"I see. Can I ask why you keep lookin' at me like that?"

"I was just thinking."

"Thinkin' what?"

"Nothing." With iron fists, stone shoulders, and steel-shod feet, words broke down the doors of his heart and forced their way into his mouth. "Your kind used to rule the Earth."

"Yeah." Rex nodded. He turned away, leaving for Roderick his serpentine tail and wide, ridged back—both the color of a grape skin that has been chewed up and spit out into the dust. "Yeah," he mumbled. "You, too."

The Wisdom of Old Earth

MICHAEL SWANWICK

Michael Swanwick had a big year in 1997, what with the publication of his new novel, *Jack Faust,* that had weekly advertisements in *The New Yorker* for a while, and the appearance of his second short story collection, *A Geography of Unknown Lands,* in trade paperback from Tigereyes Press, a small press in Pennsylvania. Tachyon Press also published a small volume of his essays on SF and fantasy. A significant portion of his fiction in recent years has been fantasy but here he returns to science fiction and at the top of his form. He calls this his Jack London story. It continues the trend noted last year of SF writers today looking back to early writers, particularly one such as London who also wrote good SF, and stealing their thunder. It certainly is tough and violent, but like the Wolfe story, has some implications that stimulate thought a good while after the first reading. It appeared in *Asimov's* and is only the first of several in this book from that magazine, which seemed to me to publish a slightly higher percentage of SF, as opposed to fantasy of various sorts, this past year.

Judith Seize-the-Day was, quite simply, the best of her kind. Many another had aspired to the clarity of posthuman thought, and several might claim some rude mastery of its essentials, but she alone came to understand it as completely as any offworlder.

Such understanding did not come easily. The human mind is slow to generalize and even slower to integrate. It lacks the quicksilver apprehension of the posthuman. The simplest truth must be repeated often to imprint even the most primitive understanding of what comes naturally and without effort to the space-faring children of humanity. Judith had grown up in Pole Star City, where the shuttles slant down through the zone of permanent depletion in order to avoid further damage to the fragile ozone layer, and thus from childhood had associated extensively with the highly evolved. It was only natural that as a woman she would elect to turn her back on her own brutish kind and strive to bootstrap herself into a higher order.

Yet even then she was like an ape trying to pass as a philosopher. For all her laborious ponderings, she did not yet comprehend the core wisdom of posthumanity, which was that thought and action must be as one. Being a human, however, when she did comprehend, she understood it more deeply and thoroughly than the posthumans themselves. As a Canadian, she could tap into the ancient and chthonic wisdoms of her race. Where her thought went, the civilized mind could not follow.

It would be expecting too much of such a woman that she would entirely hide her contempt for her own kind. She cursed the two trollish Ninglanders who were sweating and chopping a way through the lush tangles of kudzu, and drove them onward with the lash of her tongue.

"Unevolved bastard pigs!" she spat. "Inbred degenerates! If you ever want to get home to molest your dogs and baby sisters again, you'll put your backs into it!"

The larger of the creatures looked back at her with an angry gleam in his eye, and his knuckles whitened on the hilt of his machete. She only grinned humorlessly, and patted the holster of her *ankh*. Such weapons were rarely allowed humans. Her possession of it was a mark of the great respect in which she was held.

The brute returned to his labor.

It was deepest winter, and the jungle tracts of what had once been the mid-Atlantic coastlands were traversable. Traversable, that is, if one had a good guide. Judith was among the best. She had brought her party alive to the Flying Hills of southern Pennsylvania, and not many could have done that. Her client had come in search of the fabled bell of liberty, which many another party had sought in vain. She did not believe he would find it either. But that did not concern her.

All that concerned her was their survival.

So she cursed and drove the savage Ninglanders before her, until all at once they broke through the vines and brush out of shadow and into a clearing.

All three stood unmoving for an instant, staring out over the clumps and hillocks of grass that covered the foundations of what had once been factories, perhaps, or workers' housing, gasoline distribution stations, grist mills, shopping malls. . . . Even the skyline was uneven. Mystery beckoned from every ambiguous lump.

It was almost noon. They had been walking since sundown.

Judith slipped on her goggles and scanned the gray skies for navigation satellites. She found three radar beacons within range. A utility accepted their input and calculated her position: less than a hundred miles from Philadelphia. They'd made more distance than she'd expected. The empathic function mapped for her the locations of her party: three, including herself, then one, then two, then one, strung over a mile and a half of trail. That was wrong.

Very wrong indeed.

"Pop the tents," she ordered, letting the goggles fall around her neck. "Stay out of the food."

The Ninglanders dropped their packs. One lifted a refrigeration stick over his head like a spear and slammed it into the ground. A wash of cool air swept over them all. His lips curled with pleasure, revealing broken yellow teeth.

She knew that if she lingered, she would not be able to face the oppressive jungle heat again. So, turning, Judith strode back the way she'd come. Rats scattered at her approach, disappearing into hot green shadow.

The first of her party she encountered was Harry Work-to-Death. His face was pale and he shivered uncontrollably. But he kept walking, because to stop was to die. They passed each other without a word. Judith doubted he would live out the trip. He had picked up something after their disastrous spill in the Hudson. There were opiates enough in what survived of the medical kit to put him out of his misery, but she did not make him the offer.

She could not bring herself to.

Half a mile later came Leeza Child-of-Scorn and Maria Triumph-of-the-Will, chattering and laughing together. They stopped when they saw her. Judith raised her *ankh* in the air, and shook it so that they could feel its aura scrape ever so lightly against their nervous systems.

"Where is the offworlder?" The women shrank from her anger. "You abandoned him. You *dared*. Did you think you could get away with it? You were fools if you did!"

Wheedlingly, Leeza said, "The sky man knew he was endangering the rest of us, so he asked to be left behind." She and Maria were full-blooded Canadians, like Judith, free of the taint of Southern genes. They had been hired for their intelligence, and intelligence they had—a low sort of animal cunning that made them dangerously unreliable when the going got hard. "He insisted."

"It was very noble of him," Maria said piously.

"I'll give you something to be noble about if you don't turn around and lead me back to where you left him." She holstered her *ankh,* but did not lock it down. "Now!" With blows of her fists, she forced them down the trail. Judith was short, stocky, all muscle. She drove them before her like the curs that they were.

The offworlder lay in the weeds where he had been dropped, one leg twisted at an odd angle. The litter that Judith had lashed together for him had been flung into the bushes.

His clothes were bedraggled, and the netting had pulled away from his collar. But weak as he was, he smiled to see her. "I knew you would return for me." His hands fluttered up in a gesture indicating absolute confidence. "So I was careful to avoid moving. The fracture will have to be reset. But that's well within your capabilities, I'm sure."

"I haven't lost a client yet." Judith unlaced his splint and carefully straightened the leg. Posthumans, spending so much of their time in microgravity environments, were significantly less robust than their ancestral stock. Their bones broke easily. Yet when she reset the femur and tied up the splint again with lengths of nylon cord, he didn't make a sound. His kind had conscious control over their endorphin production. Judith checked his neck for ticks and chiggers, then tucked in his netting. "Be more careful with this. There are a lot of ugly diseases loose out here."

"My immune system is stronger than you'd suspect. If the rest of me were as strong, I wouldn't be holding you back like this."

As a rule, she liked the posthuman women better than their men. The men were hothouse flowers—flighty, elliptical, full of fancies and elaboration. Their beauty was the beauty of a statue; all sculptured features and chill affect. The offworlder, however, was not like that. His look was direct. He was as solid and straightforward as a woman.

"While I was lying here, I almost prayed for a rescue party."

To God, she thought he meant. Then saw how his eyes lifted briefly, involuntarily, to the clouds and the satellites beyond. Much that for humans required machines, a posthuman could accomplish with precisely tailored neural implants.

"They would've turned you down." This Judith knew for a fact. Her mother, Ellen To-the-Manner-Born, had died in the jungles of Wisconsin, eaten away with gangrene and cursing the wardens over an open circuit.

"Yes, of course, one life is nothing compared to the health of the planet." His mouth twisted wryly. "Yet still, I confess I was tempted."

"Put him back in the litter," she told the women. "Carry him gently." In the Québecois dialect, which she was certain her client did not know, she added, "Do this again, and I'll kill you."

She lagged behind, letting the others advance out of sight, so she could think. In theory she could simply keep the party together. In practice, the women could not both carry the offworlder and keep up with the men. And if she did not stay with the Ninglanders, they would not work. There were only so many days of winter left. Speed was essential.

An unexpected peal of laughter floated back to her, then silence.

Wearily, she trudged on. Already they had forgotten her, and her *ankh*. Almost she could envy them. Her responsibilities weighed heavily upon her. She had not laughed since the Hudson.

According to her goggles, there was a supply cache in Philadelphia. Once there, they could go back on full rations again.

The tents were bright mushrooms in the clearing. Work-to-Death lay dying within one of them. The women had gone off with the men into the bush. Even in this ungodly heat and humidity, they were unable or unwilling to curb their bestial lusts.

Judith sat outside with the offworlder, the refrigeration stick turned up just enough to take the edge off the afternoon heat. To get him talking, she asked, "Why did you come to Earth? There is nothing here worth all your suffering. Were I you, I'd've turned back long ago."

For a long moment, the offworlder struggled to gear down his complex thoughts into terms Judith could comprehend. At last he said, "Consider evolution. Things do not evolve from lower states to higher, as the ancients believed, with their charts that began with a fish crawling up upon the land and progressed on to mammals, apes, Neanderthals, and finally men. Rather, an organism evolves to fit its environment. An ape cannot live in the ocean. A human cannot brachiate. Each thrives in its own niche.

"Now consider posthumanity. Our environment is entirely artificial—floating cities, the Martian subsurface, the Venusian and Jovian bubbles. Such habitats require social integration of a high order. A human could survive within them, possibly, but she would not thrive. Our surround is self-defined, and therefore within it we are the pinnacle of evolution."

As he spoke, his hands twitched with the suppressed urge to amplify and clarify his words with the secondary emotive language offworlders employed in parallel with the spoken. Thinking, of course, that she did not savvy hand-sign. But as her facility with it was minimal, Judith did not enlighten him.

"Now imagine a being with more-than-human strength and greater-than-posthuman intellect. Such a creature would be at a disadvantage in the posthuman environment. She would be an evolutionary dead end. How then could she get any sense of herself, what she could do, and what she could not?"

"How does all apply to you personally?"

"I wanted to find the measure of myself, not as a product of an environment that caters to my strengths and coddles my weaknesses. I wanted to discover what I am in the natural state."

"You won't find the natural state here. We're living in the aftermath."

"No," he agreed. "The natural state is lost, shattered like an eggshell. Even if—when—we finally manage to restore it, gather up all the shards and glue them together, it will no longer be natural, but something we have decided to maintain and preserve, like a garden. It will be only an extension of our culture."

"Nature is dead," Judith said. It was a concept she had picked up from other posthumans.

His teeth flashed with pleasure at her quick apprehension. "Indeed. Even off Earth, where conditions are more extreme, its effects are muted by technology. I suspect that nature can only exist where our all-devouring culture has not yet reached. Still . . . here on Earth, in the regions where all but the simplest technologies are prohibited, and it's still possible to suffer pain and even death. . . . This is as close to an authentic state as can be achieved." He patted the ground by his side. "The past is palpable here, century upon century, and under that the strength of the soil." His hands involuntarily leapt. *This is so difficult*, they said. *This language is so clumsy.* "I am afraid I have not expressed myself very well."

He smiled apologetically then, and she saw how

exhausted he was. But still she could not resist asking, "What is it like, to think as you do?" It was a question that she had asked many times, of many posthumans. Many answers had she received, and no two of them alike.

The offworlder's face grew very still. At last he said, "Lao-tzu put it best. 'The way that can be named is not the true way. The name that can be spoken is not the eternal name.' The higher thought is ineffable, a mystery that can be experienced but never explained."

His arms and shoulders moved in a gesture that was the evolved descendant of a shrug. His weariness was palpable.

"You need rest," she said, and, standing, "let me help you into your tent."

"Dearest Judith. What would I ever do without you?"

Ever so slightly, she flushed.

The next sundown, their maps, though recently downloaded, proved to be incomplete. The improbably named Skookle River had wandered, throwing off swamps that her goggles' topographical functions could not distinguish from solid land. For two nights the party struggled southward, moving far to the west and then back again so many times that Judith would have been entirely lost without the navsats.

Then the rains began.

There was no choice but to leave the offworlder behind. Neither he nor Harry Work-to-Death could travel under such conditions. Judith put Maria and Leeza in charge of them both. After a few choice words of warning, she left them her spare goggles and instructions to break camp and follow as soon as the rains let up.

"Why do you treat us like dogs?" a Ninglander asked her when they were underway again. The rain poured down over his plastic poncho.

"Because you are no better than dogs."

He puffed himself up. "I am large and shapely. I have a fine mustache. I can give you many orgasms."

His comrade was pretending not to listen. But it was obvious to Judith that the two men had a bet going as to whether she could be seduced or not.

"Not without my participation."

Insulted, he thumped his chest. Water droplets flew. "I am as good as any of your Canadian men!"

"Yes," she agreed, "unhappily, that's true."

When the rains finally let up, Judith had just crested a small hillock that her topographics identified as an outlier of the Welsh Mountains. Spread out before her was a broad expanse of overgrown twenty-first-century ruins. She did not bother accessing the city's name. In her experience, all lost cities were alike; she didn't care if she never saw another. "Take ten," she said, and the Ninglanders shrugged out of their packs.

Idly, she donned her goggles to make sure that Leeza and Maria were breaking camp, as they had been instructed to do.

And screamed with rage.

The goggles Judith had left behind had been hung, unused, upon the flap-pole of one of the tents. Though the two women did not know it, it was slaved to hers, and she could spy upon their actions. She kept her goggles on all the way back to their camp.

When she arrived, they were sitting by their refrigeration stick, surrounded by the discarded wrappings of half the party's food and all of its opiates. The stick was turned up so high that the grass about it was white with frost. Already there was an inch of ash at its tip.

Harry Work-to-Death lay on the ground by the women, grinning loopily, face frozen to the stick. Dead.

Outside the circle, only partially visible to the goggles, lay the offworlder, still strapped to his litter. He chuckled and sang to himself. The women had been generous with the drugs.

"Pathetic weakling," Child-of-Scorn said to the off-worlder, "I don't know why you didn't drown in the rain. But I am going to leave you out in the heat until you are dead, and then I am going to piss on your corpse."

"I am not going to wait," Triumph-of-the-Will bragged. She tried to stand and could not. "In just—just a moment!"

The whoops of laughter died as Judith strode into the camp. The Ninglanders stumbled to a halt behind her, and stood looking uncertainly from her to the women and back. In their simple way, they were shocked by what they saw.

Judith went to the offworlder and slapped him hard to get his attention. He gazed up confusedly at the patch she held up before his face.

"This is a detoxifier. It's going to remove those drugs from your system. Unfortunately, as a side effect, it will also depress your endorphin production. I'm afraid this is going to hurt."

She locked it onto his arm, and then said to the Ninglanders, "Take him up the trail. I'll be along."

They obeyed. The offworlder screamed once as the detoxifier took effect, and then fell silent again. Judith turned to the traitors. "You chose to disobey me. Very well. I can use the extra food."

She drew her *ankh*.

Child-of-Scorn clenched her fists angrily. "So could we! Half-rations so your little pet could eat his fill. Work us to death carrying him about. You think I'm *stupid*. I'm not stupid. I know what you want with him."

"He's the client. He pays the bills."

"What are you to him but an ugly little ape? He'd sooner fuck a cow than you!"

Triumph-of-the-Will fell over laughing. "A cow!" she cried. "A fuh-fucking cow! Moo!"

Child-of-Scorn's eyes blazed. "You know what the sky

people call the likes of you and me? Mud-women! Sometimes they come to the cribs outside Pole Star City to get good and dirty. But they always wash off and go back to their nice clean habitats afterward. Five minutes after he climbs back into the sky, he'll have forgotten your name."

"Moooo! Moooo!"

"You cannot make me angry," Judith said, "for you are only animals."

"I am not an animal!" Child-of-Scorn shook her fist at Judith. "I refuse to be treated like one."

"One does not blame an animal for being what it is. But neither does one trust an animal that has proved unreliable. You were given two chances."

"If I'm an animal, then what does that make *you*? Huh? What the fuck does that make *you*, goddamnit?" The woman's face was red with rage. Her friend stared blankly up at her from the ground.

"Animals," Judith said through gritted teeth, "should be killed without emotion."

She fired twice.

With her party thus diminished, Judith could not hope to return to Canada afoot. But there were abundant ruins nearby, and they were a virtual reservoir of chemical poisons from the days when humans ruled the Earth. If she set the *ankh* to its hottest setting, she could start a blaze that would set off a hundred alarms in Pole Star City. The wardens would have to come to contain it. She would be imprisoned, of course, but her client would live.

Then Judith heard the thunder of engines.

High in the sky, a great light appeared, so bright it was haloed with black. She held up a hand to lessen the intensity and saw within the dazzle a small dark speck. A shuttle, falling from orbit.

She ran crashing through the brush as hard and fast as she could. Nightmarish minutes later, she topped a small rise and found the Ninglanders standing there, the offworlder between them. They were watching the shuttle come to a soft landing in the clearing its thrusters had burned in the vegetation.

"You summoned it," she accused the offworlder.

He looked up with tears in his eyes. The detoxifier had left him in a state of pitiless lucidity, with nothing to concentrate on but his own suffering. "I had to, yes." His voice was distant, his attention turned inward, on the neural device that allowed him to communicate with the ship's crew. "The pain—you can't imagine what it's like. How it feels."

A lifetime of lies roared in Judith's ears. Her mother had died for lack of the aid that came at this man's thought.

"I killed two women just now."

"Did you?" He looked away. "I'm sure you had good reasons. I'll have it listed as death by accident." Without his conscious volition, his hands moved, saying, *It's a trivial matter, let it be.*

A hatch opened in the shuttle's side. Slim figures clambered down, white med-kits on their belts. The offworlder smiled through his tears and stretched out welcoming arms to them.

Judith stepped back and into the shadow of his disregard. She was just another native now.

Two women were dead.

And her reasons for killing them mattered to no one.

She threw her head back and laughed, freely and without reserve. In that instant Judith Seize-the-Day was as fully and completely alive as any of the unworldly folk who walk the airless planets and work in the prosperous and incomprehensible habitats of deep space.

In that instant, had any been looking, she would have seemed not human at all.

The Firefly Tree

JACK WILLIAMSON

Jack Williamson is a living legend in science fiction, who has been writing and publishing SF since the 1920s, seven decades now, and it looks very much like he might make it to the eighth. Of all the writers of his era, he is the last to keep writing SF that is part of the living evolution of the literature today. His classic fantasy novel, *Darker Than You Think,* originally published in *Unknown Worlds* in the early 1940s is still influential, and his SF classics, including *The Legion of Space* and *The Humanoids,* still drop in and out of print in paperback in a decade when many newer books by others are gone. This piece appeared in *SF Age,* which has been required reading for several years now but in 1997 had its best year yet for science fiction, and is the first of several from that magazine in this volume. It is about a boy and an alien and is a moving evocation of wonder in what we might perhaps call the Ray Bradbury tradition.

They had come back to live on the old farm where his grandfather was born. His father loved it, but he felt lonely for his friends in the city. Cattle sometimes grazed through the barren sandhills beyond the barbed wire fences, but there were no neighbors. He found no friends except the firefly tree.

It grew in the old fruit orchard his grandfather had planted below the house. His mouth watered for the ripe apples and peaches and pears he expected, but when he saw the trees they were all dead or dying. They bore no fruit.

With no friends at all, he stayed with his father on the farm when his mother drove away every morning to work at the peanut mill. His father was always busy in the garden he made among the bare trees in the orchard. The old windmill had lost its wheel, but there was an electric pump for water. Cantaloupe and squash vines grew along the edge of the garden, with rows of tomatoes and beans, and then the corn that grew tall enough to hide the money trees.

His mother fretted that they might cause trouble. Once he heard her call them marijuana. His father quickly hushed her. The word was strange to him but he never asked what it meant because he saw his father didn't like it.

He found the firefly tree one day while his father was chopping weeds and moving the pipes that sprayed water on his money trees. It was still tiny then, not as tall as his knee. The leaves were odd: thin arrowheads of glossy black velvet, striped with silver. A single lovely flower had three wide sky-colored petals and a bright yellow star at the center. He sat on the ground by it, breathing its strange sweetness, till his father came by with the hoe.

"Don't hurt it!" he begged. "Please!"

"That stinking weed?" his father grunted. "Get out of the way."

Something made him reach to catch the hoe.

"Okay." His father grinned and let it stay. "If you care that much."

He called it his tree, and watched it grow. When it wilted in a week with no rain, he found a bucket and carried water from the well. It grew taller than he was, with a dozen of the great blue flowers and then a hundred. The odor of them filled the garden.

Since there was no school, his mother tried to teach him at home. She found a red-backed reader for him, and a workbook with pages for him to fill out while she was away at work. He seldom got the lessons done.

"He's always mooning over that damn weed," hie father muttered when she scolded him. "High as a kite on the stink of it."

The odor was strange and strong, but no stink at all. Not to him. He loved it and loved the tree. He carried more water and used the hoe to till the soil around it. Often he stood just looking at the huge blue blooms, wondering what the fruit would be.

One night he dreamed that the tree was swarming with fireflies. They were so real that he got out of bed and slipped out into the dark. The stars blazed brighter here than they had ever been in the city. They lit his way to the orchard, and he heard the fireflies before he came to the tree.

Their buzz rose and fell like the sound of the surf the time they went to visit his aunt who lived by the sea. Twinkling brighter than the stars, they filled the branches. One of them came to meet him. It hovered in front of his face and lit on the tip of his trembling finger, smiling at him with eyes as blue and bright as the flowers.

He had never seen a firefly close up. It was as big as a bumblebee. It had tiny hands that gripped his fingernail, and one blue eye squinted a little to study his face. The light came from a round topknot on its head. It flickered like something electric, from red to green, yellow to blue, maybe red again. The flashes were sometimes slower than his breath, sometimes so fast they blurred. He thought the flicker was meant to tell him something, but he had no way to understand.

Barefoot and finally shivering with cold, he stood there till the flickering stopped. The firefly shook its crystal wings and flew away. The stars were fading into the dawn, and the tree was dark and silent when he looked. He was back in bed before he heard his mother rattling dishes in the kitchen, making breakfast.

The next night he dreamed that he was back under the tree, with the firefly perched again on his finger. Its tiny face seemed almost human in the dream, and he understood its winking voice. It told him how the tree had grown from a sharp-pointed acorn that came from the stars and planted itself when it struck the ground.

It told him about the firefly planet, far off in the sky. The fireflies belonged to a great republic spread across the stars. Thousands of different peoples lived in peace on thousands of different worlds. The acorn ship had come to invite the people of Earth to join their republic. They were ready to teach the Earth-people how to talk across space and travel to visit the stars. The dream seemed so wonderful that he tried to tell about it at breakfast.

"What did I tell you?" His father turned red and shouted at his mother. "His brain's been addled by the stink of that poison weed. I ought to cut it down and burn it."

"Don't!" He was frightened and screaming. "I love it. I'll die if you kill it."

"I'm afraid he would." His mother made a sad little frown. "Leave the plant where it is, and I'll take him to Dr. Wong."

"Okay." His father finally nodded, and frowned at him

sternly. "If you'll promise to do your chores and stay out of the garden."

Trying to keep the promise, he washed the dishes after his mother was gone to work. He made the beds and swept the floors. He tried to do his lessons, though the stories in the reader seemed stupid to him now.

He did stay out of the garden, but the fireflies came again in his dreams. They carried him to see the shining forests on their own wonderful world. They took him to visit the planets of other peoples, people who lived under their seas, people who lived high in their skies, people as small as ants, people larger than the elephants he had seen in a circus parade and queerer than the octopus in the side show. He saw ships that could fly faster than light from star to star, and huge machines he never understood, and cities more magical than fairyland.

He said no more about the dreams till the day his mother came home from work to take him to Dr. Wong. The nurse put a thermometer under his tongue and squeezed his arm with a rubber gadget and left him to wait with his mother for Dr. Wong. Dr. Wong was a friendly man who listened to his chest and looked at the nurse's chart and asked him about the fireflies.

"They're wonderful!" He thought the doctor would believe him. "You must come at night to see them, sir. They love us. They came to show us the way to the stars."

"Listen to him!" His mother had never been out at night to see the fireflies shining. "That ugly weed has driven him out of his head!"

"An interesting case." The doctor smiled and patted his shoulder in a friendly way and turned to speak to his mother. "One for the books. The boy should see a psychiatrist."

His mother had no money for that.

"I'll just take him home," she said, "and hope he gets better."

A police car was parked in front of the house when they got there. His father sat in the back, behind a metal grill. His head was bent. He wouldn't look up, not even when his mother called through a half-open window.

The police had more cars parked around the garden. They had chopped down all the money trees and thrown them into a pile. The firefly tree lay on top. Its fragrance was lost in a reek of kerosene. The policemen made everybody move upwind and set the fire with a hissing blowtorch.

It spread slowly at first, then blazed so high they had to move farther away. Feeling sick at his stomach, he saw the branches of the tree twist and beat against the flames. He heard a long sharp scream. A cat caught in the fire, the policemen said, but he knew it wasn't a cat. Fireflies swarmed out of the thrashing branches and exploded like tiny bombs when the flames caught them.

His father was crying when the police took him away, along with a bundle of the money trees for evidence. His mother moved them back to the city. In school again, he tried to tell his new teachers about the fireflies and how they had come to invite the Earth into their great confederation of stars. The teachers said he had a great imagination and sent him to the school psychologist.

The psychologist called his mother to come for a conference. They wanted him to forget the fireflies and do his lessons and look up his old friends again, but he wanted no friends except the fireflies. He grieved for them and grieved for his father and grieved for all that might have been.

Thirteen Views of a Cardboard City

WILLIAM GIBSON

William Gibson aspired early in his career to being like J. G. Ballard, and achieving a position of literary respect for his precise and lucid and modernist (or postmodernist) works—perhaps not a huge popular success, but hugely respected and admired by a knowledgeable few. Instead he achieved immense popular success far outside the SF field. This story, from the most ambitious anthology of the year, *New Worlds,* shows Gibson staking a claim to High Modernist territory, in striking opposition to ordinary science fiction. Here he is the cold, precise, clinically-detached, observing eye, descended from Wallace Steven's great poem, "Thirteen Ways of Looking at a Blackbird," viewing through the lens of Ballard and William S. Burroughs his own place and time, the noir future city. It also somehow reminds me of Richard Brautigan's poetry collection (at least the title), *All Watched Over By Machines of Loving Grace,* and of Anna Kavan's *Ice.* This is not the direction in which his novels, such as the recent *Idoru,* now point, but it is a reminder of the range and talent and origins of this impressive writer.

ONE
DEN-EN

Low angle, deep perspective, establishing Tokyo subway station interior.

Shot with available light, long exposure; a spectral pedestrian moves away from us, into background. Two others visible as blurs of motion.

Overhead fluorescents behind narrow rectangular fixtures. Ceiling tiled with meter-square segments (acoustic baffles?). Round fixtures are ventilators, smoke-detectors, speakers? Massive square columns recede. Side of a stairwell or escalator. Mosaic tile floor in simple large-scale pattern: circular white areas in square tiles, black infill of round tiles. The floor is spotless: no litter at all. Not a cigarette butt, not a gum-wrapper.

A long train of cardboard cartons, sides painted with murals, recedes into the perspective of columns and scrubbed tile: first impression is of a children's art project, something choreographed by an aggressively creative preschool teacher. But not all of the corrugated cartons have been painted; many, particularly those farthest away, are bare brown paper. The one nearest the camera, unaltered, bright yellow, bears the Microsoft logo.

The murals appear to have been executed in poster paints, and are difficult to interpret here.

There are two crisp-looking paper shopping-bags on the tile floor: one near the murals, the other almost in the path of the ghost pedestrian. These strike a note of anomaly, of possible threat: London Transport warnings, Sarin cultists . . . Why are they there? What do they contain?

The one nearest the murals bears the logo "DEN-EN."

Deeper in the image are other cartons. Relative scale makes it easier to see that these are composites, stitched together from smaller boxes. Closer study makes the method of fastening clear: two sheets are punctured twice with narrow horizontal slits, flat poly-twine analog (white or pink) is threaded through both sheets, a knot is tied, the ends trimmed neatly. In fact, all of the structures appear to have been assembled this way.

Deepest of all, stairs. Passengers descending.

TWO
BLUE OCTOPUS

Shallow perspective, eye-level, as though we were meant to view an anamorphic painting.

This structure appears to have been braced with a pale blue, enameled, possibly spring-loaded tube with a white, non-slip plastic foot. It might be the rod for a shower-curtain, but here it is employed vertically. Flattened cartons are neatly lashed to this with poly-tie.

The murals. Very faintly, on the end of the structure, nearest the camera, against a black background, the head of the Buddha floats above something amorphous and unreadable. Above the Buddha are fastened what appear to be two packaging-units for Pooh Bear dolls. These may serve a storage function. The mural on the face of the structure is dark, intricate, and executed (acrylic paints?) with considerable technique. Body parts, a sense of claustrophobic, potentially erotic proximity. A female nude, head lost where the cardboard ends, clutches a blue octopus whose tentacles drape across the forehead of a male who seems to squat doglike at her feet. Another nude lies on her back, knees upraised, her sex shadowed in perspective. The head of a man with staring eyes and pinprick pupils hovers above her ankles; he appears to be smoking but has no cigarette.

A third nude emerges, closest to the camera: a woman whose features suggest either China or the Mexico of Diego Rivera.

A section of the station's floor, the round black tiles, is partially covered with a scrap of grayish-blue synthetic pile carpeting.

Pinned eyes.

THREE
FRONTIER INTERNATIONAL

Shot straight back into what may be a wide alcove. Regular curves of pale square tiles.

Four structures visible.

The largest, very precisely constructed, very hard-edged, is decorated with an eerie pointillist profile against a solid black background: it seems to be a very old man, his chin, lipless mouth and drooping nose outlined in blood red. In front of this is positioned a black hard-sided overnighter suitcase.

Abutting this structure stands another, smaller, very gaily painted: against a red background with a cheerful yellow bird and yellow concentric circles, a sort of Cubist ET winks out at the camera. The head of a large nail or pin, rendered in a far more sophisticated style, penetrates the thing's forehead above the open eye.

A life-sized human hand, entirely out of scale with the huge head, is reaching for the eye.

Nearby sits an even smaller structure, this one decorated with abstract squares of color recalling Klee or Mondrian. Beside it is an orange plastic crate of the kind used to transport sake bottles. An upright beer can. A pair of plastic sandals, tidily arranged.

Another, bigger structure behind this one. Something painted large-scale in beige and blue (sky?) but this is obscured by the Mondrian. A working door, hinged with poly-tie, remains unpainted: the carton employed for the door is printed with the words "FRONTIER INTERNATIONAL."

Individual styles of workmanship start to become apparent.

Deeper in the image, beyond what appears to be a stack of neatly-folded blankets, is located the blue enamel upright, braced against the ceiling tile. Another like it, to its right, supports a paper kite with the printed face of a samurai.

**FOUR
AFTER PICASSO**

Shallow perspective of what appears to be a single, very narrow shelter approximately nine meters in length. Suggests the literally marginal nature of these constructions: someone has appropriated less than a meter at the side of a corridor, and built along it, tunneling like a cardboard seaworm.

The murals lend the look of a children's cardboard theater.

Punch in the underground.

Like so many of the anonymous paintings to be found in thrift shops everywhere, these murals are somehow vaguely after Picasso. Echo of *Guernica* in these tormented animal forms. Human features rendered flounder-style: more Oxfam Cubism.

Square black cushion with black tassels at its corners, top an uncharacteristically peaked section of cardboard roof. Elegant.

The wall behind the shelter is a partition of transparent lucite, suggesting the possibility of a bizarre ant-farm existence.

FIVE
YELLOW SPERM

We are in an impossibly narrow "alley" between shelters, perhaps a communal storage area. Cardboard shelving, folded blankets.

A primitive portrait of a black kitten, isolated on a solid green ground, recalls the hypnotic stare of figures in New England folk art.

Also visible: the white plastic cowl of an electric fan, yellow plastic sake crate, pale blue plastic bucket, section of blue plastic duck-board, green plastic dustpan suspended by string, child's pail in dark blue plastic. Styrofoam takeaway containers with blue and scarlet paint suggest more murals in progress.

Most striking here is the wall of a matte-black shelter decorated with a mural of what appear to be large yellow inner-tubes with regularly spaced oval "windows" around their perimeters; through each window is glimpsed a single large yellow sperm arrested in midwriggle against a nebulous black-and-yellow background.

SIX
GOMI GUITAR

Extreme close, perhaps at entrance to a shelter.

An elaborately designed pair of black-and-purple Nike trainers, worn but clean. Behind them a pair of simpler white Reeboks (a woman's?).

A battered acoustic guitar strung with nylon. Beside it, a strange narrow case made of blue denim, trimmed with red imitation leather; possibly a golf bag intended to carry a single club to a driving range?

A self-inking German rubber stamp.

Neatly folded newspaper with Japanese baseball stars.

A battered pump-thermos with floral design.

SEVEN
108

A space like the upper berths on the Norfolk & Western sleeping cars my mother and I took when I was a child. Form following function.

The structure is wide enough to accommodate a single traditional Japanese pallet. A small black kitten sits at its foot (the subject of the staring portrait?). Startled by the flash, it is tethered with a red leash. A second, larger tabby peers over a shopping bag made of tartan paper. The larger cat is also tethered, with a length of thin white poly rope.

Part of a floral area-rug visible at foot of bed.

This space is deeply traditional, utterly culture-specific.

Brown cardboard walls, cardboard mailing tubes used as structural uprights, the neat poly-tie lashings.

On right wall:
GIC
MODEL NO: VS-30
Q'TY: 1 SET
COLOR: BLACK
C/T NO: 108
MADE IN KOREA

At the rear, near what may be assumed to be the head of the bed, are suspended two white-coated metal shelves or racks. These contain extra bedding, a spare cat-leash, a three-pack of some pressurized product (butane for a cooker?), towels.

On the right wall are hung two pieces of soft luggage, one in dark green imitation leather, the other in black leather, and a three-quarter-length black leather car coat.

On the left wall, a white towel, a pair of bluejeans, and two framed pictures (content not visible from this angle).

A section of transparent plastic has been mounted in the ceiling to serve as a skylight.

EIGHT
HAPPY HOUR

Wall with mailing-tube uprights.

A large handbill with Japanese stripper: LIVE NUDE, TOP-
LESS BOTTOMLESS, HAPPY HOUR. Menu-chart from a hamburger
franchise illustrating sixteen choices.

Beneath these, along the wall, are arranged two jars containing white plastic spoons, a tin canister containing chopsticks, eight stacked blue plastic large takeaway cups, fourteen
stacked white paper takeway cups (all apparently unused, and
inverted to protect against dust), neatly folded towels and
bedding, aluminum cookware, a large steel kettle, a pink plastic dishpan, a large wooden chopping-board.

Blanket with floral motif spread as carpet.

NINE
SANDY

A different view of the previous interior, revealing a storage
loft very tidily constructed of mailing-tubes and flattened cartons.

The similarities with traditional Japanese post-and-beam
construction is even more striking, here. This loft-space is
directly above the stacked cookware in the preceding image.
Toward its left side is a jumble of objects, some unidentifiable:
heavy rope, a child's plaid suitcase, a black plastic bowl, a
softball bat. To the right are arranged a soft, stuffed baby doll,
a plush stuffed dog, a teddy bear wearing overalls that say
"SANDY," what seems to be a plush stuffed killer whale
(shark?) with white felt teeth. The whale or shark still has the
manufacturer's cardboard label attached, just as it came from
the factory.

In the foreground, on the lower level, is a stack of glossy
magazines, a tin box that might once have held candy or some

other confection, and an open case that probably once contained a pair of sunglasses.

TEN
BOY'S BAR KYOKA

A very simple shot, camera directed toward floor, documenting another food-preparation area.

A square section of the round tiles is revealed at the bottom of the photograph. The rest of the floor is covered by layers of newspaper beneath a sheet of brown cardboard. A narrow border of exposed newsprint advertises "Boy's Bar KYOKA."

A blue thermos with a black carrying-strap. A greasy-looking paper cup covered with crumpled aluminum foil. A red soap-dish with a bar of white soap. A cooking-pot with an archaic-looking wooden lid. The pot's handle is wrapped in a white terry face cloth, secured with two rubber bands. Another pot, this one with a device for attaching a missing wooden handle, contains a steel ladle and a wooden spatula. A nested collection of plastic mixing bowls and colanders.

A large jug of bottled water, snow-capped peaks on its blue and white label.

A white plastic cutting-board, discolored with use. A white plastic (paper?) bag with "ASANO" above a cartoon baker proudly displaying some sort of loaf.

ELEVEN
J.O.

The shelters have actually-enclosed a row of pay telephones!
Dial 110 for police.
Dial 119 for fire or ambulance.
Two telephones are visible: they are that singularly bilious shade of green the Japanese reserve for pay phones.

They have slots for phone-cards, small liquid crystal displays, round steel keys. They are mounted on individual stainless-steel writing-ledges, each supported by a stout, mirror-finished steel post. Beneath each ledge is an enclosed shelf or hutch, made of black, perforated steel sheeting. Provided as a resting place for a user's parcels.

The hutches now serve as food-prep storage: four ceramic soup bowls of a common pattern, three more with a rather more intricate glaze, four white plastic bowls and several colored ones. A plastic scrubbing-pad, used.

On the floor below, on newspaper, are an aluminum teapot and what may be a package of instant coffee sachets. Three liter bottles of cooking oils.

On the steel ledge of the left-hand phone is a tin that once contained J.O. Special Blend ready-to-drink coffee.

TWELVE
NIPPON SERIES

An office.

A gap has been left in the corrugated wall, perhaps deliberately, to expose a detailed but highly stylized map of Tokyo set into the station's wall. The wall of this shelter and the wall of the station have become confused. Poly-tie binds the cardboard house directly into the fabric of the station, into the Prefecture itself.

This is quite clearly an office.

On the wall around the official, integral subway map, fastened to granite composite and brown cardboard with bits of masking tape: a postcard with a cartoon of orange-waistcoated figures escorting a child through a pedestrian crossing, a restaurant receipt (?), a newspaper clipping, a small plastic clipboard with what seem to be receipts, possibly from an ATM, a souvenir program from the 1995 Nippon Series (baseball), and two color photos of a black-

and-white cat. In one photo, the cat seems to be here, among the shelters.

Tucked behind a sheet of cardboard are four pens and three pairs of scissors. A small pocket flashlight is suspended by a lanyard of white poly-tie.

To the right, at right angles to the wall above, a cardboard shelf is cantilevered with poly-tie. It supports a box of washing detergent, a book, a dayglo orange Casio G-Shock wristwatch, a white terry face cloth, a red plastic AM/FM cassette-player, and three disposable plastic cigarette-lighters.

Below, propped against the wall, is something that suggests the bottom of an inexpensive electronic typewriter of the sort manufactured by Brother.

A box of Chinese candy, a cat-brush, a flea-collar.

**THIRTEEN
TV SOUND**

Close-up of the contents of the shelf.

The red stereo AM/FM cassette-player, its chrome antenna extended at an acute angle for better reception. It is TV Sound brand, model LX-43. Its broken handle, mended with black electrical tape, is lashed into the structure with white poly-tie. Beside the three lighters, which are tucked partially beneath the player, in a row, are an unopened moist towelette and a red fine-point felt pen. To the left of the player is a square red plastic alarm clock, the white face cloth, and the Casio G-Shock. The Casio is grimy, one of the only objects in this sequence that actually appears to be dirty. The book, atop the box of laundry detergent, is hardbound, its glossy dustjacket bearing the photograph of a suited and tied Japanese executive. It looks expensive. Inspirational? Autobiographical?

To the right of the LX-43: a rigid cardboard pack of Lucky Strike non-filters and a Pokka coffee tin with the top neatly removed (to serve as an ashtray?).

On the cardboard bulkhead above these things are taped up two sentimental postcards of paintings of kittens playing. "Cat collection" in a cursive font.

Below these are glued (not taped) three black-and-white photographs.

#1: A balding figure in jeans and a short-sleeved T-shirt squats before an earlier, unpainted version of this structure.

One of the cartons seems to be screened with the word "PLAST—". He is eating noodles from a pot, using chopsticks.

#2: The "alley" between the shelters. The balding man looks up at the camera. Somehow he doesn't look Japanese at all. He sits cross-legged among half-a-dozen others. They look Japanese. All are engrossed in something, perhaps the creation of murals.

#3: He squats before his shelter, wearing molded plastic sandals. His hands grip his knees. Now he looks entirely Japanese, his face a formal mask of suffering.

Curve of square tiles.

How long has be lived here?

With his cats, his guitar, his neatly folded blankets?

Dolly back.

Hold on the cassette player.

Behind it, almost concealed, is a Filofax.

Names.

Numbers.

Held as though they might be a map, a map back out of the underground.

The Nostalginauts

S.N. DYER

S.N. Dyer (Sharon Farber) has been writing competent, entertaining science fiction for years without attracting the recognition she deserves. She has a flair for tone and attitude that is much in evidence here, and characteristically tells an engaging tale, with bits of acute social observation. This is a witty concoction about kids today in the future after a transforming change, again from *Asimov's*, that is pretty far from hard SF (it seems to me a direct descendant of the 1950s *Galaxy* or *F&SF* stories) but still a captivating SF idea. How badly would you feel if your future selves and friends and family, and even strangers, were touristing back in time to watch you at every important moment of your life? Could you get used to it? Rise above it? Could you resist it yourself later? This is a story of teenage angst and a destabilized world. Who is to say it is not serious just because it reeks with attitude?

"**S**o, you wanna go to the prom?"

"Why?" I asked. "Like, I thought the Chess Club was going to hang on Geek-web."

It was going to be a worldwide hook-up of dateless losers. You can't say we don't know how to have a good time.

"I just think I ought to be there," Gar said. "At the prom." He shrugged. I shrugged.

We were on the steps of the old Carnegie-built library— its motto: *One hundred years, nothing controversial yet*—and were watching the church across the street. A wedding. That meant the possibility of time travelers. Or not. Entertaining either way.

"So why me?"

"What do you mean?"

"Why not Net Girl?"

"She's too popular."

True. She's only a junior and already has five electronic boyfriends. She also weighs three hundred pounds. But a hell of a website.

"Besides," he said. "You clean up nice. Remember Halloween? You were hot on Halloween."

There was action inside the church now, people opening the doors, spilling outside. We craned forward.

The happy couple emerged. Hands paused, loaded with rice . . .

Everyone looked around. The question on everyone's lips: Would *they* be there? Would the happy couple, a quarter-century older, time travel back to reexperience this day of joy? Gar and I crossed our fingers sarcastically.

Because if they didn't show, it meant they were either dead, or divorced, or dirt poor. Talk about killing the festivities by your absence.

"Any bets?" I asked.

"Loser buys at T-Bell? I say they'll come."

Suddenly the air by a late-model Honda began to crackle and fluoresce. A middle-aged duo clicked into focus, promptly waving at the newlyweds. A collectively held breath exhaled in unison. The couple waved back, and everyone cheered. From across the street, we joined in. Let's hear it for lasting marital bliss.

And then, just as suddenly, the old pair's thirty seconds were up, they clicked out—and here came more travelers. The cheery offspring. Five of them, ranging in age from near-teen to must-have-been-pregnant-on-the-big-day. The crowd went wild.

"Hot damn," I said. More life-affirming than an entire week of *Nick at Nite*.

"So, will you?"

"On Halloween I was a vampire in black velvet and red satin."

"Works for me," said Gar.

So we shook on it, and headed to T-Bell.

"You know how the lights go weird right before the dum-dums show?"

When time travelers first started showing up they were called *phantoms*. When scientists figured out what they were, the media called them *time tourists,* or *nostalginauts.* We stuck with *phantom*, pronounced *phan-dumb*, and finally just *dumdums*.

I mean, what a phenomenally stupid invention. Time travel that only takes you twenty-five years into the past, lasts half a minute, and you're insubstantial too. It makes a quest for rubber beverage containers look intelligent. Eyelash massagers. Trampoline deodorizers. Computer ventriloquists.

"But it *is* important," Gar kept saying. "It means Time is quantized. So what if the first level is trivial. . . . Maybe you can visit longer levels."

"Then we'd have boring visitors from the far future, not just people with anniversaries and reunions."

"Maybe guys from further out dress so they won't scare us or give anything away. Or the future scientists could be viewing, oh, australopithecines or trilobites or the big asteroid crash. But it means We Understand Time. Unified Theory of Everything."

I rolled my eyes toward the ceiling. Gar has a lot of emotion invested in time travel. He's convinced he's going to invent it. That's okay with me. He'll need something to keep him busy next fall when he's at MIT and doesn't have his geeky pals from the Chess Club to keep him real. (And no, we don't play chess. We call it that to scare away stupid people. It works.)

A couple of classmates of the Neanderthal persuasion stopped by our table. "Hey dorks, drowning your sorrows 'cause you don't have prom dates?"

"No," I said. "We're drowning our sorrows because it's lonely being the only ones in town with active synaptic potentials."

"Oooh, big words. I'm sooo scared!"

The bigger one tore open a couple of hot sauce packets and smeared them on my softaco. Ha ha.

I caught the moron's eye, grinned, grabbed half a dozen more packets, added them on, and took a nice happy bite.

The Neanderthals turned pale and left.

"I can't believe it," Gar said. "They're scared of spicy food!"

Good thing I hang on the Weird Cuisine SIG. And it's why I have to leave town. I want to find out if Thai restaurants really do exist in nature. But I went back to the problem at hand.

"So why are you set on the senior prom, Gar? It's not like you've ever been to a game or bought a yearbook or anything."

"Last week, something weird happened. I was in my room thinking about Time, and how the lights before the dumdums come are kind of like when I put my metal-rimmed *Pinky and the Brain* mug in the microwave, and my jaw was hanging open really stupid . . . and I realized there was someone else in my room. A dumdum."

"Wrong address?"

He shook his head. "He was looking at me, and smiling." He shuddered. Our crowd wasn't used to real smiles.

He was right. If true, it was most definitely weird.

"Maybe you were about to be murdered?"

"Yeah, of course, that's it. And now I'm dead."

Because that's the only non-nostalgia use for time travel so far—checking out unsolved crimes. Deterrent value is zero. Face it. If a dumdum shows up while you're busy ventilating a little old lady with an icepick, you don't say, *Whoa, I'm caught.* You say *Cool, I got away with it for twenty-five years!* Which to your average criminal and your average teenager is like forever.

"Okay, let's go with this as your grand moment of revelation. Kekule and the snake. Newton and the fig."

I wasn't going to let Gar's ego get any bigger. So his IQ was bigger than the gross national product of Chechnya. He was still a dateless nerd. A laughingstock. A loser whose best friends were so socially inept they could really only talk to him via modem. And of course me, the rebel without a Santa Claus. The girl for whom the guidance counselors had made up a stamp that said *bad attitude.*

"You going to remember your old friends when you've got a Nobel prize in every room?"

And then something happened. The air fluoresced and a

dumdum appeared at the next table. And stared at us, staring back, for the longest thirty seconds of my life, before disappearing again.

"Wow," I said. "Maybe I should save the hot sauce wrappers. They may be worth something someday."

Mom was in the kitchen doing her June Cleaver thing. "Hey Mom!" I yelled, plopping down in front of the TV and going right to Home Shopping so I could make fun of the boomer collectibles. Eighty bucks for a model of a bicycle. "Hey Mom, can I go to the prom tomorrow night?"

I was sort of permanently grounded since I called the principal a *neototalitarian babbitoid*. I would have been expelled too, but someone finally explained it to him and it just wasn't bad enough.

A fossilized survivor of the Partridge Family was shilling vinyl souvenirs. Makes you proud to be American.

"The *prom*?"

I jumped. Mom was right behind me. She'd run out from the kitchen, hands still covered in flour, and was wide-eyed like she was going to cry.

"The prom," I said. "It's not like Lassie just came home."

She started nervously wiping her hands on her apron. "We'll run out right now and get your hair done and a dress and . . ."

"Hey, it's just Gar, and I'll wear my black dress."

Her face fell. I almost felt bad. I hadn't realized the way the word *prom* would hit her. Stimulus response. For one microsecond I was a normal daughter, wanting the normal world of dresses and boys and family, not a changeling who wanted to go to film school and raise tattoos.

They really did get my blood tested once. They were that convinced I'd been switched in the nursery.

"So can I go?"

She sighed. "Go. Do what you want. Remember, there are only seventy-two Family Shaming Days before you go away to college."

"Thanks, Mom. When you make a joke like that, I almost believe we're related."

She flinched, started back to the kitchen, then turned.

"You know what I hope?" she said. "I hope you show up at the prom—your future self, I mean—and I hope you tell yourself what a mess you're going to make of your life. I hope to God you straighten out."

And then I shuddered. Because I thought of all those old farts at their twenty-fifth reunion, coming back en masse to look at the glory days of the prom—anyone who wasn't dead or broke or a total reject—and I didn't want it. I didn't want to be one of the jerks smiling and waving and holding snapshots of big families and big cars and big houses.

"I wouldn't do that," I muttered. "I wouldn't do anything so—so ordinary."

On the other hand, if I did feel like I had to revisit my prom, maybe I'd be cool enough to do it dressed entirely in vinyl Partridge Family souvenirs.

No corsage, but he brought me a red carnation that went with my color scheme. We started out at the Chess Club alternate prom party. Eight people, seven computers, a lot of Doritos, and two bottles of Annie Green Springs.

"God, you both look great," said Net Girl. "I love the tux. You two could be Fred and Ginger."

"Yeah, the Transylvanian dance team," said Jean-Luc. "Make it so." Poor guy had three strikes against him: he was brilliant, he was going bald at seventeen, and he liked to write philosophical essays in Klingon. But there was something in his eyes I wasn't accustomed to . . .

Great. I was now the sex goddess of the pathetic loser crowd.

"We'll be back after the dance," said Gar. "Assuming we're not hospitalized or murdered or anything."

Then we gritted our collective dentition and drove to the school gym. "I couldn't believe it when I heard you were coming," said Mrs. Trout, my homeroom teacher. She hated my guts. It was mutual. "I should have known you'd pull something like this."

"It's my best dress, ma'am," I said.

We didn't dance. I don't know how, and Gar looked dangerous to my podiatric integrity. So we stood by the wall, occasionally shouted something sarcastic at each other over the din, and were bored to tears.

Until the dumdums started to appear. You can get a lot of mileage watching eighteen-year-olds confront their forty-three-year-old selves. Like they never realized they'd get that old. And the dumdums thinking they still looked buff or cool, not realizing they were just ancient. Embarrassing.

Most of them were holding little signs or pictures of all the detritus they'd accumulated. The pictures of families, mansions, and what we could only assume were expensive cars.

I made a gagging sound. I couldn't imagine anything worse than knowing where you were going to live, how many kids you'd have. It would be like trying to read an Agatha Christie when you've already snuck a look at the last chapter.

Gar kept looking around. I guess he thought he'd show up with his Nobel around his neck. Maybe a physics groupie on each arm. It could happen. Sooner or later he'd have to grow into his face.

The class president stood at the mike and tapped it until everyone quieted down. He'd just seen his own red-nosed future self holding pictures of a car dealership and what was either a second wife or a very inappropriately clad daughter. He was primed.

The pitiful country band quieted down. Fine with me. You ever heard redneck rap?

"Now it's time to announce the Prom King and Queen . . ."

And he named us.

"Oh hell," I said. I didn't like the sound of this.

We found ourselves being pushed up to the stage. The president and my homeroom teacher pulled us up. "Your future self hasn't appeared yet, has she?" she sneered. Obviously meaning: because you couldn't afford it, or you died of a drug overdose in a gutter, or you're embarrassed by your lack of success.

"Hell no," I said. "Think I'd want to relive this boring and now humiliating piece of shit night?"

"Detention until the end of school for swearing, dear," she hissed.

The class president stuck crowns on our heads, ducked back quickly, and then the pies started to fly. But I'd been alerted, and dove behind Miss Trout, pushing her into the line of fire. Detention, hell—now it would be suspension.

Poor Gar wiped banana cream from his glasses—the idiots didn't know you were supposed to use shaving cream—and staggered to the microphone.

"You are all . . . infantile," he said. His voice was cracking, but it got stronger as he went. I stepped forward to put a hand on his shoulder. I felt kind of bad I hadn't had time to warn him.

"You're all unoriginal, boring, hopelessly conventional bourgeoisie."

"Yeah!" a Neanderthal shouted, and the football team whooped. They weren't sure what it meant, but if the four-eyed technonerd was against it, they were for it.

"And it's really all just jealousy. Because I'm leaving this hick town and *you'll* all stay, just live and die here and no one will ever remember you. But *I'm* going to be important. . . ."

"America's Most Wanted Dork!"

"Good one," I shouted. "Who writes your jokes, Flipper?"

"I'm going to contribute to human knowledge, and you'll just contribute to . . . to your own IRAs."

Gar never thought well on the fly. I should have anticipated the need for a retribution speech.

"And you'll only be remembered as the assholes who made fun of me, like the ones who laughed at Darwin and suppressed Galileo. . . ."

And that's when it got weirder, as everyone realized that attendance in the room had doubled. There were future people everywhere, looking around, recording, remembering. And all the dumdums were focused on Gar, except when they were sneering at the other prom-goers.

It was too funny. I couldn't stop laughing. They'd been trying to make fun of us and now they would be famous as the Village of Short-sighted Idiots. Spending the rest of their lives as the laughingstocks of history, trying to live it down. And in the process, no doubt, becoming even more militantly short-sighted and closeminded.

I loved it. Even as I pitied the next generation in this crappy town.

And yeah, I even caught sight of Grownup Gar the Tenured Professor. He did grow into his face, and there *are* Nobel Groupies.

I stumbled away out of the crowd. My own cozy footnote in history assured, maybe, as Gar's vampira prom date. But he didn't need me now. He was basking in the attention of the future's intelligentsia, and the air that was thick with *I Told You So.*

I walked out into the parking lot, breathing in the relatively fresh air, and leaned against the wall. I'd probably have to bum a ride to the Chess Club party, or walk. I had a feeling Gar was about to go home and pound out a theory of time. Excuse me, Time.

Something crackled out of the corner of my eye, and I

found myself looking into my own eyes. Crow's feet, middle-aged spread, and it seemed I was apparently doomed to another quarter century of bad hair days and no fashion sense.

But I still had my patented sardonic grin, as my future self flashed up something white.

"Not pictures," I moaned.

No. It was an index card. My handwriting didn't seem to have improved either. I'd scrawled, "IT HASN'T BEEN DULL."

I shrugged at me and disappeared.

It hasn't been dull.

Cool. I can live with that.

Guest Law

JOHN C. WRIGHT

John C. Wright is a new writer with a future, judging by this story. He trained in law, but dropped out of the workforce to write, and has sold a few stories only to *Asimov's*, while working on novels not yet published. This story struck me as strong, individual, and unusual right away. It has some of the submerged just anger of Cordwainer Smith, and some of his poetics. It also has some of the feel of Donald M. Kingsbury's fiction, just a bit wonderfully inhuman in its future. It has a bit of the feel of cyberspace. But primarily it has the feel of traditional SF, of great issues raised by titanic beings in the distant future, against a backdrop of uncountable stars. All in all it is the work of a strong new talent.

The night of deep space is endless and empty and dark. There is nothing behind which to hide. But ships can be silent, if they are slow.

The noble ship *Procrustes* was silent as a ghost. She was black-hulled, and ran without beacons or lights. She was made of anti-radar alloys and smooth ceramics, shark-finned with panels meant to diffuse waste-heat slowly, and tiger-striped with electronic webs meant to guide certain frequencies around the hull without rebounding.

If she ever were seen, a glance would show that she was meant to be slow. Her drive was fitted with baffle upon baffle, cooling the exhaust before it was expelled, a dark drive, non-radioactive, silent as sprayed mist. Low energy in the drive implied low thrust. Further, she had no centrifuge section, nor did she spin. This meant that her crew were lightweights, their blood and bones degenerated or adapted to microgravity, not the sort who could tolerate high boosts.

This did not mean *Procrustes* was not a noble ship. Warships can be slow; only their missiles need speed.

And so it was silently, slowly, that *Procrustes* approached the stranger's cold vessel.

"We are gathered, my gentlemen, to debate whether this new ship here viewed is noble, or whether she is unarmed; and, if so, whether and how the guest law applies. It pleases us to hear you employ the second level of speech; for this is a semi-informal occasion, and briefer honorifics we permit."

The captain, as beautiful and terrifying as something

from a children's Earth-story, floated nude before the viewing well. The bridge was a cylinder of gloom, with only control-lights winking like constellations, the viewing well shining like a full moon.

The captain made a gesture with her fan toward Smith and spoke: "Engineer, you do filth-work . . ." (by which she meant manual labor) ". . . which makes you familiar with machines." (She used the term "familiar" because it simply was not done to say a lowlife had "knowledge" or "expertise.") "It would amuse us to hear your conclusions touching and concerning the stranger's ship."

Smith was never allowed high and fore to the bridge, except when he was compelled to go, as he was now. His hands had been turned off at the wrists, since lowlifes should not touch controls.

Smith was in terror of the captain, but loved her too, since she was the only highlife who called smiths by their old title. The captain was always polite, even to tinkers or drifters or bondsman.

She had not even seemed to notice when Smith had hooked one elbow around one of the many guy-wires that webbed the dark long cylinder of the bridge. Some of the officers and knights who floated near the captain had turned away or snorted with disgust when he had clasped that rope. It was a foot-rope, meant for toes, not a hand rope. But Smith's toes were not well formed, not coordinated. He had not been born a lightweight.

Smith was as drab as a hairless monkey next to the captain's vavasors and carls, splendid in their head-to-toe tattoos which displayed heraldries and victory-emblems. These nobles all kept their heads pointed along the captain's axis (an old saying ran: "the captain's head is always up!"), whereas Smith was offset 90 degrees clockwise, legs straight, presenting a broad target. (This he did for the same reason a man under acceleration would bow or kneel; a posture where one could not move well to defend oneself showed submission.)

Smith could see the stranger's ship in the viewing well. She was a slim and handsome craft, built along classical lines, an old, a very old design, of such craftsmanship as was rarely seen today. She was sturdy: built for high accelerations, and proudly bearing long thin structures forward of antennae of a type that indicated fearlessly loud and long-range radar. The engine block was far aft on a very long and graceful insulation shaft. The craft had evidently been made in days when the safety of the engine serfs still was a concern.

Her lines were sleek. (Not, Smith thought secretly, like *Procrustes,* whose low speed and lack of spin allowed her to grow many modules, ugly extrusions, and asymmetric protuberances.)

But the stranger's ship was *old.* Rust, and ice from frozen oxygen, stained the hull where seals had failed.

Yet she still emitted, on radio, the cheerful welcome-code. Merry green-and-red running lights were still lit. Microwave detectors showed radiations from the aft section of her hull, which might still be inhabited, even though the fore sections were cold and silent. Numbers and pictoglyphs flickered on a small screen to one side of the main image, showing telemetry and specific readings.

Smith studied the cylinder's radius and rate of spin. He calculated, and then he said, "Glorious Captain, the lowest deck of the stranger ship has centrifugal acceleration of exactly 32 feet per second per second."

The officers looked eye to eye, hissing with surprise.

The chancellor nodded the gaudy plume that grew from his hair and eyebrows. "This number has ancient significance! Some of the older orders of eremites still use it. They claim that it provides the best weight for our bones. Perhaps this is a religious ship."

One of the younger knights, a thin, dapple-bellied piebald wearing silk speed-wings running from his wrists to ankles, now spoke up: "Great Captain, perhaps she is an Earth ship, inhabited by machine intelligences . . . or ghosts!"

The other nobles opened their fans, and held them in front of their faces. If no derisive smiles were seen, then there was no legal cause for duel. The young knight might be illiterate, true, most young knights were, but the long kick-talons he wore on his calves had famous names.

The captain said, "We are more concerned for the stranger's nobility, than her . . . ah . . . origin." There were a few smirks at that. A ship from Earth, indeed! All the old horror-tales made it clear that nothing properly called human was left on Earth, except, perhaps, as pets or specimens of the machines. The Earthmind had never had much interest in space.

The chancellor said, "Those racks forward . . ." (he pointed at what were obviously antennae) ". . . may house weaponry, great Captain, or particle beam weapons, if the stranger has force enough in her drive core to sustain a weapon-grade power flow."

The captain looked toward Smith, "Concerning this ship's energy architecture, Engineer, have you any feelings or intuitions?" She would not ask him for "deductions" or "conclusions," of course.

Smith felt grateful that she had not asked him directly to answer the question; he was not obligated to contradict the chancellor's idiotic assertions. Particle beam indeed! The man had been pointing at a radio dish.

Very polite, the captain, very proper. Politeness was critically important aboard a crowded ship.

The captain was an hermaphrodite. An ancient law forbade captains to marry (or to take lowlife concubines) from crew aboard. The Captain's Wife must be from off-ship, either as gift or conquest or to cement a friendly alliance.

But neither was it proper for the highest of the highlife to go without sexual pleasure, so the captain's body was modified to allow her to pleasure herself.

Her breasts were beautiful—larger, by law, than any woman's aboard—and her skin was adjusted to a royal purple melanin, opaque to certain dangerous radiations. Parallel rows of her skin cells, down her belly and back, had been adjusted to become ornaments of nacre and pearl. Her long legs ended in a second pair of hands, nails worn long to show that she was above manual work. On her wrists and on her calves were the sheaths of her gem-studded blades, and she could fight with all four blades at once.

"Permission to speak to your handmaidens, Glorious Captain?"

"Granted. We will be amused by your antics."

The handmaidens were tied by their hair to the control boards (this was no discomfort in weightlessness, and left their fingers and toes free to manipulate the controls). Some controls were only a few inches from the captain's hand, but she would not touch controls, of course. That was what handmaidens were for.

Smith diffidently suggested to the handmaidens that they focus analytical cameras on several bright stars aft of the motionless ship, and then, as *Procrustes* approached a point where those same stars were eclipsed by the emission trail behind the stranger's drive, a spectographic comparison would give clues as to the nature of the exhaust, and hence of the engine structure. Such a scan, being passive, would not betray *Procrustes'* location.

When the analysis had been done as Smith suggested, the result showed an unusally high number of parts per billion of hard gamma radiation, as well as traces of high overall electric charge. Smith gave his report, and concluded: "The high numbers of antiprotons through the plume points to a matter-antimatter reaction drive. In properly tuned drives, however, the antiprotons should have been completely consumed, so that their radiation pressure could add to the thrust. Particle decay in the plume indicates many gigaseconds have passed since the main expulsions. There is a cloud of different geometry condensed closer to the drive itself, indicating that the starship has been drifting on low power, her engines idling. But the engines are still active, Glorious Captain. She is not a hulk. She lives."

Smith was smiling when he gave this report, surprised by his own calm lightheartedness. He did not recognize the mood, at first.

It was hope. Often the guest law required the captain to display great munificence. And here was a ship clearly in need of repair, in need of a good smith.

Perhaps the captain would sell his contract to these new people; perhaps there was hope that he could leave *Procrustes,* perhaps find masters less cruel, duties less arduous. (Freedom, a home, a wife, a woman to touch, babies born with his name, a name of his own—these he did not even dream of, anymore.)

With a new ship, anything might happen. And even if Smith weren't given away, at least there would be news, new faces, and a banquet. Guest law made such chance meetings a time of celebration.

The captain waved her fan to rotate herself to face her gathered officers. "Opinions, my gentlemen?"

The chancellor said, "With respect, great Captain, we must assume she is of the noble class. If she carries antimatter, she must be armed. She may be a religious ship, perhaps a holy order on errantry or antimachine crusade. In either case, it would be against the guest law not to answer her hail. As the poet says: 'Ships are few and far in the wide expanse of night; shared cheer, shared news, shared goods, all increase our might.'"

The winged knight said: "With respect, great Captain! If this is a religious ship, then let God or His Wife Gaia look after her! Why should a ship with such potent drives be hanging idle and adrift? No natural reason! There may be plagues aboard, or bad spirits, or machines from Earth. I say pass this one by. The guest law does not require we give hospitality and aid to such unchancy vessels, or ships under curse. Does not the poet also say: 'Beware the strangeness of the stranger. Unknown things bring unknown danger'?"

A seneschal whose teeth had been grown into jewels spoke next, "Great Captain, with respect. The guest law allows us to live in the Void. Don't we share air and water and wine? Don't we swap crews and news when we meet? This is a ship unknown, too true, and a strange design. But every ship we meet is new! Einstein makes certain time will age us forever away from any future meetings with any other ship's crew. None of that matters. Captain, my peers, honored officers, listen: either that ship is noble, or she is unarmed. If she is unarmed, she owes us one tenth of her cargo and air and crew. Isn't that fair? Don't we keep the Void clear of pirates and rogues when we find them? But if she is noble, either she has survivors, or she has not. If there are no survivors, then she is a rich prize, and ours by salvage law. Look at the soundness of her structure: her center hull would make a fine new high keep; she is leaking oxygen, she must have air to spare; and the grease-monkey here says she has a drive of great power! Driven by antimatter!"

The vavasors and knights were gazing now with greedy eyes at the image in the viewing well. Antimatter, particularly anti-iron, was the only standard barter metal used throughout the Expanse. Like gold, it was always in demand; unlike radioactives, it did not decay; it was easily identifiable, it was homogenous, it was portable. It was the universal coin, because everyone needed energy.

The seneschal said, "But if she has survivors, great Captain, they must be very weak. And weak ships are often more generous than the guest law requires! More generous than any living man wants to be!"

A ripple of hissing laughter echoed from the circle of nobles. Some of them fondly touched their knives and anchorhooks.

The captain looked as if she were about to chide them for their evil thoughts, but then a sort of cruel masculine look came to her features. Smith was reminded that the womanly parts of her hermaphrodite's body were only present to serve the pleasure of the manly parts.

The captain said, "Good my gentlemen, might there be a noble woman aboard, among the survivors?"

The ship's doctor, an old, wiry man with thin hands and goggle-adapted eyes, laughed breathlessly: "Aye! Captain's in rut and high time she were married, says I! Sad when we had to choke that concubine, back last megasecond when the air-stock got low. Don't you worry, Capt'n! If there be anyone aboard that ship, whatever they is now, I'll make 'em into a woman for you! Make 'em! Even boys get to like it, you know, after you dock 'em a few times, if you got their wombs wired up right to the pleasure center of their brains!"

There was some snickering at that, but the laughter froze when the captain said in her mildest voice: "Good my ship's Surgeon, we are most pleased by your counsel, though it is not called for at this time. We remind you that an officer and a gentleman does not indulge in waggish humor or display."

Then she snapped her right fan open and held it overhead for attention. "My herald, radio to the stranger ship with my compliments and tell her to prepare for docking under the guest-law protocols. Fire-control, ready your weapons in case she answers in an ignoble or inhospitable fashion, or if she turns pirate. Quartermaster, ready ample cubic space to take on full supplies."

The nobles looked eye to eye, smiling, hands caressing weapon-hilts, nostrils dilated, smiling with blood-lust at the prospect.

The captain said with mild irony: "The stranger is weak, after all, and may be more generous than guest law or prudence requires. Go, my gentlemen, prepare your battle-dress! Look as haughty as hawks and as proud as peacocks for our guests!"

Their laughter sounded horrid to Smith's ears. He thought of the guest law, and of his hopes, and felt sick.

▲   ▲   ▲

The captain, as an afterthought, motioned with her fan toward Smith, saying to her handmaid, "And shut down the engineer. We may have need of his aptitudes soon, and we need no loose talk belowdecks the while."

A handmaiden raised a control box and pointed it at Smith, and, before he could summon the courage to plead, a circuit the ship's doctor had put in his spine and brain stem shut off his sensory nerves and motor-control.

Smith wished he had had the chance to beg for his sleep center to be turned on. He hated the hallucinations sensory deprivation brought.

Numb, blind, wrapped in a gray void, Smith tried to sleep.

When Smith slept, he dreamed of home, of his father and mother and many brothers. His native habitat was built up around the resting hulk of the exile-ship *Never Return,* in geosynchronous orbit above an ancient storm system rippling the face of a vast gas giant in the Tau Ceti system.

The habitat had a skyhook made of materials no modern man could reproduce, lowered into the trailing edge of the storm. Here the pressure caused a standing wave, larger than the surface area of most planets, which churned up pressurized metallic hydrogen from the lower atmospheres. The colonists had mined the wave for fuel for passing starships for generations.

In the time of Smith's great-grandfather, the multimillion-year-old storm began to die out. As fuel production failed, the colony grew weak, and the Nevermen were subject to raids. Some came from Oort-cloud nomads, but most were from the inner-system colonists who inhabited the asteroidal belts their ancestors had made by pulverizing the subterrestrial planets.

Smith's mother and father had been killed in the raids.

There was no law, no government, to appeal to for aid. Even on old Earth, before the machines, no single government had ever managed to control the many peoples of that one small planet. To dream of government across the Expanse was madness: the madness of sending a petition to a ruler so distant that only your remote descendants would hear a reply.

And it was too easy for anyone who wished to escape the jurisdiction of any prospective government; they need only shut down their radio and alter their orbit by a few degrees. Space is vast, and human habitats were small and silent.

(Planets? No one lived on the surface of those vulnerable rocks, suited against atmospheres humans could not endure, at gravities that they could not, by adjusting spin, control. Legends said that Earth was a world where unsuited men could walk abroad. The chances of finding a perfect twin—and the match must be perfect, for humans were evolved for only one environment—made certain that the legend would remain a legend. In the meantime, mankind lived on ships and habitats.)

After the destruction of his home, Smith himself had been sold into slavery.

Slavery? Why *not* slavery? It was not economically feasible in a technological society, true. But then again, slavery had *never* been economically feasible, even back on Old Earth. The impracticality of slavery had not abolished it. History's only period without slavery, back on Earth, happened when the civilized Western nations, led by Britain, brought the pressure of world opinion (or open war) against the nations that practiced it. The Abolitionist Movements and their ideals reached to all continents.

But, on Earth, it did not take years and generations for nearest neighbors to take note of what their neighbors did.

Endless space meant endless lawlessness.

There was, however, custom.

Radio traffic was easier to send than ships from star to star, and there was no danger in listening to it. Radio-men and scholars in every system had to keep ancient languages alive, or else the lore of the talking universe would be closed to them. Common language permitted the possibility of common custom.

Furthermore, systems that did not maintain the ancient protocols for approaching starships could not tempt captains to spend the time and fuel to decelerate. If colonists wanted news and gifts and emigrants and air, they had to announce their readiness to obey the guest law.

And, of course, there were rumors and horrid myths of supernatural retributions visited on those who broke the guest law. Smith thought that the mere existence of such rumors proved that the guest law was not, and could never be, enforced.

Smith was not awake when the heralds exchanged radio-calls and conducted negotiations between the ships.

But when the seneschal ordered him alert again, he saw the looks of guilt and fear on the faces of the highlife officers, the too-nervous laughter, too-quickly smothered.

The seneschal's cabin was sparsely decorated, merely a sphere divided by guy-ropes, without bead-webs or battle-flags or religious plant-balls growing on their tiny globules of earth. However, every other panel of the sphere was covered with a fragile screen of hemp-paper inked with iconography or calligraphy. (It was a credit to the seneschal's high-born agility that none of the hemp-paper screens were torn. When he practiced the grapples, thrusts, and slash-rebounds of zero-gravity fencing, he apparently judged his trajectories so well that he never spun or kicked into one. "Always kept his feet on the floor," as the old saying went.)

The seneschal was giving Smith instructions for a work

detail. A party was to go EVA (still called "hanging" even though the ship lacked spin) to prepare a section of hull to receive sections from the stranger's ship, once it had been cannibalized.

(Smith was secretly agonized to hear the seneschal call the beautiful strange craft "it" instead of "she," as if the ship were a piece of machinery, already dead, and no longer a living vessel.)

They were interrupted by the attention claxon in the ceremonial imperative mode. The seneschal reached out with both feet, and gracefully drew open a panel hidden behind the hemp-paper screens, to reveal a private viewing well beneath.

Shining in the image was a scene from the huge forward cargo lock. The main clamshell radiation-shockwave shields had been folded back, and the wide circle of the inner lock's docking ring glittered black in the light of many floating lanterns.

Beyond was a glimpse of the stranger ship. Here was an archaic lock, both doors open in a sign of trust. Controls of ancient fashion glinted silvery in an otherwise black axis, which opened like a dark well filled with gloom and frost, ripped guy-lines trembling like cobwebs in the gusts from irregular ventilators.

A figure came out from the gloom. He passed the lock, and slowed himself with a squirt from an antique leg-jet, raising his foot to his center of mass and spraying a cloud before him. He hovered in the center of the black ring, while the squirt of mist that hid him slowly dissipated.

The seneschal said in a voice of curiosity and fear: "It's true, then. He has no entourage! What happened to his crew?" He had apparently forgotten who was in his cabin, for he spoke in the conversational register.

"Request permission to come aboard," the stranger was calling in Anglatin.

Smith stared in wonder. The stranger was very short, even for a heavyweight. The skin of his head and hands was normal, albeit blank and untattooed, but the rest of his body was loose, wrinkled, and folded, as if his skin were contaminated with some horrible epidermal disease. Apparently he was a eunuch; there were no sex organs visible between his legs. His hair was white, and had been programmed to grow, for some reason, only on the top, back, and sides of his skull (Smith had seen religious orders modify their hair to this design, claiming such ugliness was ancient tradition).

Suddenly Smith realized that the blue material of the stranger's skin was *not* skin, but fabric, as if he were suited (with gauntlets and helm removed) from some suit too thin to protect a man from vacuum; or as if he wore a lowlifer's work-smock without pockets or adhesive pads.

"Garb," said the seneschal, obviously wondering along the same lines Smith had been. "The old word for outer skins is garb. It is used to retain heat close to the body, without the energy cost of heating the whole cabin. He must have lost environmental control long ago. That weapon at his hip is also an antique. It is called a kiri-su-gama. Very difficult to control. One must spin the ball-and-chain counter-opposite from the hook or else one rotates wildly during combat. Either the hook or the ball can be used to snare the opponent to prevent blow-rebounds. But what arrogance to carry such an antique! Back in the times when ships had large interior spaces, perhaps, perhaps! But now? Knives and cestuses are better for fighting in cabins and crawltubes. Arrogance! Arrogance! And, ugh! He wears foot-mittens instead of foot-gloves; nor do I blame him. See how his toes are deformed! Has he been walking on them? Ghastly!"

But the stranger was obviously the foreign captain. The emblems on his epaulettes were the same as those that the *Procrustes'* captain had growing from modified areas of her shoulder cells. His blue "garb" was the same color, nearly, as her pigments.

She was speaking now, granting his permission to come aboard with the words and gestures of the ancient boarding-ceremony. She concluded with: "And by what title is it proper to call our honored guest?" And her flute-dwarf gave a three-tone flourish with his pipes so that the ritual music ended as her words did.

"Call me Descender. My ship is the noble *Olympian Vendetta*. And by what title is it proper to call my generous hostess?"

"Call me Ereshkigal, captain of the noble ship *Procrustes*."

"Noble fellow-Captain, because mankind is so widely flown, and many years and light-years separate brother from brother, tell me, before I board your craft, whether my understanding of the guest law is sufficient, and whether it accords with yours at every point? Excuse this question if it seems impertinent or suspicious; nothing of the sort is meant or should be inferred; I merely wish to ensure I give no unwitting offense or that I make no unfounded assumptions. For, as the poet says, 'The wise man calculates each maneuver as he goes; ignorance and inattention feed the seeds from which all danger grows.'"

"Noble fellow-Captain, you speak well and gentlemanly," said the captain, visibly impressed with the other's humble eloquence. "No offense is taken, nor do I permit offense to be taken by my men. As the poet says, 'A gentleman learns five things to do aright: to fly, to fence, to tell the truth, to know no fear, to be polite.' And politely you have spoken, sir."

But her quote was not quite as apt as, nor did it display the learning of, the stranger's.

She called for her chancellor, who, without any show of impatience, recited the whole body of the guest law, phrase by phrase, and answered with grave care when the stranger politely asked for definitions of ambiguous wording.

There were customary rules mentioned that Smith had never heard before, or had not heard in detail, but everything seemed to be based on common sense and common politeness: Aid to be given to fellow ships met in the void, not to exceed one-tenth of total value of ships and crew; more to be exchanged if mutually agreeable; navigational data to be shared without reservation; standardized protocols for swapping air and supplies to ships in need; all maneuvering before and after docking to be determined by formula based on mass and vector, the lighter ships going farther to match velocities with the heavier, so that the total fuel expenditures were roughly equal; guests to bring their own air, plus a tithe for the host plants; common forms of politeness to be used; disembarking to be done at will after due warning; no departure from the guest-ship to be interpreted as constituting any abandonment; the code of duels to be suspended; any disagreements as to valuations of goods exchanged or veracity of informations shared to be determined by such arbitrators as shall be mutually agreed-upon. And so on.

Smith, through the viewing well, could see the gathered nobles growing uneasy, not meeting each other's eyes. Looks of sullen guilt darkened on their tattooed faces as they heard each phrase and lofty sentiment of the laws they intended to violate.

When the recitation of the law was done, Captain Descender and Captain Ereshkigal bound themselves by formidable oaths to abide by every aspect of this law. They exchanged grave and serious assurances of their honesty and good intent.

Smith, listening, felt cold.

The oathtaking concluded with Captain Ereshkigal saying: ". . . and if I am forsworn, let devils and ghosts consume me in Gaia's Wasteland, in God's Hell, and may I suffer the vengeance of the Machines of Earth."

"Exactly so," said Captain Descender, smiling.

▲   ▲   ▲

The feast-hall of the *Procrustes* was aft of the bridge, but forward of the drive core, along the axis, where it was protected by (and inward of) all lower decks. The Officers' Mess (to use the old poet's term for it) was the highest of the high country, a place of ceremony and rare delight.

Banners of translucent fabric, colored, or luminous with fantastic heraldries, ran from point to point throughout the cylinder. The fabric was meant to absorb escaping food crumbs or particles of flying wine from the air, but it also muted and colored the lights shining from the bulkheads.

For drinks (or drinkers) of low esteem, there were wineskins. But the ship's cook had outdone himself for the high wines: pleasing to the eye, the globules of high wine or winejelly gleamed and glittered, held only in skins of fishnet web. The interstices of the web were small enough to keep the wine englobed by its own surface tension. Nobles had to drink from such webs with a delicate and graceful touch, lest a sudden maneuver allow wine to splatter through the webbing.

Here was the captain, floating at the focal point of an array of banners so that she looked like a Boddhisattva of Gaia in the center of a celestial rose. She was in the Reserved Regard position; that is, right foot folded on her lap, left foot extended, foot-spoon held lightly between her toes, left hand holding an open fan, right hand overhead in graceful gesture, wearing an eating glove with different spices crusting the fingernails. As tradition required, she held a napkin in her right foot folded in a complex origami pattern. It was considered a crime against elegance to have to actually use the napkin.

Her hair was arrayed in the coiffure called Welcome Dish, braided at the ends and electrostatically charged so that it made an evenly swirled disk above and behind her head and shoulders, like a halo.

Her feast was arranged in a circle around her, little colorful moons of ripe fruit, balls of wine-jelly, spheres of lacy bread, meatballs or sausages tumbling end-over-end. As the feast progressed, she would rotate slowly clockwise, to let one delicacy after another come within reach of hand and foot (toe-foods for the foot, finger-foods for the hand) and the order of the orbiting food around her was organized by traditional culinary theory.

Since the captain's head was always "up," the feasters must be attentive, and match their rotations to the captain, eating neither too swiftly nor too slowly, nor grabbing for any favored food out of order.

Descender was the last to be escorted in. The feasting nobles formed a rough cylinder, with Captain Ereshkigal at one end and Descender's place at the other.

Smith was hovering behind Captain Ereshkigal, not to eat, of course, but to answer any technical questions the captain might demand. He had a towel wrapped around his right foot and left hand, to capture any grease that might float from the Captain's lips. He also held her charging-brush, to act as hair-page, in case any haphazard event should interfere with the flow of her locks.

Smith noticed with some surprise that there was no page near Descender's mess-station; nor were there any guy-ropes very near reach.

When Descender entered, he flew using a rotate-and-thrust technique, shifting the attitude of his body with spins of the weighted tail of his sash, then moving with wasteful spurts of jet. It was an awkward and very old-fashioned method of maneuvering, not at all like the graceful, silent glides of nobles using fans, their moves full of subtle curves and changes, deceptive to an enemy in combat. It was easy to guess the trajectories of a man using rotate-and-thrust; easy for a fighter with a knife to kill him. Smith felt the same embarrassment for the man as someone in gravity might feel seeing a grown man crawl.

When Descender took his position, he paused, blinking, evidently puzzled by the lack of a convenient anchor nearby, the lack of service.

Smith noticed that the lights facing in that direction were

focused without banners to block direct glare. Another over-sight.

All the nobles watched Descender with careful sidelong looks. Some vague pleasantries were exchanged; grace was said; the meal began.

One knight loudly called: "Look here, mate, at what a fine dish we have: we'll suck this marrow dry!" And he tossed a leg of mutton lightly across the axis to the chancellor at the captain's right.

There was a slight silence. It was considered boorish to allow any food to pass between another feaster and the captain; the leg of lamb was centered just where it would block Descender's view.

The chancellor reached out with a leg-fork and hooked the meat, kicking trembling bits of grease in Descender's direction. "Aye. At least a sheep has good sense enough to know when it is due for the slaughter-pump house!"

No one laughed.

Descender turned his head. The doors behind him had been shut, and now two shipcarls were there, arms folded, legs in a position called Deadly Lotus, where fingers and toes could touch the hilts of sheathed blades. Unlike where Descender was, the shipcarls were surrounded by a web of guy-wires, and had surfaces near to kick off from.

It was with a sinking feeling that Smith saw Descender look up and down at the food-ring they had prepared for him. All the meats and fruits in the arc nearest his head were toe-foods; finger-foods were along the lower half of the circle; he must either grab for food out of turn, or eat uncouthly.

He looked as if he wanted to say something. He opened his mouth and closed it again. Perhaps a hint of nagging fear began to show on Descender's features.

The captain herself looked a little sad. She took up the salt-ball, but instead of pushing it along the axis to the other captain (showing that he was next in priority), she took a nail-full of salt and brushed the ball toward the seneschal on her right upper.

He grinned at Descender, took a fingernail's worth of salt, but then tossed it to his left. All the knights were served before the salt-ball came to Descender. The last knight to touch it looked carefully at Descender, licked the salt-ball with his tongue, and threw it toward Descender with a jerk of his jaw.

Descender's face, by now, was an impassive mask, but his jaw was clenched. A bead of sweat floated from his forehead. He did not reach for the insulting salt-ball, but let it fly past his shoulder toward the bulk-head behind.

All the nobles had their hands near their weapons. The chamber was utterly silent.

There was something sad in Descender's eye when he smiled a weak smile and reached up for a foot-peach near his head. "I compliment my noble fellow-captain for her bountiful feast," he said, and took a bite.

There was some snickering. It was like seeing a man under acceleration eating off what, in the old times, they would have called the floor.

One of the shipcarls behind Descender opened the ventilator, so that the breezes began to slowly scatter his food. Descender paused; he grabbed one or two pieces of fruit and stuck them under his elbow to hang onto them.

It looked absurd. But nobody laughed.

It was hard to say whether or not Descender actually was frightened. His face showed no emotion. But he certainly acted like a frightened man.

He said, "I thank you for your hospitality. I wish now to return to my ship."

The chancellor said, "But we are not done with you. That ship of yours; it is a nice one, isn't it? We would be happy to accept its drives and main hulls sections as gifts. Or perhaps we can simply claim it as salvage. There's no one aboard it right now."

Descender curled his legs, and put his hands near his kiri-su-gama. He spoke softly: "She. It's more polite, good sir, to address those crafts who sustain our lives as 'her' and 'she.'"

The winged knight said loudly, "Those who carry arms are required, when honor commands, to use them. Those false lowlife debris and pokeboys who scrounge the weapons off their betters deserve a looter's air-lock. But who says a thief has any care for honor? It is to honor, gentlemen, that I propose a toast! To the honor and to the air that sustains us! Let those who will not drink be deprived of both. But look! You have no page, you who call yourself a captain! Hoy! Smith! Grease-monkey! Hand our guest his last draught of wine; your hands are the only ones fit to hand it to him!" And he took from his pouch a plastic bag from the medical stores, filled with liquid waste. The knight threw it to Smith, who caught it with trembling fingers.

This was a mortal insult. If Smith passed the bag to him, Descender could neither drink, nor could he refuse the toast, with honor. The carefully planned program of insults that had gone before, Smith guessed, had only been to see how much Descender would stomach. If he had any hidden weapons, tricks, or traps, now he would show them; Captain Ereshkigal would only lose one lesser knight; Ereshkigal could repudiate the rash young knight once he was killed, apologize, blame him; polite words and polite pretense could keep a bit of honor intact during such retreat.

That is, if he had some hidden weapon. If not . . .

Anger made Smith forget all caution. He threw down the heavy charging-brush and the sloshing bag of medical waste, so that he drifted away from the captain and out of her immediate knifereach. "Here's a poor man, innocent as innocence, and you're going to strangle him up and eat his fine ship! He's done no wrong, and answered all your slurs with kind words! Why can't you let him be?! Why can't you let him *be?!*"

The captain spoke without turning her head: "Engineer, you are insubordinate. Your air ration is hereby decreased to zero. If you report to the medical house for euthanasia, your going will be pleasant, and note will be made of your obedience in the ship's log. If you continue your insubordination, however, your name will be blotted out. I have no wish to dishonor you; go quietly."

Descender spoke in a strange and distant tone of voice: "Captain, your order is not lawful. At feast times, the code of subordination is relaxed, and free speech allowed, at least among those civilized peoples who recognize the guest law . . ." He turned and looked at Smith, addressing him directly, "Engineer, what, pray tell, is your name? Tell it to me, and I shall preserve it in my ship's log, my book of life, and it may endure longer than any record of this age."

But Smith's courage deserted him then, and he did not answer. He flapped the napkin he held as a fan, moving back to the bulkhead, where he crouched, looking each way with wide, wild eyes, ready to spring off in any direction.

Yet no one paid much heed to him. The nobles were still concentrating on Descender. There was silence in the chamber.

The gentlemen were each stealing quick glances at their neighbors. Each crouched and ready. But no one was prepared to take the final swoop to make their threats and hints come true. Perhaps there was something hard about killing a man who had not drawn his weapon; perhaps they were each thinking that now, even now, it still was not too late to back away. . . .

Then the young piebald knight with the racing-wings spoke up, kicking the sheaths off his blades, displaying steel. Now it was too late. His voice rang out, high-pitched and over-loud: "What is more hateful in the sight of God than cowardice? By Gaia, how I hate the thing (I will not call him a man) who takes a blow without a show of spleen! He smiles with his beggar's smile, his shoulders hunched, his eye wet, a tremble in his whining voice. Hatred, gentleman, hatred and disgust is what we ought to feel for those we hurt! Weakness is loathsome! And any man who will not fight deserves to die!

A lowlife heart should not dare to hide inside what seems a captain's chest. I say we cut the false heart *out!*"

Descender's face was stiff and expressionless. His voice was tense and even. His eyes were filled with dreadful calm: "You are angry because you have no good *excuse* for anger, have you? It would be easier to do the deed if I had given some offense, wouldn't it? Or if I somehow seemed less human? Noble fellow-Captain Ereshkigal! There is no need for this. What I can spare from my ship, I will freely give. Let us avoid a scene of horror. You conduct yourself as one who honors honorable conduct. Let not this feast end in tragic death!"

The young knight shouted, "Beg and beg! Must we hear the beggar mewl!? Cut his throat and silence this shrill noise!" He kicked his legs to clash his blades together, a bright crash of metallic noise.

But Captain Ereshkigal held open her fan for silence. "My brother captain asks, with dignity, that we not pretend that this is other than it is. We will not mask our deed under the code of duels. Let it openly be named: Murder, then, murder and piracy!"

There was a slight noise all around the chamber, sighs and hisses from the gentlemen. Some looked angry, or saddened, or surprised; most were stony-faced; but each face, somehow, still was dark with cruelty.

The captain continued: "But you have brought it on *yourself,* brother captain! How *dare* you have a fine hull, fine drives, and air, when we are many, and you are only one?"

"The property is mine, by right."

"And when you die, it shall be ours, by right *or* wrong."

"You have no need."

"But we *want.*"

"Captain, I beg you—"

"We wish to hear no more of begging!"

"So . . . ? Is this the rule by which you wish also to be judged? Then no plea for mercy will be heard when your own time comes."

"Judged? How dare you speak defiance to us?"

"You condemn me when I apologize, and then equally when I do not. What if I say, take my ship, but spare my life?"

"We will not even spare an ounce of air!"

"Hah! I will be more generous than you, Ereshkigal. I will spare one life; perhaps that of the scared little Smith there. He has done me no harm, and I think that he begins to suspect what I am. Yes; one person should survive to spread the tale, otherwise the exercise is useless."

"Do you think to frighten us with superstitious hints and lies? Englobe him, my gentlemen! Steward, close the ducts! We must have our drapes sop up the blood-cloud so no drops foul our air system."

Descender spoke softly while the bejeweled, beribboned, and tattooed knights and vavasors, glittering, smiling, fans waving, drew their snaring-hooks and dirks and slowly circled him.

He spoke in a voice of Jovian calm: "Who else but a machine intelligence has so long a life that it can intend to bring law and order to the Void, and yet expect to see the slow results? Civilization, gentlemen, is when all men surrender their natural habits of violence, because they fear the retribution of some power sufficient to terrify and awe them into obedience. To civilize a wilderness is long effort; and when the wilderness is astronomically vast, the terror must be vast as well."

Captain Ereshkigal, her eyes wide with growing panic, made a clumsy gesture with her fan, shrieking, "Kill him! Kill!"

Steel glittered in their hands as the shouting knights and nobles kicked off the walls and dove. With hardly any surprise at all, Smith saw the stranger beginning to shine with supernatural light, and saw him reach up with flaming fingers to pull aside what turned out to be, after all, a mask.

The Voice

GREGORY BENFORD

Gregory Benford is one of the chief spokesmen of hard SF of the last twenty years, articulate and contentious, and he has produced some of the best fiction of recent decades about scientists working, and about the riveting and astonishing concepts of cosmology and the nature of the universe, for example, *Timescape,* or *Great Sky River.* For several years he has also been a science columnist for *Fantasy & Science Fiction* (he is currently preparing a collection of his columns). His novel *Foundation's Fear,* continuing Isaac Asimov's Foundation series, was published in 1997. His new novel, *Cosm,* is out this year in hardcover. He has had a story in each of the two previous *Year's Best* volumes in this series, each one quite different from the others in tone and approach. This story appeared in *SF Age,* and in a very different version in the original anthology *Future Histories.* It starts out in Isaac Asimov territory and wanders somehow into Ray Bradbury country without losing its punch or its science.

"I don't believe it." Qent said sternly.

Klair tugged him down the musty old corridor. "Come on, turn off your Voice. Mine is—I showed you."

"Stuff on walls, whoever heard of—"

"There's another one further along."

Down the narrow, dimly lit hallway they went, to a recessed portion of the permwall. "See—another sign."

"This? Some old mark. What's a 'sign' anyway?"

"This one says—" she shaped the letters to herself carefully—"PASSAGE DENIED."

Qent thumbed on his Voice impatiently. He blinked. "That's . . . what the Voice says."

"See?"

"You've been here before and the Voice told you."

"I let you pick the corridor, remember? A fair trial."

"You cheated."

"No! I can read it." Read. The very sound of the word made her pulse thump.

Qent paused a second and she knew he was consulting the Voice again. "And 'read' means to untangle things, I see. This 'sign' tells you PASSAGE DENIED? How?"

"See those?—they're letters. I know each one—there are twenty-six, it takes a lot of work—and together they shape words."

"Nonsense," Qent said primly. "Your mouth shapes words."

"I have another way. My way."

He shook his head and she had to take him on to another sign and repeat the performance. He grimaced when the Voice told him that indeed, the markings meant ALDENTEN

SECTOR. "A trick. Your Voice is on. You just rigged your touchpad—"

"Here, take my insert!" She thrust it into his hand and made him walk to the next emblem. "MANUFAC DIST, that way."

"I know an arrow when I see it," he said sarcastically. But the rest of it—what's DIST mean?"

She had hoped he wouldn't ask that. "Maybe it means a place."

"Like a neighborhood?"

"Could be—in fact, yes, 'district.' If there wasn't room to write it all out, they'd shorten a word."

"And who were 'they'? Some magicians?"

"The ancients, I guess."

He was working his way around to being convinced, she could see. "They left wall marks? What for, when the Voice—"

"Maybe they came before the Voice."

"But what possible use—"

"I learned all this from those old papers I uncovered in the Historical Section. They were called 'Bills of Lading' but there were enough words—"

"How do you know you can 'read' something? I mean, without checking with the Voice?"

"I know. The letters group together, you see—MANU-FAC is just 'man' and this upturned letter is the sound 'you,' and—"

"You're going too fast." He grimaced, obviously not liking this at all. He was a biology specialist and tolerated her interest in antiquity, but finally he said, "Okay, show me again. Not that I really believe this, but . . ."

They spent the next few days in the oldest precinct of the Historical Sector, searching out corridors that the Imperium had not gotten around to Voicing. Klair read him signs and he started picking up the method. Progress was slow; reading was hard. Letters, words, then working up to grasping how sentences and then paragraphs had their logic and rhythms, their clues about how to extract meaning.

Still, it wasn't as though he were some Deedee, after all. After a while she recalled from her Educational Specialty training that Deedees were actually officially called the Developmentally Delayed. So if someone had once taken just the first letters of both words, that was how they had gotten their name.

Everything went well between them and they got to like having their Voices off while they strolled through the antiquated hallways, making sense of the signs.

The Voice was always available if they needed it. Linkchips embedded near both ears could pick up the pervasive waves of CompCentral. They only had basic link, no frills but constant access. Like everybody, they had used the Voice more as time went on; it was so easy.

But reading gave them a touch of the past and some silence. It was a relief, really.

They had kept their Voices nearly always on. It was easy to get used to the Voice's silky advertisements that floated just within hearing. You could pay the subscriber service for the Voice and have no ads, but none of their friends did: it was far too expensive. And anyway, the ads told you a lot about people. There was a really interesting one for sperm and egg donors to the gay/les bank, a Meritocracy program to help preserve the Gay gene. It had zoomer sonics and life histories and everything. You could amp it and hear a whole half-hour show if you wanted. For free, too. But most weren't anywhere near that good, so they were glad to be rid of them.

Reading, though, grew on them. There were advantages to reading old signs that the Voice didn't bother to translate. They showed off to a few friends but nobody believed they could really read the curious markings. It had to be some trick, for sure. Klair and Qent just smiled knowingly and dropped the subject.

Not that it was all good. At an old intersection Qent honored the GO signal by reading it, rather than listening to his Voice. The signal was off synch and he nearly got flattened by a roller car.

They debated whether to tell anyone in authority. After all, maybe nobody knew this.

"Ummm, no," Qent said. "Look at it this way—carrion eaters rule the world, in their way. Because nobody cares. Nobody wants what they like."

"So we'd be fools to make other people like reading?"

"Demand rises, supplies fall. Suppose everybody wanted those old books you found?"

She had to admit it was a sobering possibility. The carrion-eater analogy came out of his biology training, and he couldn't resist adding, "It's a smart strategy. When times are tough on everybody, the buzzards just get more to eat."

The thought was so disgusting she decided to forget about the whole question.

They came to like strolling the byways of the Megapolis, ferreting out the antiquated secrets of the signs. Lovers often find their own rituals, and this was a particularly delectable one.

Outside one vaultway there were clearly marked instructions on how to spin a dial and get in. They had to work on it for quite a while but finally they made it work. The door swung open on primitive hinges and they walked into a musty set of rooms. Exploring them proved boring; just stacks of locked compartments, all without signs. Until a guard came in with a drawn zapper.

"How'd you kids get in here?"

"It was open, sir," Qent said. He had always been quick and Klair supposed his answer was technically correct. She had opened the door.

"How the hell—? Well, get out. Out!"

He was confused and worried and hardly gave them more than a brief search. Qent asked to see the zapper, imitating a dumbo kid, and the guard brushed them off, still puzzled.

Until the vault she had not realized that her hard-won trick was anything more than a delicious secret. Klair was a scholarly type and enjoyed her hours of scanning over the decaying sheets she found in the Historical Sector's archives.

The fat ones she learned were called "books" and there was even an entry in the Compendium about them. The Voice recited the entry to her in its soft tones, the ones she had chosen for her daily work. She used a more ornate voice for social matters and a crisp, precise one for directions. In normal life that was all anyone needed, a set of pleasing Voice agents.

There was hardly any delay when she requested the book entry and the Voice told a marvelous tale. There were many kinds of books, including one called "novel." This meant new the Voice said. But the one novel Klair found in the dank, dark Antiquities Vault was obviously old, not new at all. Such confusions were inevitable in research, she realized.

Books were known also as buchs in some ancient sources, it said, in the confusing era when there were competing Voices. Not really even Voices, either, but whole different speech-methods, before Standard was discovered.

All that happened in the Narrow Age, as antiquarians termed it. A time of constrained modes, hopelessly linear and slow. People then were divided by their access to information. Thank goodness such divisive forces were now banished.

They now lived in the Emergent Age, of course. The Voice had emerged from the evolution of old style Intelligent Agents, on computers. Those would perform fetch-'em tasks. Gradually, people let their Agents do more and more. Agent merging led to more creativity, coming from the overlap of many voices, many threads in a society where all was open and clear to all, available through the Voice.

"What sop!" Qent said to this, and she sort of agreed. The Narrow Age sounded fascinating, with its books and reading. The tingling thrill of being able to hold a year's worth of Voice talk in your hand, opening it to anywhere you chose, picking out lore at will—it captivated her.

Of course, she knew the Voice was superior. Instantly it could skip to any subject or even word you liked in any record. It would explain in private, sounding just like an enormously smart person speaking to you alone, in your head. Everybody had one and could access it with an internal signal.

She looked up the Voice itself in one of the old books. The words were hard to follow and she began to wish for some way to find out what they meant. Sounding them out was hard because, even when she knew the word, the mapping from letters to sounds followed irregular rules. "What's the point of that?" Qent asked often, but he kept at it with her.

The books said that the Voice had started as an aid to people called "illiterates"—and Klair was startled to find, consulting the Voice, that everybody was one. Except her and Qent, now.

Once, lots and lots of people could read. But as the Voice got easier to use, a certain cachet attached to using only the Voice. Independence from linear "print-slavery" became fashionable, then universal. After all, the Voice could pipe the data you needed on fast-flow, a kind of compressed speech that was as fast (or in fact, by that time, faster) as people could read.

Most people got their information by eye, anyway. In a restaurant, they ordered chicken by touching the drumstick icon, or fish by the fishstick icon. And of course most of their time they spent at entertainments, which had to be visual, tactile, smell-rich—sports, 3Ds, sensos, a-morphs, realos.

She found it quite delicious to have an obscure, secret talent that none of her friends even guessed. She was going to have a party and show them all, but then she saw the big letters in the Boulevard of Aspiration, and things got complicated.

Qent said, "I make it to be—

SAVVY THIS? MEAT 13:20 @ Y."

Skeptically he eyed the poorly printed letters written in livid red on a blue wall.

"Somebody did that by hand," Klair marveled.

"Writing by yourself? How?"

"I hadn't thought anybody could. I mean, machines make letters, don't they?"

"You're the one who read all those historical books. Printing machines gave way to Voice machines, you said."

Klair traced a hand over the misshapen letters. "It's like making a drawing, only you try to imitate a machine, see? Think of letters as little art objects."

"This isn't an art exhibit."

"No, it's a message. But maybe I can . . ."

By luck she had in her side-sack her latest cherished discovery, a fat book called "Dictionary." It had many more words in it than the Voice, approximating and vernacular. Big words that nobody used any more, hadn't used for so long even the Voice didn't know them. It even told her that "@" meant "at," but not why.

"Here," she pointed forcefully at the tiny little entry. "Meat is the flesh of an animal."

"Animals do that. I heard that people used to."

"Primitivo!" she said scornfully.

"It may mean that in there, but it sounds like 'meet.'"

"Somebody made an error? Confusing the sound with another word?"

"Somebody wants people who can read the sign to meet them."

"Other readers."

"Where?" He frowned.

"It says 'Y.' That's not a word."

"Maybe it's an abbreviation, like that "MANUFAC DIST?"

"No, too short."

He snapped his fingers. "Remember where the Avenue of Aspiration branches? You can look down on it from the balcony of the Renew building. From above, it looks like that letter."

"Let's be there, then."

They showed up, but nobody else did. Instead, at the Y another crude hand-lettered sign said

MEAT CORRIDOR 63,
13:30 TOMORROW, BLOCK 129

They went home and turned off their Voices and talked. Most couples silenced the Voice only during sex. This was merely polite, even though of course no other person could be sure it was off nowadays, what with the new neuroactivated models.

They went home and sped-read some ancient texts. There was a thick book titled The Lust of the Mahicans that Qent had seen on senso. She read it—her speed was a lot higher than his—but it wasn't anything like the senso he had seen. There was no sex in it at all. Just stares of infinite longing and heavy breathing and pounding pulses and stuff like that. Still, she found it oddly stirring. Reading was funny that way.

They could not get their minds off the sign. Qent was out of sorts, irked that others had mastered their discovery. He groused about it vaguely and found excuses to change the subject.

Klair didn't see it possessively. After all, the higher moral good was to share. Reading was wickedly single-ist. Was that why she liked it so much? A reader was isolated, listening to a voice no one else could take part in. That led to differences and divisions, friction and clashes.

Still, the rapture of reading—of listening to silent sounds from ages past—was too, well, perhaps the right word was tit-illating.

She was excited by the prospect of other readers. Inevitably, they went to the site.

The man who slouched beside a rampway was not impressive. Medium height, his crimson codpiece was three years out of date. His hair was stringy and festooned with comically tattered microbirds. He said nothing, simply handed them a sheet. Miserably printed sentences covered both sides. The first paragraph was enough for Klair.

THE SECRET ASSEMBLY OF READERS MUST UNITE! WE HAVE A TALENT THE MASSES CANNOT UNDERSTAND. THEY WILL FEAR US IF THEY KNOW. A BROTHERHOOD AND SISTERHOOD OF READERS IS THE ONLY SOLUTION TO OUR ISOLATION. ARISE!

"What cliche sop!" She thrust the sheet back at him.

"True, though."

Qent said sharply, "Just tell us what you—"

"You never know when the Voice is on," the man said mysteriously.

Klair said, "And your printing is awful."

"Better than yours," he said shrewdly.

"That's not the point," Qent said. "We demand to know—"

"Come on. And shut up, huh?"

▲   ▲   ▲

They were in a wildness preserve before the man spoke. "I'm Marq. No Voice pickups here, at least according to the flow charts."

"You're an engineer?" Klair asked, admiring the oaks.

"I'm a philosopher. I make my money engineering."

"How long have you been reading?"

"Years. Started with some old manuals I found. Figured it out from scratch."

"So did we." Qent said. "It's hard, not being able to ask for help from the Voice."

Marq nodded. "I did. Dumb, huh?"

"What happened?"

"Some Spectors came by. Just casual talk, y'know, but I knew what they were after."

"Evidence?" she asked uneasily.

"When I asked the Voice there was a pause, just a little one. A priority shift, I know how to spot them. So I broke off and took the books I had to a hiding place. When I got back there were the Spectors, cool as you like, just kind of looking around my room."

"You didn't tell them . . . ?" she asked.

"You got to give them something. I had a copy of this thing about books that I couldn't understand, Centigrade 233. Kept it buried under a pseud-bush bed. They were getting funny on me so I took it out and gave it to them."

She blinked, startled. "What did they do? Arrest you?"

Marq gave her a crooked grin. "Reading's not illegal, y'know. Just anti, that's all. So they let me off with six weeks of grouping."

"Wow, do I hate those," Qent said.

Marq shrugged. "I did the time. They poked at me and I had to pretend to see the light and all. They kept the book."

"You're brave," Klair said.

"Just stupid. I should never have asked the Voice."

Qent said earnestly, "You'd think the Voice would encourage us to learn. I mean, it'd be useful in emergencies. Say the Voice goes down, we could read the info we'd need."

Marq nodded. "I figure the Voice reads. It just doesn't want competition."

She said, "The Voice is a machine."

"So?" Marq shrugged again. "Who knows how smart it is?"

"It's a service," Qent said. "That's all."

"Notice how it won't store what we say?" Marq smiled shrewdly.

Qent nodded. "It says it's trying to improve our memories."

"Reading was invented to replace memory," Klair said. "I read it in a history book."

"So it must be true?" Marq shrugged derisively, a gesture that was beginning to irk Klair a lot.

She hated politics and this was starting to sound like that. "How many books have you got?"

"Lots. I found a tunnel into a vault. I can go there any-time."

Qent and Klair gasped at his audacity as he described how for years he had burrowed into sealed-off chambers, many rich in decaying documents and bound volumes. He spoke of exotica they had never seen, tomes which were nothing but names in the Dictionary: Encyclopedias, Thesauruses, Atlases, Alamancs. He had read whole volumes of the fabled Britannica!

Would he trade? Lend? "Of course," Marq said warmly.

Their friendship began that way, a bit edgy and cautious at the margins, but dominated by the skill and secret lore they shared. Three years of clandestine reading followed before Marq disappeared.

▲   ▲   ▲

He wasn't at any of their usual meeting places. After all this time, they still did not know where he lived, or where his hoard of books might be. Marq was secretive. They searched the sprawling corridors of the complexes, but were afraid to ask the Voice for any info on him.

The Majority Games were on then so the streets were more crowded than usual. Most people were out all the time, excited and eager and happy to be in the great mobs that thronged the squares. The Games took up everybody's time—except, of course, the three hours of work everyone had to put in, no exceptions, every laborday. Klair and Qent broke up to cover more ground and spent a full week on the search. Many times Klair blamed herself for not pressing Marq about where he lived, but the man was obsessively secretive. "Suppose they grab you, make you tell about me?" he had always countered.

Now she wondered what the Spectors would do if they uncovered a lode of books like Marq's. Send him to Advanced Treatment? Or was there something even worse?

She came home after a day of dogged searching and Qent was not there. He did not appear that evening. When she awoke the next morning she burst into tears. He was gone that day and the one after.

On her way back from work, a routine counseling job, she resolved to go to the Spector. She halfheartedly watched the crowds, hoping to see Marq or Qent, and that was how she noticed that three men and a woman were moving parallel to her as she crossed the Plaza of Promise. They were all looking some other way but they formed four points of the compass around her with practiced precision.

She walked faster and they did too. They looked stern and remorseless and she could not lose them in the warrens of streets and corridors near the two-room apartment she shared with Qent. They had waited five years to get one with a tiny balcony. Even then it was just two levels up from the muddy floor of the air shaft. But if you hooked your head over to the side you could see some sky that way.

Klair kept moving in an aimless pattern and they followed. Of course she did not want to go to the apartment, where she would be trapped. But she was tired and she could not think of anything else to do.

They knocked a few minutes after she collapsed on the bed. She had hoped they might hold off for a while. She was resigned. When she spun the door open the person she least expected to see was Marq.

"You won't believe what's going on," he said, brushing past her.

"What? Where have you—"

"The Meritocrats want us."

"For what?"

"Reading!"

"But the Voice—"

"Keeps people out of touch and happy. Great idea—but it turns out you can't run everything with just the Voice." He blinked, the merest hesitation. "Somebody's got to be able to access info at a higher level. That was our gut feeling, remember—that reading was different."

"Well, yes, but the Spectors—"

"They keep people damped down, is all." A slight pause. "Anybody who's got the savvy to see the signs, the grit to learn to piece together words on their own, to process it all—those are the people the Merits want. Us!"

Klair blinked. This was too much to encompass. "But why did they take you away, and Qent—"

"Had to be sure." He gave his old familiar shrug. "Wanted to test our skills, make sure we weren't just posing. People might catch on, only pretend to read, y'know?"

"I . . . see." There was something about Marq that wasn't right. He had never had these pauses before . . . because he wasn't listening to the Voice then?

She backed away from him. "That's marvelous news. When will Qent be back?"

"Oh, soon, soon." He advanced and she backed out onto the balcony.

"So what job will you do? I mean, with reading in it?"

They were outside. She backed into the railing. The usual distant clatter and chat of the air shaft gave her a momentary sense of security. Nothing could happen here, could it?

"Oh, plenty. Looking up old stuff, comparing, y'know." He waved his hands vaguely.

It wasn't much of a drop from here. Over the railing, legs set right . . .

"It's good work, really."

Could she could get away if she jumped? Marq wasn't the athletic type and she knew that if she landed right on the mud below she wouldn't twist an ankle or anything. She had on sensible shoes. She could elude him. If she landed right.

She gave him a quick, searching look. Had he come here alone? No, probably there were Spectors outside her door, just waiting for him to talk her into surrendering. Stall for time, yes.

"How bad is it?"

He grinned. "You won't mind. They just access that part of your mind for three hours a day. Then they install a shutdown on that cerebral sector."

"Shutdown? I—"

"So you don't need to read any more. Just during work, is all. You get all you need that way. Then you're free!"

She thought it through. Jump, get away. Couldn't use the Voice for help because they could undoubtedly track her if she had her receiver on. Could she get by just reading the old signs?

Suppose she could. Then what? Find some friends she could trust. Stay underground? How? Living off what?

"It's much better. Qent will be back soon and—"

"Hold it. Don't move."

She looked down the air shaft. Was the jump worth it?

You spool out of the illusion and snap—back into the tight cocoon. The automatic sensory leads retract, giving your skin momentary pinprick goodbye kisses. Once more you feel the cool clasping surfaces of the cocoon. Now you turn and ask, "Hey, where's the rest?"

Myrph shrugs her shoulders, still busy undoing her leads. "That's all there was, I told you."

"Maybe it's just damaged?"

"No, that's the end of the cube. There must be another cube to finish the story, but this was the only one I found back in that closet."

"But how does it end? What's she do?" You lean toward her, hoping maybe she's just teasing.

"I dunno. What would you do? Jump?"

You blink, not ready for the question. "Uh, this reading thing. What is it, really?"

Myrph frowns. "It felt like a kind of your own silent voice inside your head."

"Is it real? I mean, does reading exist?"

"Never heard of it."

"So this isn't an historical at all, right? It's a fantasy."

"Must be. I've never seen those things on walls."

"Signs, she called them." You think back. "They would have worn away a long time ago, anyway."

"I guess. Felt kinda strange, didn't it, being able to find out things without the Voice?"

You bite your lip, thinking. Already the illusion of being that woman is slipping away, hard to fix in memory. She did have a kind of power all on her own with that reading thing. You liked that. "I wonder what she did?"

"Hey, it's just a story."

"What would you do?"

"I don't have to decide. It's just a story."

"But why tell it then?"

Myrph says irritably, "It's just an old illusion, missing a cube."

"Maybe there was only one."

"Look, I want illusions to take me away, not stress me out."

You remember the power of it. "Can I have it, then?"

"The cube? Sure."

Myrph tosses it over. It is curiously heavy, translucent and chipped with rounded corners. You cup it in your hand and like the weight of it.

That is how it starts. You know already that you will go and look for the signs in the corridors and that for good or ill something new has come into your world and will now never leave it.

Yeyuka

GREG EGAN

Greg Egan is one of the leading SF writers to emerge in recent decades from Australian SF onto the world stage, and the most prominent of them in the 1990s as the decade moves on toward the World SF convention in Australia in 1999. His novels include *Quarantine, Permutation City, Distress,* and *Diaspora,* and some of his best stories are collected in *Axiomatic.* This story appeared in the Australian literary magazine, *Meanjin,* and was one of several of his in 1997 that might have been chosen for this book. He is one of the strong and individual new voices in SF this decade with an invariably high level of execution in recent years. This story has an intimate quality, yet balanced (paradoxically?) by an ironic distance. More than many of his other stories it gets to the heart of cultural, social, and technological barriers that divide and segment our world today and raises the questions of those divisions, real and artificial. What do we have to give up to save others?

On my last day in Sydney, as a kind of farewell, I spent the morning on Bondi Beach. I swam for an hour, then lay on the sand and stared at the sky. I dozed off for a while, and when I woke there were half a dozen booths set up amid the sun bathers, dispensing the latest fashion: solar tattoos. On a touch-screen the size of a full-length mirror, you could choose a design and then customize it, or create one from scratch with software assistance. Computer-controlled jets sprayed the undeveloped pigments onto your skin, then an hour of UV exposure rendered all the colors visible.

As the morning wore on, I saw giant yellow butterflies perched between shoulder blades, torsos wrapped in green-and-violet dragons, whole bodies wreathed in chains of red hibiscus. Watching these images materialize around me, I couldn't help thinking of them as banners of victory. Throughout my childhood, there'd been nothing more terrifying than the threat of melanoma—and by the turn of the millennium, nothing more hip than neck-to-knee lycra. Twenty years later, these elaborate decorations were designed to encourage, to boast of, irradiation. To proclaim, not that the sun itself had been tamed, but that our bodies had. To declare that cancer had been defeated.

I touched the ring on my left index finger, and felt a reassuring pulse through the metal. Blood flowed constantly around the hollow core of the device, diverted from a vein in my finger. The ring's inner surface was covered with billions of tiny sensors, spring-loaded funnel-shaped structures like microscopic Venus fly-traps, each just a few hundred atoms wide. Every sizeable molecule in my bloodstream that collided with one of these traps was seized and shrink-wrapped, long enough and tightly enough to determine its shape and its chemical identity before it was released.

So the ring knew exactly what was in my blood. It also knew what belonged, and what didn't. Under its relentless scrutiny, the biochemical signature of a viral or bacterial infection, or even a microscopic tumor far downstream, could never escape detection for long—and once a diagnosis was made, treatment was almost instantaneous. Planted alongside the sensors were programmable catalysts, versatile molecules that could be reshaped under computer control.

The ring could manufacture a wide range of drugs from raw materials circulating in the blood, just by choosing the right sequence of shapes for these catalysts—trapping the necessary ingredients together in nooks and crannies molded to fit like plaster casts around their combined outlines.

With medication delivered within minutes or seconds, infections were wiped out before they could take hold, tiny clusters of cancer cells destroyed before they could grow or spread. Linked by satellite to a vast array of medical databases, and as much additional computing power as it required, the ring gave me a kind of electronic immune system, fast enough and smart enough to overcome any adversary.

Not everyone on the beach that morning would have had their own personal HealthGuard, but a weekly session on a shared family unit, or even a monthly check-up at their local GP, would have been enough to reduce their risk of cancer dramatically. And though melanoma was the least of my worries—fair-skinned, I was covered in sunscreen as usual; fatal or not, getting burnt was painful—with the ring standing guard against ten thousand other possibilities, I'd come to think of it as a vital part of my body. The day I'd installed it, my life expectancy had risen by fifteen years—and no doubt my bank's risk-assessment software had assumed a similar extension to my working life, since I'd be paying off the loan I'd needed to buy the thing well into my sixties.

I tugged gently at the plain metal band, until I felt a sharp warning from the needle-thin tubes that ran deep into the flesh. This model wasn't designed to be slipped on and off in an instant like the shared units, but it would only take a five minute surgical procedure under local anaesthetic to remove it. In Uganda, a single HealthGuard machine served forty million people—or rather, the lucky few who could get access to it. Flying in wearing my own personal version seemed almost as crass as arriving with a giant solar tattoo. Where I was headed, cancer had very definitely not been defeated.

Then again, nor had malaria, typhoid, yellow fever, schistosomiasis. I could have the ring immunize me against all of these and more, before removing it . . . but the malaria parasite was notoriously variable, so constant surveillance would provide far more reliable protection. I'd be no use to anyone lying in a hospital bed for half my stay. Besides, the average villager or shanty-town dweller probably wouldn't even recognize the thing, let alone resent it. I was being hypersensitive.

I gathered up my things and headed for the cycle rack. Looking back across the sand, I felt the kind of stab of regret that came upon waking from a dream of impossible good fortune and serenity, and for a moment I wanted nothing more than to close my eyes and rejoin it.

Lisa saw me off at the airport.

I said, "It's only three months. It'll fly past." I was reassuring myself, not her.

"It's not too late to change your mind." She smiled calmly; no pressure, it was entirely my decision. In her eyes, I was clearly suffering from some kind of disease—a very late surge of adolescent idealism, or a very early mid-life crisis— but she'd adopted a scrupulously non-judgmental bedside manner. It drove me mad.

"And miss my last chance ever to perform cancer surgery?" That was a slight exaggeration; a few cases would keep slipping through the HealthGuard net for years. Most of my usual work was trauma, though, which was going through changes of its own. Computerized safeguards had made traffic accidents rare, and I suspected that within a decade no one would get the chance to stick their hand in a conveyor belt again. If the steady stream of gunshot and knife wounds ever dried up, I'd have to re-train for nose jobs and reconstructing rugby players. "I should have gone into obstetrics, like you."

Lisa shook her head. "In the next twenty years, they'll crack all the molecular signals, within and between mother and fetus. There'll be no premature births, no Caesarians, no complications. The HealthGuard will smooth my job away, too." She added, deadpan, "Face it, Martin, we're all doomed to obsolescence."

"Maybe. But if we are . . . it'll happen sooner in some places than others."

"And when the time comes, you might just head off to some place where you're still needed?"

She was mocking me, but I took the question seriously. "Ask me that when I get back. Three months without mod cons and I might be cured for life."

My flight was called. We kissed goodbye. I suddenly realized that I had no idea why I was doing this. The health of distant strangers? Who was I kidding? Maybe I'd been trying to fool myself into believing that I really was that selfless—hoping all the while that Lisa would talk me out of it, offering some face-saving excuse for me to stay. I should have known she'd call my bluff instead.

I said plainly, "I'm going to miss you. Badly."

"I should hope so." She took my hand, scowling, finally accepting the decision. "You're an idiot, you know. Be careful."

"I will." I kissed her again, then slipped away.

▲   ▲   ▲

I was met at Entebbe airport by Magdalena Iganga, one of the oncologists on a small team that had been put together by Médecins Sans Frontières to help overburdened Ugandan doctors tackle the growing number of Yeyuka cases. Iganga was Tanzanian, but she'd worked throughout eastern Africa, and as she drove her battered ethanol-powered car the thirty kilometers into Kampala, she recounted some of her brushes with the World Health Organization in Nairobi.

"I tried to persuade them to set up an epidemiological database for Yeyuka. Good idea, they said. Just put a detailed proposal to the cancer epidemiology expert committee. So I did. And the committee said, we like your proposal, but oh dear, Yeyuka is a contagious disease, so you'll have to submit this to the contagious diseases expert committee instead. Whose latest annual sitting I'd just missed by a week." Iganga sighed stoically. "Some colleagues and I ended up doing it ourselves, on an old 386 and a borrowed phone line."

"Three eight what?"

She shook her head. "Paleocomputing jargon, never mind."

Though we were dead on the equator and it was almost noon, the temperature must have been thirty at most; Kampala was high above sea level. A humid breeze blew off Lake Victoria, and low clouds rolled by above us, gathering threateningly then dissipating, again and again. I'd been promised that I'd come for the dry season; at worst there'd be occasional thunderstorms. On our left, between patches of marshland, small clusters of shacks began to appear. As we drew closer to the city, we passed through layers of shanty towns, the older and more organized verging on a kind of bedraggled suburbia, others looking more like out-and-out refugee camps. The tumors caused by the Yeyuka virus tended to spread fast but grow slowly, often partially disabling people for years before killing them, and when they could no longer manage heavy rural labor, they usually headed for the nearest city in the hope of finding work. Southern Uganda had barely recovered from HIV when Yeyuka cases began to appear, around 2013; in fact, some virologists believed that Yeyuka had arisen from a less virulent ancestor after gaining a foothold within the immune-suppressed population. And though Yeyuka wasn't as contagious as cholera or tuberculosis, crowded conditions, poor sanitation and chronic malnourishment set up the shanty towns to bear the brunt of the epidemic. As we drove north between two hills, the center of Kampala appeared ahead of us, draped across a hill of its own. Compared to Nairobi, which I'd flown over a few hours before, Kampala looked uncluttered. The streets and low buildings were laid out in a widely-spaced plan, neatly organized but lacking any rigid geometry of grid lines or concentric circles. There was plenty of traffic around us, both cycles and cars, but it flowed smoothly enough, and for all the honking and shouting going on the drivers seemed remarkably good humored.

Iganga took a detour to the east, skirting the central hill. There were lushly green sports grounds and golf courses on our right, colonial-era public buildings and high-fenced foreign embassies on our left. There were no high-rise slums in sight, but there were makeshift shelters and even vegetable gardens on some stretches of parkland, traces of the shanty towns spreading inward.

In my jet-lagged state, it was amazing to find that this abstract place that I'd been imagining for months had solid ground, actual buildings, real people. Most of my second-hand glimpses of Uganda had come from news clips set in war zones and disaster areas; from Sydney, it had been almost impossible to conceive of the country as anything more than a frantically edited video sequence full of soldiers, refugees, and fly-blown corpses. In fact, rebel activity was confined to a shrinking zone in the country's far north, most of the last wave of Zairean refugees had gone home a year ago, and while Yeyuka was a serious problem, people weren't exactly dropping dead in the streets. Makerere University was in the north of the city; Iganga and I were both staying at the guest house there. A student showed me to my room, which was plain but spotlessly clean; I was almost afraid to sit on the bed and rumple the sheets. After washing and unpacking, I met up with Iganga again and we walked across the campus to Mulago Hospital, which was affiliated with the university medical school. There was a soccer team practicing across the road as we went in, a reassuringly mundane sight.

Iganga introduced me to nurses and porters left and right; everyone was busy but friendly, and I struggled to memorize the barrage of names. The wards were all crowded, with patients spilling into the corridors, a few in beds but most on mattresses or blankets. The building itself was dilapidated, and some of the equipment must have been thirty years old, but there was nothing squalid about the conditions; all the linen was clean, and the floor looked and smelled like you could do surgery on it.

In the Yeyuka ward, Iganga showed me the six patients I'd be operating on the next day. The hospital did have a CAT scanner, but it had been broken for the past six months, waiting for money for replacement parts, so flat X rays with cheap contrast agents like barium were the most I could hope for. For some tumors, the only guide to location and extent was plain old palpation. Iganga guided my hands, and kept me from applying too much pressure; she'd had a great deal more experience at this than I had, and an over-zealous beginner could do a lot of damage. The world of three-dimensional images spinning on my workstation while the software advised on the choice of incision had receded into fantasy. Stubbornly, though, I did the job myself; gently mapping the tumors by touch, picturing them in my head, marking the X rays or making sketches.

I explained to each patient where I'd be cutting, what I'd remove, and what the likely effects would be. Where necessary, Iganga translated for me—either into Swahili, or what she described as her "broken Luganda." The news was always only half good, but most people seemed to take it with a kind of weary optimism. Surgery was rarely a cure for Yeyuka, usually just offering a few years' respite, but it was currently the only option. Radiation and chemotherapy were useless, and the hospital's sole HealthGuard machine couldn't generate custom-made molecular cures for even a lucky few; seven years into the epidemic, Yeyuka wasn't yet well enough understood for anyone to have written the necessary software.

By the time I was finished it was dark outside. Iganga asked, "Do you want to look in on Ann's last operation?" Ann Collins was the Irish volunteer I was replacing.

"Definitely." I'd watched a few operations performed here, on video back in Sydney, but no VR scenarios had been available for proper "hands on" rehearsals, and Collins would only be around to supervise me for a few more days. It was a painful irony: foreign surgeons were always going to be inexperienced, but no one else had so much time on their hands. Ugandan medical students had to pay a small fortune in fees—the World Bank had put an end to the new government's brief flirtation with state-subsidized training—and it looked like there'd be a shortage of qualified specialists for at least another decade.

We donned masks and gowns. The operating theater was like everything else, clean but outdated. Iganga introduced me to Collins, the anaesthetist Eriya Okwera, and the trainee surgeon Balaki Masika.

The patient, a middle-aged man, was covered in orange Betadine-soaked surgical drapes, arranged around a long abdominal incision. I stood beside Collins and watched, entranced. Growing within the muscular wall of the small intestine was a gray mass the size of my fist, distending the peritoneum, the organ's translucent "skin," almost to the bursting point. It would certainly have been blocking the passage of food; the patient must have been on liquids for months.

The tumor was very loose, almost like a giant discolored blood clot; the hardest thing would be to avoid dislodging any cancerous cells in the process of removing it, sending them back into circulation to seed another tumor. Before making a single cut in the intestinal wall, Collins used a laser to cauterize all the blood vessels around the growth, and she didn't lay a finger on the tumor itself at any time. Once it was free, she lifted it away with clamps attached to the surrounding tissue, as fastidiously as if she was removing a leaky bag full of some fatal poison. Maybe other tumors were already growing unseen in other parts of the body, but doing the best possible job, here and now, might still add three or four years to this man's life. Masika began stitching the severed ends of the intestine together. Collins led me aside and showed me the patient's X rays on a light-box. "This is the site of origin." There was a cavity clearly visible in the right lung, about half the size of the tumor she'd just removed. Ordinary cancers grew in a single location first, and then a few mutant cells in the primary tumor escaped to seed growths in the rest of the body. With Yeyuka, there were no "primary tumors"; the virus itself uprooted the cells it infected, breaking down the normal molecular adhesives that kept them in place, until the infected organ seemed to be melting away. That was the origin of the name: yeyuka, to melt. Once set loose into the bloodstream, many of the cells died of natural causes, but a few ended up lodged in small capillaries—physically trapped, despite their lack of stickiness—where they could remain undisturbed long enough to grow into sizeable tumors.

After the operation, I was invited out to a welcoming dinner in a restaurant down in the city. The place specialized in

Italian food, which was apparently hugely popular, at least in Kampala. Iganga, Collins, and Okwera, old colleagues by now, unwound noisily; Okwera, a solid man in his forties, grew mildly but volubly intoxicated and told medical horror stories from his time in the army. Masika, the trainee surgeon, was very softly spoken and reserved. I was something of a zombie from jet lag myself, and didn't contribute much to the conversation, but the warm reception put me at ease.

I still felt like an impostor, here only because I hadn't had the courage to back out, but no one was going to interrogate me about my motives. No one cared. It wouldn't make the slightest difference whether I'd volunteered out of genuine compassion, or just a kind of moral insecurity brought on by fears of obsolescence. Either way, I'd brought a pair of hands and enough general surgical experience to be useful. If you'd ever had to be a saint to heal someone, medicine would have been doomed from the start.

I was nervous as I cut into my first Yeyuka patient, but by the end of the operation, with a growth the size of an orange successfully removed from the right lung, I felt much more confident. Later the same day, I was introduced to some of the hospital's permanent surgical staff—a reminder that even when Collins left, I'd hardly be working in isolation. I fell asleep on the second night exhausted, but reassured. I could do this, it wasn't beyond me. I hadn't set myself an impossible task.

I drank too much at the farewell dinner for Collins, but the HealthGuard magicked the effects away. My first day solo was anticlimactic; everything went smoothly, and Okwera, with no high-tech hangover cure, was unusually subdued, while Masika was as quietly attentive as ever.

Six days a week, the world shrank to my room, the campus, the ward, the operating theater. I ate in the guest house, and usually fell asleep an hour or two after the evening meal;

with the sun diving straight below the horizon, by eight o'clock it felt like midnight. I tried to call Lisa every night, though I often finished in the theater too late to catch her before she left for work, and I hated leaving messages, or talking to her while she was driving.

Okwera and his wife invited me to lunch the first Sunday, Masika and his girlfriend the next. Both couples were genuinely hospitable, but I felt like I was intruding on their one day together. The third Sunday, I met up with Iganga in a restaurant, then we wandered through the city on an impromptu tour.

There were some beautiful buildings in Kampala, many of them clearly war-scarred but lovingly repaired. I tried to relax and take in the sights, but I kept thinking of the routine—six operations, six days a week—stretching out ahead of me until the end of my stay. When I mentioned this to Iganga, she laughed. "All right. You want something more than assembly-line work? I'll line up a trip to Mubende for you. They have patients there who are too sick to be moved. Multiple tumors, all nearly terminal."

"Okay." Me and my big mouth; I knew I hadn't been seeing the worst cases, but I hadn't given much thought to where they all were.

We were standing outside the Sikh temple, beside a plaque describing Idi Amin's expulsion of Uganda's Asian community in 1972. Kampala was dotted with memorials to atrocities—and though Amin's reign had ended more than forty years ago, it had been a long path back to normality. It seemed unjust beyond belief that even now, in an era of relative political stability, so many lives were being ruined by Yeyuka. No more refugees marching across the countryside, no more forced expulsions—but cells cast adrift could bring just as much suffering.

I asked Iganga, "So why did you go into medicine?"

"Family expectations. It was either that or the law. Medicine seemed less arbitrary; nothing in the body can be overturned by an appeal to the High Court. What about you?"

I said, "I wanted to be in on the revolution. The one that was going to banish all disease."

"Ah, that one."

"I picked the wrong job, of course. I should have been a molecular biologist."

"Or a software engineer."

"Yeah. If I'd seen the HealthGuard coming fifteen years ago, I might have been right at the heart of the changes. And I'd have never looked back. Let alone sideways."

Iganga nodded sympathetically, quite unfazed by the notion that molecular technology might capture the attention so thoroughly that little things like Yeyuka epidemics would vanish from sight altogether. "I can imagine. Seven years ago, I was all set to make my fortune in one of the private clinics in Dar es Salaam. Rich businessmen with prostate cancer, that kind of thing. I was lucky in a way; before that market vanished completely, the Yeyuka fanatics were nagging me, bullying me, making little deals." She laughed. "I've lost count of the number of times I was promised I'd be co-author of a groundbreaking paper in Nature Oncology if I just helped out at some field clinic in the middle of nowhere. I was dragged into this, kicking and screaming, just when all my old dreams were going up in smoke."

"But now Yeyuka feels like your true vocation?"

She rolled her eyes. "Spare me. My ambition now is to retire to a highly paid consulting position in Nairobi or Geneva."

"I'm not sure I believe you."

"You should." She shrugged. "Sure, what I'm doing now is a hundred times more useful than any desk job, but that doesn't make it any easier. You know as well as I do that the warm inner glow doesn't last for a thousand patients; if you fought for every one of them as if they were your own family or friends, you'd go insane . . . so they become a series of clinical problems, which just happen to be wrapped in human flesh. And it's a struggle to keep working on the same problems, over and over, even if you're convinced that it's the most worthwhile job in the world."

"So why are you in Kampala right now, instead of Nairobi or Geneva?"

Iganga smiled. "Don't worry, I'm working on it. I don't have a date on my ticket out of here, like you do, but when the chance comes, believe me, I'll grab it just as fast as I can."

It wasn't until my sixth week, and my two-hundred-and-fourth operation, that I finally screwed up.

The patient was a teenaged girl with multiple infestations of colon cells in her liver. A substantial portion of the organ's left lobe would have to be removed, but her prognosis seemed relatively good; the right lobe appeared to be completely clean, and it was not beyond hope that the liver, directly downstream from the colon, had filtered all the infected cells from the blood before they could reach any other part of the body.

Trying to clamp the left branch of the portal vein, I slipped, and the clamp closed tightly on a swollen cyst at the base of the liver, full of gray-white colon cells. It didn't burst open, but it might have been better if it had; I couldn't literally see where the contents was squirted, but I could imagine the route very clearly: back as far as the Y-junction of the vein, where the blood flow would carry cancerous cells into the previously unaffected right lobe.

I swore for ten seconds, enraged by my own helplessness. I had none of the emergency tools I was used to: there was no drug I could inject to kill off the spilt cells while they were still more vulnerable than an established tumor, no vaccine on hand to stimulate the immune system into attacking them.

Okwera said, "Tell the parents you found evidence of leakage, so she'll need to have regular follow-up examinations."

I glanced at Masika, but he was silent.

"I can't do that."

"You don't want to cause trouble."

"It was an accident!"

"Don't tell her, and don't tell her family." Okwera regarded me sternly, as if I was contemplating something both dangerous and self-indulgent. "It won't help anyone if you dive into the shit for this. Not her, not you. Not the hospital. Not the volunteer program."

The girl's mother spoke English. I told her there were signs that the cancer might have spread. She wept, and thanked me for my good work.

Masika didn't say a word about the incident, but by the end of the day I could hardly bear to look at him. When Okwera departed, leaving the two of us alone in the locker room, I said, "In three or four years there'll be a vaccine. Or even HealthGuard software. It won't be like this forever."

He shrugged, embarrassed. "Sure."

"I'll raise funds for the research when I get home. Champagne dinners with slides of photogenic patients, if that's what it takes." I knew I was making a fool of myself, but I couldn't shut up. "This isn't the nineteenth century. We're not helpless anymore. Anything can be cured, once you understand it."

Masika eyed me dubiously, as if he was trying to decide whether or not to tell me to save my platitudes for the champagne dinners. Then he said, "We do understand Yeyuka. We have HealthGuard software written for it, ready and waiting to go. But we can't run it on the machine here. So we don't need funds for research. What we need is another machine."

I was speechless for several seconds, trying to make sense of this extraordinary claim. "The hospital's machine is broken—?"

Masika shook his head. "The software is unlicensed. If we used it on the hospital's machine, our agreement with HealthGuard would be void. We'd lose the use of the machine entirely."

I could hardly believe that the necessary research had been completed without a single publication, but I couldn't believe Masika would lie about it either. "How long can it take HealthGuard to approve the software? When was it submitted to them?"

Masika was beginning to look like he wished he'd kept his mouth shut, but there was no going back now. He admitted warily, "It hasn't been submitted to them. It can't be—that's the whole problem. We need a bootleg machine, a decommissioned model with the satellite link disabled, so we can run the Yeyuka software without their knowledge."

"Why? Why can't they find out about it?"

He hesitated. "I don't know if I can tell you that."

"Is it illegal? Stolen?" But if it was stolen, why hadn't the rightful owners licensed the damned thing, so people could use it?

Masika replied icily, "Stolen back. The only part you could call 'stolen' was stolen back." He looked away for a moment, actually struggling for control. Then he said, "Are you sure you want to know the whole story?"

"Yes."

"Then I'll have to make a phone call."

Masika took me to what looked like a boarding house, student accommodation in one of the suburbs close to the campus. He walked briskly, giving me no time to ask questions, or even orient myself in the darkness. I had a feeling he would have liked to have blindfolded me, but it would hardly have made a difference; by the time we arrived I couldn't have said where we were to the nearest kilometer.

A young woman, maybe nineteen or twenty, opened the door. Masika didn't introduce us, but I assumed she was the person he'd phoned from the hospital, since she was clearly expecting us. She led us to a ground floor room; someone was playing music upstairs, but there was no one else in sight.

In the room, there was a desk with an old-style keyboard and computer monitor, and an extraordinary device standing on the floor beside it: a rack of electronics the size of a chest of drawers, full of exposed circuit boards, all cooled by a fan half a meter wide.

"What is that?"

The woman grinned. "We modestly call it the Makerere supercomputer. Five hundred and twelve processors, working in parallel. Total cost, fifty thousand shillings."

That was about fifty dollars. "How—?"

"Recycling. Twenty or thirty years ago, the computer industry ran an elaborate scam: software companies wrote deliberately inefficient programs, to make people buy newer, faster computers all the time—then they made sure that the faster computers needed brand new software to work at all. People threw out perfectly good machines every three or four years, and though some ended up as landfill, millions were saved. There's been a worldwide market in discarded processors for years, and the slowest now cost about as much as buttons. But all it takes to get some real power out of them is a little ingenuity."

I stared at the wonderful contraption. "And you wrote the Yeyuka software on this?"

"Absolutely." She smiled proudly. "First, the software characterizes any damaged surface adhesion molecules it finds—there are always a few floating freely in the bloodstream, and their exact shape depends on the strain of Yeyuka, and the particular cells that have been infected. Then drugs are tailor-made to lock on to those damaged adhesion molecules, and kill the infected cells by rupturing their membranes." As she spoke, she typed on the keyboard, summoning up animations to illustrate each stage of the process. "If we can get this onto a real machine . . . we'll be able to cure three people a day."

Cure. Not just cut them open to delay the inevitable.

"But where did all the raw data come from? The RNA sequencing, the X-ray diffraction studies . . . ?"

The woman's smile vanished. "An insider at Health-Guard found it in the company archives, and sent it to us over the net."

"I don't understand. When did HealthGuard do Yeyuka studies? Why haven't they published them? Why haven't they written software themselves?"

She glanced uncertainly at Masika. He said, "Health-Guard's parent company collected blood from five thousand people in Southern Uganda in 2013. Supposedly to follow up on the effectiveness of their HIV vaccine. What they actually wanted, though, was a large sample of metastasizing cells so they could perfect the biggest selling point of the Health-Guard: cancer protection. Yeyuka offered them the cheapest, simplest way to get the data they needed."

I'd been half expecting something like this since Masika's comments back in the hospital, but I was still shaken. To collect the data dishonestly was bad enough, but to bury information that was halfway to a cure—just to save paying for what they'd taken—was unspeakable.

I said, "Sue the bastards! Get everyone who had samples taken together for a class action: royalties plus punitive damages. You'll raise hundreds of millions of dollars. Then you can buy as many machines as you want."

The woman laughed bitterly. "We have no proof. The files were sent anonymously, there's no way to authenticate their origin. And can you imagine how much HealthGuard would spend on their defense? We can't afford to waste the next twenty years in a legal battle, just for the satisfaction of shouting the truth from the rooftops. The only way we can be sure of making use of this software is to get a bootleg machine, and do everything in silence."

I stared at the screen, at the cure being played out in simulation that should have been happening three times a day in Mulago hospital. She was right, though. However hard it was to stomach, taking on HealthGuard directly would be futile.

Walking back across the campus with Masika, I kept thinking of the girl with the liver infestation, and the possibility of undoing the moment of clumsiness that would otherwise almost certainly kill her. I said, "Maybe I can get hold of a bootleg machine in Shanghai. If I knew where to ask, where to look." They'd certainly be expensive, but they'd have to be much cheaper than a commissioned model, running without the usual software and support.

My hand moved almost unconsciously to check the metal pulse on my index finger. I held the ring up in the starlight. "I'd give you this, if it was mine to give. But that's thirty years away." Masika didn't reply, too polite to suggest that if I'd owned the ring outright, I wouldn't even have raised the possibility.

We reached the University Hall; I could find my way back to the guest house now. But I couldn't leave it at that; I couldn't face another six weeks of surgery unless I knew that something was going to come of the night's revelations. I said, "Look, I don't have connections to any black market, I don't have a clue how to go about getting a machine. But if you can find out what I have to do, and it's within my power . . . I'll do it."

Masika smiled, and nodded thanks, but I could tell that he didn't believe me. I wondered how many other people had made promises like this, then vanished back into the world-without-disease while the Yeyuka wards kept overflowing.

As he turned to go, I put a hand on his shoulder to stop him. "I mean it. Whatever it takes, I'll do it."

He met my eyes in the dark, trying to judge something deeper than this easy protestation of sincerity. I felt a sudden flicker of shame; I'd completely forgotten that I was an impostor, that I'd never really meant to come here, that two months ago a few words from Lisa would have seen me throw away my ticket, gratefully.

Masika said quietly, "Then I'm sorry that I doubted you. And I'll take you at your word."

Mubende was a district capital, half a day's drive west of Kampala. Iganga delayed our promised trip to the Yeyuka clinic there until my last fortnight, and once I arrived I could understand why. It was everything I'd feared: starved of funds, understaffed and overcrowded. Patients' relatives were required to provide and wash the bed-clothes, and half of them also seemed to be bringing in painkillers and other drugs bought at the local markets—some genuine, some rip-offs full of nothing but glucose or magnesium sulfate.

Most of the patients had four or five separate tumors. I treated two people a day, with operations lasting six to eight hours. In ten days, seven people died in front of me; dozens more died in the wards, waiting for surgery.

Or waiting for something better.

I shared a crowded room at the back of the clinic with Masika and Okwera, but even on the rare occasions when I caught Masika alone, he seemed reluctant to discuss the details of getting hold of a bootleg HealthGuard. He said, "Right now, the less you know the better. When the time comes, I'll fill you in."

The ordeal of the patients was overwhelming, but I felt more for the clinic's sole doctor and two nurses; for them, it never ended. The morning we packed our equipment into the truck and headed back for Kampala, I felt like a deserter from some stupid, pointless war: guilty about the colleagues I was leaving behind, but almost euphoric with relief to be out of it myself. I knew I couldn't have stayed on here—or even in

Kampala—month after month, year after year. However much I wished that I could have been that strong, I understood now that I wasn't.

There was a brief, loud stuttering sound, then the truck squealed to a halt. The four of us were all in the back, guarding the equipment against potholes, with the tarpaulin above us blocking everything but a narrow rear view. I glanced at the others; someone outside shouted in Luganda at Akena Ibingira, the driver, and he started shouting back.

Okwera said, "Bandits."

I felt my heart racing. "You're kidding?"

There was another burst of gunfire. I heard Ibingira jump out of the cab, still muttering angrily.

Everyone was looking at Okwera for advice. He said, "Just cooperate, give them what they want." I tried to read his face; he seemed grim but not desperate—he expected unpleasantness, but not a massacre. Iganga was sitting on the bench beside me; I reached for her hand almost without thinking. We were both trembling. She squeezed my fingers for a moment, then pulled free.

Two tall, smiling men in dirty brown camouflage appeared at the back of the truck, gesturing with automatic weapons for us to climb out. Okwera went first, but Masika, who'd been sitting beside him, hung back. Iganga was nearer to the exit than me, but I tried to get past her; I had some half-baked idea that this would somehow lessen her risk of being taken off and raped. When one of the bandits blocked my way and waved her forward, I thought this fear had been confirmed.

Masika grabbed my arm, and when I tried to break free, he tightened his grip and pulled me back into the truck. I turned on him angrily, but before I could say a word he whispered, "She'll be all right. Just tell me: do you want them to take the ring?"

"What?"

He glanced nervously toward the exit, but the bandits had moved Okwera and Iganga out of sight. "I've paid them to do this. It's the only way. But say the word now and I'll give them the signal, and they won't touch the ring."

I stared at him, waves of numbness sweeping over my skin as I realized exactly what he was saying.

"You could have taken it off under anesthetic."

He shook his head impatiently. "It's sending data back to HealthGuard all the time: cortisol, adrenaline, endorphins, prostaglandins. They'll have a record of your stress levels, fear, pain . . . if we took it off under anesthetic, they'd know you'd given it away freely. This way, it'll look like a random theft. And your insurance company will give you a new one."

His logic was impeccable; I had no reply. I might have started protesting about insurance fraud, but that was all in the future, a separate matter entirely. The choice, here and now, was whether or not I let him have the ring by the only method that wouldn't raise suspicion.

One of the bandits was back, looking impatient. Masika asked plainly, "Do I call it off? I need an answer." I turned to him, on the verge of ranting that he'd willfully misunderstood me, abused my generous offer to help him, and put all our lives in danger.

It would have been so much bullshit, though. He hadn't misunderstood me. All he'd done was taken me at my word.

I said, "Don't call it off."

The bandits lined us up beside the truck, and had us empty our pockets into a sack. Then they started taking watches and jewelry. Okwera couldn't get his wedding ring off, but stood motionless and scowling while one of the bandits applied more force. I wondered if I'd need a prosthesis, if I'd still be able to do surgery, but as the bandit approached me I felt a strange rush of confidence.

I held out my hand and looked up into the sky. I knew that anything could be healed, once it was understood.

An Office Romance

TERRY BISSON

Terry Bisson just keeps writing his own way and like no one else. Last year it was virtual reality, this year it is the humdrum world of office computers, transformed. Bisson's most impressive achievement this year, though, was not in short fiction but was the completion of Walter M. Miller's second novel, *Saint Liebowitz and the Wild Horse Woman*, set in the same future as his classic *A Canticle for Leibowitz*. Miller found himself unable to complete the book after decades of work, and agreed, before his death, to have Bisson complete it. And Bisson did so with marvelous fidelity. One should note the satiric irony in Miller, so integral a part of his serious work, is the same in kind, though not in tone, as Bisson's. Miller said anyone with a sense of humor ought to be able to finish his book. Bisson certainly qualifies. This story appeared in *Playboy*. Computer nerds will love it. If you have never used a computer, worked in an office, or heard of Microsoft, you may have to have the humor explained.

The First time Ken678 saw Mary97, he was in Municipal Real Estate, queued for a pickup for Closings. She stood two spaces in front of him: blue skirt, orange tie, slightly convex white blouse, like every other female icon. He didn't know she was a Mary; he couldn't see which face she had. But she held her Folder in both hands, as old-timers often did, and when the queue scrolled forward he saw her fingernails.

They were red.

Just then the queue flickered and scrolled again, and she was gone. Ken was intrigued, but he promptly forgot about her. It was a busy time of year, and he was running like crazy from Call to Task. Later that week he saw her again, paused at an open Window in the Corridor between Copy and Send. He slowed as he passed her, by turning his Folder sideways— a trick he had learned. There were those red fingernails again. It was curious.

Fingernails were not on the Option Menu.

Red was not on the Color Menu, either.

Ken used the weekend to visit his mother at the Home. It was her birthday or anniversary or something like that. Ken hated weekends. He had grown used to his Ken face and felt uncomfortable without it. He hated his old name, which his mother insisted on calling him. He hated how grim and terrifying things were outside. To avoid panic he closed his eyes and hummed—out here, he could do both—trying to simulate the peaceful hum of the Office.

But there is no substitute for the real thing, and Ken

didn't relax until the week restarted and he was back inside. He loved the soft electron buzz of the search engines, the busy streaming icons, the dull butter shine of the Corridors, the shimmering Windows with their relaxing scenes of the environment. He loved his life and he loved his work.

That was the week he met Mary—or rather, she met him.

Ken678 had just retrieved a Folder of documents from Search and was taking it to Print. He could see by the blur of icons ahead that there was going to be a long queue at the Bus leaving Commercial, so he paused in the Corridor; waitstates were encouraged in high traffic zones.

He opened a Window by resting his Folder on the sill. There was no air, of course, but there was a nice view. The scene was the same in every Window in Microserf Office 6.9: cobblestones and quiet cafés and chestnut trees in bloom. April in Paris.

Ken heard a voice.

<Beautiful, isn't it?>

<What?> he said, confused. Two icons couldn't open the same Window, and yet there she was beside him. Red fingernails and all.

<April in Paris,> she said.

<I know. But how—>

<A little trick I learned.> She pointed to her Folder, stacked on top of his, flush right.

<—did you do that?> he finished because it was in his buffer. She had the Mary face, which, it so happened, was his favorite. And the red fingernails.

<When they are flush right the Window reads us as one icon,> she said.

<Probably reads only the right edge,> Ken said. <Neat.>

<The name's Mary,> she said. <Mary97.>

<Ken678.>

<You slowed when you passed me last week, Ken. Neat trick, too. I figure that made you almost worth an intro. Most of the workaholics here in City Hall are pretty unsociable.>

Ken showed her his Folder trick even though she seemed to know it already.

<How long have you been at City?> he asked.

<Too long.>

<How come I have never seen you before?>

<Maybe you saw me but didn't notice me,> she said. She held up a hand with red fingernails. <I didn't always have these.>

<Where'd you get them?>

<It's a secret.>

<They're pretty neat,> Ken said.

<Is that pretty or neat?>

<Both.>

<Are you flirting with me?> she asked, smiling that Mary smile.

Ken tried to think of an answer, but he was too slow. Her Folder was blinking, a waitstate interrupt, and she was gone.

A few cycles later in the week he saw her again, paused at an open Window in the Corridor between Copy and Verify. He slid his Folder over hers, flush right, and he was standing beside her, looking out into April in Paris.

<You learn fast,> she said.

<I have a good teacher,> he said. Then he said what he had been rehearsing over and over: <And what if I was?>

<Was what?>

<Flirting.>

<That would be OK,> she said, smiling the Mary smile.

Ken678 wished for the first time that the Ken face had a smile. His Folder was flickering, but he didn't want to leave yet. <How long have you been at City?> he asked again.

<Forever,> she said. She was exaggerating, of course, but in a sense it was true. She told Ken she had been at City Hall when Microserf Office 6.9 was installed. <Before Office, records were stored in a basement, in metal drawers, and accessed by hand. I helped put it all on disk. Data entry, it was called.>

<Entry?>

<This was before the neural interface. We sat *outside* and reached in through a Keyboard and looked in through a sort of window that they called a Monitor. There was nobody *in* Office. Just pictures of files and stuff. There was no April in Paris, of course. That was added later to prevent claustrophobia.>

Ken678 calculated in his head. How old did that make Mary—55? 60? It didn't matter. All icons are young, and all females are beautiful.

Ken had never had a friend before, in or out of the Office. Much less a girlfriend. He found himself hurrying his Calls and Tasks so he could cruise the Corridors looking for Mary97. He could usually find her at an open Window, gazing at the cobblestones and the little cafés, the blooming chestnut trees. Mary loved April in Paris. <It's so romantic there,> she said. <Can't you just imagine yourself walking down the boulevard?>

<I guess,> Ken said. But in fact he couldn't. He didn't like to imagine things. He preferred real life, or at least Microserf Office 6.9. He loved standing at the Window beside her, listening to her soft Mary voice, answering in his deep Ken voice.

<How did you get here?> she asked. Ken told her he had been hired as a temp, transporting scanned-in midcentury documents up the long stairway from Archives to Active.

<My name wasn't Ken then, of course,> he said. <All the temp icons wore gray, male and female alike. We were neural-

interfaced through helmets instead of earrings. None of the regular Office workers spoke to us, or even noticed us. We worked 14-, 15-cycle days.>

<And you loved it,> Mary said.

<I loved it,> Ken admitted. <I found what I was looking for. I loved being inside.> And he told her how wonderful and strange it had felt, at first, to be an icon; to see himself as he walked around, as if he were both inside and outside his own body.

<Of course, it seems normal now,> he said.

<It is,> Mary said. And she smiled that Mary smile.

Several weeks passed before Ken got up the courage to make what he thought of as "his move."

They were at the Window where he had first spoken with her, in the Corridor between Copy and Verify. Her hand was resting on the sill, red fingernails shimmering, and he put his hand exactly over it. Even though he couldn't actually feel it, it felt good.

He was afraid she would move her hand, but instead she smiled that Mary smile and said, <I didn't think you were ever going to do that.>

<I've been wanting to since I first saw you,> he said.

She moved her fingers under his. It almost tingled. <Want to see what makes them red?>

<You mean your secret?>

<It'll be our secret. You know the Browser between Deeds and Taxes? Meet me there in three cycles.>

The Browser was a circular connector with no Windows. Ken met Mary at Select All and followed her toward Insert, where the doors got smaller and closer together.

<Ever hear of an Easter Egg?> she asked.

<Sure,> Ken said. <A programmer's surprise that is hidden in the software. An unauthorized subroutine that's not in the manual. Sometimes humorous or even obscene. Easter Eggs are routinely—>

<You're just repeating what you learned in Orientation,> Mary said.

<—found and cleared from commercial software by background Debuggers and Optimizers.> Ken finished because it was already in his buffer.

<But that's OK,> she said. <Here we are.>

Mary97 led him into a small Windowless room. There was nothing in it but a tiny, heart-shaped table.

<This room was erased but never overwritten,> Mary said. <The Optimizer must have missed it. That's why the Easter Egg is still here. I discovered it by accident.>

On the table were three playing cards. Two were facedown and one was faceup: the ten of diamonds.

<Ready?> Without waiting for Ken's answer, Mary turned the ten of diamonds facedown. Her fingernails were no longer red.

<Now you try it,> she said.

Ken backed away.

<Don't get nervous. This card does not do anything; it just changes the Option. Go ahead!>

Reluctantly, Ken turned up the ten of diamonds.

Mary's fingernails were red again. Nothing happened to his own.

<That first card works just for girls,> Mary said.

<Neat,> Ken said, relaxing a little.

<There's plenty more,> Mary said. <Ready?>

<I guess.>

Mary turned up the second card. It was the queen of hearts. As soon as she turned it up, Ken heard a *clippety-clop*, and a Window opened in the Windowless room.

In the Window it was April in Paris.

Ken saw a gray horse coming straight down the center of the boulevard. It wore no harness, but its tail and mane were bobbed. Its enormous red penis was almost dragging the cobblestones.

<See the horse?> Mary97 said. She was standing beside Ken at the Window. Her convex white blouse and orange tie both were gone. She was wearing a red lace brassiere. The sheer cups were full. The narrow straps were taut. The tops of her plump breasts were round and bright as moons.

Ken678 couldn't move or speak. It was terrifying and wonderful at the same time. Mary's hands were behind her back, unfastening her brassiere. There! But just as the cups started to fall away from her breasts, a whistle blew.

The horse had stopped in the middle of the boulevard. A gendarme was running toward it, waving a stick.

The Window closed. Mary97 was standing at the table, wearing her convex white blouse and orange tie again. Only the ten of diamonds was faceup.

<You turned the card down too soon,> Ken said. He had wanted to see her nipples.

<The queen turns herself down,> Mary said. <An Easter Egg is a closed algorithm. Runs itself once it gets started. Did you like it? And don't say you guess.>

She smiled that Mary smile and Ken tried to think of what to say. But both their Folders were blinking, waitstate interrupts, and she was gone.

Ken found her a couple cycles later at their usual meeting place, at the open Window in the Corridor between Copy and Verify.

<Like it?> he said. <I loved it.>

<Are you flirting with me?> Mary97 asked.

<What if I am?> he said, and the familiar words were almost as good as a smile.

<Then come with me.>

▲   ▲   ▲

Ken678 followed Mary97 to the Browser twice more that week. Each time was the same; each time was perfect. As soon as Mary turned over the queen of hearts, Ken heard a *clippety-clop*. A Window opened in the Windowless room and there was the horse again, coming down the boulevard, its enormous penis almost dragging the cobblestones. Mary97's ripe, round, perfect breasts were spilling over the top of her red lace brassiere as she said, <See the horse?> and reached behind her back, unfastening—

Unfastening her bra! And just as the cups started to fall away, just as Ken678 was about to see her nipples, a gendarme's whistle blew and Mary97 was wearing the white blouse again and the orange tie. The Window was closed, the queen of hearts facedown.

<The only problem with Easter Eggs,> Mary said, <is that they are always the same. Whoever designed this one obviously had a case of arrested development.>

<I like always the same,> Ken replied.

As he left for the weekend, Ken678 scanned the crowd of office regulars filing down the long steps of City Hall. Which woman was Mary97? There was, of course, no way of knowing. They were all ages, all nationalities, but they all looked the same with their blank stares, neural-interface gold earrings, and mesh marks from their net gloves.

The weekend seemed to last forever. As soon as the week restarted, Ken raced through his Calls and Tasks, then cruised the Corridors until he found Mary at "their" spot, the open Window between Copy and Verify.

<Isn't it romantic?> she said, looking out into April in Paris.

<I guess,> said Ken impatiently. He was thinking of her hands behind her back, unfastening.

<What could be more romantic?> she asked, and he could tell she was teasing.

<A red brassiere,> he said.

<Then come with me,> she said.

They met in the Browser three times that week. Three times Ken678 heard the horse, three times he watched the red lace brassiere falling away, falling away. That week was the closest to happiness he would ever come.

<Do you ever wonder what's under the third card?> Mary97 asked. They were standing at the Window between Copy and Verify. A new week had barely restarted. In April in Paris the chestnuts were in bloom above the cobblestones. The cafés were empty. A few stick figures in the distance were getting in and out of carriages.

<I guess,> Ken678 said, though it wasn't true. He didn't like to wonder.

<Me too,> said Mary.

When they met a few cycles later in the Windowless room off the Browser, Mary put her red-fingernailed hand on the third card and said, <There's one way to find out.>

Ken didn't answer. He felt a sudden chill.

<We both have to do it,> she said. <You turn up the queen and I'll turn up the third card. Ready?>

<I guess,> Ken said, though it was a lie.

The third card was the ace of spades. As soon as it was turned up, Ken knew something was wrong.

Something felt different.

It was the cobblestones under his feet.

It was April in Paris and Ken678 was walking down the boulevard. Mary97 was beside him. She was wearing a low-cut, sleeveless peasant blouse and a long, full skirt.

Ken was terrified. Where was the Window? Where was the Windowless room? <Where are we?> he asked.

<We are *in* April in Paris,> Mary said. <*In*side the exvironment! Isn't it exciting?>

Ken tried to stop walking, but he couldn't. <I think we're stuck,> he said. He tried to close his eyes to avoid panic, but he couldn't.

Mary just smiled the Mary smile and they walked along the boulevard, under the blooming chestnut trees. They passed a café, they turned a corner; they passed another café, turned another corner. It was always the same. The same trees, the same café, the same cobblestones. The carriages and stick figures in the distance never got any closer.

<Isn't it romantic?> Mary said. <And don't say you guess.>

She looked different somehow. Maybe it was the outfit. Her peasant blouse was cut very low. Ken tried to look down it but couldn't.

They passed another café. This time Mary97 turned in, and Ken was sitting across from her at a small sidewalk table.

<Voilà!> she said. <This Easter Egg is more interactive. You just have to look for new ways to do things.> She was still smiling that Mary smile. The table was heart-shaped, like the table in the Windowless room. Ken leaned across it but still couldn't see down her blouse.

<Isn't it romantic!> Mary said. <Why don't you let me order?>

<It's time to head back,> Ken said. <I'll bet our Folders—>

<Don't be silly,> Mary said, opening the menu.

<—are blinking like crazy,> he finished because it was already in his buffer.

A waiter appeared. He wore a white shirt and black pants. Ken tried to look at his face, but he didn't exactly have one. There were only three items on the menu:

WALK
ROOM
HOME

Mary pointed at ROOM, and before she had closed the menu they were in a wedge-shaped attic room with French doors, sitting on the edge of a bed. Now Ken could see down Mary97's blouse. In fact he could see his two hands reach out and pull it down, uncovering her two plump, perfect breasts. Her nipples were as big and as brown as cookies. Through the French doors Ken could see the Eiffel Tower and the boulevard.

<Mary,> he said as she helped him pull up her skirt. Smiling that Mary smile, she lay back with her blouse and skirt both bunched around her waist. Ken heard a familiar *clippety-clop* from the boulevard below as Mary spread her plump, perfect thighs wide.

<April in Paris,> she said. Her red-tipped fingers pulled her little French underpants to one side and

He kissed her sweet mouth. <Mary!> he said.

Her red-tipped fingers pulled her little French underpants to one side and

He kissed her sweet red mouth. <Mary!> he said.

Her red-tipped fingers pulled her little French underpants to one side and

He kissed her sweet red cookie mouth. <Mary!> he said.

A gendarme's whistle blew and they were back at the sidewalk café. The menu was closed on the heart-shaped table. <Did you like that?> Mary asked. <And don't say you guess.>

<Like it? I loved it,> Ken said. <But shouldn't we head back?>

<Back?> Mary shrugged. Ken didn't know she could shrug. She was holding a glass of green liquid.

Ken opened the menu and the faceless waiter appeared.

There were three items on the menu. Before Mary could point, Ken pointed at HOME, and the table and the waiter were gone. He and Mary97 were in the Windowless room, and the cards were facedown except for the ten of diamonds.

<Why do you want to spoil everything?> Mary said.

<I don't—> Ken started, but he never got to finish. His Folder was blinking, waitstate interrupt, and he was gone.

<It *was* romantic,> Ken678 insisted a few cycles later when he joined Mary97 in their usual spot, at the Window in the Corridor between Copy and Verify. <And I did love it.>

<Then why were you so nervous?>

<Was I nervous?>

She smiled that Mary smile.

<Because I just get nervous,> Ken said. <Because April in Paris is not really part of Microserf Office 6.9.>

<Sure it is. It's the exvironment.>

<It's just Wallpaper. We're not supposed to be *in* there.>

<It's an Easter Egg,> Mary97 said. <We're not supposed to be having an office romance, either.>

<An office romance,> Ken said. <Is that what we're having?>

<Come with me and I'll show you,> Mary said, and he did. And she did.

And he did and she did and they did. He met her three times that week and three times the next week, every spare moment, it seemed. The cobblestones and the cafés still made Ken678 nervous, but he loved the wedge-shaped attic room. He loved Mary's nipples as big and as brown as cookies; loved her blouse and skirt bunched around her waist as she lay on her back with her plump, perfect thighs spread wide; loved the *clippety-clop* and her red-tipped fingers and her little French underpants pulled to one side; loved her.

It was, after all, a love affair.

The problem was, Mary97 never wanted to go back to Microserf Office 6.9. After the wedge-shaped room she wanted to walk on the boulevard under the blooming chestnut trees, or sit in a café watching the stick figures get in and out of carriages in the distance.

 <Isn't it romantic?> she would say, swirling the green liquid in her glass.

 <Time to head back,> Ken would say. <I'll bet our Folders are blinking like crazy.>

 <You always say that,> Mary would always say.

Ken678 had always hated weekends because he missed the warm electron buzz of Microserf Office 6.9, but now he missed it during the week as well. If he wanted to be with Mary97 (and he did, he did!) it meant April in Paris. Ken missed "their" Window in the Corridor between Copy and Verify. He missed the busy streaming icons and the Folders bulging with files and blinking with Calls and Tasks. He missed the red brassiere.

 <What happens,> Ken asked late one week <if we turn over just the queen?>

 He was turning over just the queen.

 <Nothing,> Mary answered. <Nothing but the red brassiere.>

 She was already turning over the ace.

<We need to talk,> Ken678 said finally. It was April in Paris, as usual. He was walking with Mary97 along the boulevard, under the blooming chestnut trees.

 <What about?> she asked. She turned a corner, then another.

 <Things,> he said.

 <Isn't it romantic?> she said as she turned into a café.

 <I guess,> he said. <But—>

<I hate it when you say that,> Mary said.

<—I miss the Office,> Ken finished because it was already in his buffer.

Mary97 shrugged. <To each his own.> She swirled the green liquid in her glass. It was thick as syrup; it clung to the sides of the glass. Ken had the feeling she was looking through him instead of at him. He tried to see down her peasant blouse but couldn't.

<I thought you wanted to talk,> Mary said.

<I did. We did,> Ken said. He reached for the menu.

Mary pulled it away. <I'm not in the mood.>

<We should be getting back, then,> Ken said. <I'll bet our Folders are blinking like crazy.>

Mary shrugged. <Go ahead,> she said.

<What?>

<You miss the Office. I don't. I'm going to stay here.>

<Here?> Ken tried to look around. He could look in only one direction, toward the boulevard.

<Why not?> Mary said. <Who's going to miss me there?> She took another drink of the green liquid and opened the menu. Ken was confused. Had she been drinking it all along?

And why were there four items on the menu?

<Me,> Ken suggested.

But the waiter had already appeared; he, at least, was still the same.

<Go ahead, go for it,> Mary said, and Ken pointed at HOME. Mary was pointing at the new item on the menu: STAY.

That weekend was the longest of Ken678's life. As soon as the week restarted, he hurried to the Corridor between Copy and Verify, hoping against hope. But there was no Window open and, of course, no Mary97.

He looked for her between Calls and Tasks, checking every queue, every Corridor. Finally, toward the middle of the week, he went to the Windowless room off the Browser by himself, for the first time.

Mary97's Folder was gone. The cards on the tiny, heart-shaped table were facedown, except the ten of diamonds.

He turned up the queen of hearts, but nothing happened. He wasn't surprised.

He turned up the ace of spades and felt the cobblestones under his feet. It was April in Paris. The chestnuts were in bloom, but Ken678 felt no joy. Only a sort of thick sorrow.

He turned into the first café and there she was, sitting at the heart-shaped table.

<Look who's here,> she said.

<Your Folder is gone,> Ken said. <It was in the room when I got back, blinking like crazy. But that was before the weekend. Now it's gone.>

Mary shrugged. <I'm not going back there anyway.>

<What happened to us?> Ken asked.

<Nothing happened to us,> Mary said. <Something happened to me. Remember when you found what you were looking for? Well, I found what I was looking for. I like it here.>

Mary pushed the glass of green liquid toward him. <You could like it here, too,> she said.

Ken didn't answer. He was afraid if he did he would start to cry, even though Kens can't cry.

<But it's OK,> Mary97 said. She even smiled her Mary smile. She took another sip and opened the menu. The waiter appeared, and she pointed to ROOM, and Ken knew somehow that this was to be the last time.

In the wedge-shaped attic room, he could see down Mary's blouse perfectly. Then his hands were cupping her plump, perfect breasts for the last time. Through the French doors he could see the Eiffel Tower and the boulevard. <Mary!> he said, and she lay back with her blouse and skirt both bunched around her waist, and he knew somehow it was the last time. He heard a familiar *clippety-clop* from the boulevard as she spread her perfect thighs and said <April in Paris!> Her red-tipped fingers pulled her little French underpants to one side and Ken knew somehow it was the last time.

He kissed her sweet red cookie mouth. <Mary!> he said. She pulled her little French underpants to one side and he knew somehow it was the last time.

<Mary!> he said.

It was the last time.

A gendarme's whistle blew and they were back at the sidewalk café. The menu was closed on the heart-shaped table. <Are you flirting with me?> Mary asked.

What a sad joke she is making, Ken678 thought. He tried to smile even though Kens can't smile.

<You're supposed to answer, What if I am?> Mary said. She took another drink of the green liquid. She swirled it jauntily. No matter how much she drank there was always plenty left.

<Time to head back,> Ken said. <My Folder will be blinking like crazy.>

<I understand. It's OK. Come and see me sometime,> she said. <And don't say, I guess.>

Ken678 nodded even though Kens can't nod. It was more like a stiff bow. Mary97 opened the menu. The waiter came and Ken pointed to HOME.

Ken678 spent the next two weeks working like crazy. He was all over Microserf Office 6.9. As soon as his Folder blinked he was off, on Call, triple Tasking, burning up the Corridors. He avoided the Corridor between Copy and Verify, though, just as he avoided the Browser. He almost paused at an open Window once. But he didn't want to look at April in Paris. It was too lonely without Mary.

Four weeks passed before Ken678 went back to the Windowless room in the Browser. He dreaded seeing the cards on the heart-shaped table. But the cards were gone. Even the table was gone. Ken saw the scuff marks along the wall, and he realized that the Optimizer had been through. The room had been erased again and was being overwritten.

When he left the room he was no longer lonely. He was accompanied by a great sorrow.

The next week he went by the room again and found it filled with empty Folders. Perhaps one of them was Mary97's. Now that the Easter Egg was gone, Ken678 no longer felt guilty about not going to see Mary97. He was free to love Microserf Office 6.9 again, free to enjoy the soft electron buzz, the busy streaming icons and the long, silent queues. But at least once a week he stops by the Corridor between Copy and Verify and opens the Window. You might find him there even now, looking out into April in Paris. The chestnuts are in bloom, the cobblestones shine, the carriages are letting off stick figures in the distance. The cafés are almost empty. A lone figure sits at a tiny table, a figure that might be her.

They say you never get over your first love. Then Mary97 must have been my first love, Ken678 likes to think. He has no interest in getting over her. He loves to remember her red fingernails, her soft Mary voice and her Mary smile, her nipples as big and as brown as cookies, her little French underpants pulled to one side—her.

The figure in the café must be Mary97. Ken678 hopes so. He hopes she is OK in April in Paris. He hopes she is as happy as she once made, is still making, him. He hopes she is as wonderfully sad.

But look: His Folder is blinking like crazy, a waitstate interrupt, and it's time to go.

Itsy Bitsy Spider

JAMES PATRICK KELLY

———

James Patrick Kelly has been in each volume of this year's best series to date, and for good reason. Although not prolific, he is building one of the most impressive bodies of short fiction in SF in this part of the decade, at the rate of a couple or three good stories a year. This year, his story collection, *Think Like a Dinosaur*, was the first hardcover release of an ambitious new publisher, Golden Gryphon, and this story was published in *Asimov's*. There were several SF stories this year about retired and infirm family members. I suppose it is that another generation of SF writers is arriving at middle age and seeing in the declining health of their parents' generation a wintry prognostication for the future, something to be got around in some science fictional way without violating the need for empathy, or indeed logic. It is an easy subject to get depressed about but Kelly avoided that, so I liked this one best.

When I found out that my father was still alive after all these years and living at Strawberry Fields, I thought he'd gotten just what he deserved. Retroburbs are where the old, scared people go to hide. I'd always pictured the people in them as deranged losers. Visiting some fantasy world like the disneys or Carlucci's Carthage is one thing, *moving* to one is another. Sure, 2038 is messy, but it's a hell of a lot better than nineteen-sixty-whatever.

Now that I'd arrived at 144 Bluejay Way, I realized that the place was worse than I had imagined. Strawberry Fields was pretending to be some long-lost suburb of the late twentieth century, except that it had the sterile monotony of cheap VR. It was clean, all right, and neat, but it was everywhere the same. And the scale was wrong. The lots were squeezed together and all the houses had shrunk—like the dreams of their owners. They were about the size of a one-car garage, modular units tarted up at the factory to look like ranches, with old double-hung storm windows and hardened siding of harvest gold, barn red, forest green. Of course, there were no real garages; faux Mustangs and VW buses cruised the quiet streets. Their carbrains were listening for a summons from Barbara Chesley next door at 142, or the Goltzes across the street, who might be headed to Penny Lanes to bowl a few frames, or the hospital to die.

There was a beach chair with blue nylon webbing on the front stoop of 144 Bluejay Way. A brick walk led to it, dividing two patches of carpet moss, green as a dream. There were names and addresses printed in huge lightstick letters on all the doors in the neighborhood; no doubt many Strawberry

Fielders were easily confused. The owner of this one was Peter Fancy. He had been born Peter Fanelli, but had legally taken his stage name not long after his first success as Prince Hal in *Henry IV Part 1*. I was a Fancy too; the name was one of the few things of my father's I had kept.

I stopped at the door and let it look me over. "You're Jen," it said.

"Yes." I waited in vain for it to open or to say something else. "I'd like to see Mr. Fancy, please." The old man's house had worse manners than he did. "He knows I'm coming," I said. "I sent him several messages." Which he had never answered, but I didn't mention that.

"Just a minute," said the door. "She'll be right with you."

She? The idea that he might be with another woman now hadn't occurred to me. I'd lost track of my father a long time ago—on purpose. The last time we'd actually visited overnight was when I was twenty. Mom gave me a ticket to Port Gemini, where he was doing the Shakespeare in Space program. The orbital was great, but staying with him was like being under water. I think I must have held my breath for the entire week. After that, there were a few, sporadic calls, a couple of awkward dinners—all at his instigation. Then twenty-three years of nothing.

I never hated him, exactly. When he left, I just decided to show solidarity with Mom and be done with him. If acting was more important than his family, then to hell with Peter Fancy. Mom was horrified when I told her how I felt. She cried and claimed the divorce was as much her fault as his. It was too much for me to handle; I was only eleven years old when they separated. I needed to be on *someone's* side and so I had chosen her. She never did stop trying to talk me into finding him again, even though after a while it only made me mad at her. For the past few years, she'd been warning me that I'd developed a warped view of men.

But she was a smart woman, my mom—a winner. Sure,

she'd had troubles, but she'd founded three companies, was a millionaire by twenty-five. I missed her.

A lock clicked and the door opened. Standing in the dim interior was a little girl in a gold-and-white checked dress. Her dark, curly hair was tied in a ribbon. She was wearing white ankle socks and black Mary Jane shoes that were so shiny they had to be plastic. There was a Band-Aid on her left knee.

"Hello, Jen. I was hoping you'd really come." Her voice surprised me. It was resonant, impossibly mature. At first glance I'd guessed she was three, maybe four; I'm not much good at guessing kids' ages. Now I realized that this must be a bot—a made person.

"You look just like I thought you would." She smiled, stood on tiptoe and raised a delicate little hand over her head. I had to bend to shake it. The hand was warm, slightly moist, and very realistic. She had to belong to Strawberry Fields; there was no way my father could afford a bot with skin this real.

"Please come in." She waved on the lights. "We're so happy you're here." The door closed behind me.

The playroom took up almost half of the little house. Against one wall was a miniature kitchen. Toy dishes were drying in a rack next to the sink; the pink refrigerator barely came up to my waist. The table was full-sized; it had two normal chairs and a booster chair. Opposite this was a bed with a ruffled Pumpkin Patty bedspread. About a dozen dolls and stuffed animals were arranged along the far edge of the mattress. I recognized most of them: Pooh, Mr. Moon, Baby Rollypolly, the Sleepums, Big Bird. And the wallpaper was familiar too: Oz figures like Toto and the Wizard and the Cowardly Lion on a field of Munchkin blue.

"We had to make a few changes," said the bot. "Do you like it?"

The room seemed to tilt then. I took a small, unsteady step and everything righted itself. *My* dolls, *my* wallpaper, the chest of drawers from Grandma Fanelli's cottage in Hyannis. I stared at the bot and recognized her for the first time.

She was me.

"What is this," I said, "some kind of sick joke?" I felt like I'd just been slapped in the face.

"Is something wrong?" the bot said. "Tell me. Maybe we can fix it."

I swiped at her and she danced out of reach. I don't know what I would have done if I had caught her. Maybe smashed her through the picture window onto the patch of front lawn or shaken her until pieces started falling off. But the bot wasn't responsible, my father was. Mom would never have defended him if she'd known about *this*. The old bastard. I couldn't believe it. Here I was, shuddering with anger, after years of feeling nothing for him.

There was an interior door just beyond some shelves filled with old-fashioned paper books. I didn't take time to look as I went past, but I knew that Dr. Seuss and A.A. Milne and L. Frank Baum would be on those shelves. The door had no knob.

"Open up," I shouted. It ignored me, so I kicked it. "Hey!"

"Jennifer." The bot tugged at the back of my jacket. "I must ask you . . ."

"You can't have me!" I pressed my ear to the door. Silence. "I'm not this thing you made." I kicked it again. "You hear?"

Suddenly an announcer was shouting in the next room. ". . . *Into the post to Russell, who kicks it out to Havlicek all alone at the top of the key, he shoots . . . and Baylor with the strong rebound.*" The asshole was trying to drown me out.

"If you don't come away from that door right now," said the bot, "I'm calling security."

"What are they going to do?" I said. "I'm the long-lost daughter, here for a visit. And who the hell are *you*, anyway?"

"I'm bonded to him, Jen. Your father is no longer competent to handle his own affairs. I'm his legal guardian."

"Shit." I kicked the door one last time, but my heart wasn't in it. I shouldn't have been surprised that he had slipped over the edge. He was almost ninety.

"If you want to sit and talk, I'd like that very much." The bot gestured toward a banana yellow beanbag chair. "Otherwise, I'm going to have to ask you to leave."

It was the shock of seeing the bot, I told myself—I'd reacted like a hurt little girl. But I was a grown woman and it was time to start behaving like one. I wasn't here to let Peter Fancy worm his way back into my feelings. I had come because of Mom.

"Actually," I said, "I'm here on business." I opened my purse. "If you're running his life now, I guess this is for you." I passed her the envelope and settled back, tucking my legs beneath me. There is no way for an adult to sit gracefully in a beanbag chair.

She slipped the check out. "It's from Mother." She paused, then corrected herself, "Her estate." She didn't seem surprised.

"Yes."

"It's too generous."

"That's what I thought."

"She must've taken care of you too?"

"I'm fine." I wasn't about to discuss the terms of Mom's will with my father's toy daughter.

"I would've liked to have known her," said the bot. She slid the check back into the envelope and set it aside. "I've spent a lot of time imagining Mother."

I had to work hard not to snap at her. Sure, this bot had at least a human equivalent intelligence and would be a free citizen someday, assuming she didn't break down first.

But she had a cognizor for a brain and a heart fabricated in a vat. How could she possibly imagine my mom, especially when all she had to go on was whatever lies *he* had told her?

"So how bad is he?"

She gave me a sad smile and shook her head. "Some days are better than others. He has no clue who President Huong is or about the quake, but he can still recite the dagger scene from *Macbeth*. I haven't told him that Mother died. He'd just forget it ten minutes later."

"Does he know what you are?"

"I am many things, Jen."

"Including me."

"You're a role I'm playing, not who I am." She stood. "Would you like some tea?"

"Okay." I still wanted to know why Mom had left my father four hundred and thirty-eight thousand dollars in her will. If he couldn't tell me, maybe the bot could.

She went to her kitchen, opened a cupboard, and took out a regular-sized cup. It looked like a bucket in her little hand. "I don't suppose you still drink Constant Comment?"

His favorite. I had long since switched to rafallo. "That's fine." I remembered that when I was a kid my father used to brew cups for the two of us from the same bag because Constant Comment was so expensive. "I thought they went out of business long ago."

"I mix my own. I'd be interested to hear how accurate you think the recipe is."

"I suppose you know how I like it?"

She chuckled.

"So, does he need the money?"

The microwave dinged. "Very few actors get rich," said the bot. I didn't think there had been microwaves in the sixties, but then strict historical accuracy wasn't really the point of Strawberry Fields. "Especially when they have a weakness for Shakespeare."

"Then how come he lives here and not in some flop? And how did he afford *you?*"

She pinched sugar between her index finger and thumb, then rubbed them together over the cup. It was something I still did, but only when I was by myself. A nasty habit; Mom used to yell at him for teaching it to me. "I was a gift." She shook a teabag loose from a canister shaped like an acorn and plunged it into the boiling water. "From Mother."

The bot offered the cup to me; I accepted it nervelessly. "That's not true." I could feel the blood draining from my face.

"I can lie if you'd prefer, but I'd rather not." She pulled the booster chair away from the table and turned it to face me. "There are many things about themselves that they never told us, Jen. I've always wondered why that was."

I felt logy and a little stupid, as if I had just woken from a thirty-year nap. "She just gave you to him?"

"And bought him this house, paid all his bills, yes."

"But why?"

"*You* knew her," said the bot. "I was hoping you could tell me."

I couldn't think of what to say or do. Since there was a cup in my hand, I took a sip. For an instant, the scent of tea and dried oranges carried me back to when I was a little girl and I was sitting in Grandma Fanelli's kitchen in a wet bathing suit, drinking Constant Comment that my father had made to keep my teeth from chattering. There were knots like brown eyes in the pine walls and the green linoleum was slick where I had dripped on it.

"Well?"

"It's good," I said absently and raised the cup to her. "No, really, just like I remember."

She clapped her hands in excitement. "So," said the bot. "What was Mother like?"

It was an impossible question, so I tried to let it bounce off me. But then neither of us said anything; we just stared at each other across a yawning gulf of time and experience. In the silence, the question stuck. Mom had died three months ago and this was the first time since the funeral that I'd thought of her as she really had been—not the papery ghost in the hospital room. I remembered how, after she divorced my father, she always took my calls when she was at the office, even if it was late, and how she used to step on imaginary brakes whenever I drove her anywhere, and how grateful I was that she didn't cry when I told her that Rob and I were getting divorced. I thought about Easter eggs and raspberry Pop Tarts and when she sent me to Antibes for a year when I was fourteen and that perfume she wore on my father's opening nights and the way they used to waltz on the patio at the house in Waltham.

"*West is walking the ball upcourt, setting his offense with fifteen seconds to go on the shot clock, nineteen in the half . . .*"

The beanbag chair that I was in faced the picture window. Behind me, I could hear the door next to the bookcase open.

"*Jones and Goodrich are in each other's jerseys down low and now Chamberlain swings over and calls for the ball on the weak side . . .*"

I twisted around to look over my shoulder. The great Peter Fancy was making his entrance.

Mom once told me that when she met my father, he was typecast playing men that women fall hopelessly in love with. He'd had great successes as Stanley Kowalski in *Streetcar* and Skye Masterson in *Guys and Dolls* and the Vicomte de Valmont in *Les Liaisons Dangereuses*. The years had eroded his good looks but had not obliterated them; from a distance he was still a handsome man. He had a shock of close-cropped white hair. The beautiful cheekbones were still there;

the chin was as sharply defined as it had been in his first head-shot. His gray eyes were distant and a little dreamy, as if he were preoccupied with the War of the Roses or the problem of evil.

"Jen," he said, "what's going on out here?" He still had the big voice that could reach into the second balcony without a mike. I thought for a moment he was talking to me.

"We have company, Daddy," said the bot, in a four-year-old trill that took me by surprise. "A lady."

"I can see that it's a lady, sweetheart." He took a hand from the pocket of his jeans, stroked the touchpad on his belt and his exolegs walked him stiffly across the room. "I'm Peter Fancy," he said.

"The lady is from Strawberry Fields." The bot swung around behind my father. She shot me a look that made the terms and conditions of my continued presence clear: if I broke the illusion, I was out. "She came by to see if everything is all right with our house." The bot disturbed me even more, now that she sounded like young Jen Fancy.

As I heaved myself out of the beanbag chair, my father gave me one of those lopsided, flirting grins I knew so well. "Does the lady have a name?" He must have shaved just for the company, because now that he had come close I could see that he had a couple of fresh nicks. There was a button-sized patch of gray whiskers by his ear that he had missed altogether.

"Her name is Ms. Johnson," said the bot. It was my ex, Rob's, last name. I had never been Jennifer Johnson.

"Well, Ms. Johnson," he said, hooking thumbs in his pants pockets. "The water in my toilet is brown."

"I'll . . . um . . . see that it's taken care of." I was at a loss for what to say next, then inspiration struck. "Actually, I had another reason for coming." I could see the bot stiffen. "I don't know if you've seen *Yesterday,* our little newsletter? Anyway, I was talking to Mrs. Chesley next door and she told me that you were an actor once. I was wondering if I might interview you. Just a few questions, if you have the time. I think your neighbors might . . ."

"Were?" he said, drawing himself up. "*Once?* Madame, I am now an actor and will always be."

"My Daddy's famous," said the bot.

I cringed at that; it was something I used to say. My father squinted at me. "What did you say your name was?"

"Johnson," I said. "Jane Johnson."

"And you're a reporter? You're sure you're not a critic?"

"Positive."

He seemed satisfied. "I'm Peter Fancy." He extended his right hand to shake. The hand was spotted and bony and it trembled like a reflection in a lake. Clearly whatever magic— or surgeon's skill—it was that had preserved my father's face had not extended to his extremities. I was so disturbed by his infirmity that I took his cold hand in mine and pumped it three, four times. It was dry as a page of one of the bot's dead books. When I let go, the hand seemed steadier. He gestured at the beanbag.

"Sit," he said. "Please."

After I had settled in, he tapped the touchpad and stumped over to the picture window. "Barbara Chesley is a broken and bitter old woman," he said, "and I will not have dinner with her under any circumstances, do you understand?" He peered up Bluejay Way and down.

"Yes, Daddy," said the bot.

"I believe she voted for Nixon, so she has no reason to complain now." Apparently satisfied that the neighbors weren't sneaking up on us, he leaned against the windowsill, facing me. "Mrs. Thompson, I think today may well be a happy one for both of us. I have an announcement." He paused for effect. "I've been thinking of Lear again."

The bot settled onto one of her little chairs. "Oh, Daddy, that's wonderful."

"It's the only one of the big four I haven't done," said my father. "I was set for a production in Stratford, Ontario, back in '99; Polly Matthews was to play Cordelia. Now there was an actor; she could bring tears to a stone. But then my wife Hannah had one of her bad times and I had to withdraw so I could take care of Jen. The two of us stayed down at my mother's cottage on the Cape; I wasted the entire season tending bar. And when Hannah came out of rehab, she decided that she didn't want to be married to an underemployed actor anymore, so things were tight for a while. She had all the money, so I had to scramble—spent almost two years on the road. But I think it might have been for the best. I was only forty-eight. Too old for Hamlet, too young for Lear. My Hamlet was very well received, you know. There were overtures from PBS about a taping, but that was when the BBC decided to do the Shakespeare series with that doctor, what was his name? Jonathan Miller. So instead of Peter Fancy, we had Derek Jacobi, whose brilliant idea it was to roll across the stage, frothing his lines like a rabid raccoon. You'd think he'd seen an alien, not his father's ghost. Well, that was another missed opportunity, except, of course, that I was too young. Ripeness is all, eh? So I still have Lear to do. Unfinished business. My comeback."

He bowed, then pivoted solemnly so that I saw him in profile, framed by the picture window. "Where have I been? Where am I? Fair daylight?" He held up a trembling hand and blinked at it uncomprehendingly. "I know not what to say. I swear these are not my hands."

Suddenly the bot was at his feet. "O look upon me, sir," she said, in her childish voice, "and hold your hand in benediction o'er me."

"Pray, do not mock me." My father gathered himself in the flood of morning light. "I am a very foolish, fond old man, fourscore and upward, not an hour more or less; and to deal plainly, I fear I am not in my perfect mind."

He stole a look in my direction, as if to gauge my reaction to his impromptu performance. A frown might have stopped him, a word would have crushed him. Maybe I should have, but I was afraid he'd start talking about Mom again, telling me things I didn't want to know. So I watched instead, transfixed.

"Methinks I should know you . . ." He rested his hand briefly on the bot's head. ". . . and know this stranger." He fumbled at the controls and the exolegs carried him across the room toward me. As he drew nearer, he seemed to sluff off the years. "Yet I am mainly ignorant what place this is; and all the skill I have remembers not these garments, nor I know not where I did lodge last night." It was Peter Fancy who stopped before me; his face a mere kiss away from mine. "Do not laugh at me; for, as I am a man, I think this lady to be my child. Cordelia."

He was staring right at me, into me, knifing through make-believe indifference to the wound I'd nursed all these years, the one that had never healed. He seemed to expect a reply, only I didn't have the line. A tiny, sad squeaky voice within me was whimpering, *You left me and you got exactly what you deserve*. But my throat tightened and choked it off.

The bot cried, "And so I am! I am!"

But she had distracted him. I could see confusion begin to deflate him. "Be your tears wet? Yes, faith. I pray . . . weep not. If you have poison for me, I will drink it. I know you do not love me . . ."

He stopped and his brow wrinkled. "It's something about the sisters," he muttered.

"Yes," said the bot, "'. . . for your sisters have done me wrong . . .'"

"Don't feed me the fucking lines!" he shouted at her. "I'm Peter Fancy, god damn it!"

After she calmed him down, we had lunch. She let him make the peanut butter and banana sandwiches while she heated up some Campbell's tomato and rice soup, which she poured from a can made of actual metal. The sandwiches were lumpy because he had hacked the bananas into chunks the size of walnuts. She tried to get him to tell me about the daylilies blooming in the backyard, and the old Boston Garden, and the time he and Mom had had breakfast with Bobby Kennedy. She asked whether he wanted TV dinner or pot pie for supper. He refused all her conversational gambits. He only ate half a bowl of soup.

He pushed back from the table and announced that it was her nap time. The bot put up a perfunctory fuss, although it was clear that it was my father who was tired out. However, the act seemed to perk him up. Another role for his resume: the doting father. "I'll tell you what," he said. "We'll play your game, sweetheart. But just once—otherwise you'll be cranky tonight."

The two of them perched on the edge of the bot's bed next to Big Bird and the Sleepums. My father started to sing and the bot immediately joined in.

"The itsy bitsy spider went up the water spout."

Their gestures were almost mirror images, except that his ruined hands actually looked like spiders as they climbed into the air.

"Down came the rain, and washed the spider out."

The bot beamed at him as if he were the only person in the world.

"Out came the sun, and dried up all the rain.

"And the itsy bitsy spider went up the spout again."

When his arms were once again raised over his head, she giggled and hugged him. He let them fall around her, returning her embrace. "That's a good girl," he said. "That's my Jenny."

The look on his face told me that I had been wrong: this was no act. It was as real to him as it was to me. I had tried hard not to, but I still remembered how the two of us always used to play together, Daddy and Jenny, Jen and Dad.

Waiting for Mommy to come home.

He kissed her and she snuggled under the blankets. I felt my eyes stinging.

"But if you do the play," she said, "when will you be back?"

"What play?"

"That one you were telling me. The king and his daughters."

"There's no such play, Jenny." He sifted her black curls through his hands. "I'll never leave you, don't worry now. Never again." He rose unsteadily and caught himself on the chest of drawers.

"Nighty noodle," said the bot.

"Pleasant dreams, sweetheart," said my father. "I love you."

"I love you too."

I expected him to say something to me, but he didn't even seem to realize that I was still in the room. He shambled across the playroom, opened the door to his bedroom and went in.

"I'm sorry about that," said the bot, speaking again as an adult.

"Don't be," I said. I coughed—something in my throat. "It was fine. I was very . . . touched."

"He's usually a lot happier. Sometimes he works in the garden." The bot pulled the blankets aside and swung her legs out of the bed. "He likes to vacuum."

"Yes."

"I take good care of him."

I nodded and reached for my purse. "I can see that." I had to go. "Is it enough?"

She shrugged. "He's my daddy."

"I meant the money. Because if it's not, I'd like to help."

"Thank you. He'd appreciate that."

The front door opened for me, but I paused before stepping out into Strawberry Fields. "What about . . . after?"

"When he dies? My bond terminates. He said he'd leave the house to me. I know you could contest that, but

I'll need to sell in order to pay for my twenty-year maintenance."

"No, no. That's fine. You deserve it."

She came to the door and looked up at me, little Jen
Fancy and the woman she would never become.

"You know, it's *you* he loves," she said. "I'm just a
stand-in."

"He loves his little girl," I said. "Doesn't do me any
good—I'm forty-seven."

"It could if you let it." She frowned. "I wonder if that's
why Mother did all this. So you'd find out."

"Or maybe she was just plain sorry." I shook my head.
She was a smart woman, my mom. I would've liked to have
known her.

"So, Ms. Fancy, maybe you can visit us again sometime."
The bot grinned and shook my hand. "Daddy's usually in a
good mood after his nap. He sits out front on his beach chair
and waits for the ice cream truck. He always buys us some.
Our favorite is Yellow Submarine. It's vanilla with fat butter-
scotch swirls, dipped in white chocolate. I know it sounds
kind of odd, but it's good."

"Yes," I said absently, thinking about all the things Mom
had told me about my father. I was hearing them now for the
first time. "That might be nice."

Beauty in the Night

ROBERT SILVERBERG

Robert Silverberg breaks new ground in the SF short story in 1997. He published two stories in *SF Age* in this same setting, a near future Earth invaded by superior and powerfully destructive aliens. They will apparently be integrated into a forthcoming Silverberg novel, *The Alien Years,* to be published in 1998. In an era when alien invasion has been most often reduced to parody or to stupid power fantasies in the movies or on TV, Silverberg restores a good bit of the original power to the Wellsian idea he has updated by clever characterization and technique. It is interesting to compare this story to Gibson's—there's a similar precise and cold observation of detail. Here, though, there is at least implied a sympathy for the human suffering portrayed, along with a very strong evocation of that suffering. How do you fight, why do you fight, when resistance is futile?

ONE: NINE YEARS FROM NOW

He was a Christmas child, was Khalid—Khalid the Entity-Killer, the first to raise his hand against the alien invaders who had conquered Earth in a single day, sweeping aside all resistance as though we were no more than ants to them. Khalid Haleem Burke, that was his name, English on his father's side, Pakistani on his mother's, born on Christmas Day amidst his mother's pain and shame and his family's grief. Christmas child though he was, nevertheless he was not going to be the new Savior of mankind, however neat a coincidence that might have been. But he would live, though his mother had not, and in the fullness of time he would do his little part, strike his little blow, against the awesome beings who had with such contemptuous ease taken possession of the world into which he had been born.

To be born at Christmastime can be an awkward thing for mother and child, who even at the best of times must contend with the risks inherent in the general overcrowding and understaffing of hospitals at that time of year. But prevailing hospital conditions were not an issue for the mother of the child of uncertain parentage and dim prospects who was about to come into the world in unhappy and disagreeable circumstances in an unheated upstairs storeroom of a modest Pakistani restaurant grandly named Khan's Mogul Palace in Salisbury, England, very early in the morning of this third

Christmas since the advent of the conquering Entities from the stars.

Salisbury is a pleasant little city that lies to the south and west of London and is the principal town of the county of Wiltshire. It is noted particularly for its relatively unspoiled medieval charm, for its graceful and imposing thirteenth-century cathedral, and for the presence, eight miles away, of the celebrated prehistoric megalithic monument.

Which, in the darkness before the dawn of that Christmas Day, was undergoing one of the most remarkable events in its long history; and, despite the earliness (or lateness) of the hour, a goodly number of Salisbury's inhabitants had turned out to witness the spectacular goings-on.

But not Haleem Khan, the owner of Khan's Mogul Palace, nor his wife Aissha, both of them asleep in their beds. Neither of them had any interest in the pagan monument that was Stonehenge, let alone the strange thing that was happening to it now. And certainly not Haleem's daughter Yasmeena Khan, who was seventeen years old and cold and frightened, and who was lying half-naked on the bare floor of the upstairs storeroom of her father's restaurant, hidden between a huge sack of raw lentils and an even larger sack of flour, writhing in terrible pain as shame and illicit motherhood came sweeping down on her like the avenging sword of angry Allah.

She had sinned. She knew that. Her father, her plump, reticent, overworked, mortally weary, and in fact already dying father, had several times in the past year warned her of sin and its consequences, speaking with as much force as she had ever seen him muster, and yet she had chosen to take the risk. Just three times, three different boys, only one time each, all three of them English and white.

Andy. Eddie. Richie.

Names that blazed like bonfires in the neural pathways of her soul.

Her mother—no, not really her mother, her true mother had died when Yasmeena was three; this was Aissha, her father's second wife, the robust and stolid woman who had raised her, had held the family and the restaurant together all these years—had given her warnings too, but they had been couched in entirely different terms. "You are a woman now, Yasmeena, and a woman is permitted to allow herself some pleasure in life," Aissha had told her. "But you must be careful." Not a word about sin, just taking care not to get into trouble.

Well, Yasmeena had been careful, or thought she had, but evidently not careful enough. Therefore she had failed Aissha. And failed her sad quiet father too, because she had certainly sinned despite all his warnings to remain virtuous, and Allah now would punish her for that. Was punishing her already. Punishing her terribly.

She had been very late discovering she was pregnant. She had not expected to be. Yasmeena wanted to believe that she was still too young for bearing babies, because her breasts were so small and her hips were so narrow, almost like a boy's. And each of those three times when she had done It with a boy—impulsively, furtively, half-reluctantly, once in a musty cellar and once in a ruined omnibus and once right here in this very storeroom—she had taken precautions afterward, diligently swallowing the pills she had secretly bought from the smirking Hindu woman at the shop in Winchester, two tiny green pills in the morning and the big yellow one at night, five days in a row.

The pills were so nauseating that they had to work. But they hadn't. She should never have trusted pills provided by a Hindu, Yasmeena would tell herself a thousand times over, but by then it was too late.

The first sign had come only about four months before. Her breasts suddenly began to fill out. That had pleased her, at first. She had always been so scrawny; but now it seemed that her body was developing at last. Boys liked breasts. You could see their eyes quickly flicking down to check out your chest, though they seemed to think you didn't notice it when they did. All three of her lovers had put their hands into her blouse to feel hers, such as they were; and at least one—Eddie, the second—had actually been disappointed at what he found there. He had said so, just like that: "Is that *all?*"

But now her breasts were growing fuller and heavier every week, and they started to ache a little, and the dark nipples began to stand out oddly from the smooth little circles in which they were set. So Yasmeena began to feel fear, and when her bleeding did not come on time, she feared even more. But her bleeding had never come on time. Once last year it had been almost a whole month late, and she an absolute pure virgin then.

Still, there were the breasts; and then her hips seemed to be getting wider. Yasmeena said nothing, went about her business, chatted pleasantly with the customers, who liked her because she was slender and pretty and polite, and pretended all was well. Again and again at night her hand would slide down her flat boyish belly, anxiously searching for hidden life lurking beneath the taut skin. She felt nothing.

But something was there, all right, and by early October it was making the faintest of bulges, only a tiny knot pushing upward below her navel, but a little bigger every day. Yasmeena began wearing her blouses untucked, to hide the new fullness of her breasts and the burgeoning rondure of her belly. She opened the seams of her trousers and punched two new holes in her belt. It became harder for her to do her work, to carry the heavy trays of food all evening long and to put in the hours afterward washing the dishes, but she forced herself to be strong. There was no one else to do the job. Her father took the orders and Aissha did the cooking and Yasmeena served the meals and cleaned up after the restaurant closed. Her brother Khalid was gone, killed defending Aissha from a mob of white men during the riots that had broken out after the Entities came, and her sister Leila was too small, only five, no use in the restaurant.

No one at home commented on the new way Yasmeena

was dressing. Perhaps they thought it was the current fashion. Life was very strange, in these early years of the Conquest.

Her father scarcely glanced at anyone these days; preoccupied with his failing restaurant and his failing health, he went about bowed over, coughing all the time, murmuring prayers endlessly under his breath. He was forty years old and looked sixty. Khan's Mogul Palace was nearly empty, night after night, even on the weekends. People did not travel any more, now that the Entities were here. No rich foreigners came from distant parts of the world to spend the night at Salisbury before going on to visit Stonehenge. The inns and hotels closed; so did most of the restaurants, though a few, like Khan's, struggled on because their proprietors had no other way of earning a living. But the last thing on Haleem Khan's mind was his daughter's changing figure.

As for her stepmother, Yasmeena imagined that she saw her giving her sideways looks now and again, and worried over that. But Aissha said nothing. So there was probably no suspicion. Aissha was not the sort to keep silent, if she suspected something.

The Christmas season drew near. Now Yasmeena's swollen legs were as heavy as dead logs and her breasts were hard as boulders and she felt sick all the time. It was not going to be long, now. She could no longer hide from the truth. But she had no plan. If her brother Khalid were here, he would know what to do. Khalid was gone, though. She would simply have to let things happen and trust that Allah, when He was through punishing her, would forgive her and be merciful.

Christmas Eve, there were four tables of customers. That was a surprise, to be so busy on a night when most English people had dinner at home. Midway through the evening Yasmeena thought she would fall down in the middle of the room and send her tray, laden with chicken biriani and mutton vindaloo and boti kebabs and schooners of lager, spewing across the floor. She steadied herself then; but an hour later she did fall; or, rather, sagged to her knees, in the hallway between the kitchen and the garbage bin where no one could see her. She crouched there, dizzy, sweating, gasping, nauseated, feeling her bowels quaking and strange spasms running down the front of her body and into her thighs; and after a time she rose and continued on with her tray toward the bin.

It will be this very night, she thought. And for the thousandth time that week she ran through the little calculation in her mind: *December 24 minus nine months is March 24, therefore it is Richie Burke, the father. At least he was the one who gave me pleasure also.*

Andy, he had been the first. Yasmeena couldn't remember his last name. Pale and freckled and very thin, with a beguiling smile, and on a humid summer night just after her sixteenth birthday when the restaurant was closed because her father was in the hospital for a few days with the beginning of his trouble, Andy invited her dancing and treated her to a couple of pints of brown ale and then, late in the evening, told her of a special party at a friend's house that he was invited to, only there turned out to be no party, just a shabby stale-smelling cellar room and an old spavined couch, and Andy's busy hands roaming the front of her blouse and then going between her legs and her trousers coming off and then, quick, *quick!*, the long hard narrow reddened thing emerging from him and sliding into her, done and done and done in just a couple of moments, a gasp from him and a shudder and his head buried against her cheek and that was that, all over and done with. She had thought it was supposed to hurt, the first time, but she had felt almost nothing at all, neither pain nor anything that might have been delight. The next time Yasmeena saw him in the street Andy grinned and turned crimson and winked at her, but said nothing to her, and they had never exchanged a word since.

Then Eddie Glossop, in the autumn, the one who had found her breasts insufficient and told her so. Big broad-shouldered Eddie, who worked for the meat merchant and who had an air of great worldliness about him. He was old, almost twenty-five. Yasmeena went with him because she knew there was supposed to be pleasure in it and she had not had it from Andy. But there was none from Eddie either, just a lot of huffing and puffing as he lay sprawled on top of her in the aisle of that burned-out omnibus by the side of the road that went toward Shaftesbury. He was much bigger down there than Andy, and it hurt when he went in, and she was glad that this had not been her first time. But she wished she had not done it at all.

And then Richie Burke, in this very storeroom on an oddly warm night in March, with everyone asleep in the family apartments downstairs at the back of the restaurant. She tiptoeing up the stairs, and Richie clambering up the drainpipe and through the window, tall, lithe, graceful Richie who played the guitar so well and sang and told everyone that some day he was going to be a general in the war against the Entities and wipe them from the face of the Earth. A wonderful lover, Richie. Yasmeena kept her blouse on because Eddie had made her uneasy about her breasts. Richie caressed her and stroked her for what seemed like hours, though she was terrified that they would be discovered and wanted him to get on with it; and when he entered her, it was like an oiled shaft of smooth metal gliding into her, moving so easily, easily, easily, one gentle thrust after another, on and on and on until marvelous palpitations began to happen inside her and then she erupted with pleasure, moaning so loud that Richie had to put his hand over her mouth to keep her from waking everyone up.

That was the time the baby had been made. There could be no doubt of that. All the next day she dreamed of marrying Richie and spending the rest of the nights of her life in his arms. But at the end of that week Richie disappeared from Salisbury—some said he had gone off to join a secret underground army that was going to launch guerrilla warfare against the Entities—and no one had heard from him again.

Andy. Eddie. Richie.

And here she was on the floor of the storeroom again, with her trousers off and the shiny swollen hump of her belly sending messages of agony and shame through her body. Her only covering was a threadbare blanket that reeked of spilled cooking oil. Her water had burst about midnight. That was when she had crept up the stairs to wait in terror for the great disaster of her life to finish happening. The contractions were coming closer and closer together, like little earthquakes within her. Now the time had to be two, three, maybe four in the morning. How long would it be? Another hour? Six? Twelve?

Relent and call Aissha to help her?

No. No. She didn't dare. Earlier in the night voices had drifted up from the streets to her. The sound of footsteps. That was strange, shouting and running in the street, this late. The Christmas revelry didn't usually go on through the night like this. It was hard to understand what they were saying; but then out of the confusion there came, with sudden clarity:

"The aliens! They're pulling down Stonehenge, taking it apart!"

"Get your wagon, Charlie, we'll go and see!"

Pulling down Stonehenge. Strange. Strange. Why would they do that? Yasmeena wondered. But the pain was becoming too great for her to be able to give much thought to Stonehenge just now, or to the Entities who had somehow overthrown the invincible white men in the twinkling of an eye and now ruled the world, or to anything else except what was happening within her, the flames dancing through her brain, the ripplings of her belly, the implacable downward movement of—of—

Something.

"Praise be to Allah, Lord of the Universe, the Compassionate, the Merciful," she murmured timidly. "There is no god but Allah, and Mohammed is His prophet."

And again: "Praise be to Allah, Lord of the Universe."

And again.

And again.

The pain was terrible. She was splitting wide open.

"Abraham, Isaac, Ishmael!" That *something* had begun to move in a spiral through her now, like a corkscrew driving a hot track in her flesh. "Mohammed! Mohammed! Mohammed! There is no god but Allah!" The words burst from her with no timidity at all, now. Let Mohammed and Allah save her, if they really existed. What good were they, if they would not save her, she so innocent and ignorant her life barely begun? And then, as a spear of fire gutted her and her pelvic bones seemed to crack apart, she let loose a torrent of other names—Moses, Solomon, Jesus, Mary, and even the forbidden Hindu names, Shiva, Krishna, Shakti, Kali,—anyone at all who would help her through this, anyone, anyone, anyone, anyone—

She screamed three times, short, sharp, piercing screams.

She felt a terrible inner wrenching and the baby came spurting out of her with astonishing swiftness. A gushing Ganges of blood followed it, a red river that spilled out over her thighs and would not stop flowing.

Yasmeena knew at once that she was going to die.

Something wrong had happened. Everything would come out of her insides and she would die. That was absolutely clear to her. Already, just moments after the birth, an eerie new calmness was enfolding her. She had no energy left now for further screaming, or even to look after the baby. It was somewhere down between her spread thighs, that was all she knew. She lay back, drowning in a rising pool of blood and sweat. She raised her arms toward the ceiling and brought them down again to clutch her throbbing breasts, stiff now with milk. She called now upon no more holy names. She could hardly remember her own.

She sobbed quietly. She trembled. She tried not to move, because that would surely make the bleeding even worse.

An hour went by, or a week, or a year.

Then an anguished voice high above her in the dark: "What? Yasmeena? Oh, my god, my god, my god! Your father will perish!"

Aissha, it was. Bending to her, engulfing her. The strong arm raising her head, lifting it against the warm motherly bosom, holding her tight.

"Can you hear me, Yasmeena? Oh, Yasmeena! My god, my god!" And then an ululation of grief rising from her step-mother's throat like some hot volcanic geyser bursting from the ground. "Yasmeena! Yasmeena!"

"The baby?" Yasmeena said, in the tiniest of voices.

"Yes! Here! Here! Can you see?"

Yasmeena saw nothing but a red haze.

"A boy?" she asked, very faintly.

"A boy, yes."

In the blur of her dimming vision she thought she saw something small and pinkish-brown, smeared with scarlet, resting in her stepmother's hands. Thought she could hear him crying, even.

"Do you want to hold him?"

"No. No." Yasmeena understood clearly that she was going. The last of her strength had left her. She was moored now to the world by a mere thread.

"He is strong and beautiful," said Aissha. "A splendid boy."

"Then I am very happy." Yasmeena fought for one last fragment of energy. "His name—is—Khalid. Khalid Haleem Burke."

"Burke?"

"Yes. Khalid Haleem Burke."

"Is that the father's name, Yasmeena? Burke?"

"Burke. Richie Burke." With her final sliver of strength she spelled the name.

"Tell me where he lives, this Richie Burke. I will get him. This is shameful, giving birth by yourself, alone in the dark, in this awful room! Why did you never say anything? Why did you hide it from me? I would have helped. I would—"

But Yasmeena Khan was already dead. The first shaft of morning light now came through the grimy window of the upstairs storeroom. Christmas Day had begun.

Eight miles away, at Stonehenge, the Entities had finished their night's work. Three of the towering alien creatures had supervised while a human work crew, using hand-held pistol-like devices that emitted a bright violet glow, had uprooted every single one of the ancient stone slabs of the celebrated megalithic monument on windswept Salisbury Plain as though they were so many jackstraws. And had rearranged them so that what had been the outer circle of immense sandstone blocks now had become two parallel rows running from north to south; the lesser inner ring of blue slabs had been moved about to form an equilateral triangle; and the sixteen-foot-long block of sandstone at the center of the formation that people called the Altar Stone had been raised to an upright position at the center.

A crowd of perhaps two thousand people from the adjacent towns had watched through the night from a judicious distance as this inexplicable project was being carried out. Some were infuriated; some were saddened; some were indifferent; some were fascinated. Many had theories about what was going on, and one theory was as good as another, no better, no worse.

▲   ▲   ▲

TWO: SIXTEEN YEARS FROM NOW

You could still see the ghostly lettering over the front door of the former restaurant, if you knew what to look for, the pale greenish outlines of the words that once had been painted there in bright gold: KHAN'S MOGUL PALACE. The old swinging sign that had dangled above the door was still lying out back, too, in a clutter of cracked basins and discarded stewpots and broken crockery.

But the restaurant itself was gone, long gone, a victim of the Great Plague that the Entities had casually loosed upon the world as a warning to its conquered people, after an attempt had been made at an attack on an Entity encampment. Half the population of Earth had died so that the Entities could teach the other half not to harbor further rebellious thoughts. Poor sad Haleem Khan himself was gone too, the ever-weary little brown-skinned man who in ten years had somehow saved five thousand pounds from his salary as a dishwasher at the Lion and Unicorn Hotel and had used that, back when England had a queen and Elizabeth was her name, as the seed money for the unpretentious little restaurant that was going to rescue him and his family from utter hopeless poverty. Four days after the Plague had hit Salisbury, Haleem was dead. But if the Plague hadn't killed him, the tuberculosis that he was already harboring probably would have done the job soon enough. Or else simply the shock and disgrace and grief of his daughter Yasmeena's ghastly death in childbirth two weeks earlier, at Christmastime, in an upstairs room of the restaurant, while bringing into the world the bastard child of the long-legged English boy, Richie Burke, the future traitor, the future quisling.

Haleem's other daughter, the little girl Leila, had died in the Plague also, three months after her father and two days before what would have been her sixth birthday. As for Yasmeena's older brother, Khalid, he was already two years gone by then. That was during the time that now was known as the Troubles. A gang of long-haired yobs had set forth late one Saturday afternoon in fine English wrath, determined to vent their resentment over the conquest of the Earth by doing a lively spot of Paki-bashing in the town streets, and they had encountered Khalid escorting Aissha home from the market. They had made remarks; he had replied hotly; and they beat him to death.

Which left, of all the family, only Aissha, Haleem's hardy and tireless second wife. She came down with the Plague, too, but she was one of the lucky ones, one of those who managed to fend the affliction off and survive—for whatever that was worth—into the new and transformed and diminished world. But she could hardly run the restaurant alone, and in any case, with three quarters of the population of Salisbury dead in the Plague, there was no longer much need for a Pakistani restaurant there.

Aissha found other things to do. She went on living in a couple of rooms of the now gradually decaying building that had housed the restaurant, and supported herself, in this era when national currencies had ceased to mean much and strange new sorts of money circulated in the land, by a variety of improvised means. She did housecleaning and laundry for those people who still had need of such services. She cooked meals for elderly folks too feeble to cook for themselves. Now and then, when her number came up in the labor lottery, she put in time at a factory that the Entities had established just outside town, weaving little strands of colored wire together to make incomprehensibly complex mechanisms whose nature and purpose were never disclosed to her.

And when there was no such work of any of those kinds available, Aissha would make herself available to the truck drivers who passed through Salisbury, spreading her powerful muscular thighs in return for meal certificates or corporate scrip or barter units or whichever other of the new versions of money they would pay her in. That was not something she would have chosen to do, if she had had her choices. But she would not have chosen to have the invasion of the Entities, for that matter, nor her husband's early death and Leila's and Khalid's, nor Yasmeena's miserable lonely ordeal in the upstairs room, but she had not been consulted about any of those things, either. Aissha needed to eat in order to survive; and so she sold herself, when she had to, to the truck drivers, and that was that.

As for why survival mattered, why she bothered at all to care about surviving in a world that had lost all meaning and just about all hope, it was in part because survival for the sake of survival was in her genes, and—mostly—because she wasn't alone in the world. Out of the wreckage of her family she had been left with a child to look after—her grandchild, her dead stepdaughter's baby, Khalid Haleem Burke. The child of shame. Khalid Haleem Burke had survived the Plague too. It was one of the ugly little ironies of the epidemic that the Entities had released upon the world that children who were less than six months old generally did not contract it. Which created a huge population of healthy but parentless babes.

He was healthy, all right, was Khalid Haleem Burke. Through every deprivation of those dreary years, the food shortages and the fuel shortages and the little outbreaks of diseases that once had been thought to be nearly extinct, he grew taller and straighter and stronger all the time. He had his mother's wiry strength and his father's long legs and dancer's grace. And he was lovely to behold. His skin was tawny golden-brown, his eyes were a glittering blue-green, and his hair, glossy and thick and curly, was a wonderful bronze color, a magnificent Eurasian hue. Amidst all the sadness and loss of Aissha's life, he was the one glorious beacon that lit the darkness for her.

There were no real schools, not any more. Aissha taught little Khalid herself, as best she could. She hadn't had much schooling, but she could read and write, and showed him how, and begged or borrowed books for him wherever she might. She found a woman who understood arithmetic, and scrubbed her floors for her in return for Khalid's lessons. There was an old man at the south end of town who knew the Koran by heart, and Aissha, though she was not a strongly religious woman herself, sent Khalid to him once a week for instruction in Islam. The boy was, after all, half Moslem. Aissha felt no responsibility for the Christian part of him, but she did not want to let him go into the world unaware that there was—somewhere, *somewhere!*—a god known as Allah, a god of justice and compassion and mercy, to whom obedience was owed, and that he would, like all people, ultimately come to stand before that god upon the Day of Judgment.

"And the Entities?" Khalid asked her. He was six, then. "Will they be judged by Allah too?"

"The Entities are not people. They are jinn."

"Did Allah make them?"

"Allah made all things in Heaven and on Earth. He made us out of potter's clay and the jinn out of smokeless fire."

"But the Entities have brought evil upon us. Why would Allah make evil things, if He is a merciful god?"

"The Entities," Aissha said uncomfortably, aware that wiser heads than hers had grappled in vain with that question, "*do* evil. But they are not evil themselves. They are merely the instruments of Allah."

"Who has sent them to us to do evil," said Khalid. "What kind of god is that, who sends evil among His own people, Aissha?"

She was getting beyond her depth in this conversation, but she was patient with him. "No one understands Allah's ways, Khalid. He is the One God and we are nothing before him. If He had reason to send the Entities to us, they were good reasons, and we have no right to question them." *And also to send sickness,* she thought, *and hunger, and death, and the English boys who killed your uncle Khalid in the street, and even the English boy who put you into your mother's belly and then ran away. Allah sent all of those into the world, too.* But then she reminded herself that if Richie Burke had not crept secretly into this house to sleep with Yasmeena, this beautiful child would not be standing here before her at this moment. And so good sometimes could come forth from evil. Who were we to demand reasons from Allah? Perhaps even the Entities had been sent here, ultimately, for our own good.

Perhaps.

Of Khalid's father, there was no news all this while. He was supposed to have run off to join the army that was fighting the Entities; but Aissha had never heard that there was any such army, anywhere in the world.

Then, not long after Khalid's seventh birthday, when he returned in mid-afternoon from his Thursday Koran lesson at the house of old Iskander Mustafa Ali, he found an unknown white man sitting in the room with his grandmother, a man with a great untidy mass of lightcolored curling hair and a lean, angular, almost fleshless face with two cold, harsh blue-green eyes looking out from it as though out of a mask. His skin was so white that Khalid wondered whether he had any blood in his body. It was almost like chalk. The strange white man was sitting in his grandmother's own armchair, and his grandmother was looking very edgy and strange, a way Khalid had never seen her look before, with glistening beads of sweat along her forehead and her lips clamped together in a tight thin line.

The white man said, leaning back in the chair and crossing his legs, which were the longest legs Khalid had ever seen, "Do you know who I am, boy?"

"How would he know?" his grandmother said.

The white man looked toward Aissha and said, "Let me do this, if you don't mind." And then, to Khalid: "Come over here, boy. Stand in front of me. Well, now, aren't we the little beauty? What's your name, boy?"

"Khalid."

"Khalid. Who named you that?"

"My mother. She's dead now. It was my uncle's name. He's dead too."

"Devil of a lot of people are dead who used to be alive, all right. Well, Khalid, my name is Richie."

"Richie," Khalid said, in a very small voice, because he had already begun to understand this conversation.

"Richie, yes. Have you ever heard of a person named Richie? Richie *Burke.*"

"My—father." In an even smaller voice.

"Right you are! The grand prize for that lad! Not only handsome but smart, too! Well, what would one expect, eh? Here I be, boy, your long-lost father! Come here and give your long-lost father a kiss."

Khalid glanced uncertainly toward Aissha. Her face was still shiny with sweat, and very pale. She looked sick. After a moment she nodded, a tiny nod.

He took half a step forward and the man who was his father caught him by the wrist and gathered him roughly in, pulling him inward and pressing him up against him, not for an actual kiss but for what was only a rubbing of cheeks. The grinding contact with that hard, stubbly cheek was painful for Khalid.

"There, boy. I've come back, do you see? I've been away seven worm-eaten miserable years, but now I'm back, and I'm going to live with you and be your father. You can call me 'dad.'"

Khalid stared, stunned.

"Go on. Do it. Say, 'I'm so very glad that you've come back, dad.'"

"Dad," Khalid said uneasily.

"The rest of it too, if you please."

"I'm so very glad—" He halted.

"That I've come back."

"That you've come back—"

"*Dad.*"

Khalid hesitated. "Dad," he said.

"There's a good boy! It'll come easier to you after a while. Tell me, did you ever think about me while you were growing up, boy?"

Khalid glanced toward Aissha again. She nodded surreptitiously.

Huskily he said, "Now and then, yes."

"Only now and then? That's all?"

"Well, hardly anybody has a father. But sometimes I met someone who did, and then I thought of you. I wondered where you were. Aissha said you were off fighting the Entities. Is that where you were, dad? Did you fight them? Did you kill any of them?"

"Don't ask stupid questions. Tell me, boy, do you go by the name of Burke or Khan?"

"Burke. Khalid Haleem Burke."

"Call me 'sir' when you're not calling me 'dad.' Say, 'Khalid Haleem Burke, sir.'"

"Khalid Haleem Burke, sir. Dad."

"One or the other. Not both." Richie Burke rose from the chair, unfolding himself as though in sections, up and up and up. He was enormously tall, very thin. His slenderness accentuated his great height. Khalid, though tall for his age, felt dwarfed beside him. The thought came to him that this man was not his father at all, not even a man, but some sort of demon, rather, a jinni, a jinni that had been let out of its bottle, as in the story that Iskander Mustafa Ali had told him. He kept that thought to himself. "Good," Richie Burke said. "Khalid Haleem Burke. I like that. Son should have his father's name. But not the Khalid Haleem part. From now on your name is—ah—Kendall. Ken for short."

"Khalid was my—"

"—uncle's name, yes. Well, your uncle is dead. Practically everybody is dead, Kenny. Kendall Burke, good English name. Kendall *Hamilton* Burke, same initials, even, only English. Is that all right, boy? What a pretty one you are,

Kenny! I'll teach you a thing or two, I will. I'll make a man out of you."

Here I be, boy, your long-lost father!

Khalid had never known what it meant to have a father, nor ever given the idea much examination. He had never known hatred before, either, because Aissha was a fundamentally calm, stable accepting person, too steady in her soul to waste time or valuable energy hating anything, and Khalid had taken after her in that. But Richie Burke, who taught Khalid what it meant to have a father, made him aware of what it was like to hate, also.

Richie moved into the bedroom that been Aissha's, sending Aissha off to sleep in what had once been Yasmeena's room. It had long since gone to rack and ruin, but they cleaned it up, some, chasing the spiders out and taping oil-cloth over the missing windowpanes and nailing down a couple of floorboards that had popped up out of their proper places. She carried her clothes-cabinet in there by herself, and set up on it the framed photographs of her dead family that she had kept in her former bedroom, and draped two of her old saris that she never wore any more over the bleak places on the wall where the paint had flaked away.

It was stranger than strange, having Richie living with them. It was a total upheaval, a dismaying invasion by an alien lifeform, in some ways as shocking in its impact as the arrival of the Entities had been.

He was gone most of the day. He worked in the nearby town of Winchester, driving back and forth in a small, brown, pre-Conquest automobile. Winchester was a place where Khalid had never been, though his mother had, to purchase the pills that were meant to abort him. Khalid had never been far from Salisbury, not even to Stonehenge, which now was a center of Entity activity anyway, and not a tourist sight. Few people in Salisbury traveled anywhere these days. Not many had automobiles, because of the difficulty of obtaining petrol, but Richie never seemed to have any problem with that.

Sometimes Khalid wondered what sort of work his father did in Winchester, but he asked about it only once. The words were barely out of his mouth when his father's long arm came snaking around and struck him across the face, splitting his lower lip and sending a dribble of blood down his chin.

Khalid staggered back, astounded. No one had ever hit him before. It had not occurred to him that anyone would.

"You must never ask that again!" his father said, looming mountain-high above him. His cold eyes were even colder, now, in his fury. "What I do in Winchester is no business of yours, nor anyone else's, do you hear me, boy? It is my own private affair. My own—private—affair."

Khalid rubbed his cutlip and peered at his father in bewilderment. The pain of the slap had not been so great: but the surprise of it, the shock—that was still reverberating through his consciousness. And went on reverberating for a long while thereafter.

He never asked about his father's work again, no. But he was hit again, more than once, indeed with fair regularity. Hitting was Richie's way of expressing irritation. And it was difficult to predict what sort of thing might irritate him. Any sort of intrusion on his father's privacy, though, seemed to do it. Once, while talking with his father in his bedroom, telling him about a bloody fight between two boys that he had witnessed in town, Khalid unthinkingly put his hand on the guitar that Richie always kept leaning against his wall beside his bed, giving it only a single strum, something that he had occasionally wanted to do for months; and instantly, hardly before the twanging note had died away, Richie unleashed his arm and knocked Khalid back against the wall. "You keep your filthy fingers off that instrument, boy!" Richie said. And after that Khalid did. Another time Richie struck him for leafing through a book he had left on the kitchen table, that had pictures of naked women in it; and another time, it was for staring too long at Richie as he stood before the mirror in the morning, shaving. So Khalid learned to keep his distance from his father but still he found himself getting slapped for this reason and that and sometimes for no reason at all. The blows were rarely as hard as the first one had been, and never ever created in him that same sense of shock. But they were blows, all the same. He stored them all up in some secret receptacle of his soul.

Occasionally Richie hit Aissha, too—when dinner was late, or when she put mutton curry on the table too often, or when it seemed to him that she had contradicted him about something. That was more of a shock to Khalid than getting slapped himself, that anyone should dare to lift his hand to Aissha.

The first time it happened, which occurred while they were eating dinner, a big carving knife was lying on the table near Khalid, and he might well have reached for it had Aissha not, in the midst of her own fury and humiliation and pain, sent Khalid a message with her furious blazing eyes that he absolutely was not to do any such thing. And so he controlled himself, then and any time afterward when Richie hit her. It was a skill that Khalid had, controlling himself—one that in some circuitous way he must have inherited from the ever-patient, all-enduring grandparents whom he had never known and the long line of oppressed Asian peasants from whom they descended. Living with Richie in the house gave Khalid daily opportunity to develop that skill to a fine art.

Richie did not seem to have many friends, at least not friends who visited the house. Khalid knew of only three.

There was a man named Arch who sometimes came, an older man with greasy ringlets of hair that fell from a big bald spot on the top of his head. He always brought a bottle of whiskey, and he and Richie would sit in Richie's room with the door closed, talking in low tones or singing raucous songs. Khalid would find the empty whiskey bottle the following morning, lying on the hallway floor. He kept them, setting them up in a row amidst the restaurant debris behind the house, though he did not know why.

The only other man who came was Syd, who had a flat nose and amazingly thick fingers, and gave off such a bad smell that Khalid was able to detect it in the house the next day. Once, when Syd was there, Richie emerged from his room and called to Aissha, and she went in there and shut the door behind her and was still in there when Khalid went to sleep. He never asked her about that, what had gone on while she was in Richie's room. Some instinct told him that he would rather not know.

There was also a woman: Wendy, her name was, tall and gaunt and very plain, with a long face like a horse's and very bad skin, and stringy tangles of reddish hair. She came once in a while for dinner, and Richie always specified that Aissha was to prepare an English dinner that night, lamb or roast beef, none of your spicy Paki curries tonight, if you please. After they ate, Richie and Wendy would go into Richie's room and not emerge again that evening, and the sounds of the guitar would be heard, and laughter, and then low cries and moans and grunts.

One time in the middle of the night when Wendy was there, Khalid got up to go to the bathroom just at the time she did, and encountered her in the hallway, stark naked in the moonlight, a long white ghostly figure. He had never seen a woman naked until this moment, not a real one, only the pictures in Richie's magazine: but he looked up at her calmly, with that deep abiding steadiness in the face of any sort of surprise that he had mastered so well since the advent of Richie. Coolly he surveyed her, his eyes rising from the long thin legs that went up and up and up from the floor and halting for a moment at the curious triangular thatch of woolly hair at the base of her flat belly, and from there his gaze mounted to the round little breasts set high and far apart on her chest, and at last came to her face, which, in the moonlight had unexpectedly taken on a sort of handsomeness if not actual comeliness, though before this Wendy had always seemed to him to be tremendously ugly. She didn't seem displeased at being seen like this. She smiled and winked at him, and ran her hand almost coquettishly through her straggly hair, and blew him a kiss as she drifted on past him toward the bathroom. It was the only time that anyone associated with Richie had ever been nice to him, had even appeared to notice him at all.

But life with Richie was not entirely horrid. There were some good aspects.

One of them was simply being close to so much strength and energy, what Khalid might have called *virility*, if he had known there was any such word. He had spent all his short life thus far among people who kept their heads down and went soldiering along obediently, people like patient plodding Aissha, who took what came to her and never complained; and shriveled old Iskander Mustafa Ali, who understood that Allah determined all things and one had no choice but to comply; and the quiet, tight-lipped English people of Salisbury, who had lived through the Conquest, and the Great Silence when the aliens had turned off all the electrical power in the world, and the Troubles, and the Plague, and who were prepared to be very, very English about whatever horror was coming next.

Richie was different, though. Richie hadn't a shred of passivity in him. "We shape our lives the way we want them to be, boy," Richie would say again and again. "We write our own scripts. It's all nothing but a bloody television show, don't you see that, Kenny-boy?"

That was a startling novelty to Khalid, that you might actually have any control over your own destiny: that you could say "no" to this and "yes" to that and "not right now" to this other thing, and that if there was something you wanted, you could simply reach out and take it. There was nothing Khalid wanted. But the *idea* that he might even have it, if only he could figure out what it was, was fascinating to him.

Then, too, for all of Richie's roughness of manner, his quickness to curse you or kick out at you or slap you when he had had a little too much to drink, he did have an affectionate side, even a charming one. He often sat with them and played his guitar, and taught them the words of songs, and encouraged them to sing along with them, though Khalid had no idea what the songs were about and Aissha did not seem to know either. It was fun, all the same, the singing; and Khalid had known very little fun. Richie was immensely proud of Khalid's good looks and agile, athletic grace, also, and would praise him for them, something that no one had ever done before, not even Aissha. Even though Khalid understood in some way that Richie was only praising himself, really, he was grateful even so.

Richie took him out behind the building and showed him how to throw and catch a ball. How to kick one, too, a different kind of ball. And sometimes there were cricket matches in a field at the edge of town; and when Richie played in these, which he occasionally did, he brought Khalid along to watch. Later, at home, he showed Richie how to hold the bat, how to guard a wicket.

Then there were the drives in the car. These were rare, a great privilege. But sometimes, of a sunny Sunday, Richie would say, "Let's take the old flivver for a spin, eh, Kenny, lad?" And off they would go into the green countryside, usually no special destination in mind, only driving up and down the quiet lanes, Khalid gawking in wonder at this new world beyond the town. It made his head whirl in a good way, as he came to understand that the world actually did go on and on past the boundaries of Salisbury, and was full of marvels and splendors.

So, though at no point did he stop hating Richie, he could

see at least some mitigating benefits that had come from his presence in their home. Not many. Some.

THREE: NINETEEN YEARS FROM NOW

Once Richie took him to Stonehenge. Or as near to it as was possible now for humans to go. It was the year Khalid turned ten: a special birthday treat.

"Do you see it out there in the plain, boy? Those big stones? Built by a bunch of ignorant prehistoric buggers who painted themselves blue and danced widdershins in the night. Do you know what 'widdershins' means, boy? No, neither do I. But they did it, whatever it was. Danced around naked with their thingummies jiggling around, and then at midnight they'd sacrifice a virgin on the big altar stone. Long, long ago. Thousands of years. Come on, let's get out and have a look."

Khalid stared. Huge gray slabs, set out in two facing rows flanking smaller slabs of blue stone set in a three-cornered pattern, and a big stone standing upright in the middle. And some other stones laying sideways on top of a few of the gray ones. A transparent curtain of flickering reddish-green light surrounded the whole thing, rising from hidden vents in the ground to nearly twice the height of a man. Why would anyone have wanted to build such a thing? It all seemed like a tremendous waste of time.

"Of course, you understand this isn't what it looked like back then. When the Entities came, they changed the whole business around from what it always was, buggered it all up. Got laborers out here to move every single stone. And they put in the gaudy lighting effects, too. Never used to be lights, certainly not that kind. You walk through those lights, you die, just like a mosquito flying through a candle flame. Those stones there, they were set in a circle originally, and those blue ones there—hey, now, lad, look what we have! You ever see an Entity before, Ken?"

Actually, Khalid had: twice. But never this close. The first one had been right in the middle of the town at noontime. It had been standing outside the entrance of the cathedral cool as you please, as though it happened to be in the mood to go to church: a giant purple thing with orange spots and big yellow eyes. But Aissha had put her hand over his face before he could get a good look, and had pulled him quickly down the street that led away from the cathedral, dragging him along as fast as he was able to go. Khalid had been about five then. He dreamed of the Entity for months thereafter.

The second time, a year later, he had been with friends, playing within sight of the main highway, when a strange vehicle came down the road, an Entity car that floated on air instead of riding on wheels, and two Entities were standing in it, looking right out at them for a moment as they went floating by. Khalid saw only the tops of their heads that time: their great eyes again, and a sort of a curving beak below, and a great V-shaped slash of a mouth, like a frog's. He was fascinated by them. Repelled, too, because they were so bizarre, these strange alien beings, these enemies of mankind, and he knew he was supposed to loathe and disdain them. But fascinated. Fascinated. He wished he had been able to see them better.

Now, though, he had a clear view of the creatures, three of them. They had emerged from what looked like a door that was set right in the ground, out on the far side of the ancient monument, and were strolling casually among the great stones like lords or ladies inspecting their estate, paying no heed whatever to the tall man and the small boy standing beside the car parked just outside the fiery barrier. It amazed Khalid, watching them teeter around on the little ropy legs that supported their immense tubular bodies, that they were able to keep their balance, that they didn't simply topple forward and fall with a crash.

It amazed him, too, how beautiful they were. He had suspected that from his earlier glances, but now their glory fell upon him with full impact.

The luminous golden-orange spots on the glassy, gleaming purple skin—like fire, those spots were. And the huge eyes, so bright, so keen: you could read the strength of their minds in them, the power of their souls. Their gaze engulfed you in a flood of light. Even the air about the Entities partook of their beauty, glowing with a liquid turquoise radiance.

"There they be, boy. Our lords and masters. You ever see anything so bloody hideous?"

"Hideous?"

"They ain't pretty, isn't that right?" Khalid made a noncommittal noise. Richie was in a good mood; he always was, on these Sunday excursions. But Khalid knew only too well the penalty for contradicting him in anything. So he looked upon the Entities in silence, lost in wonder, awed by the glory of these strange gigantic creatures, never voicing a syllable of his admiration for their elegance and majesty.

Expansively Richie said. "You heard correctly, you know, when they told you that when I left Salisbury just before you were born, it was to go off and join an army that meant to fight them. There was nothing I wanted more than to kill Entities, nothing. Christ Eternal, boy, did I ever hate those creepy bastards! Coming in like they did, taking our world away quick as you please. But I got to my senses pretty fast, let me tell you. I listened to the plans the underground army people had for throwing off the Entity yoke, and I had to laugh. I had to *laugh!* I could see right away that there wasn't a hope in hell of it. This was even before they put the Great Plague upon us, you understand. I knew. I damn well knew, I did. They're as powerful as gods. You want to fight against a bunch of gods, lots of luck to you. So I quit the underground then and there. I still hate the bastards, mind you, make no mistake about that, but I know it's foolish even to dream about overthrowing them. You just have to fashion your accommodation with them, that's all there is. You just have to make your peace within yourself and let them have their way. Because anything else is a fool's own folly."

Khalid listened. What Richie was saying made sense. Khalid understood about not wanting to fight against gods. He understood also how it was possible to hate someone and yet go on unprotestingly living with him.

"Is it all right, letting them see us like this?" he asked. "Aissha says that sometimes when they see you, they reach out from their chests with the tongues that they have there and snatch you up, and they take you inside their buildings and do horrible things to you there."

Richie laughed harshly. "It's been known to happen. But they won't touch Richie Burke, lad, and they won't touch the son of Richie Burke at Richie Burke's side. I guarantee you that. We're absolutely safe."

Khalid did not ask why that should be. He hoped it was true, that was all.

Two days afterward, while he was coming back from the market with a packet of lamb for dinner, he was set upon by two boys and a girl, all of them about his age or a year or two older, whom he knew only in the vaguest way. They formed themselves into a loose ring just beyond his reach and began to chant in a high-pitched, nasal way: *"Quisling, quisling, your father is a quisling!"*

"What's that you call him?"

"Quisling."

"He is not."

"He is! He is! *Quisling, quisling, your father is a quisling!*"

Khalid had no idea what a quisling was. But no one was going to call his father names. Much as he hated Richie, he knew he could not allow that. It was something Richie had taught him: *Defend yourself against scorn, boy, at all times.* He meant against those who might be rude to Khalid because he was part Pakistani; but Khalid had experienced very little of that. Was a quisling someone who was English but had had a child with a Pakistani woman? Perhaps that was it. Why would these children care, though? Why would anyone?

"Quisling, quisling—"

Khalid threw down his package and lunged at the closest boy, who darted away. He caught the girl by the arm, but he would not hit a girl, and so he simply shoved her into the other boy, who went spinning up against the side of the market building. Khalid pounced on him there, holding him close to the wall with one hand and furiously hitting him with the other.

His two companions seemed unwilling to intervene. But they went on chanting, from a safe distance, more nasally than ever.

"Quis-ling, quis-ling, your fa-ther is a quis-ling!"

"Stop that!" Khalid cried. "You have no right!" He punctuated his words with blows. The boy he was holding was bleeding, now, his nose, the side of his mouth. He looked terrified.

"Quis-ling, quis-ling—"

They would not stop, and neither would Khalid. But then he felt a hand seizing him by the back of his neck, a big adult hand, and he was yanked backward and thrust against the market wall himself. A vast meaty man, a navvy, from the looks of him, loomed over Khalid. "What do you think you're doing, you dirty Paki garbage? You'll kill the boy!"

"He said my father was a quisling!"

"Well, then, he probably is. Get on with you, now, boy! Get on with you!"

He gave Khalid one last hard shove, and spat and walked away. Khalid looked sullenly around for his three tormentors, but they had run off already. They had taken the packet of lamb with them, too.

That night, while Aissha was improvising something for dinner out of yesterday's rice and some elderly chicken, Khalid asked her what a quisling was. She spun around on him as though he had cursed Allah to her ears. Her face all ablaze with a ferocity he had not seen in it before, she said, "Never use that word in this house, Khalid. Never! Never!" And that was all the explanation she would give. Khalid had to learn, on his own, what a quisling was; and when he did, which was soon thereafter, he understood why his father had been unafraid, that day at Stonehenge when they stood outside that curtain of light and looked upon the Entities who were strolling among the giant stones. And also why those three children had mocked him in the street. *You just have to fashion your accommodation with them, that's all there is.* Yes. Yes. Yes. To fashion your accommodation.

FOUR: TWENTY YEARS FROM NOW

It was after the time that Richie beat Aissha so severely, and then did worse than that—violated her, raped her—that Khalid definitely decided that he was going to kill an Entity.

Not kill Richie.

Kill an Entity.

It was a turning point in Khalid's relationship with his father, and indeed in Khalid's whole life, and in the life of any number of other citizens of Salisbury, Wiltshire, England, that time when Richie hurt Aissha so. Richie had been treating Aissha badly all along, of course. He treated everyone badly. He had moved into her house and had taken possession of it as though it were his own. He regarded her as a servant, there purely to do his bidding, and woe betide her if she failed to meet his expectations. She cooked; she cleaned the house; Khalid understood now that sometimes, at his whim, Richie would make her come into his bedroom to amuse him or his friend Syd or both of them together. And there was never a word of complaint from her. She did as he wished; she showed no sign of anger or even resentment; she had given herself over entirely to the will of Allah. Khalid, who had not yet managed to find any convincing evidence of Allah's existence, had not. But he had learned the art of accepting the unacceptable from Aissha. He knew better than to try to change what was unchangeable. So he lived with his hatred of Richie, and that was merely a fact of daily existence, like the fact that rain did not fall upward.

Now, though, Richie had gone too far.

Coming home plainly drunk, red-faced, enraged over something, muttering to himself. Greeting Aissha with a growling curse, Khalid with a stinging slap. No apparent reason for either. Demanding his dinner early. Getting it, not liking what he got. Aissha offering mild explanations of why beef had not been available today. Richie shouting that beef bloody well *should* have been available to the household of Richie Burke.

So far, just normal Richie behavior when Richie was having a bad day. Even sweeping the serving bowl of curried mutton off the table, sending it shattering, thick oily brown sauce splattering everywhere, fell within the normal Richie range.

But then, Aissha saying softly, despondently, looking down at what had been her prettiest remaining sari now spotted in twenty places, "You have stained my clothing" And Richie going over the top. Erupting. Berserk. Wrath out of all measure to the offense, if offense there had been.

Leaping at her, bellowing, shaking her, slapping her. Punching her, even. In the face. In the chest. Seizing the sari at her midriff, ripping it away, tearing it in shreds, crumpling them and hurling them at her. Aissha backing away from him, trembling, eyes bright with fear, dabbing at the blood that seeped from her cut lower lip with one hand, spreading the other one out to cover herself at the thighs.

Khalid staring, not knowing what to do, horrified, furious.

Richie yelling. "I'll stain you, I will! I'll give you a sodding stain!" Grabbing her by the wrist, pulling away what remained of her clothing, stripping her all but naked right there in the dining room. Khalid covering his face. His own grandmother, forty years old, decent, respectable, naked before him: How could he look? And yet how could he tolerate what was happening? Richie dragging her out of the room, now, toward his bedroom, not troubling even to close the door. Hurling her down on his bed, falling on top of her. Grunting like a pig, a pig, a pig, a pig.

I must not permit this.

Khalid's breast surged with hatred: a cold hatred, almost dispassionate. The man was inhuman, a jinni. Some jinn were harmless, some were evil; but Richie was surely of the evil kind, a demon.

His father. An evil jinni.

But what did that make him? What? What? What? What?

Khalid found himself going into the room after them, against all prohibitions, despite all risks. Seeing Richie plunked between Aissha's legs, his shirt pulled up, his trousers pulled down, his bare buttocks pumping in the air. And Aissha staring upward past Richie's shoulder at the frozen Khalid in the doorway, her face a rigid mask of horror and shame: gesturing to him, making a repeated brushing movement of her hand through the air, wordlessly telling him to go away, to get out of the room, not to watch, not to intervene in any way.

He ran from the house and crouched cowering amid the rubble in the rear yard, the old stewpots and broken jugs and his own collection of Arch's empty whiskey bottles. When he returned, an hour later, Richie was in his room, chopping malevolently at the strings of his guitar, singing some droning tune in a low, boozy voice. Aissha was dressed again, moving about in a slow, downcast way, cleaning up the mess in the dining room. Sobbing softly. Saying nothing, not even looking at Khalid as he entered. A sticking-plaster on her lip. Her cheeks looked puffy and bruised. There seemed to be a wall around her. She was sealed away inside herself, sealed from all the world, even from him.

"I will kill him," Khalid said quietly to her.

"No. That you will not do." Aissha's voice was deep and remote, a voice from the bottom of the sea.

She gave him a little to eat, a cold chapati and some of yesterday's rice, and sent him to his room. He lay awake for hours, listening to the sounds of the house, Richie's endless drunken droning song, Aissha's barely audible sobs. In the morning nobody said anything about anything.

Khalid understood that it was impossible for him to kill his own father, however much he hated him. But Richie had to be punished for what he had done. And so, to punish him, Khalid was going to kill an Entity.

The Entities were a different matter. They were fair game.

For some time now, on his better days, Richie had been taking Khalid along with him as he drove through the countryside, doing his quisling tasks, gathering information that the Entities wanted to know and turning it over to them by some process that Khalid could not even begin to understand, and by this time Khalid had seen Entities on so many different occasions that he had grown quite accustomed to being in their presence.

And had no fear of them. To most people, apparently, Entities were scary things, ghastly alien monsters, evil, strange; but to Khalid they still were, as they always had been, creatures of enormous beauty. Beautiful the way a god would be beautiful. How could you be frightened by anything so beautiful? How could you be frightened of a god?

They didn't ever appear to notice him at all. Richie would go up to one of them and stand before it, and some kind of transaction would take place. While that was going on, Khalid simply stood to one side, looking at the Entity, studying it, lost in admiration of its beauty. Richie offered no explanations of these meetings and Khalid never asked.

The Entities grew more beautiful in his eyes every time he saw one. They were beautiful beyond belief. He could almost have worshipped them. It seemed to him that Richie felt the same way about them: that he was caught in their spell, that he would gladly fall down before them and bow his forehead to the ground.

And so . . .

I will kill one of them, Khalid thought.

Because they are so beautiful. Because my father, who works for them, must love them almost as much as he loves himself, and I will kill the thing he loves. He says he hates them, but I think it is not so. I think he loves them, and that is why he works for them. Or else he loves them and hates them both. He may feel the same way about himself. But I see the light that comes into his eyes when he looks upon them.

So I will kill one, yes. Because by killing one of them I will be killing some part of *him*. And maybe there will be some other value in my doing it, besides.

FIVE: TWENTY-TWO YEARS FROM NOW

Richie Burke said, "Look at this goddamned thing, will you, Ken? Isn't it the goddamnedest fantastic piece of shit anyone ever imagined?"

They were in what had once been the main dining room of the old defunct restaurant. It was early afternoon. Aissha was elsewhere, Khalid had no idea where. His father was holding something that seemed something like a rifle, or perhaps a highly streamlined shotgun, but it was like no rifle or shotgun he had ever seen. It was a long, slender tube of greenish-blue metal with a broad flaring muzzle and what might have been some type of gunsight mounted midway down the barrel, and a curious sort of computerized trigger arrangement on the stock. A one-of-a-kind sort of thing, custom made, a home inventor's pride and joy.

"Is it a weapon, would you say?"

"A weapon? A weapon? What the bloody hell do you think it is, boy? It's a fucking Entity-killing gun! Which I confiscated this very day from a nest of conspirators over Warminster way. The whole batch of them are under lock and key this very minute, thank you very much, and I've brought Exhibit A home for safe-keeping. Have a good look, lad. Ever seen anything so diabolical?"

Khalid realized that Richie was actually going to let him handle it. He took it with enormous care, letting it rest on both his outstretched palms. The barrel was cool and very smooth, the gun lighter than he had expected it to be.

"How does it work, then?"

"Pick it up. Sight along it. You know how it's done. Just like an ordinary gunsight."

Khalid put it to his shoulder, right there in the room. Aimed at the fireplace. Peered along the barrel.

A few inches of the fireplace were visible in the crosshairs, in the most minute detail. Keen magnification, wonderful optics. Touch the right stud, now, and the whole side of the house would be blown out, was that it? Khalid ran his hand along the butt.

"There's a safety on it," Richie said. "The little red button. There. That. Mind you don't hit it by accident. What we have here, boy, is nothing less than a rocket-powered grenade gun. A bomb-throwing machine, virtually. You wouldn't believe it, because it's so skinny, but what it hurls is a very graceful little projectile that will explode with almost incredible force and cause an extraordinary amount of damage, altogether extraordinary. I know because I tried it. It was amazing, seeing what that thing could do."

"Is it loaded now?"

"Oh, yes, yes, you bet your little brown rump it is! Loaded and ready! An absolutely diabolical Entity-killing machine, the product of months and months of loving work by a little band of desperadoes with marvelous mechanical skills. As stupid as they come, though, for all their skills . . . Here, boy, let me have that thing before you set it off somehow."

Khalid handed it over.

"Why stupid?" he asked. "It seems very well made."

"I *said* they were skillful. This is a goddamned triumph of miniaturization, this little cannon. But what makes them think they could kill an Entity at all? Don't they imagine anyone's ever tried? Can't be done, Ken, boy. Nobody ever has, nobody ever will."

Unable to take his eyes from the gun, Khalid said obligingly, "And why is that, sir?"

"Because they're bloody unkillable!"

"Even with something like this? Almost incredible force, you said, sir. An extraordinary amount of damage."

"It would fucking well blow an Entity to smithereens, it would, if you could ever hit one with it. Ah, but the trick is to succeed in firing your shot, boy! Which cannot be done. Even as you're taking your aim, they're reading your bloody mind, that's what they do. They know exactly what you're up to, because they look into our minds the way we would look into a book. They pick up all your nasty little unfriendly thoughts about them. And then—bam!—they give you the bloody Push, the thing they do to people with their minds, you know, and you're done for, piff paff poof. We've heard of four cases, at least. Attempted Entity assassination. Trying to take a shot as an Entity went by. Found the bodies, the weapons, just so much trash by the roadside." Richie ran his hands up and down the gun, fondling it almost lovingly. "This gun here, it's got an unusually great range, terrific sight, will fire upon the target from an enormous distance. Still wouldn't work, I wager you. They can do their telepathy on you from three hundred yards away. Maybe five hundred. Who knows, maybe a thousand. Still, a damned good thing that we broke this ring up in time. Just in case they could have pulled it off somehow."

"It would be bad if an Entity was killed, is that it?" Khalid asked.

Richie guffawed. "Bad? Bad? It would be a bloody catastrophe. You know what they did, the one time anybody managed to damage them in any way? No, how in hell would you know? It was right around the moment you were getting born. Some buggerly American idiots launched a laser attack from space on an Entity building. Maybe killed a few, maybe didn't, but the Entities paid us back by letting loose a plague on us that wiped out damn near every other person there was in the world. Right here in Salisbury they were keeling over like flies. Had it myself. Thought I'd die. Damned well hoped I would, I felt so bad. Then I arose from my bed of pain and threw it off. But we don't want to risk bringing down another plague, do we, now? Or any other sort of miserable punishment that they might choose to inflict. Because they certainly will inflict one. One thing that has been clear from the beginning is that our masters will take no shit from us, no, lad, not one solitary molecule of shit."

He crossed the room and unfastened the door of the cabinet that had held Khan's Mogul Palace's meager stock of wine in the long-gone era when this building had been a licensed restaurant. Thrusting the weapon inside, Richie said, "This is where it's going to spend the night. You will make no reference to its presence when Aissha gets back. I'm expecting Arch to come here tonight, and you will make no reference to it to him, either. It is a top secret item, do you hear me? I show it to you because I love you, boy, and because I want you to know that your father has saved the world this day from a terrible disaster, but I don't want a shred of what I have shared with you just now to reach the ears of another human being. Or another inhuman being for that matter. Is that clear, boy? Is it?"

"I will not say a word," said Khalid.

▲   ▲   ▲

And said none. But thought quite a few.

All during the evening, as Arch and Richie made their methodical way through Arch's latest bottle of rare pre-Conquest whiskey, salvaged from some vast hoard found by the greatest of good luck in a Southampton storehouse, Khalid clutched to his own bosom the knowledge that there was, right there in that cabinet, a device that was capable of blowing the head off an Entity, if only one could manage to get within firing range without announcing one's lethal intentions.

Was there a way of achieving that? Khalid had no idea.

But perhaps the range of this device was greater than the range of the Entities' mind-reading capacities. Or perhaps not. Was it worth the gamble? Perhaps it was. Or perhaps not.

Aissha went to her room soon after dinner, once she and Khalid had cleared away the dinner dishes. She said little these days, kept mainly to herself, drifted through her life like a sleepwalker. Richie had not laid a violent hand on her again since that savage evening several years back, but Khalid understood that she still harbored the pain of his humiliation of her, that in some ways she had never really recovered from what Richie had done to her that night. Nor had Khalid.

He hovered in the hall, listening to the sounds from his father's room until he felt certain that Arch and Richie had succeeded in drinking themselves into their customary stupor. Ear to the door. Silence. A faint snore or two, maybe.

He forced himself to wait another ten minutes. Still quiet in there. Delicately he pushed the door, already slightly ajar, another few inches open. Peered cautiously within.

Richie slumped head down at the table, clutching in one hand a glass that still had a little whiskey in it, cradling his guitar between his chest and knee with the other. Arch on the floor opposite him, head dangling to one side, eyes closed, limbs sprawled every which way. Snoring, both of them. Snoring. Snoring. Snoring.

Good. Let them sleep very soundly.

Khalid took the Entity-killing gun now from the cabinet. Caressed its satiny barrel. It was an elegant thing, this weapon. He admired its design. He had an artist's eye for form and texture and color, did Khalid: some fugitive gene out of forgotten antiquity miraculously surfacing in him after a dormancy of centuries, the eye of a Gandharan sculptor, of a Rajput architect, a Gujerati miniaturist coming to the fore in him after passing through all those generations of the peasantry. Lately he had begun doing little sketches, making some carvings. Hiding everything away so that Richie would not find it. That was the sort of thing that might offend Richie, his taking up such piffling pastimes. Sports, drinking, driving around—those were proper amusements for a man.

On one of his good days last year Richie had brought a bicycle home for him: a startling gift, for bicycles were rarities, nowadays, none having been available, let alone manufactured, in England in ages. Where Richie had obtained it, from whom, with what brutality, Khalid did not like to think. But he loved his bike. Rode long hours through the countryside on it, every chance he had. It was his freedom; it was his wings. He went outside now, carrying the grenade gun, and carefully strapped it to the bicycle's basket.

He had waited nearly three years for this moment to make itself possible.

Nearly every night nowadays, Khalid knew, one could usually see Entities traveling about on the road between Salisbury and Stonehenge, one or two at a time, riding in those cars of theirs that floated a little way above the ground on cushions of air. Stonehenge was a major center of Entity activities nowadays and there were more and more of them in the vicinity all the time. Perhaps there would be one out there this night, he thought. It was worth the chance: he would not get a second opportunity with this captured gun that his father had brought home.

About halfway out to Stonehenge there was a place on the plain where he could have a good view of the road from a little copse several hundred yards away. Khalid had no illusion that hiding in the copse would protect him from the mind-searching capacities the Entities were said to have. If they could detect him at all, the fact that he was standing in the shadow of a leafy tree would not make the slightest difference. But it was a place to wait, on this bright moonlit night. It was a place where he could feel alone, unwatched.

He went to it. He waited there.

He listened to night-noises: an owl; the rustling of the breeze through the trees; some small nocturnal animal scrabbling in the underbrush.

He was utterly calm.

Khalid had studied calmness all his life, with his grandmother Aissha as his tutor. From his earliest days he had watched her stolid acceptance of poverty, of shame, of hunger, of loss, of all kinds of pain. He had seen her handling the intrusion of Richie Burke into her household and her life with philosophical detachment, with stoic patience. To her it was all the will of Allah, not to be questioned. Allah was less real to Khalid than He was to Aissha, but Khalid had drawn from her her infinite patience and tranquility, at least, if not her faith in God. Perhaps he might find his way to God later on. At any rate, he had long ago learned from Aissha that yielding to anguish was useless, that inner peace was the only key to endurance, that everything must be done calmly, unemotionally, because the alternative was a life of unending chaos and suffering. And so he had come to understand from her that it was possible even to hate someone in a calm, unemotional way. And had contrived thus to live calmly, day by day, with the father whom he loathed.

For the Entities he felt no loathing at all. Far from it. He had never known a world without them, the vanished world where humans had been masters of their own destinies. The Entities, for him, were an innate aspect of life, simply there, as were hills and trees, the moon, or the owl that roved the night above him now, cruising for squirrels or rabbits. And they were very beautiful to behold, like the moon, like an owl moving silently overhead, like a massive chestnut tree.

He waited, and the hours passed, and in his calm way he began to realize that he might not get his chance tonight, for he knew he needed to be home and in his bed before Richie awakened and could find him and the weapon gone. Another hour, two at most, that was all he could risk out here.

Then he saw turquoise light on the highway, and knew that an Entity vehicle was approaching, coming from the direction of Salisbury. It pulled into view a moment later, carrying two of the creatures standing serenely upright, side by side, in their strange wagon that floated on a cushion of air.

Khalid beheld it in wonder and awe. And once again marveled, as ever, at their elegance of these Entities, their grace, their luminescent splendor.

How beautiful you are! Oh, yes. Yes.

They moved past him on their curious cart as though traveling on a river of light, and it seemed to him, dispassionately studying the one on the side closer to him, that what he beheld here was surely a jinni of the jinn: Allah's creature, a thing made of smokeless fire, a separate creation. Which nonetheless must in the end stand before Allah in judgment, even as we.

How beautiful. How beautiful.

I love you.

He loved it, yes. For its crystalline beauty. A jinni? No, it was a higher sort of being than that; it was an angel. It was a being of pure light—of cool clear fire, without smoke. He was lost in rapt admiration of its angelic perfection.

Loving it, admiring it, even worshipping it, Khalid calmly lifted the grenade gun to his shoulder, calmly aimed, calmly stared through the gunsight. Saw the Entity, distant as it was, transfixed perfectly in the crosshairs. Calmly he released the safety, as Richie had inadvertently showed him how to do. Calmly put his finger to the firing stud.

His soul was filled all the while with love for the beautiful creature before him as—calmly, calmly, calmly—he pressed the stud. He heard a whooshing sound and felt the weapon kicking back against his shoulder with astonishing force, sending him thudding into a tree behind him and for a moment knocking the breath from him; and an instant later the left side of the beautiful creature's head exploded into a cascading fountain of flame, a shower of radiant fragments. A greenish-red mist of what must be alien blood appeared and went spreading outward into the air.

The stricken Entity swayed and fell backward, dropping out of sight on the floor of the wagon.

In that same moment the second Entity, the one that was riding on the far side, underwent so tremendous a convulsion that Khalid wondered if he had managed to kill it, too, with that single shot. It stumbled forward, then back, and crashed against the railing of the wagon with such violence that Khalid imagined he could hear the thump. Its great tubular body writhed and shook, and seemed even to change color, the purple hue deepening almost to black for an instant and the orange spots becoming a fiery red. At so great a distance it was hard to be sure, but Khalid thought, also, that its leathery hide was rippling and puckering as if in a demonstration of almost unendurable pain.

It must be feeling the agony of its companion's death, he realized. Watching the Entity lurch around blindly on the platform of the wagon in what had to be terrible pain, Khalid's soul flooded with compassion for the creature, and sorrow, and love. It was unthinkable to fire again. He had never had any intention of killing more than one; but in any case he knew that he was no more capable of firing a shot at this stricken survivor now than he would be of firing at Aissha.

During all this time the wagon had been moving silently onward as though nothing had happened; and in a moment more it turned the bend in the road and was gone from Khalid's sight, down the road that led toward Stonehenge.

He stood for a while watching the place where the vehicle had been when he had fired the fatal shot. There was nothing there now, no sign that anything had occurred. *Had* anything occurred? Khalid felt neither satisfaction nor grief nor fear nor, really, any emotion of any other sort. His mind was all but blank. He made a point of keeping it that way, knowing he was as good as dead if he relaxed his control even for a fraction of a second.

Strapping the gun to the bicycle basket again, he pedaled quietly back toward home. It was well past midnight; there was no one at all on the road. At the house, all was as it had been; Arch's car parked in front, the front lights still on, Richie and Arch snoring away in Richie's room.

Only now, safely home, did Khalid at last allow himself the luxury of letting the jubilant thought cross his mind, just for a moment, that had been flickering at the threshold of his consciousness for an hour.

Got you, Richie! Got you, you bastard!

He returned the grenade gun to the cabinet and went to bed, and was asleep almost instantly, and slept soundly until the first bird-song of dawn.

In the tremendous uproar that swept Salisbury the next day, with Entity vehicles everywhere and platoons of the glossy balloon-like aliens that everybody called Spooks going from house to house, it was Khalid himself who provided the key clue to the mystery of the assassination that had occurred in the night.

"You know, I think it might have been my father who did it," he said almost casually, in town, outside the market, to a boy named Thomas whom he knew in a glancing sort of way. "He came home yesterday with a strange sort of big gun. Said it was for killing Entities with, and put it away in a cabinet in our front room."

Thomas would not believe that Khalid's father was capable of such a gigantic act of heroism as assassinating an Entity. No, no, no, Khalid argued eagerly, in a tone of utter and sublime disingenuousness: He did it, I know he did it, he's always talked of wanting to kill one of them one of these days, and now he has.

He has?

Always his greatest dream, yes, indeed.

Well, then—

Yes. Khalid moved along. So did Thomas. Khalid took care to go nowhere near the house all that morning. The last person he wanted to see was Richie. But he was safe in that regard. By noon Thomas evidently had spread the tale of Khalid Burke's wild boast about the town with great effectiveness, because word came traveling through the streets around that time that a detachment of Spooks had gone to Khalid's house and had taken Richie Burke away.

"What about my grandmother?" Khalid asked. "She wasn't arrested too, was she?"

"No, it was just him," he was told. "Billy Cavendish saw them taking him, and he was all by himself. Yelling and screaming, he was, the whole time, like a man being hauled away to be hanged."

Khalid never saw his father again.

During the course of the general reprisals that followed the killing, the entire population of Salisbury and five adjacent towns was rounded up and transported to walled detention camps near Portsmouth. A good many of the deportees were executed within the next few days, seemingly by random selection, no pattern being evident in the choosing of those who were put to death. At the beginning of the following week the survivors were sent on from Portsmouth to other places, some of them quite remote, in various parts of the world.

Khalid was not among those executed. He was merely sent very far away.

He felt no guilt over having survived the death-lottery while others around him were being slain for his murderous act. He had trained himself since childhood to feel very little indeed, even while aiming a rifle at one of Earth's beautiful and magnificent masters. Besides, what affair was it of his, that some of these people were dying and he was allowed to live? Everyone died, some sooner, some later. Aissha would have said that what was happening was the will of Allah. Khalid more simply put it that the Entities did as they pleased, always, and knew that it was folly to ponder their motives.

Aissha was not available to discuss these matters with. He was separated from her before reaching Portsmouth and Khalid never saw her again, either. From that day on it was necessary for him to make his way in the world on his own.

He was not quite thirteen years old. Often, in the years ahead, he would look back at the time when he had slain the Entity; but he would think of it only as the time when he had rid himself of Richie Burke, for whom he had had such hatred. For the Entities he had no hatred at all, and when his mind returned to that event by the roadside on the way to Stonehenge, to the alien being centered in the crosshairs of his weapon, he would think only of the marvelous color and form of the two starborn creatures in the floating wagon, of that passing moment of beauty in the night.

Mr. Pale

RAY BRADBURY

Ray Bradbury is one of the great SF writers of the century. His most transforming and influential work was written in the 1940s and 1950s: the stories collected in *Dark Carnival, The October Country* and *The Martian Chronicles, The Golden Apples of the Sun* and *The Illustrated Man;* the novels *Fahrenheit 451, Dandelion Wine,* and *Something Wicked This Way Comes.* There has always been a strong strain of moral allegory in his fiction, and he often combines fantasy and the supernatural with science fiction. Although he has devoted most of his effort in succeeding decades to poetry and plays, and a couple of nostalgic mystery novels, he has never entirely abandoned short fiction, and every once in a while reminds us of what he has done and can still do in that form. Most of his fiction of this decade has been fantasy. This is one of his now scarce hybrids, which takes us back to his 50s best.

"**H**e's a very sick man."

"Where is he?"

"Up above on Deck C. I got him to bed."

The doctor sighed. "I came on this trip for a vacation. All right, all right. Excuse me," he said to his wife. He followed the private up through the ramps of the spaceship and the ship, in the few minutes while he did this, pushed itself on in red and yellow fire across space, a thousand miles a second.

"Here we are," said the orderly.

The doctor turned in at the portway and saw the man lying on the bunk, and the man was tall and his flesh was sewed tight to his skull. The man was sick, and his lips fluted back in pain from his large, discolored teeth. His eyes were shadowed cups from which flickers of light peered, and his body was as thin as a skeleton. The color of his hands was that of snow. The doctor pulled up a magnetic chair and took the sick man's wrist.

"What seems to be the trouble?"

The sick man didn't speak for a moment, but only licked a colorless tongue over his sharp lips.

"I'm dying," he said, at last, and seemed to laugh.

"Nonsense, we'll fix you up, Mr. . . . ?"

"Pale, to fit my complexion. Pale will do."

"Mr. Pale." This wrist was the coldest wrist he had ever touched in his life. It was like the hand of a body you pick up and tag in the hospital morgue. The pulse was gone from the cold wrist already. If it was there at all, it was so faint that the doctor's own fingertips, pulsing, covered it.

"It's bad, isn't it?" asked Mr. Pale.

The doctor said nothing but probed the bared chest of the dying man with his silver stethoscope.

There was a faint far clamor, a sigh, a musing upon distant things, heard in the stethoscope. It seemed almost to be a regretful wailing, a muted screaming of a million voices, instead of a heartbeat, a dark wind blowing in a dark space and the chest cold and the sound cold to the doctor's ears and to his own heart, which gave pause in hearing it.

"I was right, wasn't I?" said Mr. Pale.

The doctor nodded. "Perhaps you can tell me . . ."

"What caused it?" Mr. Pale closed his eyes smilingly over his colorlessness. "I haven't any food. I'm starving."

"We can fix that."

"No, no, you don't understand," whispered the man. "I barely made it to this rocket in time to get aboard. Oh, I was really healthy there for a while, a few minutes ago."

The doctor turned to the orderly. "Delirious."

"No," said Mr. Pale, "no."

"What's going on here?" said a voice, and the captain stepped into the room. "Hello, who's this? I don't recall . . ."

"I'll save you the trouble," said Mr. Pale. "I'm not on the passenger list. I just came aboard."

"You couldn't have. We're ten million miles away from Earth."

Mr. Pale sighed. "I almost didn't make it. It took all my energy to catch you. If you'd been a little farther out . . ."

"A stowaway, pure and simple," said the captain. "And drunk, too, no doubt."

"A very sick man," said the doctor. "He can't be moved. I'll make a thorough examination . . ."

"You'll find nothing," said Mr. Pale, faintly, lying white and long and alone in the cot, "except I'm in need of food."

"We'll see about that," said the doctor, rolling up his sleeves.

An hour passed. The doctor sat back down on his magnetic chair. He was perspiring. "You're right. There's nothing wrong with you, except you're starved. How could you do this to yourself in a rich civilization like ours?"

"Oh, you'd be surprised," said the cold, thin, white man. His voice was a little breeze blowing ice through the room. "They took all my food away an hour or so ago. It was my own fault. You'll understand in a few minutes now. You see, I'm very very old. Some say a million years, some say a billion. I've lost count. I've been too busy to count."

Mad, thought the doctor, utterly mad.

Mr. Pale smiled weakly as if he had heard this thought. He shook his tired head and the dark pits of his eyes flickered. "No, no. No, no. Old, very old. And foolish. Earth was mine. I owned it. I kept it for myself. It nurtured me, even as I nurtured it. I lived well there, for a billion years, I lived high. And now here I am, in the name of all that's darkest, dying too. I never thought I could die. I never thought I could be killed, like everyone else. And now *I* know what the fear is, what it will be like to die. After a billion years I know, and it is frightening, for what will the universe be without me?"

"Just rest easily, now, we'll fix you up."

"No, no. No, no, there's nothing you can do. I overplayed my hand. I lived as I pleased. I started wars and stopped wars. But this time I went too far, and committed suicide, yes, I did. Go to the port there and look out." Mr. Pale was trembling, the trembling moved in his fingers and his lips. "Look out. Tell me what you see."

"Earth. The planet Earth, behind us."

"Wait just a moment, then," said Mr. Pale.

The doctor waited.

"Now," said Mr. Pale, softly. "It should happen about *now*."

A blind fire filled the sky.

The doctor cried out. "My God, my God, this is terrible!"

"What do you see?"

"Earth! It's caught fire. It's burning!"

"Yes," said Mr. Pale.

The fire crowded the universe with a dripping blue yellow flare. Earth blew itself into a thousand pieces and fell away into sparks and nothingness.

"Did you see?" said Mr. Pale.

"My God, my God." The doctor staggered and fell against the port, clawing at his heart and his face. He began to cry like a child.

"You see," said Mr. Pale, "what a fool I was. Too far. I went too far. I thought, What a feast. What a banquet. And now, and now, it's over."

The doctor slid down and sat on the floor, weeping. The ship moved in space. Down the corridors, faintly, you could hear running feet and stunned voices, and much weeping.

The sick man lay on his cot, saying nothing, shaking his head slowly back and forth, swallowing convulsively. After five minutes of trembling and weeping, the doctor gathered himself and crawled and then got to his feet and sat on the chair and looked at Mr. Pale who lay gaunt and long there, almost phosphorescent, and from the dying man came a thick smell of something very old and chilled and dead.

"Now do you see?" said Mr. Pale. "I didn't want it this way."

"Shut up."

"I wanted it to go on for another billion years, the high life, the picking and choosing. Oh, I was king."

"You're mad!"

"Everyone feared me. And now *I'm* afraid. For there's no one left to die. A handful on this ship. A few thousand left on Mars. That's why I'm trying to get there, to Mars, where I can live, if I make it. For in order for me to live, to be talked about, to have an existence, others must be alive to die, and when all the living ones are dead and no one is left to die, then Mr. Pale himself must die, and he most assuredly does not want that. For you see, life is a rare thing in the universe. Only Earth lived, and only I lived there because of the living men. But now I'm so weak, so weak. I can't move. You must help me."

"Mad, mad!"

"It's another two days to Mars," said Mr. Pale, thinking it through, his hands collapsed at his sides. "In that time you must feed me. I can't move or I would tend myself. Oh, an hour ago, I had great power, think of the power I took from so much and so many dying at once. But the effort of reaching this ship dispersed the power, and the power is self-limiting. For now I have no reason to live, except you, and your wife, and the twenty other passengers and crew, and those few on Mars. My incentive, you see, weakens, weakens . . ." His voice trailed off into a sigh. And then, after swallowing, he went on, "Have you wondered, Doctor, why the death rate on Mars in the six months since you established bases there has been nil? I can't be everywhere. I was born on Earth on the same day as life was born. And I've waited all these years to move on out into the star system. I should have gone months ago, but I put it off, and now, I'm sorry. What a fool, what a greedy fool."

The doctor stood up, stiffening and pulling back. He clawed at the wall. "You're out of your head."

"Am I? Look out the port again at what's left of Earth."

"I won't listen to you."

"You must help me. You must decide quickly. I want the captain. He must come to me first. A transfusion, you might call it. And then the various passengers, one by one, just to keep me on the edge, to keep me alive. And then, of course, perhaps even you, or your wife. You don't want to live forever, do you? That's what would happen if you let me die."

"You're raving."

"Do you dare believe I am raving? Can you take that chance? If I die, all of you would be immortal. That's what man's always wanted, isn't it? To live forever. But I tell you, it would be insanity, one day like another, and think of the immense burden of memory! Think! Consider."

The doctor stood across the room with his back to the wall, in shadow.

Mr. Pale whispered, "Better take me up on this. Better die when you have the chance than live on for a million billion years. Believe me. I *know*. I'm almost glad to die. Almost, but not quite. Self-preservation. Well?"

The doctor was at the door. "I don't believe you."

"Don't go," murmured Mr. Pale. "You'll regret it."

"You're lying."

"Don't let me die . . ." The voice was so far away now, the lips barely moved. "Please don't let me die. You need me. All life needs me to make life worthwhile, to give it value, to give it contrast. Don't . . ."

Mr. Pale was thinner and smaller and now the flesh seemed to melt faster. "No," he sighed. "No . . ." said the wind behind the hard yellowed teeth. "Please . . ." The deep-socketed eyes fixed themselves in a stare at the ceiling.

The doctor crashed out the door and slammed it and bolted it tight. He lay against it, weeping again, and through the ship he could see the people standing in groups staring back at the empty space where Earth had been. He heard cursing and wailing. He walked unsteadily and in great unreality for an hour through the ship's corridors until he reached the captain.

"Captain, no one is to enter that room where the dying man is. He has a plague. Incurable. Quite insane. He'll be dead within the hour. Have the room welded shut."

"What?" said the captain. "Oh, yes, yes. I'll attend to it. I will. Did you see? See Earth go?"

"I saw it."

They walked numbly away from each other. The doctor sat down beside his wife who did not recognize him for a moment until he put his arm around her.

"Don't cry," he said. "Don't cry. Please don't cry."

Her shoulders shook. He held her very tightly, his eyes

clenched in on the trembling in his own body. They sat this way for several hours.

"Don't cry," he said. "Think of something else. Forget Earth. Think about Mars, think about the future."

They sat back in their seats with vacant faces. He lit a cigarette and could not taste it, and passed it to her and lit another for himself. "How would you like to be married to me for another ten million years?" he asked.

"Oh, I'd like that," she cried out, turning to him and seizing his arm in her own, fiercely wrapping it to her. "I'd like that very much!"

"*Would* you?" he said.

The Pipes of Pan

BRIAN STABLEFORD

Brian Stableford is one of the finest living critics and historians of SF and fantasy (he is the author of large chunks of both *The Encyclopedia of Science Fiction* and *The Encyclopedia of Fantasy*) and is another of the leading short-fiction writers in SF in this decade, and a significant novelist. His novels in recent years, such as the alternate universe extravaganza, *The Hunger and Ecstasy of Vampires*, have had a fantasy cast and have somewhat taken a back seat to his shorter fiction, which is regularly on award nomination ballots and various "best" lists. For most of the 1990s he has been writing stories such as "Inherit the Earth" and in a large future history setting, as yet unnamed, spanning centuries and focusing on immense changes in human society and in humanity due primarily to advances in the biological sciences. "The Pipes of Pan" appeared in *Fantasy & Science Fiction* and is one of these.

In her dream Wendy was a pretty little girl living wild in a magical wood where it never rained and never got cold. She lived on sweet berries of many colors, which always tasted wonderful, and all she wanted or needed was to be happy.

There were other girls living wild in the dream-wood but they all avoided one another, because they had no need of company. They had lived there, untroubled, for a long time—far longer than Wendy could remember.

Then, in the dream, the others came: the shadow-men with horns on their brows and shaggy legs. They played strange music on sets of pipes which looked as if they had been made from reeds—but Wendy knew, without knowing how she knew or what sense there was in it, that those pipes had been fashioned out of the blood and bones of something just like her, and that the music they played was the breath of her soul.

After the shadow-men came, the dream became steadily more nightmarish, and living wild ceased to be innocently joyful. After the shadow-men came, life was all hiding with a fearful, fluttering heart, knowing that if ever she were found she would have to run and run and run, without any hope of escape—but wherever she hid, she could always hear the music of the pipes.

When she woke up in a cold sweat, she wondered whether the dreams her parents had were as terrible, or as easy to understand. Somehow, she doubted it.

▲   ▲   ▲

There was a sharp rat-a-tat on her bedroom door.

"Time to get up, Beauty." Mother didn't bother coming in to check that Wendy responded. Wendy always responded. She was a good girl.

She climbed out of bed, took off her night-dress, and went to sit at the dressing-table, to look at herself in the mirror. It had become part of her morning ritual, now that her awakenings were indeed awakenings. She blinked to clear the sleep from her eyes, shivering slightly as an image left over from the dream flashed briefly and threateningly in the depths of her emergent consciousness.

Wendy didn't know how long she had been dreaming. The dreams had begun before she developed the sense of time which would have allowed her to make the calculation. Perhaps she had always dreamed, just as she had always got up in the morning in response to the summoning rat-a-tat, but she had only recently come by the ability to remember her dreams. On the other hand, perhaps the beginning of her dreams had been the end of her innocence.

She often wondered how she had managed not to give herself away in the first few months, after she first began to remember her dreams but before she attained her present level of waking self-control, but any anomalies in her behavior must have been written off to the randomizing factor. Her parents were always telling her how lucky she was to be thirteen, and now she was in a position to agree with them. At thirteen, it was entirely appropriate to be a little bit inquisitive and more than a little bit odd. It was even possible to get away with being too clever by half, as long as she didn't overdo it.

It was difficult to be sure, because she didn't dare interrogate the house's systems too explicitly, but she had figured out that she must have been thirteen for about thirty years, in mind and body alike. She was thirteen in her blood and her bones, but not in the privacy of her head.

Inside, where it counted, she had now been unthirteen for at least four months.

If it would only stay inside, she thought, *I might keep it a secret forever. But it won't. It isn't. It's coming out. Every day that passes is one day closer to the moment of truth.*

She stared into the mirror, searching the lines of her face for signs of maturity. She was sure that her face looked thinner, her eyes more serious, her hair less blond. All of that might be mostly imagination, she knew, but there was no doubt about the other things. She was half an inch taller, and her breasts were getting larger. It was only a matter of time before that sort of thing attracted attention, and as soon as it was noticed the truth would be manifest. Measurements couldn't lie. As soon as they were moved to measure her, her parents would know the horrid truth.

Their baby was growing up.

"Did you sleep well, dear?" Mother said, as Wendy took her seat at the breakfast-table. It wasn't a trick question; it was just part of the routine. It wasn't even a matter of pretending, although her parents certainly did their fair share of that. It was just a way of starting the day off. Such rituals were part and parcel of what they thought of as *everyday life.* Parents had their innate programming too.

"Yes thank you," she replied, meekly.

"What flavor manna would you like today?"

"Coconut and strawberry please." Wendy smiled as she spoke, and Mother smiled back. Mother was smiling because Wendy was smiling. Wendy was supposed to be smiling because she was a smiley child, but in fact she was smiling because saying "strawberry and coconut" was an authentic and honest *choice,* an exercise of freedom which would pass as an expected manifestation of the randomizing factor.

"I'm afraid I can't take you out this morning, Lovely," Father said, while Mother punched out the order. "We have to wait in for the house-doctor. The waterworks still aren't right."

"If you ask me," Mother said, "the real problem's the water table. The aproots are doing their best but they're having to go down too far. The system's fine just so long as we get some good old-fashioned rain once in a while, but every time there's a dry spell the whole estate suffers. We ought to call a meeting and put some pressure on the landscape engineers. Fixing a water table shouldn't be too much trouble in this day and age."

"There's nothing wrong with the water table, dear," Father said, patiently. "It's just that the neighbors have the same in-dwelling systems that we have. There's a congenital weakness in the root-system; in dry weather the cell-terminal conduits in the phloem tend to get gummed up. It ought to be easy enough to fix—a little elementary somatic engineering, probably no more than a single-gene augment in the phloem—but you know what doctors are like, they never want to go for the cheap and cheerful cure if they can sell you something more complicated."

"What's phloem?" Wendy asked. She could ask as many questions as she liked, to a moderately high level of sophistication. That was a great blessing. She was glad she wasn't an eight-year-old, reliant on passive observation and a restricted vocabulary. At least a thirteen-year-old had the right equipment for thinking all set up.

"It's a kind of plant tissue," Father informed her, ignoring the tight-lipped look Mother was giving him because he'd contradicted her. "It's sort of equivalent to your veins, except of course that plants have sap instead of blood."

Wendy nodded, but contrived to look as if she hadn't really understood the answer.

"I'll set the encyclopedia up on the system," Father said. "You can read all about it while I'm talking to the house-doctor."

"She doesn't want to spend the morning reading what

the encyclopedia has to say about phloem," Mother said, peevishly. "She needs to get out into the fresh air." That wasn't mere ritual, like asking whether she had slept well, but it wasn't pretense either. When Mother started talking about Wendy's supposed wants and needs she was usually talking about her own wants and supposed needs. Wendy had come to realize that talking that way was Mother's preferred method of criticizing Father; she was paying him back for disagreeing about the water table.

Wendy was fully conscious of the irony of the fact that she really did want to study the encyclopedia. There was so much to learn and so little time. Maybe she didn't *need* to do it, given that it was unlikely to make any difference in the long run, but she wanted to understand as much as she could before all the pretense had to end and the nightmare of uncertainty had to begin.

"It's okay, Mummy," she said. "Honest." She smiled at them both, attempting to bring off the delicate trick of pleasing Father by taking his side while simultaneously pleasing Mother by pretending to be as heroically long-suffering as Mother liked to consider herself.

They both smiled back. All was well, for now. Even though they listened to the news every night, they didn't seem to have the least suspicion that it could all be happening in their own home, to their own daughter.

It only took a few minutes for Wendy to work out a plausible path of icon selection which got her away from translocation in plants and deep into the heart of child physiology. Father had set that up for her by comparing phloem to her own circulatory system. There was a certain danger in getting into recent reportage regarding childhood diseases, but she figured that she could explain it well enough if anyone took the trouble to consult the log to see what she'd been doing. She didn't think anyone was likely to, but she simply couldn't help being anxious about the possibility—there were, it seemed, a lot of things one simply couldn't help being anxious about, once it was possible to be anxious at all.

"I wondered if I could get sick like the house's roots," she would say, if asked. "I wanted to know whether my blood could get clogged up in dry weather." She figured that she would be okay as long as she pretended not to have understood what she'd read, and conscientiously avoided any mention of the word *progeria*. She already knew that progeria was what she'd got, and the last thing she wanted was to be taken to a child-engineer who'd be able to confirm the fact.

She called up a lot of innocuous stuff about blood, and spent the bulk of her time pretending to study elementary material of no real significance. Every time she got hold of a document she really wanted to look at she was careful to move on quickly, so it would seem as if she hadn't even bothered to look at it if anyone did consult the log to see what she'd been doing. She didn't dare call up any extensive current affairs information on the progress of the plague or the fierce medical and political arguments concerning the treatment of its victims.

It must be wonderful to be a parent, she thought, *and not have to worry about being found out—or about anything at all, really.*

At first, Wendy had thought that Mother and Father really did have worries, because they talked as if they did, but in the last few weeks she had begun to see through the sham. In a way, they *thought* that they did have worries, but it was all just a matter of habit, a kind of innate restlessness left over from the olden days. Adults must have had authentic anxieties at one time, back in the days when everybody could expect to die young and a lot of people never even reached seventy, and she presumed that they hadn't quite got used to the fact that they'd changed the world and changed themselves. They just hadn't managed to lose the habit. They probably would, in the fullness of time. Would they still need children then, she wondered, or would they learn to do without? Were children just another habit, another manifestation of innate restlessness? Had the great plague come just in time to seal off the redundant umbilical cord which connected mankind to its evolutionary past?

We're just betwixts and betweens, Wendy thought, as she rapidly scanned a second-hand summary of a paper in the latest issue of *Nature* which dealt with the pathology of progeria. *There'll soon be no place for us, whether we grow older or not. They'll get rid of us all.*

The article which contained the summary claimed that the development of an immunoserum was just a matter of time, although it wasn't yet clear whether anything much might be done to reverse the aging process in children who'd already come down with it. She didn't dare access the paper itself, or even an abstract—that would have been a dead giveaway, like leaving a bloody thumbprint at the scene of a murder.

Wendy wished that she had a clearer idea of whether the latest news was good or bad, or whether the long-term prospects had any possible relevance to her now that she had started to show physical symptoms as well as mental ones. She didn't know what would happen to her once Mother and Father found out and notified the authorities; there was no clear pattern in the stories she glimpsed in the general newsbroadcasts, but whether this meant that there was as yet no coherent social policy for dealing with the rapidly escalating problem she wasn't sure.

For the thousandth time she wondered whether she ought simply to tell her parents what was happening, and for the thousandth time, she felt the terror growing within her at the thought that everything she had might be placed in jeopardy, that she might be sent back to the factory or handed over to the researchers or simply cut adrift to look after herself. There was no way of knowing, after all, what really lay behind the rituals which her parents used in dealing with her, no way of knowing what would happen when their thirteen-year-old daughter was no longer thirteen.

Not yet, her fear said. *Not yet. Hang on. Lie low . . . because once you can't hide, you'll have to run and run and run and there'll be nowhere to go. Nowhere at all.*

She left the workstation and went to watch the house-doctor messing about in the cellar. Father didn't seem very glad to see her, perhaps because he was trying to talk the house-doctor round to his way of thinking and didn't like the way the house-doctor immediately started talking to her instead of him, so she went away again, and played with her toys for a while. She still enjoyed playing with her toys—which was perhaps as well, all things considered.

"We can go out for a while now," Father said, when the house-doctor had finally gone. "Would you like to play ball on the back lawn?"

"Yes please," she said.

Father liked playing ball, and Wendy didn't mind. It was better than the sedentary pursuits which Mother preferred. Father had more energy to spare than Mother, probably because Mother had a job that was more taxing physically. Father only played with software; his clever fingers did all his work. Mother actually had to get her hands inside her remote-gloves and her feet inside her big red boots and get things moving. "Being a ghost in a machine," she would often complain, when she thought Wendy couldn't hear, "can be bloody hard work." She never swore in front of Wendy, of course.

Out on the back lawn, Wendy and Father threw the ball back and forth for half an hour, making the catches more difficult as time went by, so that they could leap about and dive on the bone-dry carpet-grass and get thoroughly dusty.

To begin with, Wendy was distracted by the ceaseless stream of her insistent thoughts, but as she got more involved in the game she was able to let herself go a little. She couldn't quite get back to being thirteen, but she could get to a state of mind which wasn't quite so fearful. By the time her heart was pounding and she'd grazed both her knees and one of her elbows she was enjoying herself thoroughly, all the more so because Father was evidently having a good time. He was in a good mood anyhow, because the house-doctor had obligingly confirmed everything he'd said about the normality of the water-table, and had then backed down gracefully when he saw that he couldn't persuade Father that the house needed a whole new root-system.

"Those somatic transformations don't always take," the house-doctor had said, darkly but half-heartedly, as he left. "You might have trouble again, three months down the line."

"I'll take the chance," Father had replied, breezily. "Thanks for your time."

Given that the doctor was charging for his time, Wendy had thought, it should have been the doctor thanking Father, but she hadn't said anything. She already understood that kind of thing well enough not to have to ask questions about it. She had other matters she wanted to raise once Father collapsed on the baked earth, felled by healthy exhaustion, and demanded that they take a rest.

"I'm not as young as you are," he told her, jokingly. "When you get past a hundred and fifty you just can't take it the way you used to." He had no idea how it affected her to hear him say *you* in that careless fashion, when he really meant *we*: a *we* which didn't include her and never would.

"I'm bleeding," she said, pointing to a slight scratch on her elbow.

"Oh dear," he said. "Does it hurt?"

"Not much," she said, truthfully. "If too much leaks out, will I need injections, like the house's roots?"

"It won't come to that," he assured her, lifting up her

arm so that he could put on a show of inspecting the wound. "It's just a drop. I'll kiss it better." He put his lips to the wound for a few seconds, then said: "It'll be as good as new in the morning."

"Good," she said. "I expect it'd be very expensive to have to get a whole new girl."

He looked at her a little strangely, but it seemed to Wendy that he was in such a light mood that he was in no danger of taking it too seriously.

"Fearfully expensive," he agreed, cheerfully, as he lifted her up in his arms and carried her back to the house. "We'll just have to take very good care of you, won't we?"

"Or do a somatic whatever," she said, as innocently as she possibly could. "Is that what you'd have to do if you wanted a boy for a while?"

He laughed, and there appeared to be no more than the merest trace of unease in his laugh. "We love you just the way you are, Lovely," he assured her. "We wouldn't want you to be any other way."

She knew that it was true. That was the problem.

She had ham and cheese manna for lunch, with real greens home-grown in the warm cellar-annex under soft red lights. She would have eaten heartily had she not been so desperately anxious about her weight, but as things were she felt it better to peck and pretend, and she surreptitiously discarded the food she hadn't consumed as soon as Father's back was turned.

After lunch, judging it to be safe enough, she picked up the thread of the conversation again. "Why did you want a girl and not a boy?" she asked. "The Johnsons wanted a boy." The Johnsons had a ten-year-old named Peter. He was the only other child Wendy saw regularly, and he had not as yet exhibited the slightest sign of disease to her eager eye.

"We didn't want *a girl*," Father told her, tolerantly. "We wanted you."

"Why?" she asked, trying to look as if she were just fishing for compliments, but hoping to trigger something a trifle more revealing. This, after all, was *the* great mystery. Why her? Why anyone? Why did adults think they needed children?

"Because you're beautiful," Father said. "And because you're Wendy. Some people are Peter people, so they have Peters. Some people are Wendy people, so they have Wendys. Your Mummy and I are definitely Wendy people—probably the Wendiest people in the world. It's a matter of taste."

It was all baby-talk, all gobbledygook, but she felt that she had to keep trying. Some day, surely, one of them would let a little truth show through their empty explanations.

"But you have different kinds of manna for breakfast, lunch and dinner," Wendy said, "and sometimes you go right off one kind for weeks on end. Maybe some day you'll go off me, and want a different one."

"No we won't, darling," he answered, gently. "There are matters of taste and matters of taste. Manna is fuel for the body. Variety of taste just helps to make the routine of eating that little bit more interesting. Relationships are something else. It's a different kind of need. We love you, Beauty, more than anything else in the world. Nothing could ever replace you."

She thought about asking about what would happen if Father and Mother ever got divorced, but decided that it would be safer to leave the matter alone for now. Even though time was pressing, she had to be careful.

They watched TV for a while before Mother came home. Father had a particular fondness for archive film of extinct animals—not the ones which the engineers had re-created but

smaller and odder ones: weirdly shaped sea-dwelling creatures. He could never have seen such creatures even if they
had still existed when he was young, not even in an aquarium;
they had only ever been known to people as things on film.
Even so, the whole tone of the tapes which documented their
one-time existence was nostalgic, and Father seemed genuinely affected by a sense of personal loss at the thought of the
sterilization of the seas during the last ecocatastrophe but one.

"Isn't it beautiful?" he said, of an excessively tentacled
sea anemone which sheltered three vivid clown-fish while
ungainly shrimps passed by. "Isn't it just *extraordinary?*"

"Yes," she said, dutifully, trying to inject an appropriate
reverence into her tone. "It's lovely." The music on the soundtrack was plaintive; it was being played on some fluty wind-
instrument, possibly by a human player. Wendy had never
heard music like it except on TV sound-tracks; it was as if the
sound were the breath of the long-lost world of nature, teem-
ing with undesigned life.

"Next summer," Father said, "I want us to go out in one
of those glass-bottomed boats that take sight-seers out to the
new barrier reef. It's not the same as the original one, of
course, and they're deliberately setting out to create something modern, something new, but they're stocking it with
some truly weird and wonderful creatures."

"Mother wants to go up the Nile," Wendy said. "She
wants to see the sphinx, and the tombs."

"We'll do that the year after," Father said. "They're just
ruins. They can wait. Living things . . ." He stopped. "Look at
those!" he said, pointing at the screen. She looked at a host of
jellyfish swimming close to the silvery surface, their bodies
pulsing like great translucent hearts.

It doesn't matter, Wendy thought. *I won't be there. I
won't see the new barrier reef or the sphinx and the tombs.
Even if they find a cure, and even if you both want me cured,
I won't be there. Not the real me. The real me will have died,
one way or another, and there'll be nothing left except a girl*

who'll be thirteen forever, and a randomizing factor which will make it seem that she has a lively mind.

Father put his arm around her shoulder, and hugged her fondly.

Father must really love her very dearly, she thought. After all, he had loved her for thirty years, and might love her for thirty years more, if only she could stay the way she was . . . if only she could be returned to what she had been before. . . .

The evening TV schedules advertised a documentary on progeria, scheduled for late at night, long after the nation's children had been put to bed. Wendy wondered if her parents would watch it, and whether she could sneak downstairs to listen to the soundtrack through the closed door. In a way, she hoped that they wouldn't watch it. It might put ideas into their heads. It was better that they thought of the plague as a distant problem: something that could only affect other people; something with which they didn't need to concern themselves.

She stayed awake, just in case, and when the luminous dial of her bedside clock told her it was time she silently got up, and crept down the stairs until she could hear what was going on in the living room. It was risky, because the randomizing factor wasn't really supposed to stretch to things like that, but she'd done it before without being found out.

It didn't take long to ascertain that the TV wasn't even on, and that the only sound to be heard was her parents' voices. She actually turned around to go back to bed before she suddenly realized what they were talking about.

"Are you *sure* she isn't affected mentally?" Mother was saying.

"Absolutely certain," Father replied. "I watched her all afternoon, and she's perfectly normal."

"Perhaps she hasn't got it at all," Mother said, hopefully.

"Maybe not the worst kind," Father said, in a voice that was curiously firm. "They're not sure that even the worst cases are manifesting authentic self-consciousness, and there's a strong contingent which argues that the vast majority of cases are relatively minor dislocations of programming. But there's no doubt about the physical symptoms. I picked her up to carry her indoors and she's a stone heavier. She's got hair growing in her armpits and she's got tangible tits. We'll have to be careful how we dress her when we take her to public places."

"Can we do anything about her food—reduce the calorific value of her manna or something?"

"Sure—but that'd be hard evidence if anyone audited the house records. Not that anyone's likely to, now that the doctor's been and gone, but you never know. I read an article which cites a paper in the latest *Nature* to demonstrate that a cure is just around the corner. If we can just hang on until then . . . she's a big girl anyhow, and she might not put on more than an inch or two. As long as she doesn't start behaving oddly, we might be able to keep it secret."

"If they do find out," said Mother, ominously, "there'll be hell to pay."

"I don't think so," Father assured her. "I've heard that the authorities are quite sympathetic in private, although they have to put on a sterner face for publicity purposes."

"I'm not talking about the bloody bureaucrats," Mother retorted, "I'm talking about the estate. If the neighbors find out we're sheltering a center of infection . . . well, how would you feel if the Johnsons' Peter turned out to have the disease and hadn't warned us about the danger to Wendy?"

"They're not certain how it spreads," said Father, defensively, "They don't know what kind of vector's involved—until they find out there's no reason to think that Wendy's endangering Peter just by living next door. It's not as if they spend much time together. We can't lock her up—that'd be suspicious in itself. We have to pretend that things are absolutely normal, at least until we know how this thing is going to turn out. I'm not prepared to run the risk of their taking her away—not if there's the slightest chance of avoiding it. I don't care what they say on the newstapes—this thing is getting out of control and I really don't know how it's going to turn out. I'm not letting Wendy go anywhere, unless I'm absolutely forced. She may be getting heavier and hairier, but *inside* she's still Wendy, and *I'm not letting them take her away.*"

Wendy heard Father's voice getting louder as he came toward the door, and she scuttled back up the stairs as fast as she could go. Numb with shock, she climbed back into bed. Father's words echoed inside her head: "I watched her all afternoon and she's perfectly normal . . . *inside* she's still Wendy. . . ."

They were putting on an act too, and she hadn't known. She hadn't been able to tell. She'd been watching them, and they'd seemed perfectly normal . . . but *inside,* where it counted . . .

It was a long time before she fell asleep, and when she finally did, she dreamed of shadow-men and shadow-music, which drew the very soul from her even as she fled through the infinite forest of green and gold.

The men from the Ministry of Health arrived next morning, while Wendy was finishing her honey and almond manna. She saw Father go pale as the man in the gray suit held up his identification card to the door camera. She watched Father's lip trembling as he thought about telling the man in the gray suit that he couldn't come in, and then realized that it wouldn't do any good. As Father got up to go to the door he exchanged a bitter glance with Mother, and murmured: "That bastard house-doctor."

Mother came to stand behind Wendy, and put both of

her hands on Wendy's shoulders. "It's all right, darling," she said. Which meant, all too clearly, that things were badly wrong.

Father and the man in the gray suit were already arguing as they came through the door. There was another man behind them, dressed in less formal clothing. He was carrying a heavy black bag, like a rigid suitcase.

"I'm sorry," the man in the gray suit was saying. "I understand your feelings, but this is an epidemic—a national emergency. We have to check out all reports, and we have to move swiftly if we're to have any chance of containing the problem."

"If there'd been any cause for alarm," Father told him, hotly, "I'd have called you myself." But the man in the gray suit ignored him; from the moment he had entered the room his eyes had been fixed on Wendy. He was smiling. Even though Wendy had never seen him before and didn't know the first thing about him, she knew that the smile was dangerous.

"Hello, Wendy," said the man in the gray suit, smoothly. "My name's Tom Cartwright. I'm from the Ministry of Health. This is Jimmy Li. I'm afraid we have to carry out some tests."

Wendy stared back at him as blankly as she could. In a situation like this, she figured, it was best to play dumb, at least to begin with.

"You can't do this," Mother said, gripping Wendy's shoulders just a little too hard. "You can't take her away."

"We can complete our initial investigation here and now," Cartwright answered, blandly. "Jimmy can plug into your kitchen systems, and I can do my part right here at the table. It'll be over in less than half an hour, and if all's well we'll be gone in no time." The way he said it implied that he didn't really expect to be gone in no time.

Mother and Father blustered a little more, but it was only a gesture. They knew how futile it all was. While Mr. Li opened up his bag of tricks to reveal an awesome profusion of gadgets forged in metal and polished glass Father came to stand beside Wendy, and like Mother he reached out to touch her.

They both assured her that the needle Mr. Li was preparing wouldn't hurt when he put it into her arm, and when it did hurt—bringing tears to her eyes in spite of her efforts to blink them away—they told her the pain would go away in a minute. It didn't, of course. Then they told her not to worry about the questions Mr. Cartwright was going to ask her, although it was as plain as the noses on their faces that they were terrified by the possibility that she would give the wrong answers.

In the end, though, Wendy's parents had to step back a little, and let her face up to the man from the Ministry on her own.

I mustn't play too dumb, Wendy thought. *That would be just as much of a giveaway as being too clever. I have to try to make my mind blank, let the answers come straight out without thinking at all. It ought to be easy. After all, I've been thirteen for thirty years, and unthirteen for a matter of months . . . it should be easy.*

She knew that she was lying to herself. She knew well enough that she had crossed a boundary that couldn't be re-crossed just by stepping backward.

"How old are you, Wendy?" Cartwright asked, when Jimmy Li had vanished into the kitchen to play with her blood.

"Thirteen," she said, trying to return his practiced smile without too much evident anxiety.

"Do you know *what* you are, Wendy?"

"I'm a girl," she answered, knowing that it wouldn't wash.

"Do you know what the difference between children and adults is, Wendy? Apart from the fact that they're smaller."

There was no point in denying it. At thirteen, a certain

amount of self-knowledge was included in the package, and even thirteen-year-olds who never looked at an encyclopedia learned quite a lot about the world and its ways in the course of thirty years.

"Yes," she said, knowing full well that she wasn't going to be allowed to get away with minimal replies.

"Tell me what you know about the difference," he said.

"It's not such a big difference," she said, warily. "Children are made out of the same things adults are made of—but they're made so they stop growing at a certain age, and never get any older. Thirteen is the oldest—some stop at eight."

"Why are children made that way, Wendy?" Step by inexorable step he was leading her toward the deep water, and she didn't know how to swim. She knew that she wasn't clever enough—yet—to conceal her cleverness.

"Population control," she said.

"Can you give me a more detailed explanation, Wendy?"

"In the olden days," she said, "there were catastrophes. Lots of people died, because there were so many of them. They discovered how not to grow old, so that they could live for hundreds of years if they didn't get killed in bad accidents. They had to stop having so many children, or they wouldn't be able to feed everyone when the children kept growing up, but they didn't want to have a world with no children in it. Lots of people still wanted children, and couldn't stop wanting them— and in the end, after more catastrophes, those people who really wanted children a lot were able to have them . . . only the children weren't allowed to grow up and have more children of their own. There were lots of arguments about it, but in the end things calmed down."

"There's another difference between children and adults, isn't there?" said Cartwright, smoothly.

"Yes," Wendy said, knowing that she was supposed to have that information in her memory and that she couldn't refuse to voice it. "Children can't think very much. They have *limited self-consciousness*." She tried hard to say it as though it were a mere formula, devoid of any real meaning so far as she was concerned.

"Do you know why children are made with limited self-consciousness?"

"No." She was sure that *no* was the right answer to that one, although she'd recently begun to make guesses. It was so they wouldn't know what was happening if they were ever sent back, and so that they didn't *change* too much as they learned things, becoming un-childlike in spite of their appearance.

"Do you know what the word *progeria* means, Wendy?"

"Yes," she said. Children watched the news. Thirteen-year-olds were supposed to be able to hold intelligent conversations with their parents. "It's when children get older even though they shouldn't. It's a disease that children get. It's happening a lot."

"Is it happening to you, Wendy? Have *you* got progeria?"

For a second or two she hesitated between *no* and *I don't know,* and then realized how bad the hesitation must look. She kept her face straight as she finally said: "I don't think so."

"What would you think if you found out you *had* got progeria, Wendy?" Cartwright asked, smug in the knowledge that she must be way out of her depth by now, whatever the truth of the matter might be.

"You can't ask her that!" Father said. "She's thirteen! Are you trying to scare her half to death? Children can be scared, you know. They're not *robots.*"

"No," said Cartwright, without taking his eyes off Wendy's face. "They're not. Answer the question, Wendy."

"I wouldn't like it," Wendy said, in a low voice. "I don't want anything to happen to me. I want to be with Mummy and Daddy. I don't want anything to happen."

While she was speaking, Jimmy Li had come back into the room. He didn't say a word and his nod was almost imperceptible, but Tom Cartwright wasn't really in any doubt.

"I'm afraid it has, Wendy," he said, softly. "It *has* happened, as you know very well."

"*No she doesn't!*" said Mother, in a voice that was halfway to a scream. "She doesn't know any such thing!"

"It's a very mild case," Father said. "We've been watching her like hawks. It's purely physical. Her behavior hasn't altered at all. She isn't showing any mental symptoms whatsoever."

"You can't take her away," Mother said, keeping her shrillness under a tight rein. "We'll keep her in quarantine. We'll join one of the drug-trials. You can monitor her *but you can't take her away.* She doesn't understand what's happening. She's just a little girl. It's only slight, only her body."

Tom Cartwright let the storm blow out. He was still looking at Wendy, and his eyes seemed kind, full of concern. He let a moment's silence endure before he spoke to her again.

"Tell them, Wendy," he said, softly. "Explain to them that it isn't slight at all."

She looked up at Mother, and then at Father, knowing how much it would hurt them to be told. "I'm still Wendy," she said, faintly. "I'm still your little girl. I . . ."

She wanted to say *I always will be,* but she couldn't. She had always been a good girl, and some lies were simply too difficult to voice.

I wish I was a randomizing factor, she thought, fiercely wishing that could be true, that it might be true. *I wish I was . . .*

Absurdly, she found herself wondering whether it would have been more grammatical to have thought *I wish I were . . .*

It was so absurd that she began to laugh, and then she began to cry, helplessly. It was almost as if the flood of tears could wash away the burden of thought—almost, but not quite.

▲   ▲   ▲

Mother took her back into her bedroom, and sat with her, holding her hand. By the time the shuddering sobs released her—long after she had run out of tears—Wendy felt a new sense of grievance. Mother kept looking at the door, wishing that she could be out there, adding her voice to the argument, because she didn't really trust Father to get it right. The sense of duty which kept her pinned to Wendy's side was a burden, a burning frustration. Wendy didn't like that. Oddly enough, though, she didn't feel any particular resentment at being put out of the way while Father and the Ministry of Health haggled over her future. She understood well enough that she had no voice in the matter, no matter how unlimited her self-consciousness had now become, no matter what progressive leaps and bounds she had accomplished as the existential fetters had shattered and fallen away.

She was still a little girl, for the moment.

She was still Wendy, for the moment.

When she could speak, she said to Mother: "Can we have some music?"

Mother looked suitably surprised. "What kind of music?" she countered.

"Anything," Wendy said. The music she was hearing in her head was soft and fluty music, which she heard as if from a vast distance, and which somehow seemed to be the oldest music in the world, but she didn't particularly want it duplicated and brought into the room. She just wanted something to fill the cracks of silence which broke up the muffled sound of arguing.

Mother called up something much more liquid, much more upbeat, much more modern. Wendy could see that Mother wanted to speak to her, wanted to deluge her with reassurances, but couldn't bear to make any promises she wouldn't be able to keep. In the end, Mother contented herself with hugging Wendy to her bosom, as fiercely and as tenderly as she could.

When the door opened it flew back with a bang. Father came in first.

"It's all right," he said, quickly. "They're not going to take her away. They'll quarantine the house instead."

Wendy felt the tension in Mother's arms. Father could work entirely from home much more easily than Mother, but there was no way Mother was going to start protesting on those grounds. While quarantine wasn't exactly *all right* it was better than she could have expected.

"It's not generosity, I'm afraid," said Tom Cartwright. "It's necessity. The epidemic is spreading too quickly. We don't have the facilities to take tens of thousands of children into state care. Even the quarantine will probably be a short-term measure—to be perfectly frank, it's a panic measure. The simple truth is that the disease can't be contained no matter what we do."

"How could you let this happen?" Mother said, in a low tone bristling with hostility. "How could you let it get this far out of control? With all modern technology at your disposal you surely should be able to put the brake on a simple virus."

"It's not so simple," Cartwright said, apologetically. "If it really had been a freak of nature—some stray strand of DNA which found a new ecological niche—we'd probably have been able to contain it easily. We don't believe that any more."

"It was *designed*," Father said, with the airy confidence of the well-informed—though even Wendy knew that this particular item of wisdom must have been news to him five minutes ago. "Somebody cooked this thing up in a lab and let it loose *deliberately*. It was all planned, in the name of liberation . . . in the name of chaos, if you ask me."

Somebody did this to me! Wendy thought. *Somebody actually set out to take away the limits, to turn the randomizing factor into . . . into what, exactly?*

While Wendy's mind was boggling, Mother was saying: "Who? How? Why?"

"You know how some people are," Cartwright said, with a fatalistic shrug of his shoulders. "Can't see an apple-cart without wanting to upset it. You'd think the chance to live for a thousand years would confer a measure of maturity even on the meanest intellect, but it hasn't worked out that way. Maybe someday we'll get past all that, but in the mean-time . . ."

Maybe someday, Wendy thought, *all the things left over from the infancy of the world will go. All the crazinesses, all the disagreements, all the diehard habits.* She hadn't known that she was capable of being quite so sharp, but she felt per-versely proud of the fact that she didn't have to spell out—even to herself, in the brand new arena of her private thoughts—the fact that one of those symptoms of craziness, one of the focal points of those disagreements, and the most diehard of all those habits, was keeping children in a world where they no longer had any biological function—or, rather, keeping the *ghosts* of children, who weren't really children at all because they were *always* children.

"They call it liberation," Father was saying, "but it really is a disease, a terrible affliction. It's the destruction of *inno-cence.* It's a kind of mass murder." He was obviously pleased with his own eloquence, and with the righteousness of his wrath. He came over to the bed and plucked Wendy out of Mother's arms. "It's all right, Beauty," he said. "We're all in this together. We'll face it together. You're absolutely right. You're still our little girl. You're still Wendy. Nothing terrible is going to happen."

It was far better, in a way, than what she'd imagined—or had been too scared to imagine. There was a kind of relief in not having to pretend any more, in not having to keep the secret. That boundary had been crossed, and now there was no choice but to go forward.

Why didn't I tell them before? Wendy wondered. *Why*

didn't I just tell them, and trust them to see that everything would be all right? But even as she thought it, even as she clutched at the straw, just as Mother and Father were clutching, she realized how hollow the thought was, and how meaningless Father's reassurances were. It was all just sentiment, and habit, and pretense. Everything couldn't and wouldn't be "all right," and never would be again, unless . . .

Turning to Tom Cartwright, warily and uneasily, she said: "Will I be an adult now? Will I live for a thousand years, and have my own house, my own job, my own . . . ?"

She trailed off as she saw the expression in his eyes, realizing that she was still a little girl, and that there were a thousand questions adults couldn't and didn't want to hear, let alone try to answer.

It was late at night before Mother and Father got themselves into the right frame of mind for the kind of serious talk that the situation warranted, and by that time Wendy knew perfectly well that the honest answer to almost all the questions she wanted to ask was: "Nobody knows."

She asked the questions anyway. Mother and Father varied their answers in the hope of appearing a little wiser than they were, but it all came down to the same thing in the end. It all came down to desperate pretense.

"We have to take it as it comes," Father told her. "It's an unprecedented situation. The government has to respond to the changes on a day-by-day basis. We can't tell how it will all turn out. It's a mess, but the world has been in a mess before—in fact, it's hardly ever been out of a mess for more than a few years at a time. We'll cope as best we can. *Everybody* will cope as best they can. With luck, it might not come to violence—to war, to slaughter, to ecocatastrophe. We're entitled to hope that we really are past all that now, that we really are capable of handling things *sensibly* this time."

"Yes," Wendy said, conscientiously keeping as much of the irony out of her voice as she could. "I understand. Maybe we won't just be sent back to the factories to be scrapped . . . and maybe if they find a cure, they'll ask us whether we want to be cured before they use it." *With luck,* she added, silently, *maybe we can all be* adult *about the situation.*

They both looked at her uneasily, not sure how to react. From now on, they would no longer be able to grin and shake their heads at the wondrous inventiveness of the randomizing factor in her programming. From now on, they would actually have to try to figure out what she *meant,* and what unspoken thoughts might lie behind the calculated wit and hypocrisy of her every statement. She had every sympathy for them; she had only recently learned for herself what a difficult, frustrating and thankless task that could be.

This happened to their ancestors once, she thought. *But not as quickly. Their ancestors didn't have the kind of headstart you can get by being thirteen for thirty years. It must have been hard, to be a thinking ape among unthinkers. Hard, but . . . well, they didn't ever want to give it up, did they?*

"Whatever happens, Beauty," Father said, "we love you. Whatever happens, you're our little girl. When you're grown up, we'll still love you the way we always have. We always will."

He actually believes it, Wendy thought. *He actually believes that the world can still be the same, in spite of everything. He can't let go of the hope that even though everything's changing, it will all be the same underneath. But it won't. Even if there isn't a resource crisis—after all, grown-up children can't eat much more than un-grown-up ones—the world can never be the same. This is the time in which the adults of the world have to get used to the fact that there can't be any more families, because from now on children will have to be rare and precious and strange. This is the time when the old people will have to recognize that the day of their silly stopgap solutions to imag-*

inary problems is over. This is the time when we all have to grow up. If the old people can't do that by themselves, then the new generation will simply have to show them the way.

"I love you too," she answered, earnestly. She left it at that. There wasn't any point in adding: "I always have," or "I can mean it now," or any of the other things which would have underlined rather than assuaged the doubts they must be feeling.

"And we'll be all right," Mother said. "As long as we love one another, and as long as we face this thing together, we'll be all right."

What a wonderful thing true innocence is, Wendy thought, rejoicing in her ability to think such a thing freely, without shame or reservation. *I wonder if I'd be able to cultivate it, if I ever wanted to.*

That night, bedtime was abolished. She was allowed to stay up as late as she wanted to. When she finally did go to bed she was so exhausted that she quickly drifted off into a deep and peaceful sleep—but she didn't remain there indefinitely. Eventually, she began to dream.

In her dream Wendy was living wild in a magical wood where it never rained. She lived on sweet berries of many colors. There were other girls living wild in the dream-wood but they all avoided one another. They had lived there for a long time but now the others had come: the shadow-men with horns on their brows and shaggy legs who played strange music, which was the breath of souls.

Wendy hid from the shadow-men, but the fearful fluttering of her heart gave her away, and one of the shadow-men found her. He stared down at her with huge baleful eyes, wiping spittle from his pipes onto his fleecy rump.

"Who are you?" she asked, trying to keep the tremor of fear out of her voice.

"I'm the devil," he said.

"There's no such thing," she informed him, sourly.

He shrugged his massive shoulders. "So I'm the Great God Pan," he said. "What difference does it make? And how come you're so smart all of a sudden?"

"I'm not thirteen anymore," she told him, proudly. "I've been thirteen for thirty years, but now I'm growing up. The whole world's growing up—for the first and last time."

"Not me," said the Great God Pan. "I'm a million years old and I'll *never* grow up. Let's get on with it, shall we? I'll count to ninety-nine. You start running."

Dream-Wendy scrambled to her feet, and ran away. She ran and she ran and she ran, without any hope of escape. Behind her, the music of the reed-pipes kept getting louder and louder, and she knew that whatever happened, her world would never fall silent.

When Wendy woke up, she found that the nightmare hadn't really ended. The meaningful part of it was still going on. But things weren't as bad as all that, even though she couldn't bring herself to pretend that it was all just a dream which might go away.

She knew that she had to take life one day at a time, and look after her parents as best she could. She knew that she had to try to ease the pain of the passing of their way of life, to which they had clung a little too hard and a little too long. She knew that she had to hope, and to trust, that a cunning combination of intelligence and love would be enough to see her and the rest of the world through—at least until the next catastrophe came along.

She wasn't absolutely sure that she could do it, but she was determined to give it a bloody good try.

And whatever happens in the end, she thought, *to live will be an awfully big adventure.*

Always True to Thee, in My Fashion

NANCY KRESS

Nancy Kress is well known for her deeply complex medical SF stories, and for her biological and evolutionary extrapolations in such classics as "Beggars in Spain," *Beggars and Choosers*, and *Beggars Ride*. Her stories are rich in texture and in the details of the inner life of character, and like only a few others, such as Bruce Sterling and James Patrick Kelly, she manages often to satisfy both the readers of hard SF and the self-styled Humanists. She is in fact one of the few writers to incorporate much of the aesthetic of Modernist fiction into SF. This story, however, from *Asimov's,* is another side of Nancy Kress, the feminine juggernaut, uproarious and unstoppable—who would want to? The more you think about it, the funnier it gets, rather like vintage Connie Willis. This is first-rate satire, extending that tradition that flowered in the 1950s, that was perhaps the center of 50s SF, into the late 90s. My ideal SF convention would have both Connie Willis and Nancy Kress as co-guests of honor, always speaking at the same time and picking up on each other's lines.

Relationships for the autumn season were casual and unconstructed, following a summer where fashion had been unusually colorful and intense. Suzanne liked wearing the new feelings. They were light and cool, allowing her a lot of freedom of movement. The off-hand affection made her feel unencumbered, graceful.

Cade wasn't so sure.

"It sounds bloody boring," he said to Suzanne, holding the pills in his hand. "Love isn't supposed to be so boring. At least the summer fashions offered a few surprises."

Boxes from the couture houses spilled around their bedroom. Suzanne, of course, had done the ordering. Karl Lagerfeld, Galliano, Enkia for Christian LaCroix, and of course Suzanne's own special designer and friend, Sendil. Cade stood in the middle of an explosion of slouchy tweeds and off-white linen, wearing his underwear and his stubborn look.

"But the summer feelings were so heavy," Suzanne said. She dropped a casual kiss on the top of Cade's head. "Come on, Cadie, at least give it a try. You have the body for casual emotions, you know. They look so good on you."

This was true. Cade was lean and loose-jointed, with a small head on a long neck: a body made for easy carelessness. Backlit by their wide bedroom windows, he already looked coolly nonchalant: an Edwardian aristocrat, perhaps, or one of those marvelously blasé American riverboat gamblers who couldn't be bothered to sweat. The environment helped, of course. Suzanne always did their V-R, and for autumn she'd programmed unlined curtains, cool terra cotta tiles, oyster-white walls. All very informal and composed, nothing trying very hard. But she'd left the windows natural. That, too, was perfect: too nonchalant about the view of London to bother reprogramming its ugliness. Only Suzanne would have thought of this touch. Their friends would be so jealous.

"Come on, Cade, try the feelings on." But he only went on looking troubled, holding the pills in his long-fingered hand.

Suzanne began to feel impatient. Cade was wonderful, of course, but he could be so conservative. He really hadn't liked the summer fashions—and they had been so much fun! Suzanne knew she looked good in those kinds of dramatic, highly colored feelings. They went well with her voluptuous body and small, sharp teeth. People had noticed. She'd had two passionate adulteries, one knife-fight with Kittery, one duel fought over her, two midnight reconciliations, and one weepy parting from Cade at sunset on the edge of a sea, which had been V-R'd into wine-dark roils for the occasion. Very satisfying.

But the summer was over. Really, Cade should be more willing to vary his emotional wardrobe. Sometimes she even wondered if she might be better off with another lover . . . Mikhail, maybe, or even Jastinder . . . but no, of course not. She loved Cade. They belonged to each other forever. Cade was the bedrock of her life. If only he weren't so stubborn!

"Have you ever thought," he said, not looking at her, "that we might skip a fashion season? Just let it go by and wear something old, off alone together? Or even go naked?"

"What an idea," she said lightly.

"We could try it, Suzanne."

"We could also move out of the towers and live down there along the Thames among the starving and dirty-mattressed thugs. Equally appealing."

Wrong, wrong. Cade turned away from her. In another minute he would put the pills back in their little bottle. Suzanne decided to try playfulness. She twined her arms around his neck, and flashed her eyes at him. "You are vast,

Cade. You contain multitudes. Do you really think it's fair, mmmm, that you deny me all your multitudes, when I'm so ready to love them all?"

Reluctantly, he smiled. "'Multitudes,' is it?"

"And I *want* them all. All the Cades. I'm greedy, you know." She rubbed against him.

"Well . . ."

"Come on, Cade. For me." Another rub, and after it she danced away, laughing.

He could never resist her. He swallowed the pills, then reached out his arms. Suzanne eluded them.

"Not yet. After they take effect."

"Suzanne . . ."

"Tomorrow." Casually, she blew him an affectionate kiss and sauntered toward the door, leaving him gazing after her. Cade wanting her, and she off-hand and insouciant.

It was going to be a wonderful autumn.

The next day was unbelievably exciting, more arousing even than when she'd walked in on Cade and Kittery in the summer bedroom and they'd had the shouting and pleading and knife fight. This was arousing in a different way. Suzanne had strolled into the apartment in mid-morning, half an hour late. "There you are, then," she'd said casually to Cade.

He looked up from his reader, his long-limbed body sprawled across the chair. "Oh, hallo."

"How are you?"

He shrugged, then made a negligent gesture with one graceful slim-fingered hand.

Suzanne draped herself across his lap, gazing abstractedly out the window. Today London looked even uglier than usual: cold, gray, dirty.

"Do you mind awfully?" Cade said. "I'm in the middle of this article."

"And so absorbed that you don't notice me, mmmmm?" Suzanne moved against him.

Cade smiled, pecked her cheek, and gave her a careless nudge. "Off you go, then." He returned to his reader. Suzanne stood and stretched.

The rush of blood to her nipples and thighs startled her. He really was indifferent to her! She would have to actually work at getting him interested, winning him from his casual reading . . . God, it was exciting!

She would succeed, of course. She always did. But why hadn't she ever realized before how much more interesting the victory was when she'd have to struggle for it? She hadn't been this aroused in years.

"Cade . . ." She leaned over him and nibbled on his ear. "Sweet Cade . . ."

He tilted his head to look up at her, eyebrows raised. The drugs had done something to his eyes, or to her perception of them; they looked lighter, more opaque. Suzanne laughed softly. "Come on, it will be so good. . . ."

"Oh, all right. If you insist."

He rose from his chair, turned to pick up the dropped reader. He nudged an antique vase a quarter inch to the right on one of Sendil's occasional tables. He rubbed his left elbow, gazing out the window. Suzanne took his hand, and they ambled toward the bedroom.

And it was wonderful. The most interesting show in years. Really, the fashion designers were geniuses.

"Cade, Flavia and Mikhail have invited us to a water fete on Saturday. Do you want to go?"

He looked up from his screen, where he was checking his portfolio on the New York Stock Exchange. He didn't even look annoyed that she'd interrupted. "Do you want to go?"

"I asked *you*."

"I don't care."

Suzanne bit her lip. "Well, what shall I tell Flavia?"

"Whatever you like, love."

"Well, then . . . I thought I might fly to Paris this weekend." She paused. "To see Guillaume."

He didn't even twitch. "Whatever you like, love."

"Cade—do you care if I visit Guillaume? For an entire weekend?" In the summer, a threat to visit Guillaume, a former lover who still adored Suzanne, had produced drama that went on for sixteen straight hours.

"Oh, Suzanne, don't be tiresome. Of course you can visit Guillaume if you want." Cade blew her a casual kiss.

She charged across the room, seized his hand, and dragged him away from the terminal. His eyebrows rose slightly.

But afterward, as Cade lay deeply asleep, Suzanne wondered. Maybe he'd actually been right, after all, about the current fashions. Not that it hadn't been exciting to work at arousing him, but . . . she wasn't supposed to be working. She was supposed to feel just as detached and casual as Cade. That was the bloody trouble with fashion—no matter what the designers said, one size never did fit all. The individual drug responses were too different. Well, no matter. Tomorrow she'd just increase her dosage. Until she, and not Cade, was the more casual. The sought after, rather than the seeker.

The way it was supposed to be.

"Cade . . . Cade?"

"Oh, Suzanne. Do come in."

He sat up in bed, unselfconscious, unruffled. Beside him, Flavia emerged languidly from the off-white sheets. She said, "Suzanne, darling. I *am* sorry. We didn't expect you so soon. Shall I leave?"

Suzanne crossed the room to the dresser. This was more like it. A little movement, for a change—a little *action*. Really, casual was all very well, but how many evenings could one spend in off-hand conversation? Almost she was grateful to Flavia. Not that she would show it, of course. But Flavia was giving her the perfect excuse to put on an entirely different demeanor. She had rather missed changing for dinner.

From the dresser top she picked up a string of pearls and toyed with them, a careful appearance of anger suppressed under a facade of sophisticated control. "Cade . . . how could you?"

Flavia said, "Perhaps I *had* better leave, hadn't I? See you later, darlings." She activated a V-R dress from her necklace—easy unconstricting lines in a subtle taupe, Suzanne noted—and left.

Cade said, "Suzanne—"

"I trusted you, Cade!"

"Oh, rot," he said. "You're making a fuss over nothing."

"Nothing! You call—"

"Really, Suzanne. Flavia hardly matters."

"'Hardly'? And just what does that mean?"

"Oh, Suzanne, you know what it means. Really, don't make yourself ridiculous over trifles." And Cade yawned, stretched, and went to sleep.

To sleep.

Suzanne thought of waking him. She thought of pounding on him with her small fists, of dumping him on the floor, of packing her bags and leaving a note. But, really, all those things *would* look rather ridiculous. People would hear about it, snicker . . . and even if they didn't, even if Cade kept her bad taste to himself, there was still the fact that the two of them would know it had happened. Suzanne had lost her cool poise. She had been as embarrassing as Kittery, the season Kittery showed up at a geisha party dressed in the crude emotions of a political revolutionary. Even if Cade were to keep this incident private, Suzanne winced at the idea of his thinking her as gauche as Kittery, as capable of such a major fashion faux pas. No, no. Better to let it pass.

Cade snored softly, Suzanne lay beside him, fists clenched, waiting for winter.

Finally, the new fashions were out! Suzanne went to Paris for the preseason shows, sitting in the first row at each important couture house, exultant. She saw, and was seen, and was happy.

The designers had outdone themselves, especially Suwela for Karl Lagerfield. The feeling was tremulous, ingenue, all the tentative sharp sweetness of virgin love. Pink, pale blue, white—lots of white—with indrawn gasps and wide-eyed sexual exploration. Ruffles and flowers and heart flutterings at a lingering look. Gianfranco Ferrè showed a marvelous silk, flowing biocloth abloom with living forget-me-nots, accessorized with innocence barely daring to touch the male model's hand. At Galliano, the jackets were matched with flounced bonnets and a blushing fear that a too-passionate kiss would lead . . . where? The models' knees trembled with nervous anticipation. And the ever-faithful Sendil showed an empire-waist ballgown in muslin—muslin!—that, he whispered to Suzanne, had been inspired solely by her.

Suzanne wanted everything. She spent more money than ever before at a preview. She could hardly wait for the official opening of the season. Càde and she, once more thirteen years old, with love new and sparkling and fraught with sweet tension. . . . While she waited for opening day she had her hair grown long, her hips slimmed, and her eyes widened and colored, to huge blue orbs.

Maybe they could give a party. Everyone tremulous with anticipation and virgin hopes . . . wasn't there something called "spin the bottle"? She could ask the computer.

It was going to be a wonderful winter.

▲   ▲   ▲

"No," Cade said.

"No?"

"Oh, don't look so crushed, love. Well, maybe, then. I mean, what does it matter, really?"

"What does it *matter*?" Suzanne cried. "Cade, it's the start of the season!"

He eyed her with amusement. But under the amusement was something else, the now-familiar feeling that he found her faintly ridiculous, casually distasteful. God, she couldn't wait to get him out of this wretched understated nonchalance.

Suzanne made an effort to speak lightly. "Well, if it doesn't matter, then there's no reason not to go for a bit of a change, is there?"

He flicked at a speck of dust on his sleeve. "I suppose not. But, then, love, no reason to go for change either, is there? This suits us well enough, don't you think?"

Suzanne tried not to bite her lip clear through. It was too close to opening day for tissue repair. "Well, perhaps, but one wants some variety, all the same. . . ."

He shrugged. "I don't, actually."

She cried, "But, Cade—!"

"Oh, Suzanne, don't get so worked up, it's quite tiresome. Can't we discuss it later?"

"But—"

"I have lunch with Jastinder. Or Kittery. Or somebody. Care to come? No? Well, suit yourself, love."

He waved to her and sauntered out.

She couldn't budge him. He didn't resist her; he just wasn't interested. Careless. Indifferent.

Opening day came. Suzanne stood in the bedroom, biting

her bottom lip. What to do? Everything was ready. She'd programmed the room for pale pink walls with white wood molding, filmy curtains fluttering in the breeze, a view of gardens filled with lavender and June roses and wisteria and anything else the computer said was old-fashioned. The scent simulator was running overtime. Around Suzanne were the half-unpacked boxes of flouncy silks and sweet girlish slip-dresses and little kid slippers. Plus, of course, the white jackets and copper-toed boots for Cade. Who had glanced at the entire thing with amused negligence, and then gone out somewhere for a stroll.

"But you can't!" Suzanne had cried. "It's opening day! And you're still dressed in . . . *that.*"

"Oh, love, what does it matter?" Cade had said. "I'm comfortable. And isn't all this stuff just a bit . . . twee? Isn't it, now?"

"But Cade—"

"I rather like what I'm used to."

"You're not used to it!" Suzanne had cried in anguish. "You can't be! You've only had it for a season!"

"Really? I guess so. Seems longer," Cade said. "See you later, love. Or not."

Now Suzanne scowled at the pills in her hand. There was a real problem here. If she took them, she would be garbed in the gentle sweet tremulousness of youth. Gentle, sweet, tremulous—and ineffective. That was the whole point. Ingenues were acted upon, not actors. But without the whole force of her will, could she persuade Cade to stop being such an ass?

On the other hand, if she didn't take the pills, she would be dressed wrong for the occasion. She pictured showing up at the Donnison lunch in the Alliani Towers, at the afternoon reception in the Artificial Islands, at Kittery's party tonight, dressed badly, shabbily, in last season's worn-out feelings . . . no, *no.* She couldn't. She had a reputation to maintain. And everyone would think that she couldn't afford new feelings, that she had lost all her money in data-atoll speculation or some other ghastly nouveau thing . . . damn Cade!

He came back from his stroll a few hours later, whistling carelessly. The vid was already crammed with "Where are you?" messages from their friends at the Donnison lunch. Breathless, ingenue messages, from people having a wonderful youthful time. And there was Cade, cool and off-hand in those detestable boring tweeds, daring to *whistle*. . . .

"Where have you *been*?" Suzanne said. "Don't you know how late we are? Come on, get dressed!"

"Don't whine, Suzanne, it's terribly unattractive."

"I never whine!" she cried, stung.

"Well, then, don't do whatever you're doing. Come lie down beside me instead."

It was the most assertive thing he'd said in months. Encouraged, Suzanne lay with him on the bed, trying to control her panic. Maybe if she were sweet enough to him . . .

"You haven't dressed yet, either, have you, love?" Cade said. He was smiling. "That isn't the tentative embrace of an ingenue."

"Would you like that?" Suzanne said hopefully. "I can just change. . . ."

"Actually, no. I've been thinking, Suzanne. I don't want to get all tricked out as some sort of ersatz boy-child, and you don't want to go on wearing these casual emotions. So what about what I suggested at the end of last summer? Let's just go naked for a while. See what it's like."

"No!" Suzanne shrieked.

She hadn't known she was going to do it. She never shrieked like that—not she, Suzanne! Except, of course, when fashion decreed it, and that didn't really count. . . . What was she thinking? Of course it counted, it was the only thing that kept them all safe. To go *naked* in front of each other! Good God, what was Cade *thinking*? Civilized people didn't parade around naked, everything personal on display for any passing observer to pick over and chortle at, nude and helplessly exposed in their deepest feelings!

Or lack of them.

She struggled to sound casual. And she succeeded—or last season's pills did. "Cade . . . I don't want to go naked. Really, I don't think you're being very fair. We had it your way for a season. Now it should be my turn."

A long silence. For a moment Suzanne thought he'd actually fallen asleep. If he had *dared* . . .

"Suzanne," he said finally, "it's my detached impression that you always have it your way."

It hurt so much that Suzanne's legs trembled as she climbed off the bed. How could he say that? She always thought in terms of the two of them! Always! She went into the bathroom and closed the door. Shaky, she leaned against the wall, and caught sight of herself in the mirror. She looked lovely. Blue eyes wide with surprised hurt, pale lip trembling, like a young girl suddenly cut to her vulnerable heart . . . .

And she hadn't even yet taken the season's pills!

Cade would have to come around. He would simply *have* to.

He didn't. Suzanne argued. She stormed. She begged. Finally, after missing three days of wonderful parties—irreplaceable parties, a season only opened once, after all—she dressed herself in the pills and a white cotton frock, and pleaded with him tremulously, weeping delicate sweet tears. Cade only laughed affectionately, and hugged her casually, and went off to do something else off-hand and detestable.

She dissolved the pills in his burgundy.

It bothered her, a little. They had always been honest with each other. And besides, it was such a scary thing for a young girl to do, her fingers shook the whole time as she broke open the capsules and a single shining crystalline tear dropped into the glass (how much salt would one tear add? Cade had a keen palate). But she did it. And, wide-eyed, she handed him the glass, her girlish bosom heaving with silent emotion. Then she excused herself and went to take a scented bath in pink bubbles and to do her hair in long drooping ringlets.

By the time she came out, Cade was waiting for her. He held a single pink rose, and his eyes met hers shyly, for just a moment, as he handed it to her. They went for a walk before dinner along a beach, and the stars came out one by one, and when he took her hand, Suzanne thought, her heart would burst. At the thought that he might kiss her, the V-R waves blurred a little, and her breath came faster.

It was going to be a wonderful winter.

"Suzanne," Cade said, very low. "Sweet Suzanne . . ."

"Yes, Cade?"

"I have something to tell you."

"Yes?" Emotion thrilled through her.

"I don't like burgundy."

"What . . . but you . . ."

"At least not that burgundy. I didn't drink it. But I did run it through the molecular analyzer."

She pulled away from his hand. Suddenly, she was very afraid.

"I'm so disappointed in you, Suzanne. I rather hoped that whatever fashion said, we at least trusted each other."

"What . . ." she had trouble getting the words out, damn this tremulous high-pitched voice—"What are you going to do?"

"Do?" He laughed carelessly. "Why do anything? It's not really worth making a fuss over, is it?"

Relief washed over her. It was last season's fashion. He was still wearing it, and it was keeping him casual about her betrayal. Nonchalant, off-hand. Oh, thank heavens . . .

"But I think maybe we should live apart for a bit. Till things sort themselves out. Don't you think that would be best?"

"Oh no! No!" Girlish protest, in a high sweet girlish voice. When what she wanted was to grab him and force her body against his and convince him to change his mind by sheer brute sexuality . . . but she couldn't. Not dressed like this. It would be ludicrous.

"Cade . . ."

"Oh, don't take it so hard, love. I mean, it's not the end of the world, is it? You're still you, and I'm still me. Be good, now." And he loped off down the beach and out the apartment door.

Suzanne turned off the V-R. She sat in the bare-walled apartment and cried. She loved Cade, she really did. Maybe if she agreed to go naked for a season . . . but, no. That wasn't how she loved Cade, or how he loved her, either. They loved each other for their multiplicity of selves, their basic and true complexity, expressed outwardly and so well through the art of change. That was what kept love fresh and romantic, wasn't it? Change. Growth. Variety.

Suzanne cried until she had no tears left, until she was completely drained. (It felt rather good, actually. Ingenues were allowed so much wild sorrow.) Then she called Sendil, at home, on a shielded frequency.

"Sendil? Suzanne."

"Suzanne? What is it? I can't see you, my dear."

"The vid's malfunctioning, I have audio only. Sendil, I've got some rather awful news."

"What? Oh, are you all right?"

"I'm . . . oh, please understand! I'm so alone! I need you!" Her voice trembled. She had his complete attention.

"Anything, love. Anything at all!"

"I'm . . ." Her girlish voice dropped to a whisper drenched in shame. "I'm . . . *enceinte*. And Cade . . . Cade won't marry me!"

"Suzanne!" Sendil cried. "Oh my God! What a master stroke! Are you going to keep it going all season?"

"I'm . . . I'm going away. I can't . . . face anyone."

"No, of course not. Oh my God, darling, this will just *make* your reputation!"

Suzanne said acidly, "I was under the impression it was already made," realized her mistake, and dropped back into ingenue. It wasn't hard, really; all she had to do was take a deep breath and give herself up to the drugs. She said gaspingly, "But I can't . . . I can't face it completely by myself. I'm just not strong enough. So you're the only person I'm telling. Will you come see me in my shame?"

"Oh, Suzanne, of course I'll stand by you." Sendil said, boyish emotion making his voice husky. Sendil always took a dose and a half of fashion.

"I leave tomorrow," Suzanne gasped. "I'll write you, dear faithful Sendil, to tell you where to visit me. . . ." She'd get a holo of her body looking pregnant custom-made. "Oh, he just threw me away! I feel so wretched!"

"Of course you do," Sendil breathed. "Poor innocent! Seduced and abandoned! What can I do to cheer you up?"

"Nothing. Oh, wait . . . maybe if I know my shame won't go on forever . . . but, oh, Sendil, I couldn't ask you what follows this season! I know you'd never let out a peep in advance!"

"Well, not ordinarily, of course, but in this case, for you . . ."

"You're the *only* one I'm going to let visit me, to hear about everything that happens. Everyone else will simply have to play along with you."

"Ahh." Sendil's voice thickened with emotion. "I'd do anything to cheer you up, darling. And believe me, you'll love the next season. After a whole season away, everyone will be panting to see how you look, every eye will be trained on you . . . and the look is going to be a return to military! You're just made for it, darling, and it for you!"

"Military," Suzanne breathed. Sendil was right. It was perfect. Uniforms' and swords and guns and stern, disciplined command breaking into bawdy barracks-room physicality at night . . . Officers pulling rank in the bedroom . . . *That's an order, soldier—Yes, sir!* . . . The sexual and social possibilities were tremendous. And Cade would never skip two seasons of fashion. She would come back from the winter's exile with everyone buzzing about her, and then Cade in the uniform of, say, the old Royal Guards . . . and herself outranking him (she'd find out somehow what rank he'd chosen, bribery or something), able to command his allegiance, keeping a military bearing and so having to give away nothing of herself. . . .

It was going to be a wonderful spring.

Canary Land

TOM PURDOM

————————————

Tom Purdom has been writing solid science fiction since the 1960s. His first story was published in 1957 and his second novel, *The Tree Lord of Imeten,* was the other side of an Ace Double from a Samuel R. Delany novel. Other novels followed and he was an active writer for a decade or so. Then he more or less disappeared from SF between the mid–1970s and the early 1990s, but he has been back with a vengeance in this decade with some first-rate fiction. One of the things he did in the meantime was to become music critic for a Philadelphia newspaper, which contributes to this story. He has not yet published a novel in the 90s, but his stories, mainly in *Asimov's* (as this one was), are deeply grounded in setting and have a pleasant complexity of motivation. "Canary Land" has those virtues in spades, and a surprising turn of plot that substitutes music and harmony for a more normal cathartic moment. Sometimes life is like this.

Back home in Delaware County, in the area that was generally known as the "Philadelphia region," the three guys talking to George Sparr would probably have been descended from long dead ancestors who had immigrated from Sicily. Here on the Moon they were probably the sons of parents who had been born in Taiwan or Thailand. They had good contacts, the big one explained, with the union that "represented" the musicians who played in eateries like the Twelve Sages Café. If George wanted to continue sawing on his viola twelve hours a day, thirteen days out of fourteen, it would be to his advantage to accept their offer. If he declined, someone else would take his place in the string quintet that the diners and lunchers ignored while they chatted.

On Earth, George had played the viola because he wanted to. The performance system he had planted in his nervous system was top-of-the-line, state-of-the-art. There had been weeks, back when he had been a normal take-it-as-it-comes American, when he had played with a different trio or quartet every night, including Saturday, and squeezed in two sessions on Sunday. Now his performance system was the only thing standing between him and the euphoric psychological states induced by malnutrition. Live music, performed by real live musicians, was one of the lowest forms of unskilled labor. Anybody could do it, provided they had attached the right information molecules to the right motor nerves. It was, in short, the one form of employment you could count on, if you were an American immigrant who was, when all was said and done, only a commonplace, cookbook kind of biodesigner.

▲   ▲   ▲

George's grasp of Techno-Mandarin was still developing. He had been scraping for money when he had left Earth. He had sold almost everything he owned—including his best viola—to buy his way off the planet. The language program he had purchased had been a cheap, quick-and-dirty item that gave him the equivalent of a useful pidgin. The three guys were talking *very* slowly.

They wanted to slip George into one of the big artificial ecosystems that were one of the Moon's leading economic resources. They had a contact who could stow him in one of the carts that delivered supplies to the canaries—the "long term research and maintenance team" who lived in the ecosystem. The contact would think she was merely transferring a container that had been loaded with a little harmless recreational material.

George was only five-eight, which was one reason he'd been selected for the "opportunity." He would be wearing a guaranteed, airtight isolation suit. Once inside, he would hunt down a few specimens, analyze their genetic makeup with the equipment he would be given, and come out with the information a member of a certain Board of Directors was interested in. Robots could have done the job, but robots had to be controlled from outside, with detectable radio sources. The Director (George could hear the capital, even with his limited knowledge of the language), the Director wanted to run some tests on the specimens without engaging in a direct confrontation with his colleagues.

There was, of course, a very real possibility the isolation suit might be damaged in some way. In that case, George would become a permanent resident of the ecosystem—a destiny he had been trying to avoid ever since he had arrived on the Moon.

The ride to the ecosystem blindsided George with an unexpected rush of emotion. There was a moment when he wasn't certain he could control the sob that was pressing against the walls of his throat.

He was sitting in a private vehicle. He was racing along a strip of pavement, with a line of vehicles ahead of him. There was sky over his head and a landscape around him.

George had spent his whole life in the car-dominated metropolitan sprawls that had replaced cities in the United States. Now he lived in a tiny one-room apartment, in a corridor crammed with tiny one-room apartments rented by other immigrants. His primary form of transportation was his own legs. When he did actually ride in a vehicle, he hopped aboard an automated cart and shared a seat with someone he had never seen before. He could understand why most of the people on the Moon came from Asiatic countries. They had crossed two hundred and fifty thousand miles so they could build a new generation of Hong Kongs under the lunar surface.

The sky was black, of course. The landscape was a rolling desert composed of craters pockmarked by craters that were pockmarked by craters. The cars on the black strip were creeping along at fifty kilometers per hour—or less—and most of the energy released by their batteries was powering a life support system, not a motor. Still, he looked around him with some of the tingling pleasure of a man who had just been released from prison.

The trio had to explain the job to him and some of the less technical data slipped out in the telling. They were also anxious, obviously, to let him know their "client" had connections. One of the corporation's biggest products was the organic interface that connected the brains of animals to electronic control devices. The company's major resource was a woman named Ms. Chao who was a big expert at developing such interfaces. Her company had become one of the three competitors everybody in the field wanted to beat.

In this case the corporation was upgrading a package that connected the brains of surveillance hawks to the electronics that controlled them. The package included genes that modified the neurotransmitters in the hawk's brain and it actually altered the hawk's intelligence and temperament. The package created, in effect, a whole new organ in the brain. You infected the brain with the package and the DNA in the package built a new organ—an organ that responded to activity within the brain by releasing extra transmitters, dampening certain responses, etc. Some of the standard, medically approved personality modifications worked exactly the same way. The package would increase the efficiency of the hawk's brain and multiply the number of functions its owners could build into the control interface.

Their Director, the trio claimed, was worried about the ethics of the *other* directors. The reports from the research and development team indicated the project was months behind schedule.

"Our man afraid he victim big cheat," the big one said, in slow Techno-Mandarin pidgin. With lots of emphatic, insistent hand gestures.

It had been the big one, oddly enough, who had done most of the talking. In his case, apparently, you couldn't assume there was an inverse relationship between muscle power and brain power. He was one of those guys who was so massive he made you feel nervous every time he got within three steps of the zone you thought of as your personal space.

The artificial ecosystems had become one of the foundations of the lunar economy. One of the Moon's greatest resources, it had turned out, was its lifelessness. Nothing could live on the surface of the Moon—not a bacterium, not a fungus, not the tiniest dot of a nematode, *nothing*.

Temperatures that were 50 percent higher than the temperature of boiling water sterilized the surface during the lunar day. Cold that was grimmer than anything found at the Antarctic sterilized it during the night. Radiation and vacuum killed anything that might have survived the temperature changes.

And what happened if some organism somehow managed to survive all of the Moon's hazards and cross the terrain that separated an ecosystem from one of the lunar cities? It still had to cross four hundred thousand kilometers of vacuum and radiation before it reached the real ecosystems that flowered on the blue sphere that had once been George's home.

The Moon, obviously, was the place to develop new life forms. The designers themselves could sit in Shanghai and Bangkok and ponder the three-dimensional models of DNA molecules that twisted across their screens. The hands-on work took place on the Moon. The organisms that sprouted from the molecules were inserted in artificial ecosystems on the Moon and given their chance to do their worst.

Every new organism was treated with suspicion. Anything—even the most trivial modification of a minor insect—could produce unexpected side effects when it was inserted into a terrestrial ecosystem. Once a new organism had been designed, it had to be maintained in a sealed lunar ecosystem for at least three years. Viruses and certain kinds of plants and insects had to be kept imprisoned for periods that were even longer.

According to the big guy, Ms. Chao claimed she was still developing the new hawk control interface. The Director, for some reason, was afraid she had already finished working on it. She could have turned it over to another company, the big guy claimed. And the new company could lock it in another ecosystem. And get it ready for market while the Director thought it was still under development inside the *old* company's ecosystem.

"Other directors transfer research other company," the big guy said. "Show him false data. Other company make money. Other directors make money. His stock—down."

"Stock no worth chips stock recorded on," the guy with the white scar on the back of his fingers said.

"You not commit crime," the big one said, with his hands pushing at the air as if he were trying to shove his complicated ideas into George's dumb immigrant's brain. "You not burglar. You work for Director. Stockholder. Director have right to know."

Like everything else on the Moon, the ecosystem was buried under the surface. George crawled into the back of the truck knowing he had seen all of the real Topside landscape he was going to see from now until he left the system. The guy with the scarred hand kept a camera on while he stood in the sterilizing unit and they talked him through the "donning procedure." The suit had already been sterilized. The donning procedure was supposed to reduce the contamination it picked up as he put it on. The sterilizing unit flooded him with UV light and other, less obvious forms of radiation while he wiggled and contorted. The big guy got some bobs and smiles from the third member of the trio when he made a couple of "jokes" about the future of George's chromosomes. Then the big guy tapped a button on the side of the unit and George stood there for five minutes, completely encased in the suit, while the unit supposedly killed off anything the suit had attracted while he had been amusing them with his reverse strip tease. The recording they were making was for his benefit, the big guy assured him. If he ran into any legal problems, they had proof they had administered all the standard safety precautions before he had entered the ecosystem.

⋅

The thing that really made George sweat was the struggle to emerge from the container. It was a cylinder with a big external pressure seal and they had deliberately picked one of the smaller sizes. *We make so small, nobody see think person,* the big guy had explained.

The trick release on the inside of the cylinder worked fine, but after that he had to maneuver his way through the neck without ripping his suit. Any tear—any puncture, any *pinhole*—would activate the laws that governed the quarantine.

The best you could hope for, under the rules, was fourteen months of isolation. You could only hope for that, of course, if you had entered the ecosystem legitimately, for a very good reason. If you had entered it illegally, for a reason that would make you the instant enemy of most of the people who owned the place, you would be lucky if they let you stay inside it, in one piece, for the rest of whatever life you might be willing to endure before you decided you were better off dead.

The people on the "long term research and maintenance team" did some useful work. An American with his training would be a valuable asset—a high level assistant to the people on the other side of the wall who really directed the research. But everybody knew why they were really there. There wasn't a person on the Moon who didn't know that coal miners had once taken canaries into their tunnels, so they would know they were breathing poisoned air as soon as the canaries keeled over. The humans locked in the ecosystem were the living proof the microorganisms in the system hadn't evolved into something dangerous.

The contact had placed the container, as promised, in the tall grasses that grew along a small stream. The ecosystem was supposed to mimic a "natural" day-night cycle on Earth and it was darker than any place George had ever visited on the real planet. He had put on a set of night vision goggles before he had closed the hood of the suit but he had to stand still for a moment and let his eyes adjust anyway.

His equipment pack contained two cases. The large flat case looked like it had been designed for displaying jewelry. The two moths fitted into its recesses would have drawn approving nods from people who were connoisseurs of bioelectronic craftsmanship.

The hawks he was interested in were living creatures with modified brains. The cameras and computers plugged into their bodies were powered by the energy generated by their own metabolism. The two moths occupied a different part of the great borderland between the world of the living and the world of the machine. Their bodies had been formed in cocoons but their organic brains had been replaced by electronic control systems. They drew all their energy from the batteries he fitted into the slots just behind each control system. Their wings were a little wider than his hand but the big guy had assured him they wouldn't trigger any alarms when a surveillance camera picked them up.

Insect like this in system. Not many. But enough.

The first moth flitted away from George's hand as soon as he pressed on the battery with his thumb. It fluttered aimlessly, just above the tops of the river grasses, then turned to the right and headed toward a group of trees about a hundred meters from its launch site.

At night the hawks were roosters, not flyers. They perched in trees, dozing and digesting, while the cameras mounted in their skulls continued to relay data to the security system.

George had never paid much attention when his parents had discussed their family histories. He knew he had ancestors who came from Romania, Italy, Austria, and the less prominent regions of the British Isles. Most of them had emigrated in the nineteenth century, as far as he could tell. One of his grandmothers had left some country in Europe when it fell apart near the end of the twentieth century.

Most of them had emigrated because they couldn't make a living in the countries they had been born in. That seemed to be clear. So why shouldn't he "pull up stakes" (whatever that meant) and head for the booming economy in the sky? Didn't that show you were made of something special?

George's major brush with history had been four sets of viewer-responsive videos he had studied as a child, to meet the requirements listed on his permanent educational transcript. His parents had chosen most of his non-technical educational materials and they had opted for a series that emphasized human achievements in the arts and sciences. The immigrants he was familiar with had overcome poverty and bigotry (there was always some mention of bigotry) and become prize-winning physicists and world famous writers and musicians. There had been no mention of immigrants who wandered the corridors of strange cities feeling like they were stumbling through a fog. There had been no indication any immigrant

had ever realized he had traded utter hopelessness for permanent, lifelong poverty.

There had been a time, as George understood it, when
the music in restaurants had been produced by electronic
sound systems and unskilled laborers had carried food to
the tables. Now unskilled labor provided the music and
carts took orders and transported the food. Had any of his
ancestors been invisible functionaries who toted plates of
food to customers who were engrossed in intense conversations about the kind of real work people did in real work
spaces like laboratories and offices? He had never heard his
parents mention it.

*Battery good twenty minutes. No more. Moth not come back
twenty minutes—not come back ever.*

He almost missed the light the moth flicked on just before
it settled into the grass. He *would* have missed it, in fact, if
they hadn't told him he should watch for it. It was only a blip,
and it was really a glow, not a flash. He crept toward it in an
awkward hunch, with both cases in his hands and his eyes
fixed on the ground in front of his boots.

The small square case contained his laboratory. The collection tube attached to the moth's body fitted into a plug on
the side of the case and he huddled over the display screen
while the unit ran its tests. If everything was on the up and up,
the yellow lines on the screen would be the same length as the
red lines. If the "Director" was being given false information,
they wouldn't.

It was a job that could have been handled by 80 percent—at least—of the nineteen million people currently living
on the Moon. In his lab on Earth, there had been *carts* that did
things like that. A four-wheeled vehicle a little bigger than
the lab case could have carried the two moths and automatically plugged the collection tube into the analyzer. He was

lurching around in the dark merely because a cart would have required a wireless communications link that *might* have been detectable.

The first yellow line appeared on the screen. It was a few pixels longer than the red line—enough to be noticeable, not enough to be significant.

The second yellow line took its place beside the second red line like a soldier coming to attention beside a partner who had been chosen because they were precisely the same height. The third line fell in beside its red line, there was a pause that lasted about five hard beats of George's pulse, and the last two yellow lines finished up the formation.

The moth had hovered above the hawk's back and jabbed a long, threadlike tube into its neck. The big changes in the bird's chemistry would take place in its brain, but some of the residue from the changes would seep into its bloodstream and produce detectable alterations in the percentages of five enzymes. The yellow lines were the same length as the red lines: ergo, the hawks were carrying a package exactly like the package they were supposed to be carrying.

Which was good news for the Director. Or George presumed it was, anyway. And bad news for him.

If the result had been positive—if he had collected proof there was something wrong with the hawks—he could have radioed the information in an encrypted one-second blip and headed straight for the nearest exit. His three bodyguards would have helped him through the portal—they'd *said* they would, anyway—and he would have been home free. Instead, he had to pick up his equipment, close all his cases, and go creeping through the dark to the other hawk nest in the system. He was supposed to follow the small stream until it crossed a dirt utility road, the big guy had said. Then he was supposed to follow the road for about four kilometers, until it intersected another stream. And work his way through another two kilometers of tangled, streamside vegetation.

The habitat reproduced three hundred square kilometers of temperate zone forest and river land. It actually supported more plant, animal, and insect species than any stretch of "natural" terrain you could visit on the real twenty-first century Earth. Samples of Earth soil had been carried to the Moon with all their microorganisms intact. Creepers and crawlers and flying nuisances had been imported by the hundreds of thousands.

You couldn't understand every relationship in a system, the logic ran. *People* might not like gnats and snakes but that didn't mean the system could operate without them. The relationship you didn't think about might be the very relationship you would disrupt if you created a wonderful, super-attractive new species and introduced it into a real habitat on Earth. A change in relationship X might lead to an unexpected change in relationship Y. Which would create a disruption in relationship C. . . .

And so on.

It was supposed to be one of the basic insights of modern biological science and George Sparr was himself one of the fully credentialed, fully trained professionals who turned that science into products people would voluntarily purchase in the free market. The fact was, however, that he *hated* insects and snakes. He could have lived his whole life without one second of contact with the smallest, most innocuous member of either evolutionary line. What he liked was riding along in a fully enclosed, air conditioned or heated (depending on the season) automobile, with half a dozen of his friends chattering away on the communications screen, while a first class, state-of-the-art control system guided him along a first class, state-of-the-art highway to a building where he would work in air-conditioned or heated ease and continue to be totally indifferent to temperature, humidity, illumination, or precipitation.

Which was what he had had. Along with pizzas, steak, tacos, turkey club sandwiches, and a thousand other items that had flavor and texture and the great virtue that they were not powdered rice flavored with powdered flavor.

There had been women whose hair tossed across their necks as they gave him little glances across their music stands while they played quartets with him. (He had made the right decision, he had soon realized, when he had chosen the viola. The world was full of violinists and cellists looking for playing partners who could fill in the middle harmonies.) There had even been the pleasure of expressing your undiluted contempt for the human robots who were hustling like mad in China, Thailand, India, and all the other countries where people had discovered they, too, could enjoy the satisfactions of electronic entertainment, hundred year lifespans, and lifelong struggles against obesity and high cholesterol levels.

George Sparr was definitely not a robot. Robots lived to work. Humans worked to live. Work was a *means*, not an end. *Pleasure* was an end. *Art* was an end. *Love* and *friendship* were ends.

George had worked for four different commercial organizations in the eleven years since he had received his Ph.D. He had left every one of them with a glowing recommendation. Every manager who had ever given him an evaluation had agreed he was a wonderful person to have on your payroll on the days when he was actually physically present. And actually concentrating on the job you were paying him to do.

▲   ▲   ▲

The dogs weren't robots, either. They were real muscle-and-tooth living organisms, and they had him boxed in—right and left, front and back, with one prowling in reserve—before he heard the first warning growl. The light mounted on the dog in the front position overwhelmed his goggles before the control system could react. An amplified female voice blared at him from somewhere beyond the glare.

"Stand absolutely still. There is no possibility the dogs can be outrun. You will not be harmed if you stand absolutely still."

She was speaking complete sentences of formal Techno-Mandarin but the learning program she had used hadn't eliminated her accent—whatever the accent was. It didn't matter. He didn't have to understand every word. He knew the dogs were there. He knew the dogs had teeth. He knew the teeth could cut through his suit.

"I'm afraid you may have a serious problem, patriot. As far as I can see, there's only one candidate for the identity of this director they told you about—assuming they were telling you the truth, of course."

The ecosystem was surrounded by tunnels that contained work spaces and living quarters. They had put him in a room that looked like it was supposed to be some kind of art gallery. Half the space on the walls was covered with watercolors, prints, and freehand crayon work. Shelves held rock sculptures. He was still wearing his suit and his goggles, but the goggles had adjusted to the illumination and he could see the lighting and framing had obviously been directed by professional-level programs.

They had left him alone twice, but there had been no danger he would damage anything. The dog sitting two steps from his armchair took care of that.

The man sitting in the other armchair was an American and he was doing his best to make this a one-immigrant-to-another conversation. He happened to be the kind of big-bellied, white-faced, fast-food glutton George particularly disliked, but he hadn't picked up the contempt radiating from George's psyche. He probably wouldn't, either, given the fact that he had to observe his surroundings through the fat molecules that puffed up his eyelids and floated in his brain.

George could understand people who choked their arteries eating steaks and lobster. But when they did it stuffing down food that had less flavor than the containers it came in . . .

"Do you understand who Ms. Chao is?" big-belly said.

George shrugged. "You can't do much biodesign without learning something about Ms. Chao."

The puffy head nodded once. They hadn't asked George about his vocational history but he was assuming they had looked at the information he had posted in the databanks. The woman had asked him for his name right after she had taken him into custody and he had given it to her without a fuss.

"Your brag screen looked very promising, patriot. It looks like you might have made it to the big leagues under the right circumstances."

"I worked for four of the largest R&D companies in the United States."

"But you never made it to the big leagues, right?"

George focused his attention on his arms and legs and consciously made himself relax. He pasted a smile on his face, and tried to make it big enough so that Mr. Styrofoam could see it through his eye slits.

"The closest I ever got to the other side of the Pacific was a weekend conference on La Jolla Beach."

"That's closer than I ever got. I was supposed to be a hardwired program genius—a Prince of the Nerds himself— right up to the moment I got my transcript certified. I thought if I came here I could show them what somebody with my brain circuits could do. And make it to Shanghai the long way round."

George nodded: the same sympathetic nod and the same sympathetic expression—he *hoped* it was sympathetic any- way—that he offered all the people who told him the same kind of story when they sat beside him on the transportation carts. Half of them usually threw in a few remarks to the effect that "doughfaces" didn't stand a chance anymore. He would usually nod in sympathy when they said that, too, but he wasn't sure that would be a good idea in this situation. His interrogator was putting on a good act, but the guy could be Ms. Chao's own son, for all George knew. George had never seen an Asian who looked that gross, but Styrofoam's mother could have decided anybody cursed with American genes had to possess a special, uniquely American variation on the human digestive tract.

"The database says you're a musician."

"I've been working in a restaurant. I bought a perfor- mance system when I was on Earth—one of the best."

"And now you're serenading the sages and samurai while they dine."

"That's why I'm here. They told me I'd be thrown out of my job if I turned them down."

"Ms. Chao had a husband. Mr. Tan. Do you know him?"

"I've heard about the Tan family. They're big in Copernicus, right?"

"They're one of the families that control the Copernicus industrial complex. And make it such a wonderful place to work and raise children. This Mr. Tan—it's clear he's con- nected, but nobody knows how much. Ms. Chao married him. They went through a divorce. Somehow he's still sitting on the Board. With lots of shares."

"And he thinks his ex-wife is trying to put something over on him? Is that what this is all about?"

Chubby hands dug into the arms of the other chair. Arm muscles struggled against the low lunar gravity as they raised the bloated body to an upright position. The Prince of the Nerds turned toward the door and let George admire the width of his waistline as he made his exit.

"You're the one who's supposed to be coming up with answers, patriot. We're supposed to be the people with the questions."

There was a timestrip built into the base of George's right glove. It now read 3:12. When they had brought him into the working and living area, it had read 3:46.

George's suit was totally self-contained. He could breathe and rebreathe the same air over and over again. But nothing comes free. Bacteria recycled the air as it passed through the filtering system. Other bacteria generated the chemicals in the organic battery that powered the circulation system. Both sets of bacteria drew their energy from a sugar syrup. In three hours and twelve minutes, the syrup would be exhausted. And George could choose between two options. He could open the suit. Or he could smother to death.

The second interrogator was a bony, stoop shouldered woman. She spoke English with a British accent but her hand gestures and her general air of weary cynicism looked European to George's eye. She glanced at the timestrip—it now read 2:58—and sat down without making any comments.

The woman waved her hand as if she was chasing smoke

away from her face. "You were hired by three people. They coerced you. They claimed you would lose your job if you didn't work for them."

"I didn't have any choice. I could come here or I could find a good space to beg. Believe me—this is the last place I want to be."

"You'd rather play little tunes in a restaurant than work in a major ecosystem? Even though your screens say you're a trained, experienced biodesigner?"

George offered her one of his more sincere smiles. "Actually, we play almost everything we want to most of the time. Mozart quintets. Fauré. Kryzwicki. Nobody listens anyway."

"The three men who hired you told you they were hired by Mr. Tan. Is that correct?"

So far George had simply told them the truth—whatever they wanted to know. Now he knew he had to think. Was she telling him they wanted him to testify against Mr. Tan? Was Ms. Chao trying to get something on her ex-husband?

Was it possible they had something else in mind? Could they be testing him in some way?

"They're very tough people," George said. "They made a lot of threats."

"They told you all the things Mr. Tan could do if you talked? They described his connections?"

"They made some very big threats. Terminating my job was only part of it. That's all I can tell you. They made some very big threats."

The woman stood up. She bent over his timestrip. She raised her head and ran her eyes over his suit.

▲   ▲   ▲

George didn't have to tell the canaries he didn't want to join them. Nobody wanted to be a canary. In theory, canaries didn't have it bad. They didn't pay rent. The meals they ate were provided free, so their diets could be monitored. They got all the medical care they needed and some they could have done without. They could save their wages. They could work their way out of their cage.

Somehow, it didn't work that way. There was always something extra you couldn't do without—videos, games, a better violin to help you pass the time. The artificial ecosystems were a little over thirty years old. So far, approximately fifteen people had actually left them while they still had the ability to eat and drink and do anything of consequence with women whose hair tossed around their neck while they played Smetana's first quartet.

And what would you really have, when you added it up? George had done the arithmetic. After twenty-five years in an ecosystem—if you did everything right—you could live in the same kind of room he was living in now, in the same kind of "neighborhood." With the same kind of people.

The other possibility would be to buy yourself a return trip to Earth. You'd even have some money left over when you stepped off the shuttle.

The timestrip read 2:14 when the woman came back. This time she put a glass bottle on a shelf near the door. George couldn't read the label but he could see the green and blue logo. The thick brown syrup in the bottle would keep the bacteria in his life support system functioning for at least ten hours.

▲   ▲   ▲

He was perfectly willing to lie. He had no trouble with that. If they wanted him to claim his three buddies had told him they were working for Mr. Tan, then he would stand up in front of the cameras, and place his hand on the American flag, or a leather bound copy of the last printed edition of *The Handbook of Chemistry and Physics,* or some similar object of reverence, and swear that he had clearly heard one of his abductors say they were employees of the said Mr. Tan. That wasn't the problem. Should he lie before the canaries let him out? And hope they *would* let him out? Or should he insist they let him out first? *Before* he perjured himself?

And what if that *wasn't* what they wanted? What if there was something *else* going on here? Something he didn't really understand?

The people he was talking to were just the fronts. Back in the city there were offices and labs where the babus who really counted made the real choices. Somewhere in one of those offices, somebody was looking at him through one of the cameras mounted in the corners of the room. Right now, when he looked up at the camera in the front left hand corner, he was looking right into the eyes of someone who was sitting in front of a screen sixty kilometers away.

If they would take away the cameras, he could just ask her. *Just tell me what they want, lady. We're both crawling around at the bottom of the food chain. Tell me what I should do. Will they let me out of here if I cooperate first? Will I get a better deal if I tough it out right to the last minute? Are all of you really working for Mr. Tan?*

And what would he have done with her answers when he got them? Did any of the people in this place understand the situation any better than he did? In the city, he hobbled around in a permanent psychological haze, surrounded by people who made incomprehensible mouth noises and hurried from one place to another on incomprehensible missions. In the ecosystem, the canaries puttered with their odd jobs and created their picture of the world from the information that trickled onto their screens.

"I understand there's a visitors' lounge attached to the outside of the ecosystem," George said.

"And?" the woman said.

"I'll be glad to tell you anything I know. I just want to get out of here—out of the system itself. There's no way I can get away if you let me get that far—just to the lounge. I'll still need transportation back to the city, right?"

The woman stood up. She stopped in front of the syrup bottle and picked it up. She turned it around in her hand as if she were reading the label. She put it back on the shelf. She glanced at the dog. She slipped out the door.

The time strip read 0:54 the next time the woman came back. The dog turned her way and she shook her head when she saw the soulful look in its eyes.

"You're putting a strain on his toilet training," the woman said.

"Suppose I do give you a statement? Is there any guarantee you'll let me go?"

"Are you trying to bargain with us?"

"Would you expect me to do anything else?"

"You think you're better than us? You think you deserve all that *opportunity* you thought they were going to give you when you left Earth?"

George shrugged. "I couldn't get a job on Earth. Any kind of job. I just came here to survive."

"They wouldn't even pay you to play that music you like?"

"On Earth? There would have been twenty thousand people lined up ahead of me."

"There's no way you can bargain with us, George. *You* answer the questions. *We* relay the answers. *They* decide what to do. There's only one thing I can guarantee."

"In fifty-four minutes, I'll have to open the suit and stay here."

"Right."

They didn't let him out when they had his statement. Instead the woman poured syrup into the flask that fueled his life support system. Then she walked out and left him sitting there.

The urine collection system on his leg was a brand name piece of equipment but he couldn't empty the receptacle without opening the suit. He had already used the system once, about an hour after they had captured him. He didn't know what would happen the next time he used it. No one had thought about the possibility he might wear the suit more than five hours.

The woman smiled when she re-entered the room and caught him fidgeting. The first dog had been replaced a few minutes after it had communicated its message but no one even mentioned *his* problem.

The woman had him stand up in the middle of the room and face the left hand camera. He repeated all his statements. He told them, once again, that the guy with the scarred fingers had mentioned Mr. Tan by name.

The timestrip said 3:27 when they left him alone this time. They had given him a full five hour refill when they had poured in the syrup.

▲   ▲   ▲

The timestrip read 0:33 when they put him in the security portal. Big-belly and the woman and three other people stared through the little square windows. A no-nonsense voice talked him through the procedure in Hong Kong British.

He was reminded that a lapse in the procedure could result in long-term isolation. He stood in an indentation in the floor. He stuck his hands into a pair of holes above his head. Robot arms stripped the suit. Heat and radiation poured into the portal.

George had never been a reader, but he had played in orchestras that accompanied two operatic versions of the Orpheus legend. He kept his eyes half shut and tried not to look at the door that would take him back to the ecosystem. When he did glance back, after the other door had swung open, the woman and big-belly looked, it seemed to him, like disappointed gargoyles. He started to wave at them and decided that would still be too risky. He walked through the door with his shoulders hunched. And started looking for the two things he needed most: clothes and a bathroom.

The lounge was just a place where drivers and visitors could stretch their legs. There was a bathroom. There was a water fountain. There was a kitchen that checked his credit when he stuck his thumb in the ID unit. And offered him a menu that listed the kind of stuff he had been eating since he arrived on the Moon.

He queried taxi services on the phone screen and discovered a trip back to the city would cost him a week's wages. He had never been naked in a public place before and he didn't know how to act. Were the canaries watching him on the single camera mounted in the ceiling?

"I didn't do this because I wanted to," he told the cameras. "I don't even know what's going on. I just want to get out of here. Is that too much to ask?"

▲   ▲   ▲

A truck entered the garage space under the lounge. A woman who was old enough to be his mother appeared in one of the doors and handed him a wad of cloth. The shirt was too long for him but it was the only thing she had. He stood around for an hour while she ate a meal and talked to people on the phone. He couldn't shake off the feeling he was wearing a dress.

He had missed a full shift at the Twelve Sages Café but the first violinist had left him a message assuring him they had only hired a temporary replacement. They could all see he was jumpy and preoccupied when he joined them at the start of the next shift but no one said anything. He had always been popular with the people he played with. He had the right temperament for a viola player. He took his part seriously but he understood the give-and-take that is one of the primary requirements of good chamber playing.

The big guy lumbered into the Twelve Sages Café a month later. He smiled at the musicians playing in the corner. He threw George a big wave as he sat down.

They were playing the slow movement of Mendelssohn's A Major quintet. George actually stumbled out of the room with his hands clutching his stomach. He managed to come back before the next movement started but he lost his place three times.

The second violinist took him aside after the last movement and told him he was putting all their jobs in danger. She came back to his apartment after the shift ended.

▲   ▲   ▲

Six months later a woman came up to George during a break and asked him if he gave lessons in style, interpretation, and the other subjects you could still teach. Eight months after that he had seven students. The second violinist moved in with him.

Then the first violinist discovered one of the most famous restaurants in the city was looking for a new quartet. And George did something that surprised him just as much as it surprised every one else. He told the first violinist they should abandon the other viola player, develop their interpretation of two of the most famous quartets in the repertoire, and audition for the other job. They would have to spend all their leisure, non-sleeping hours studying Chi-Li's Opus 12 and Beethoven's Opus 59, No. 2, but the second violinist backed him up. The other two were dubious but they caught fire as George guided them through the recordings and interpretative commentaries he selected from the databanks. The restaurant owner and her husband actually stood up and applauded when they finished the last note of the Chi-Li.

The restaurant paid unskilled labor real money. It was also a place, George discovered, where some of the customers actually listened to the music. They were busy people—men and women who were making fortunes. Someday they might buy performance systems themselves and enjoy the pleasure of experiencing music from the inside. For now, they sat at their tables like barons and duchesses and let the commoners do the work. Once every three or four days somebody dropped the musicians a tip that was bigger than all the money their old quintet had received in a week.

The other members of the quartet knew they owed it all to George. Anyone could buy a performance system and play the notes. George was the guy who understood the shadings and the instrumental interactions that turned sounds into real music. He had created a foursome that worked well together—

a unit that accepted his ideas without a lot of argument.

George had occasionally exercised that kind of leadership when he had been playing for pleasure on Earth. Now he did it with all the intensity of someone who knew his livelihood depended on it.

George searched the databanks twice. He didn't like to spend money on things he didn't need, even after he began to feel more secure. As far as he could tell, Ms. Chao was still the chief designer in her company. Mr. Tan had resigned from the board four months after George's visit to the canary cage. Then he had rejoined the board six months later. It occurred to George that Ms. Chao had somehow tricked Mr. Tan into doing something that looked stupid. But why did she let him rejoin the board later?

The second violinist thought it might have something to do with family ties.

"Everybody says the Overseas Chinese have always been big on family ties," the second violinist pointed out. "Why should the off-Earth Chinese be any different?"

The whole business became even more puzzling when one of George's students told him she was really glad "Tan Zem" had recommended him. Three of his first four students, George discovered, had looked him up because Mr. Tan had steered them his way. Had Mr. Tan felt guilty? Had he been motivated by some kind of criminal code of honor? Finally George stopped trying to figure it out. He had a bigger apartment. He had a better job. He had the second violinist. He had become—who would have believed it?—the kind of immigrant the other immigrants talked about when they wanted to convince themselves a determined North American could create a place for himself in the new society humanity was building on the Moon.

He had become—by immigrant standards—a success.

Universal Emulators

TOM COOL

Tom Cool (it's an Irish name) is a Commander in the U.S. Navy. His first SF novel, *Infectress,* came out in paperback in 1997, and his second, *Secret Realms,* is due out this year. This story is one of his thus far few pieces of short fiction. It shows an impressive storytelling talent at work and clever plotting. Its thematic underpinnings, on the nature of identity, give it extra substance. It was published in *Fantasy & Science Fiction,* which published a relatively low percentage of science fiction this year. There is something about the energy and drive of this story that reminds me of the adventure fiction of Roger Zelazny, and that landed it in this anthology. Heaven knows, SF could use another talent like him, any time.

Having circumnavigated the globe several times, I had thought that I had known the sea. My limited experience had been deceptive. All of my voyages had been in tropical zones, circling the warm waist of the world. In a typhoon, the southern seas had been furious and horrifying, but never bleak. East of Iceland, as the *Sephora* steamed north, I learned how indifferent is the ocean. It has no color, mood or nature of its own, slavishly reflecting in hue and temperament the aspect of its master, the sky.

East of Iceland the sky was a cold, dreary expanse of lifeless gray cloud. Underneath it the ocean crawled on its belly like a cur at its master's feet. The ocean, which had seduced me while wearing the profoundest blue in nature, the blue of the tropical ocean under clear skies, crawled with a heavy gray, a hue more lifeless than slate, more dispiriting than the gray of rain-slickened tree branches in winter. Underscoring its bleakness was the knowledge that, if a man were to fall into these arctic waters, in five minutes the ocean would suck from him all his living warmth.

The *Sephora* was pitching as it bounded over the cold choppy rollers of the North Atlantic. Since the sea was following, the ship was rolling hardly at all. I stood in the private sponson off the master's cabin where no one could see me. And there was none to see. *Sephora* was a robotically controlled ship. No one was aboard except Cecilia and Coupon.

How many of my off-hours had I spent here, enjoying the tropical sun, smearing myself with sun-block to prevent burning a shade darker than my paradigm, Coupon. Now I had to worry about wind-burn, as the frigid wind sliced past my face.

Zealously I applied lip balm. My lips could not be chapped and brittle, while Coupon's were moist and pliant.

Taking more weather than he did was a dangerous proposition. Yet I craved the weather deck, where, alone, I could try to remember who or what I was, other than one of the most deeply bonded emulators in the world. That day, the bleak scenery of the subarctic ocean reinforced my mood. My thoughts were heavy and troubled. I wondered how much longer I could go on. The end of my indenture seemed impossibly distant.

A sharp double rap—his signature knock—called me away from my own thoughts. I undogged the hatch and stepped back into the master's cabin. Here the warm air was scented with rosewood. The furnishings were simple but opulent; every plush chair and love-seat was bolted through the deep wool carpeting into the deck. The lighting was muted and indirect.

Looming before me was Coupon, my mirror image (or, more properly, I was his mirror image). We had the same tall, narrow head, cold gray eyes (gray as the sea, I realized), thin lips. We were wearing identical mess dress of Coupon's design: black slacks, gold satin cummerbunds, white short waist jackets with miniature medals, a light cotton shirt with a soft choker decorated with a ruby brooch at the throat.

"Is it too much?" he demanded. "Is it too much to ask that you wait for me here? I've got the Japanese calling every five minutes, the ball-and-chain wants a private word, I'm trying to visualize the next generation of SEE, and you can't tear yourself away from the weather deck for five minutes."

I bobbed my head. It was a mannerism learned from my Universal Emulators coach in client relations, a Japanese man rumored to have doubled for the Emperor for fifteen years. "I'm sorry, master," I said. "How may I serve you now?"

"The ball-and-chain . . . Nah, I'll take her this time. I want you to run interference with the Japanese. Keep them off my back for two more days. Don't promise anything except they'll be happy when I pitch the concept."

"Yes, master," I said, disappointed he had chosen that task rather than interfacing with his wife. I worried that he was beginning to mistrust how convincingly I played the role of the husband.

I brushed past Coupon and pressed the ceiling-height mirror, which popped open to reveal the doorway into my cabin. Once safely inside, I logged into the covert surveillance network, so that I could monitor him through the rest of the day. Our knowledge of each other's activities had to be kept complete, lest one of us betray the other. Then I donned Coupon's business avatar and began to answer requests for communication, beginning with Morita, the Sony vice-president in charge of site-entrenched entertainment.

"Mr. Coupon, how are you?" Morita began. He was wearing his typical business avatar, a two-sworded samurai in green silks. Coupon's avatar was also retro, silk brocades based on the court dress of the Sun King.

"Fine, Mr. Vice President. How pleasant to see you. Are you feeling as fit as you look?" I asked in Coupon's most dulcet tones. In doing so, in posing as Coupon, I was committing several felonies simultaneously . . . and since he had shared his cryptocode with me, so was my paradigm.

An overseas Japanese, Morita was direct. "We here in Portland are very excited about your preliminary proposal. We are anxiously awaiting the full proposal."

By now I was wearing my paradigm's head. I was not acting like Coupon. I was Coupon, yet Coupon informed by my better judgment. It was a delicate balance, responding authentically as Coupon, but Coupon on one of his best days. I knew that he would have retorted irritably because of the recent stress, but I responded with a soft answer.

"Yes, well, I'm hard at work on that now. So much of the shine is in the polish, don't you think?"

"Of course you're right," Morita said. "Simply that we

have a board meeting tomorrow. It might strengthen the project's support from the board if I could show them something. Perhaps a two-D rendering?"

"Let me see if anything is worthy. One moment please . . ."

My avatar froze as I linked off-line with Coupon, who snarled, but shot me a two-D rendering of the new entertainment, an immersive Valhalla optimized for Russian males.

"How intriguing," Morita said, as the samurai studied a photograph of Nordic paradise. "And how much is natural?"

"Certainly all the mead," I said, chuckling. "Please, let me save the rest for the proposal. With your kind permission."

"Of course," Morita said, thankfully placated. "By the way, how is the sailing?"

We exchanged small talk for several minutes, then Morita as the superior took the initiative to sign off. In the confines of my secret room, I heaved a sigh and checked my other. Coupon was arguing with his wife. We needed him to work on the proposal. He should have sent me to see her. I scanned the transcript of the argument to date. I needed to return to the communication queues, but the fight was too distracting. It upset me. Here I was dedicating the best days of the best years of my life to him, shouldering his most tedious burdens, taking the brunt of his personal and professional shocks, freeing him so that he could create. Day after day, night after night, I proved that I could be everything that he was, I could do everything that he did, yet he had the name. My name was almost forgotten. Because the lightning bolt of employment had struck him and not me, I had no dreams of my own. I dreamed his dreams. I accepted his insults. All that I asked was to serve him. And here he was, squandering the time and the emotional energy that I saved for him on yet another stupid argument with Cecilia. He was savaging her, too. Sometimes I thought he brutalized her just to upset me.

". . . getting fat and lazy," Coupon was shouting. "Don't

you understand that I've got work to do? I've got to earn the money that you're so fond of spending."

"We're rich enough already, Frederick," Cecilia said in her pleading voice. "I just want more of your time. It gets lonely in here—"

"You're the one who wants to see St. Petersburg in February, well, here you are, complaining about how boring an Arctic passage is."

"I thought we might have some time together," Cecilia wailed. Then she said something unnerving: "I don't understand you! Sometimes you're so wonderful and understanding, and other times, like now, you're so bloody beastly—"

Coupon roared with anger. I stood up, afraid that he was going to hit her again. He loomed over her, his fists clenched. I fought my own compulsion to bolt from my hiding hole, dash down to her cabin and pull my twin away from her. Thankfully, he managed to chain the demon of his temper, venting it only in screams of obscenity. Coupon turned his heel and left Cecilia sobbing.

Moments later, he tore open the door to my room, crowding inside where his shouts would be doubly sound-proofed.

"What have you been doing to my wife?" he demanded. His face was flushed, the cords of his neck muscles strained. I could see the pulse in his jugular veins.

"You know what," I said. "What you've ordered."

"You're making her fall in love with you!" he shouted.

Looking up into his flushed face, seeing the blood-shot eyes and spit-speckled lips, I wondered how I could ever have considered ourselves handsome.

"I'm making her fall in love with you," I answered.

"I said that you could make love to her!" Coupon shouted. "I didn't say to go on about it for an hour!"

"We were having a good day," I retorted.

Coupon clenched his fist and swung at my face. Abruptly

I stood, my left arm deflecting the blow, as I grabbed him by the lapels and jacked him up against the bulkhead.

"Never again," I hissed.

He could feel my strength. Our identical faces were almost nose-to-nose. I stared into his eyes and sought the glint of fear I knew would surface. When it gleamed like something arisen to the surface of a dark pool, I repeated, "Never again. You will never hit me again. And you'll . . ."

I hesitated, because it occurred to me that instructing the client not to beat his wife exceeded my brief as a professional emulator. Uncertain, I released his lapels, reflexively crushing my own so that once again our appearances matched. Coupon's breath stank as he hyperventilated so close to me.

"We're—sorry, master," I said. "We're under pressure. We've got the deadline. Why don't you retire to the study, work on the proposal. I'll finish your communications. Later, we'll have calmed down enough. You could go to Cecilia then. Apologize."

"I'll be damned if I apologize to her," Coupon snapped. "But you will. And make it good, too."

"Yes, master."

"I don't want to have to bother with her again for two days. Or with you. I've got a deadline, dammit! I've got to pitch a 300 trillion yen SEE in two days, and the damned 3D models aren't even done, let alone the animations. Aren't I paying you to make my life easier?"

"Yes, master. I'm trying."

"Well, give the communications back-log the same attention you give to my future ex-wife and maybe we'll get something accomplished!"

Coupon turned on his heel, checked the spy hole to ensure no one was in his stateroom and left me alone with only his odor. I sat and wondered. After I had glimpsed the fear in his eyes, something else had surfaced, something colder and more deadly. Hate. In that moment, Coupon hated me, his other self. I hugged my ribs. I began to fear for my life.

It would be so easy. He could poison me or simply tip me overboard. A privileged conversation with the president of Universal Emulators, a surrendering of his employee insurance premium and I would not even be history. It would be as if I had never existed.

Then, the sister idea presented its seductive self: how easy would it be for me simply to tip him overboard. If I managed to avoid DNA typing for the rest of my life, then I could be Coupon. Not emulate him. Be him.

A new fantasy, so much richer and darker than the workaday one of fleeing with Cecilia. "My future ex-wife . . ." Lately, he had taken to referring to her as such. Was he doing it to torment me, because he had learned to read my thoughts as thoroughly as I read his?

I shook my head, then turned my attention to the communications. There were now eighteen high-ranking requests to communicate, plus hundreds of messages in his in-boxes across the Nets. Soon I fell into the rhythm of communicating as Coupon. It was soothing. While he began to orchestrate the overall presentation in the study, I tended to the hundreds of details. The Korean animators needed a tongue-lashing; imagine trying to use stock backgrounds in a Coupon presentation! Alexi, chief of the user group in St. Petersburg, had an interesting point about the spouse-acceptance factor; I summarized his drunken ramblings and shot the summary to Coupon. And that Zurich professor was still whining about historiocity! Was that even a word?

Hours later, I worked down to the textual interchanges. Fan mail from Duluth. Blue-sky futurizing with the MIT media lab. High-priced gossip about Microsoft's next move. He really was an incurable networker. If only he had built up a real staff and controlled his interactions, then he would never have needed an emulator. Yet that's how these employed people were: so fearful of losing control, so terrified of becoming one of the huge majority of the unemployed. The Net allowed them to be virtually everywhere all the time, so they worked until they stressed themselves to uselessness, shot themselves or hired an emulator to pose as them, first in the little things, gradually, in all things, even the most important . . . except presentations to the sponsors. After all, in the Net, you were who your crypto-key said you were.

And if your competition used class-B emulators, then naturally you wanted a class-A: some poor dupe, highly educated but otherwise unemployable, who was desperate enough after squandering his youth preparing for a nonexistent job that he was willing to market his very self. Cosmetic gene therapy. Bone splints and grafts, hormonal treatments so that he smelled like you. Voice, posture, walking, sitting lessons. Someone willing to break himself upon the rock of economic necessity and heal in bonds so that he could emulate you during those tiresome cocktail parties. Someone who could even service your spouse while you were busy preparing for your next professional triumph.

Someone very much like me. Coupon's emulator. Whose name was just a scrawl on a contract locked up in a Yokohama bank, but when I remembered it, it was Jack. Jack Quimby, who had been a poor British boy raised in America before he became an American tax refugee, or at least the shadow of such.

So I worked the queue until they were down to only one, which I thought had been garbled in transmission since I couldn't decode it. Then I noticed the routing codes. Someone in Yokohama was replying to a message Coupon had sent. Was he communicating with my service in a personal code unknown to me? Perhaps he was checking the details on the clause of the contract that dealt with the sudden and inexplicable disappearance of the emulator.

I wrapped the message in a shell and shipped it for decoding to a discreet black arts group in Taiwan. Checking the time, I saw that it was almost four in the morning. Coupon was still working in the study. Now he was drinking; the alcoholic phase of his work marathons typically lasted twenty hours. That would give us time enough to crash, sleep, work another day and then make the presentation.

And so to bed. My paradigm had ordered me to Cecilia, and so I went.

She was lying in the dark with her back to the door. I shut the stateroom door and undressed silently. The curtains were pulled back from the portals, which glowed as redly as demon's eyes. Beyond the glass, the ship's running light was firing the swirling mists of a heavy sea fog. The weather was worsening. As the ship was beginning to roll, I stumbled as I crawled into bed.

I could tell she was awake, although she didn't move. Settling into bed, I began to hope that I would spend a peaceful night.

"Don't you love me?" she asked, her voice small and vulnerable.

"Yes, of course," I said, but on whose behalf I was uncertain.

"Why do you treat me so horribly?"

"One word, Cecilia. Stress."

She turned, so that the red light outlined hazily the curve of her cheekbone. Her eyes were black pools in shadow, yet they gleamed.

"Why do you keep pushing yourself so? Is it worth it?"

"Sometimes . . ." I said, intending to say, *Sometimes I wonder,* but I pulled myself up short. It wouldn't do to negotiate the master into a position with which he was uncomfortable. How well I knew that his priorities were work first, second and third, with Cecilia somewhere in the double digits.

"Sometimes . . . it may not seem like it's worth it," I said, speaking now for him. "But it's what I do, Cecilia. It's who I am."

"Who are you?" she asked sharply. "Who are you really?"

In the darkness, it was impossible to read her eyes. I

couldn't tell at what level she was asking, so I answered at the level most comfortable for Coupon.

"Frederick Coupon, CEO of Bonus Enterprises."

"I don't think you know who you are," Cecilia said.

"Maybe not. All I see in the mirror is the reflection of a man's face. I don't see myself except when I look at something that I made and I know that no one else could possibly have made it."

"I don't think you exist outside of the things you make," she said. "I don't think you're for real."

"Yet somehow the reality of my money is convincing," I said. That was pure Coupon, but she had wounded me.

"I want a divorce," Cecilia said.

"A divorce will only get you two million yen, if you remember the terms of the prenuptial. I'll give you three million yen right now if you would kindly shut the fuck up."

Slowly Cecilia raised herself to sit. I wondered if she had a butcher knife among the bedclothes. How unfair it would be to die as Coupon!

"That was good," she said. "But that was just getting too much like Coupon."

There followed a profound silence.

"Excuse me?" I said.

"You do him really well," she said. "It bothers me that you're making it harder to tell the difference. I always liked you better. I don't think I should have to put up with two Coupons. A tag team of jerks. I've only been putting up with him for so long because I liked you. Don't you get like him."

"I am him," I offered feebly.

"I think you're getting confused on the issue," Cecilia said. "But you are definitely not him."

"Who am I, then?" I asked.

"I've been wondering that for two years," Cecilia said. "Who are you?"

"I don't know."

"Who did you use to be?"

"Jack. Jack Quimby."

The lights flared. Coupon stormed into the room.

"That's just great!" he shouted. "You're fired, you idiot."

"No, you can't fire him," Cecilia said.

"What! He's fired!"

"It's going to cost you half of everything, then, Fred," Cecilia said. We both winced. Nobody called us Fred, just as nobody pronounced Coupon with the accent on the first syllable, at least not after the first transgression. "Because the prenuptial is void in the case of infidelity."

"But I've been faithful to you!"

"No you haven't," Cecilia said coldly. "When you sent this employee, this double, into our bed, you violated the monogamy of our marriage. Any judge would see it that way."

Coupon staggered. It was obvious that he saw the piercing, twisted truth of Cecilia's logic.

"And so until you're willing to give me half of everything you own," Cecilia said, "I'm calling the shots. And I don't want to see you anymore. And I want Jack here to . . . protect me. I feel threatened right now. Go away because I feel the deep urge for him to protect me."

Coupon's jaw sagged. He took a step forward, then one back, then he turned and fled from the stateroom.

Cecilia hugged me from the rear, her arms warm around my shoulders, her breasts pressed against my back.

"You do want to protect me, don't you, Jack?"

"If you'll protect me," I answered.

"Deal."

I collapsed into her arms. We made urgent love. She seemed to delight in murmuring my name, "Jack" and hearing her murmur it and then shout it and finally scream it was a perfect tonic for my wounded soul. When we were done, I felt more like my own self than I had in years.

"Who are you?" she asked, as I lay, head on her breast as she stroked my hair.

"An emulator. Universal—"

"No, who are you *really?*"

"Just . . . a fool who refused to be useless," I said. "I studied and trained for so many years. I always felt certain that I would be the one good enough to get a job. The months passed and then the years. And I found out that there were millions of men like me. Do you know what that's like?"

"Yes," Cecilia said softly, her voice deep with emotion.

"And I am good," I said. "He never would have gotten the Miami contract without me. Now I don't know what we're going to do. We can't go on like this, can we?"

"Oh no," Cecilia said. "He'll kill us first."

My mind resisted the thought, but I knew that she was right.

"We'll have to go away," I said.

"Oh no," she said. "*He'll* have to go away. Do you really think that he would let us live, knowing that he's committed fraud thousands of times? His name is his reputation and his reputation is his business. We could ruin him. He'll never allow us to have that power over him."

"Why hasn't he . . ."

"He's thinking about it now," she said. "You know he is. He's been watching us make love and now he's thinking about what we're saying. He's working it out at just about the speed that you're working it out."

"So?"

"So I think you had better start looking for a weapon."

"But—"

"If you want to save yourself, you have to do it, Jack. So do it."

"And what about you?"

"You're more his match, Jack. Go."

Slowly I rose from the bed.

We had no weapons on board. Coupon didn't trust them. On legs as nerveless as wood, I stumbled toward the galley for a butcher knife, but then I realized that was where he would go. Since the study was closer to the galley than the master stateroom, he would beat me there. Looking for a weapon, I would only find him there, armed. So I turned and hurried aft and then downward toward the engine room, where surely there would be a heavy tool such as a crowbar.

Then I stopped short. Would he second-guess me and go to the engine room instead of the galley?

For a long moment I stood swaying. The deck was increasingly unsteady as the weather topside grew nastier. It seemed that he was reading my thoughts and countering each impulse. Although I couldn't see him, our knowledge of each other seemed like a long tunnel of mirror images, each image slightly smaller, less precise and askew.

His almost perfect possession of my own mind enraged me. "I am *not* you!" I shouted.

Downward I hustled. I burst into the engine room, where I found emergency equipment secured to the wall. I had my choice of a sledgehammer, a fireman's ax and a crowbar. I chose the crowbar.

Back up the ladders I hurried. Coupon was cowering in the galley, no doubt, clutching the butcher knife—

A sharp sudden agony pierced my back. Reflexively I wheeled, striking out with the crowbar. Through a haze of pain that reddened my sight, I saw the tip of the crowbar clip the temple of the head identical to mine. The lucky blow stunned him. I raised the crowbar again, but it seemed we both were down. I remember wanting to strike, but I don't remember striking.

Hours later, I rose once again to consciousness. I was face-down in a postoperative sling so all I could see was a communications station moving, while my own body hung unmoved. The screen fired into the image of Cecilia's face.

"Jack," she said. "You're going to be all right."

"I feel fine," I said. "I feel wonderful."

"You're heavily sedated," she said. "The surgery system

had to fuse your left kidney and repair some nerve and muscle damage. It'll take you a few weeks. But you'll be fine."

"Yes. Yes. And . . ."

"He's gone," she said. "You left quite a mess, but it's been cleaned up. I'm wiping the janitor system's memory now."

"He's . . . in the ocean?"

"Under the ocean. Chained to ten kilogram free weights."

"Gone."

"Never talk about him again," Cecilia said. "Now, are you up to making the Morita pitch in eight hours?"

"Possibly."

"It would be better. Failing to make the pitch would be suspicious."

"I know. And it's such an important pitch. Let me check how far he got in pulling the pieces together."

"Give me the cryptokey, darling, and I'll help."

"It's nothing you can help me with."

"Yes I can," Cecilia said. "I'm an emulator too."

Her naked statement stunned me. For a long moment, I stared into the image of her eyes, finally beginning to see the truth.

"On whose behalf?" I asked.

"I don't know," she said. "Either she put me in place because she wanted to escape from him, or he put me here because he killed her. It's a double blind contract. I don't know. I think she's dead. But I'm trained, Jack. I can help you. Give me the cryptokey, please."

"No," I said.

"Why not? Don't you trust me?"

"Trust you? I don't even know who you are."

"I'm the same as you, Jack. The same. Just a poor girl who didn't want to be useless. You're hurt, darling. Let me help."

Despite my medicated state, I was beginning to feel

increasingly uncomfortable with the situation. Having been stabbed in the back hours previously did nothing to raise my confidence in human nature. Strangely, I felt betrayed, because while I had made love to Cecilia as Coupon, this stranger had made love to me as Cecilia.

And why was she telecommunicating? Why wasn't she at my side?

"Where are you?" I asked.

"In the communications center," she said. "I've got to overwrite the memory of fifteen different systems. Some of them are cryptolocked with your code . . . with Coupon's code, Jack. I've got to have it."

"I'll clean them out later," I said. "There's time."

"You don't trust me!" she wailed.

"No," I said. "But maybe I will later. Give me time."

Cecilia's image stared at me. For a moment she seemed to have frozen.

"All right," she said. "That's fair. Let's just get through this bloody presentation."

"There's a lot of work ahead of us," I said.

"I'll help you, Jack."

"I need your help . . . Cecilia."

"I'm Luiza," she said. "Luiza Johnson."

"Luiza."

"Call me Cecilia, though, Ja—Fred. Cecilia. Otherwise we'll have to keep rewriting over the memories. And someday you might slip in front another person."

"Cecilia."

"Yes, Fred."

"Frederick."

"Of course. Frederick."

We muddled through the presentation. I healed well enough that I was able to attend the necessary meetings in

St. Petersburg. At the first opportunity, however, Cecilia and I escaped in the *Sephora*. We set course for the lesser Antilles. By the time we anchored off the Ochos Rios recreational complex, Cecilia's and my relationship had taken its new, more loving form. To all the world, it seemed as if Mr. and Mrs. Frederick Coupon had undergone a marital renaissance.

We grew into a good team. Besides her emulator training, Cecilia refused to talk about her past. For my own part, it was difficult to try to explain who or what a Jack Quimby was or once had been. Our work together seemed the most fruitful topic of conversation. Eventually I came to believe that a romantic relationship is a complex of behaviors and chemistries, with identity having little to do with it. Did it really matter? Men had loved women throughout history, but what man had ever claimed to know them?

Yet I was beginning to trust her enough that I was contemplating sharing Coupon's cryptokey. As luck would have it, I was on the cusp of deciding to do so, the day the message came in from the Taiwanese black arts enterprise.

Unlocking the code with Coupon's cryptokey, I read the following message:

> Most excellent Mr. Coupon,
>
> We of Red Dragon Semantic Arts have been honored with your patronage. We regret the tardiness of our delivery, but since the outer message code was irreducible, we had to resort to special actions to obtain the key. Decoding the inner code, of course, relies on your own private key.
>
> We have billed the indicated account by 50 MYen. May we suggest that you exercise the utmost delicacy in your further dealings with Universal Emulators. We look forward to the next opportunity to be of service.

I tapped in the two large prime numbers which consti-
tuted Coupon's private key. The original text then became
sense:

────────── start transmission ──────────

Special Emulator Reichmanf,

Your most recent request to allow Emulator
Quimby to relieve you on station is most emphati-
cally denied. The current team in place is highly
functional. We will not entertain any more communications on this issue. You will continue to perform your duties as stipulated by your indenture
contract, which will not be up for renegotiation for
another three years, six months, eleven days.
        Find comfort in the knowledge that your private
account now totals over 39 trillion yen.

────────── end transmission ──────────

I studied the message for long minutes, unable to comprehend. Finally, when I did understand, I wondered if
Emulator Reichmanf had taken the place of the original
Coupon, or had he merely assumed the place of an n–1 generation copy?

And who was I? Nothing about me seemed so important
as the fact that I was the only man in the world who held
Coupon's private cryptokey. Reichmanf had shared it with
me and it had been the death of him.

Out on the sponson, staring at the hypocritical blue face
of the tropical ocean, I realized down to my grafted bones
who I was.

The bearer of Coupon's cryptokey. In other words,
Coupon.

Fair Verona

R. GARCIA Y ROBERTSON

R. Garcia y Robertson is the author of a fantasy, *The Spiral Dance;* several SF novels, including *The Virgin and the Dinosaur;* and the recent historical novel (but only in the sense that *Berger's Little Big Man* is an historical novel—it has a contemporary sensibility) *American Woman.* His stories have appeared in *Fantasy & Science Fiction* and *Asimov's* with some regularity for the last ten years and are characterized by their broad range of concerns, stylistic sophistication, and attention to historical detail. Garcia has tended toward time travel or historical settings both for his fantasy and SF stories. His fiction has been underappreciated since the small flash of critical and peer attention garnered by his first novel, *The Spiral Dance.* This story, from *Asimov's,* shows all his strengths, but is particularly fine at plot surprises. This is the work of a fully accomplished writer.

"In fair Verona, where we lay our scene . . ."
—*Romeo and Juliet,* Prologue

THE NOBLE DOG

Antonio first saw her in the night, at Carnival on the Via Cappello. He had just staggered out of the inn that came to be called the Casa di Giulietta, because of its marble balcony. A surge of revelers filled the torchlit street. Harlequins, lace doves, street minstrels, and drunken louts—laughing, dancing, singing, and colliding, tripping over cobbles, falling into fountains, and pissing on the bonfires.

Standing under "Romeo's" balcony, with enough good red bardolino aboard to float a boat, Antonio wondered what mischief he meant to get into. Should it be a woman, or a fight? Or maybe both. Then he saw her. His heavenly vision. Lady Love in a gold lace mask and a wide-sleeved gown. She turned, winked, blew a kiss, then was gone, whirled away by the throng.

Without taking fuddled eyes off the crowd, he grabbed Proteus, his manservant, who was busy tipping the innkeeper. "Did you see her? Who was she?"

Proteus pushed a silver groat on the barkeep, then turned to his drunken master. "Who was who?"

"The woman in the gold mask. She was shockingly beautiful."

Proteus looked askance at the crowd. No woman seemed to stand out. "How could you tell? She was masked."

"I can tell," Antonio insisted. He had seen it in the smile above her swan white throat. "You can tell a beautiful woman by her walk. By the way she carries her head."

"Doubtless." Proteus slipped a spare bottle of bardolino into his jacket. The way tonight was headed, his master would be brought to bed soused. Or not at all.

"She has to be the most beautiful lady at Carnival. I'd stake my life on it. My fortune. My estates. Even my slim hope of seeing salvation."

"I have nothing to match against that," Proteus admitted.

That she was a lady was obvious. Her gown, her gold-linked belt, her wig powdered with gold dust—were all beyond the means of Verona's most industrious courtesans. Plunging cloth-of-gold décolletage had shown off sculpted neck and shoulders, and round firm breasts, right down to the nipples. But Antonio would have been wild for her if she had worn sack cloth. Or a nun's habit.

Pushing Proteus aside, he lurched into the street. The crowd parted smartly for him. Despite his black-feathered mask, none could mistake the prince's nephew in tight hose and pearl-studded jacket, sword at his side and spurred like a Tartar.

He looked up toward the Piazza Erbe, the herb market atop the ancient forum. Nothing. Turning toward the Via Stella, he spotted a flash of gold in the throng. Antonio took off, spurs striking sparks on the pavement.

The crowd parted even more promptly. Antonio Cansignorio della Scala was so used to such deference, he barely noticed. Everything in Verona seemed arranged for his pleasure. He was the Noble Dog. Tall and handsome, an accomplished troubadour, a skilled condottiere, a passable silversmith, and a good Catholic—but an enemy of the Pope. Most of all, he had the good luck to be a nephew to Cangrande della Scala, the "Big Dog" who lorded over Verona. Directly descended from Mastino I, the Mastiff, founder of the Scaligeri dynasty.

The woman in gold turned a corner, headed for the Piazza Bra. Antonio dashed down a side street, cutting her off.

But when he got to the Piazza, he could not pick her out of the costumed crowd. Had he lost her? He doubled back up an alley. There was only one other way she could have gone. Ahead loomed the Arena, Verona's ancient Roman amphitheater. Second only to the Colosseum in size, its colonnade blocked off the entire eastern side of the Piazza Bra. He had her trapped. Unless she hid in the Arena itself, hardly the place for a woman alone on Carnival Night.

Then he spotted her. Beyond the mouth of the alley, framed in one of the Arena's dark cavernous archways, a gold icon in a black niche. He called to her to stop. She turned to look back, standing still and composed. Waiting. She had the good sense to know when the game had gone far enough.

Two costumed men stepped out of the gloom at the head of the alley, coming between her and him. One wore a jester's belled cap and floppy straw boots. The other was tall, wearing the black cloak and white bird-faced mask of a plague doctor. Both had swords at their sides.

The Jester called out, "Montague or Capulet?" The worst words any honest Veronan could hear in a dark alley.

"Neither, swine!" Antonio swore, drawing sword and dagger, not for an instant thinking that this was some honest mistake. Masked or not, all men knew the prince's nephew. Nor would it be the first time that a street feud was used to cover murder. "A thousand pardons, we thought the man was a Montague."

And Antonio had enemies aplenty. Mighty enemies. A godawful long list. Headed by Pope Clement V, Christ's Vicar on Earth, and lapdog of Philip the Fair. Guelfs in general hated him. So did the Visconti vipers of Milan. Then there were the French, a blasphemous nation of traitors and ingrates. Whole hosts of people would be happy to hear that the Noble Dog had died in some dark alley. Some would even take the trouble to arrange it.

But it was easier wished than done. He glanced past the two men to the woman. She took no active part, standing motionless, lips parted in horror—or perhaps excitement; her mask made it impossible to tell.

"Drop your sword," the Jester shouted. "We only mean to talk."

"Just a word," the Plague Doctor assured him.

"My word is 'Begone,'" Antonio retorted. "Draw if you be men!"

The Jester drew blade, saying over his shoulder, "Back me."

Antonio sprang to meet him. Swords clashed and grated. Bells rang on the Jester's cap as he backpedaled, parrying briskly. Fighting drunk, and full of anger, Antonio easily forced them back. Too easily. Both men swiftly gave ground. Suddenly the Jester slipped in his floppy boots, going down on one knee with a shriek of fear.

Piss-poor acting. Instead of trying to get in past the man's guard, Antonio spun about, putting his back to a wall.

A third assassin, dressed like a Saracen in a cloak and turban, leaped from a doorway. His scimitar sliced empty air, where the Noble Dog had been.

The trap had been obvious even to the half-drunk Antonio. Two men falling back before one, while the ringing bells on the Jester's cap covered the third attacker's footsteps. Antonio had seen it done before. And better.

He slashed at the Saracen's throat, feeling the solid jar of contact down the length of his sword arm. Sure of his kill, the Saracen never had time to parry. Blood sprayed the width of the alley. The assassin crumpled, his head hanging sideways.

Antonio congratulated himself. Not bad for fighting on a head full of bardolino! It was two to one again.

The Jester scrambled back to his feet, cursing. He called to the Doctor, "Come, man, make worm's meat out of him!"

The Jester met Antonio's drunken attack, while the black-cloaked Plague Doctor tried to get at the Noble Dog's left side. Cool professionals, they acted unfazed by the death of their comrade. But the narrowness of the alley fought for Antonio, keeping them from both getting to him at once.

Abandoning his caution, the Jester pressed Antonio hard, trying to create an opening for the Doctor. Swords met, rasped, struck sparks. Antonio parried with his dagger, thrusting past the Jester's guard. His point pierced the Jester's jacket, which was sewn with playing cards. Striking metal, the Noble Dog's blade bounced back. There was steel hidden beneath the card-sewn jacket. The Jester's boldness was explained—his ringing Fool's Cap hid the clang of armor.

Grinning, the Jester came on, bolder than ever, hacking and slashing. He did not fear a body blow, and probably had an armored codpiece to boot.

Antonio feinted low, as though going for the groin. The Jester rose on his toes, aiming a downward slash. Antonio again parried high with the dagger—this time aiming his sword thrust beneath the upraised arm. His grandfather had been on the losing side at Benevento, and never tired of telling how King Manfred's German mercenaries were cut down by French knights striking *à l'estoc* into the armpit. His point slid through the Jester's sleeve, and over the cuirass.

The Belled Fool folded up, staggered, and fell gasping against the Doctor. He had the impudence to take Antonio's blade with him, its point tangled in the puffed sleeve and the top of his lung.

Letting go of the sword, Antonio sprang forward with just his dagger, staking everything on a single drunken rush. Pushing the dying Jester aside, the bird-faced Doctor aimed a sweeping blow at Antonio. Too late. The Noble Dog got inside his guard, grabbing the Doctor's right wrist, slamming him against the alley wall. His dagger at the man's throat, he hissed, "Yield."

Helpless, the Doctor let his blade fall. His white bird mask looked blankly at the Noble Dog.

Antonio glanced up to see the woman disappear into the Arena archway. Damn. Missed her again. The man beneath him would die for that. But first . . .

Keeping the dagger clenched in his hand, he grabbed the beak of the white bird-mask, wrenching it back. Finding the face beneath irritatingly familiar. He *knew* this man from somewhere. "Why?" Antonio demanded. "Why dare to accost me?"

Amazingly calm, despite sure death at his throat, the man managed a devil-may-care smirk. "There is a call on your service. Clients are coming down the Beanstalk."

HEARTBREAK HOTEL

Tearing off his headset, Toni stared at the 3V deck resting on his knees. Naked thighs shone slick and white in the artificial light. Disoriented and drenched in sweat, it took time for the truth to sink in. Those were *his* thighs. He was no longer in Verona. No longer the Noble Dog. No longer wearing pants.

An audio beeper indicated incoming messages. Toni ignored it, still fixed on Verona. Who was she? Had she really gone into the Arena?

Beeps increased in volume, dragging him into the here-and-now, badgering him with incoming calls. He hated that. Hated being jerked out of the program. Hell, he hated being out of the program *period*. Hated being anywhere but Verona.

Shutting down the beeper, he stared at the stained white ceiling of the sanitary unit. Sitting bare-assed in a dingy portable toilet, fed by a glucose drip, was a piss-poor substitute for being a prince's nephew at Carnival time. Or at any time.

Setting aside the 3V deck, he climbed up on his exercise bike, thankful that Ariel's pull was only .5g. Any more, and he never would have made it off the toilet seat. Toni found physical exercise boring—but most realtime activities were essentially tedious. So Toni put his tedium to maximum use, telling Proteus—Programmed Techno-Environmental Utilization Service—"Give me the priority messages."

The housekeeping program obeyed. Grunting atop the bike, Toni responded to his calls as best he could.

"Check. Hunting party headed down the Beanstalk."

"Yes. Of course I still think of you."

"Fuck off."

"2100 tomorrow—at the soonest."

"Will call back."

"Shit. OK, OK, I'll get to it."

When he could not take any more, he told Proteus, "Dump everything over forty hours old. Hold the rest."

Toni got down off the bike, inserted the glucose drip, and set the deck on his lap, tempted to return at once to Verona. He had to follow her into the Arena. And . . .

His hand hovered above the deck, fingers itching to hit VERONA. He hit DRAGON HUNT instead.

Instantly, Toni was outside—standing at the base of the Beanstalk, looking out over Freeport with infrared eyes. Geodomes and apartment blocks glowed softly from internal heat. Powered filters showed as bright firefly streaks. Pair-a-Dice Beanstalk towered above him, piercing the dawn sky, connecting Freeport to the Pair-a-Dice geosync platform thousands of klicks overhead. The topless stalk cast a thin shadow onto the cloud plain, a dark razor-straight line disappearing in the direction of Nightside.

It was early morning. Prospero had just cut a notch in the cloud plain surrounding Mt. Beanstalk. Another long drawn-out day had begun. This far into the Twilight Belt, it was always dawn or dusk. Ariel kept the same face turned toward her primary, Prospero. Orbital libration produced a slow-mode version of day and night; long cool mornings alternating with shady twilights. Prospero never climbed too high in the sky, nor sank too low below the horizon.

A Transgalactic Liner was in on Pair-a-Dice. Tourists

jammed the slidewalk, wearing tinsel wigs and chrome yellow pompoms—laughing, joking, and generally embarrassing themselves. Toni was not in the mood to be amused by rich fools with nothing to do. And he could have done something about it. At the moment he was three meters tall, standing head and shoulders above the crowd on duraluminum legs. His metal arms—all four of them—could have scythed through the throng, braining the lot of them without so much as raising a sweat. Plasti-metal does not perspire.

But he had better things to do. Better as in *paid*. Otherwise, he would have deleted Freeport completely, and gone straight to Verona. He flipped off the infrared filters. The last time he had inhabited the cyborg body had been for a Nightside hunt. Here, he did not need them.

Ali, Harpo, and Doc came striding up. They too were three meters tall, with plasti-metal bodies. Except for Ali, who was a head shorter, nonchalantly carrying his cyborg cranium tucked under his arm. The helmeted head, with its radar dome, sonar receptors, and binocular lenses, looked up at Toni. "Draw if you be men," the head dared him. Its speak-box exactly mimicked the Noble Dog's accent.

Toni glared at the talking head.

"Or we'll make worm's meat of you," Harpo added.

"Shut up with the Shakespeare," Toni growled. In Verona, he could have had the three of them flayed.

The cyborgs laughed. In Ali's case, the chuckle came from under his arm. He hefted the head and screwed it—still laughing—onto his shoulders. "We had to come for you."

"But not just then. I was *this* close." Toni lifted his upper left hand, holding two heavy gauntleted fingers a micron apart.

"Gives you a reason to go back." Harpo's attempt at a grin looked like the front end of a ground car. As if Toni *needed* a reason. As if any of them did. They all had their private Veronas. They enjoyed jerking him out merely because misery loves company. He would get them back.

A soft subsonic buzz warned that their Pair-a-Dice capsule had arrived. The pressure door at the base of the Beanstalk began to disgorge luggage. Hand-tooled leather flight bags. Fancy holographic camcorders. Field shelters. Night glasses and freeze-dried gourmet rations. An autobar and a silver tea-service. Along with sufficient ancillary equipment to start a small colony.

Port workers in mint-green candy-striped coveralls attacked the mountain of belongings, loading them onto gravity sleds, working briskly, but without enthusiasm. They wore electronic shackles and shock collars. Most were government employees—addicts, vagrants, debtors, and moral degenerates, working off their debt to society.

Then came the hunting party. First the Client, flanked by a pair of SuperChimp bodyguards, looking sure of himself and overly successful. He had a squat bald head, cropped ears, beady eyes, pink jowls, several chins, and no noticeable neck. His lace-trimmed purple doublet and parti-colored hose merely made him look more grotesque, like Quasimodo in a clown suit. Anyone who could easily afford biosculpt, but still looked that ugly, obviously did not give a damn what an age of artificial beauty thought. People had to take him as he was, or not at all. His walk matched his looks, brusque and self-absorbed. Oblivious to underlings scurrying around him, he talked through an open comlink to someone in orbit. Toni told Proteus to put a name to the face.

Proteus obeyed—(*Alexander Gracchus,* CEO of Transgalactic for the Deneb Kaitos, offices in Mt. Zion in Mt. Zion system, on Aesir III and Vanir II in the Twin Systems, and on Pair-a-Dice in Prospero System. Personal residences: Baldar, main moon of Aesir VII, Sylvan Hall on Vanir II, and a lodge in the Quartz Peaks Hunt Preserve on Aesir III. Three wives, five children, 2s. 3d.)

The rest of the party looked tiny compared to Gracchus and his hulking bodyguards. Two of them were women. Proteus identified them as Gracchus's younger wives—Selene and Pandora. Selene, older and senior, had blond hair and fair skin dusted with silver. She wore a feathered, flaring gown better suited to a ballet than a Wyvyrn hunt. Pandora, the junior wife, was more sensibly dressed, wearing thigh-length boots and a leopard-skin leotard. Alert and self-reliant, she had a friendly, curious face framed by untidy lacquered hair trimmed to ten-centimeter spikes. Like the stevedores, she wore an electronic slave collar—only diamond-studded.

Pandora immediately took charge of the baggage, helping to stow it aboard a big aerial barge docked by the Beanstalk. Working briskly and cheerfully in her spiked hair and leotards, she encouraged the convict labor by passing out stim tabs from a pillbox on her wrist. Toni lumbered over to lend his four mechanical hands. If he could not be in Verona, he meant to be doing *something*.

The baggage pile vanished into the barge, and Pandora (whose name meant "All-giving") emptied the contents of her pillbox, passing out extra tabs as rewards. A guard wearing a purple skin-suit with broad white vertical stripes strolled over, one hand resting on a holstered riot pistol. He signed for her to stop. Without saying a word, Pandora whipped a miniature chrome holocam off her wrist. Smiling, she handed the holocam to the guard, who pocketed it, turning his back on the proceedings.

One port worker refused the pills. An older woman with graying hair, she glared at Pandora, saying that she did not need "hoppers." Whatever crime the woman had to work off probably didn't come close to passing out drugs to convicts. Or bribing a trustee.

Pandora deftly handed her tabs to the next guy. Reaching up, she removed two sapphire chip earrings, putting them in the older woman's palm. "No one should work for nothing."

The woman gaped at the tiny blue stones, then swiftly closed her hand before the guard could see.

Pandora smiled ruefully up at Toni. What could you give a three-meter-tall cyborg? "Maybe later," she said, and shrugged. Toni did not answer—totally uninterested in whatever she had to offer.

The hunting party trooped aboard the barge and lifted off into dawn light. Freeport and Pair-a-Dice Beanstalk fell behind them. The barge was big, resting on huge rounded helium tanks, with a wide observation deck forward, and a jet-powered hover car sitting on the fantail. Toni stood on the foredeck, staring out across tens of thousands of square klicks of dazzling white cloud plain, wishing he were in Verona. Beneath him, below the cloud plain, lay Ariel's surface, a pressure-cooked caldron of searing hot winds and greenhouse gases. Partial terraforming had given the planet a rudimentary biosphere based on mountaintops and high plateaus. Incompletely habitable, Ariel was very much a work in progress.

Telescopic vision let Toni make out their destination, the ringwall of Elysium poking through the sea of clouds. A massive volcanic caldera rearing up into the biosphere, Elysium formed a huge natural amphitheater more than a hundred klicks across, a great green bowl of misty jungle, surrounded by stadium-like walls.

Seeing Elysium ringwall reminded Toni of the Arena in Verona—the ancient Roman amphitheater that the Lady-in-Gold had vanished into. Seized by the image, his mind immediately tried to catapult back to Verona. Toni fought the impulse. Such spontaneous flashbacks terrified him. They were symptoms of acute mental feedback, severe glitches in his neural circuitry. A hazard Toni would rather not think about—and one he had to hide from his employers at all cost. If Dragon Hunt suspected him of having cybernetic seizures, they would yank his program—stranding him in real time.

The jolt of landing helped jerk Toni back to reality. The landing zone sat on a cleared semicircle blasted out of the crater rim, big enough for the barge and a base camp. A trail sloped downward, choked with cycad fronds and tall bamboo. Vines and creepers kept Toni from seeing more than a couple of meters into the tangle.

Happy to be back in control of his augmented psyche, Toni helped with the unloading, piling safari supplies about the landing site. Turning up his hypersensitive hearing, he tried to tell if the Hunt Guide had noticed his lapse.

". . . but with the brain shot the angle of entry varies too much to rely on surface features. Don't count on aiming between the eye cells. Or above the mandibles." The Guide was giving a short lecture on the best way to scramble a Wyvyrn's neuroanatomy.

"What *should* I aim for?" Gracchus asked. His weapon hung loosely from one huge hand—a long gray 30mm recoilless minicannon, with a padded shoulder rest and a broad ugly snout.

"Imagine a line running between the bases of the primary antennae. The Wyvyrn's cerebrum is a barbell-shaped pair of ganglia midway along that line."

Gracchus grunted. "Sounds tricky."

"It is," the Guide admitted, "unless you're close enough to tickle its tonsils. You might want to try for heart number one. It is located in the center of the second segment back from the head. . . ."

Fine. The Guide was too busy bullshitting Gracchus to care what his cyborgs were up to. It surprised Toni that someone so obviously successful as Gracchus could fall for such a shuck. But the allure—and expense—of a *real* hunt, with *real* prey, was too much for folks with more money than sense.

Toni had a true 3V addict's contempt for "real" adventure. For a tiny fraction of the cost, Gracchus could be a 3V Beowulf, or Siegfried. He could kill Fafnir, battle sea serpents, and fuck Brunhilde, all without leaving home. But that would be too much like the plebs.

Toni looked about, seeing the impassive Chimp bodyguards. And Gracchus's two wives, now drenched in sweat.

Selene's fairy gown was drooping, and smeared with silver dust. Pandora looked cooler in her leopard-spotted leotard. Neither dared to complain.

Why haul everyone through this? Dragging folks about in the flesh—just to show that Gracchus had the power and money to make it happen. The Guide's little bullshit lecture made no mention of *collared* Wyvyrn. Wyvyrn were flying megafauna from Beta Hydri IV. Huge hundred-meter, semi-intelligent, flying omnivores, with less reason to tangle with humans than lions had. Humans didn't taste good to them— and normally they had sense enough to stay out of their way. To get them to cooperate, Dragon Hunt went into Elysium ahead of time and collared a couple of prime specimens. Once collared, the Wyvyrn could be made to stick around. Even attack. Without control collars, Gracchus would be lucky to *see* a Wyvyrn, much less get off a "brain" shot.

It was all as phony as 3V. Only less comfortable, and a damned sight more expensive. Which, alas, was the point. So long as Toni was paid, he kept his complaints to himself. Besides, who cared what a cyborg thought?

The Guide signaled with his hand, and they set out. Harpo went ahead, hacking out a path. Toni lifted a field shelter, ration case, and microstove, along with a hundred-odd kilos of baggage and ammunition, falling in behind Doc.

The first couple of klicks were dense brush, a claustrophobic pile of creepers and wrist-thick bamboo, crisscrossed with lianas and strangler vine. Toni kept station a dozen meters behind Doc, turning when he turned.

Without warning, the tangle suddenly opened overhead. Toni strode into a cool cathedral forest of kilometer-tall trees festooned with great red perfumed blossoms. Slanting Prospero light glittered off the wings of giant insects flitting from flower to flower. A forest imp flew by, a tiny pale humanoid with huge gold eyes, riding on the back of a two-meter dragonfly.

Toni kept his optical sensors aimed low, trying not to

tread on the humans hidden by tall ferns and elephant grass.
Ten more hours of slogging and he could go back to Verona.

> *"Myself was from Verona banished*
> *For practicing to steal away a lady . . ."*
> —*Two Gentlemen of Verona*, Act IV

VIA VENEZIA

At first light, the morning after Carnival, the Noble Dog rode
across the *Ponte Romano*, the ancient stone bridge over the
Adige, leaving Verona. Green suburban hills rose up on the
far bank, dotted with palaces, pleasure gardens, churches, and
Roman ruins. After him came Proteus with the led horses.

Antonio now had a name to put behind the mask—a
name, but not a face. His Lady-in-Gold was Silvia Lucetta
Visconti, the daughter of Matteo Visconti, exiled Lord of
Milan, reputed to be the most beautiful woman in northern
Italy. Proteus had come up with this news, along with word
that she had taken the road east toward Padua and Venice.
Antonio's manservant was a wizard at ferreting out information—part Gypsy and part thief—never failing to turn up a
useful fact. Always anticipating Antonio's wants, and seeing
to his needs.

That he had still not seen Silvia made her all the more
attractive. Every woman Antonio knew paled in comparison
to how he pictured her—no flesh-and-blood female could
hope to compete with his imagination.

This obsession led to caustic words between Antonio and
his uncle Cangrande, the Big Dog—sparking a family argument that rebounded off the romanesque arches of Cangrande's audience chamber, keeping servants and mistresses
awake well after midnight. The Lord of Verona had an
absurdly cherubic face, pierced by a pair of sharp compelling
eyes. Dismissing Silvia Visconti out of hand, he reminded his

nephew of the "bad blood in that family." (The Vipers of
Milan were infamous for savage despotism, murderous cruelty, and engaging in all manner of sexual manias—in addi-
tion to giving good government and encouraging the arts.)
How could the daughter of an exiled enemy be a fit object for
marriage?

"Who said I mean to marry her?" Antonio retorted.
Being obsessed with a woman was a poor excuse to wed her.

The Big Dog was not mollified. "What if you get her in
pup? The bitch could be bait. I do not want any half-Visconti
bastards running about, hoping to be put up as heirs to
Verona."

Down-and-out though they were, it remained the
Visconti dream to hold all the Piedmont, plus as much of
Tuscany and the Veneto as they could grab. Even in exile,
they were far too cozy with the Emperor—and would happily use Verona as a step to regain Milan. "Have no more
to do with her," Cangrande commanded, his habitual inane
grin masking a ruthless will no sane nephew dared brook.

Bidding the Big Dog a stormy farewell, Antonio stalked
off to do as he pleased. His obsession might be unhealthy—
but by God it was *his*. If he wanted a horse or a dog, he got
it. Women were at least as important. True, he did feel a little like that old fool Dante, who still mooned over some
woman he had glimpsed in the market decades ago. But at
least Antonio was going *after* his Silvia, not locking himself
away in a borrowed room, wasting paper on some impossible *terza rima* epic to her.

On the east bank of the Adige, he passed the *Teatro
Romano*, the ancient open-air theater, and the old cathedral of Santo Stefano with its great octagonal red-brick
campanile. There he paused, treating himself to a last view
of the city, wreathed in breakfast smoke and still recovering
from Carnival. Then he was off, riding through the *Porta
Vescovo*, with Proteus at his heels.

The *Corso Venezia,* the dusty via Venezia that led to
Padua, Venice, and the sea, rolled through green pastures cut
with stone fences. Antonio stopped only once near Soave to
rest the horses, and put in a supply of light, dry white wine.
On his left, vineyards came right down to the road. In the
hazy distance he could see the Alps.

At the bridge over the Alpone, he caught up with her. Just
past the fork that leads to Belfiore, Antonio spotted the
woman a few hundred paces ahead, riding a pretty black
mare. Even at a distance, there was no mistaking her. She
wore the same lace mask, and her gold-link belt glittered in
the sun. Besides, by now Antonio knew her style. There was
not another young noblewoman in North Italy likely to be
riding alone on the Venice road. She gave him a single over-
the-shoulder glance, then, with a flick of her mare's tail, she
made for the bridge.

Giving spur, Antonio set off at a gallop. Mounted on a
blooded stallion with twice the strength of her little mare, he
felt certain that he had her. As they neared the bridge, he cut
her lead to two hundred paces. Then one hundred. Then fifty.
Then twenty. He could see the Visconti serpents on her horse
cloth.

But by then they were into the bridge traffic, peddlers
pushing handcarts, and a big hay wagon half-blocking the
ramp. Peasants with their bundles leaped into the ditches
rather than be trampled, but the carts could not be brushed
aside. Antonio had to rein in. Weaving deftly between the
obstacles, she beat him to the bridge, and, as soon as she was
over it, she picked up speed, opening the gap.

Cursing like a *condottiere,* Antonio forced his way
through the throng with the flat of his sword. On the far side
of the bridge was the town of Villanova, where the road
forked. The right fork ran south along the Alpone through the
marshes to Arcola. The left fork kept on along the line of the
Chiampo, headed for Venice and Padua.

Again, Antonio had to rein in. There was no telling which fork she had taken. But she was headstrong and willful, not likely to change direction just because a man was after her. So he put spurs to his stallion and took the left fork, keeping to the Via Venezia.

Beyond San Bonifacio, he caught sight of her. Giving a great hurrah, he redoubled his efforts. But by now, his horse was blown. Her mare must have been better rested—as well as carrying a lighter load. Getting her second wind, the filly easily kept her distance, daring his stallion to catch her. The chase slowed from a gallop, to a canter, then finally to a tired trot, with his winded mount unable to gain on her mare.

Antonio heard a hail behind him. Twisting in his saddle, he turned to see Proteus pounding up behind him with the led horses—just when he needed the man most.

Proteus had a spare mount already saddled and ready to ride. Tired as he was, Antonio did not bother to rein in. Instead, Proteus brought the fresh horse up alongside his, and Antonio leaped aboard his new mount without breaking stride, shouting his thanks. Proteus handed him the horse's reins, then dropped back, taking charge of the winded stallion. He was one manservant in a million—worth the price of a duchy!

Surging forward on his fresh mount, Antonio ran head-down at full gallop, the mane whipping his face. Silvia's tired mare had no chance. The distance shrank rapidly—two hundred paces. One hundred. Fifty. They hit a long stretch of rising ground, doubly favoring his fresh horse. He closed the gap, tasting her dust in his mouth, seeing little clods thrown up by the hooves of her flagging mare. Her blue eyes showed in the mask holes when she looked back. Tall towers and castle battlements reared above the hill ahead, overlooking Montecchio Maggiore, but Antonio meant to have her long before she reached the town.

Three horsemen appeared atop the rise, emerging silently from the trees along the road to stand silhouetted at the crest.

They were dressed in carnival garb—a Saracen, a Jester, and a Plague Doctor. Parting ranks, they let Silvia pass between them. As she disappeared over the crest, they closed up, cutting Antonio off.

Damn. Another emergency call. This was more than Toni could take. He found his cyborg body right where he had left it, sitting on a mossy jungle trail beside a pile of baggage. Great vine covered tree-ferns towered over him, their huge fronds shading the path.

He stood up, shooing off the forest imps that were climbing curiously over the baggage pile. "What is it? And it better be bad."

"The worst." That was Harpo.

"We lost the client." Doc cut in.

Toni was up and trotting down the trail, leaving the baggage to the forest imps. "Wasn't he radio-tagged?"

"Not lost like in misplaced. Lost like in *dead*."

"Torn to pieces," Harpo explained.

"Wyvyrn got him," Ali added.

They were nervous as hell, all talking at once. "Bullshit!" Toni retorted, giving his snap professional opinion.

"See for yourself," Harpo suggested.

Toni got to see it all different ways. First in 3V, then through his own optical sensors. The kill site looked like some huge mowing machine had gone berserk. Shattered tree-ferns leaned at crazy angles. Big lycopods lay broken and uprooted. Even the mossy forest floor was gouged and furrowed. A great gaping hole ripped in the canopy overhead showed where the Wyvyrn had made its exit.

And there was blood all about. Big splotches of it stained the moss. Smaller drops speckled the torn fronds. In the center of the broken clearing sat a SuperChimp's head, glaring at the mess.

Reviewing recordings was singularly unproductive. The Guide had gone on ahead to "flush" the Wyvyrn. Gracchus and his bodyguards had been waiting, armed with enough firepower to take out a platoon of light tanks—staring at the surrounding wall of cycads, fern fronds, hanging lianas, and vine covered trunks, all about as transparent as green-painted reactor shielding. Until you've been on a Wyvyrn hunt, you'll never be able to imagine how hard it is to spot a hundred-meter flying monster in dense cover.

A faint rustle off to the right caught everyone's attention. Then the Wyvyrn burst on them.

There was no time for a brain shot, heart shot, or even a frantic toe stab. Toni got to see the carnage from three different angles—from the point of view of Gracchus and his two Chimp bodyguards. One of the Chimps lasted the longest, but all he saw was his master being shredded before the Wyvyrn turned on him. So much for realtime adventure.

And the sickest part was that Dragon Hunt had set it all up, using the Wyvyrn's control collar, electronically torturing a semi-intelligent omnivore until it turned killer. Some "sport." Brutal, but *real*. Which was what Gracchus had paid for—at least he got his money's worth.

Meticulous search of the area turned up a profusion of body parts, some of them human. But only one object of interest—a torn diamond neck piece, and several loose stones. Toni recognized it as soon as Harpo showed it to him. "It's Pandora's slave collar."

"She's missing," Harpo informed him.

Toni scoffed, "No shit."

"The blood on the stones came from a Chimp," Doc added. "She could still be alive."

"Right." Toni remembered her at the dock, cheerfully handing out stim pills—and a pair of earrings. "But for how long?" If the Wyvyrn carried her off, they were going to have a godawful time finding the body.

"Well, we've got to make the attempt." That was Ali, always the optimist.

Toni could see an absolutely pointless search stretching out ahead of them. Of course they had to make the attempt. But Elysium covered thousands of square klicks, most of it as dense as the morass around them. Given time and patience, each square centimeter could be gone over for clues, until something turned up. But when they did find parts of Pandora, so what? Dragon Hunt was dead. They had just killed one of the richest men in the galaxy. No one was going to award them points for bringing back pieces of his most junior wife.

THE COURT OF A MILLION LIES

Antonio arrived in Venice by boat, one of the small lateen-rigged craft that ply the lagoon, with their strange hooked masts and old-fashioned side rudders. A crude, ungainly means of transport, utterly beneath his station—but the easiest way to enter the island republic, unless you had wings, or were willing to swim.

Braced against the curved prow, he watched "Byzantium's Favorite Daughter" draw closer, seeming to rise up out of the low gleaming lagoon chop. At first, all he could see were roofs and upper floors, topped by bell towers, cupolas, oriental battlements, fancifully colored domes, and the lace-like stone facades that gave the city her Eastern cast. A vision built on mud flats. Then came the jumble of walkways, bridges, streets, canals, and the great mass of pilings that kept Venice from washing out to sea. Venice had no city gates, no rich or poor quarters. Lines of wash hung over side canals and small alleys. Ships' masts moved among the steeples.

At the Cannaregio docks, Antonio sent Proteus prowling into the city for news of his quarry, while he changed to a black gondola, setting out down the "Canal Regio." Cats prowled near the Campo San Giobbe—but the nearby church stood empty. Bells were gone from the church towers, packed away in straw. Venice lay under a papal interdict. A theological calamity that meant no masses, no communion, no Holy Mother Church to stand between the people of Venice and the fires of Hell. Worse yet, God-fearing merchants were free to renounce their debts to Venice and plunder her cargoes.

Uncorking a bottle of bardolino, Antonio offered it to the gondolier, asking what he thought of the ban. The man stopped poling, took a swig, and thought it through. He was a blunt broad-shouldered brute who made his living with his back, and clearly cared little for mainland nobility. He admitted in thick Venetian, "I miss the bells. But interdict also means no marriage and no confession. Twin blessings there!"

Antonio laughed and called him a scoundrel.

He took a second swig. "And no Holy Inquisition."

Antonio ventured that Venice was coming out well ahead.

"So it would be, were it not for the dead."

"Death undoes us all," Antonio agreed, eyeing the houses piled one atop the other. No church burials badly burdened a city that saw deaths every day but lacked fields to take the bodies. Dig too deeply and they'd be burying folks at sea.

"What is your lordship's religion?" the gondolier asked.

"I don't speak French." Antonio's stock reply. It was what some Flemish burgher said to Robert of Artois, brother-in-law to King Philip of France, before braining the Count with a club at the battle of Courtrai.

The gondolier laughed, handed back the bottle, and began poling again. The French had managed to put religion to shame, beating one Pope to death and poisoning the next. Clement V was their creature, afraid to set foot in Rome, keeping the Papacy in Babylonian Captivity at Avignon— which the French claimed to be part of Italy since Avignon was a fief of the Two Sicilies, making a farce of both faith and geography. Clement V and Philip the Fair had gone on to commit the crime of the century, looting the treasury of the Knights Templars, burning and torturing innocent knights—including the aged Grand Master, who was godfather to Philip's children. It was hard to fear a church that put faith and justice up for sale.

The Canal Regio ran right into the Canalazzo, the Grand Canal, a magnificent S-shaped waterway that cut sweeping backward curves through the heart of Venice, following the bed of an ancient river now buried beneath wharves, *palazzi*, and granaries. Barges and pleasure boats crowded the city's greatest thoroughfare, grand showpiece, and primary sewer. Merchant princes could walk out of their doors onto a gangway and not step ashore again until they were in Marseilles or Alexandria.

Antonio got off at the Rialto, in the city center, beside the only bridge spanning the Grand Canal. Cogs and trading galleys unloaded in the shadow of the silent and empty San Giacomo, disgorging wares from around the world—wheat, figs, frankincense, almonds, Byzantine glass, and slaves from the East. Proteus caught up with him at a stall selling perfumed lace and dyed wax. "Tonight she'll be at the Court of a Million Lies, attending a fete in her honor."

Antonio nodded. He knew this type of commercial soirée stocked with overfed ignoramuses and flirtatious women. Ordinarily, he found them as inviting as the plague.

"And on the morrow," Proteus added, "she will be gone."

"Gone? Where?" Would she ever stop running?

"A merchant galley is waiting at San Marco to take her to the East."

"In God's name, *why?*"

"She is heiress to Visconti lands in the Levant worth millions of ducats. Word is she wants a new life."

What woman did not? Antonio aimed to give her one.

"If you are to succeed with her, it must be tonight, at the Court of a Million Lies."

"Of course I'll succeed." Antonio never failed.

"Naturally." His manservant made a mocking bow. If Proteus weren't irreplaceable, Antonio would have booted him into a canal.

The Court of a Million Lies, just north of the Rialto on the outskirts of Cannaregio, was really two courts: the Court of the First Million Lies, and the Court of the Second Million Lies. Both were owned by the Polo family, Venice's most notorious merchant adventurers. A villainous-looking Tartar, with dark slanted eyes and a devil's leer, greeted guests at the door. He wore Polo livery and had been christened "Peter" after the doorman to Heaven.

Inside, the crowd was equally mixed. Antonio saw brown, black, and tan faces, beneath fur hats, damask turbans, and scented peacock feathers. He heard Greek, Spanish, Arabic, and every type of Italian—mostly in male tones. Venice took after the East, where good wives stayed at home and only whores walked the streets. But Silvia was there, attended by old Marco Polo's own daughters, acting the gracious guest of honor. (A Visconti Pope had blessed the Polo mission to Kublai Khan.) She had exchanged her mask for a gold half-veil. Blue eyes flashed Antonio a greeting as he came in.

He hastened to present himself to Master Marco, who was busy spinning tales of the East to drunken skeptics. An Italian scoffer waved a wine cup, asking if the holy *yogis* of India really went about buck-naked, "With their members hanging out. They sound as shameless as Dominicans."

"So they do," Marco assured him. "But by living in abstinence, they do not use the male member for sin. They say it is no more sinful to show it than your hand or your face."

Someone snickered, "And what about those who sin with hand and face?" The skeptic still looked doubtful, "With all this abstinence, how can there be so *many* of them?"

Marco shrugged. "The East is vast, with multitudes of people and customs. In some provinces in Cathay, they care so little for chastity that wives take in strangers off the road. If a husband finds a traveler's cloak hanging by the door, he stays away, even for days at a time."

Men laughed. Stories like this had earned him the name Marco of the Million Lies. "Sounds like France," someone suggested. "The poor sods. Our wives at least have the Christian decency to do it behind our backs!"

"That's not the way they see it," Polo protested. "The traveler leaves the wife some token payment, a trinket, or bit of cloth. Both husband and wife see him off, waving the token. 'This was yours,' they say 'Now it is ours. What are you taking away with *you*? Nothing at all!'"

A woman's favors might well be nothing, but Antonio had ridden halfway across Italy for one particular woman. Thanking his host, he strode across the court to where Silvia waited alongside a fountain whose demi-god faces spit wine into a silver basin. He could see her lively eyes above the veil. The same eyes that laughed at him in Verona at Carnival. He bowed. "Silvia Luoetta Visconti."

"Bold Antonio, you have caught me at last."

"Not without effort," he admitted. It was the first time he had heard her voice, but already it sounded familiar—as familiar as the form he had been chasing for days.

"Are you ready to lift my veil, and claim your reward?"

"More than ready." Antonio had never seen a minx so secure in her mystery. He reached out, seizing her veil, triumphantly drawing it aside. When he saw her face, his hand froze. He stared speechless. Beneath the gold veil and blond wig was the face of Pandora—Gracchus's junior wife—last seen at the site of the Wyvyrn attack. Her lips parted. "Save me," she whispered. "Save me, bold Antonio."

> "... I am but a shadow;
> And to your shadow will make true love."
> —Proteus, *Two Gentlemen of Verona*, Act IV

BUT A SHADOW

Toni jerked off his headset, staring at the walls of the sanitary unit. This was way worse than any flashback. Virtual junkies got used to being dumped into the middle of a street brawl at Carnival or having long dead friends tap you on the shoulder. But nothing topped a whiff of reality invading your dreams. He punched PROTEUS.

An answer flashed back: PROGRAM ERROR— PLEASE WAIT—FREE FOUR HOUR UPGRADE.

Four free hours. Wow! How generous. Way *too* generous for some little program glitch. Upgrades usually came measured in minutes. PROTEUS was going to great expense to get him to sit tight and not ask questions, waiting for his reward like one of Pavlov's dogs.

Toni leapt up, jerking the glucose drip out of his arm, shutting down his life-support pack, pulling on his pants. He might be an addict, but he wasn't an idiot. Toni knew what happened to lab dogs when they were no longer needed.

Tucking his deck and his life-support pack under his arm, he hit the release on the sanitary unit door. He hated leaving the exercise bike. Bright slanting sunlight nearly blinded him. Half-blind and wobbly on his feet, he steadied himself against the open door, getting his eyes in focus. "Elvis Saves," was scrawled above the words OUT OF ORDER.

Peeling OUT OF ORDER off the door, he put the letters in his pocket to use later—if he ever got the chance. Then he set off at a stumbling run down a wooded path. The sanitary unit sat in a little-used part of a public park. Kilometer-tall trees soared overhead. Brightly colored flying eels snaked between vine-covered trunks.

For the first time in days, Toni had to move under his own

power. He did not find it easy. Or comfortable. Were it not for Ariel's .5 gravity, he would have had to do it on all fours. He tottered up a side trail leading to a cargo field on the shoulder of Mt. Beanstalk. Above him towered the peak, with the razor-straight Beanstalk disappearing into the deep blue stratosphere.

Toni did not see the spark falling from orbit, but he heard the blast as it hit. Shock waves rattled the foliage, showering him with twigs. Scratch one sanitary unit. Alarms rang across the cargo field. Cargo handlers in mint-striped coveralls raced over, peering into the vegetation, though there was nothing left to see. Whoever offered him FOUR FREE HOURS had not even waited two minutes before blowing his dingy cubicle to bits. They must have assumed he was a moron. Hopefully, they now assumed he was a dead moron.

As guards came running up to take their look, Toni walked casually the other way. Women in shorn hair and green-striped coveralls grinned at him. Smiles were all they had to offer—their only way to look attractive.

Disheveled and out of shape, breathing hard from the run up slope, Toni did not fancy himself overly handsome. But these women had gone months, maybe years, without a man. The mere fact that he was walking free put him way ahead of the guys they were used to seeing. Swiftly, he searched out a matronly female trustee in loading and packaging, offering his life-support pack for cargo-class passage to Elysium. Toni had a bulging credit file, but dared not touch it—not so long as he planned to stay dead.

She readily agreed. What he wanted was only mildly illegal—and the support pack was crammed with drugs and paraphernalia. Stuff that could keep you entertained for weeks in lockup. Giggling mint-striped prisoners loaded him into a cushioned bio-container. The trustee, easily twice Toni's age, with a long sentence behind her, leaned in and kissed him, pressing her breasts against him beneath the coveralls. Whispering "Sweet dreams," she closed the lid. The box sealed.

Curled in the dark, Toni reviewed the news channels. ("The armed merchant cruiser *M. Licinius Crassus* regrets the accidental launching of an Osiris orbit-to-surface missile. Luckily, the missile impacted in a sparsely populated area, causing no significant structural damage except to a public toilet.") But the top story remained the hunting death of Transgalactic tycoon Alexander Gracchus. ("A member of his party is still listed as missing.") Much bigger news than some blown-up outhouse.

Presently, he felt himself being loaded aboard a ballistic cargo carrier, Toni could still smell the warm odor of the woman who had tucked him in, reminding him how shitty some people's "real" lives were. What had she done to deserve a lonely, single-sex realtime existence, locked away when she was not working. Not much, he bet. Whoever murdered Alexander Gracchus was bound to be doing way better.

And murder it was. Whatever slim chance had existed that this was all some ghastly hunting mishap had been punctured by Pandora turning up alive in Verona. Alive and on the run. Having known, or seen, too much. Clearly, she was supposed to have died along with Gracchus and his Chimp bodyguards. But she must have seen it coming, and set up her escape ahead of time—using PROTEUS to get Toni's attention. Damn it, why had she picked *him*? Didn't she know he was an addict?

Answer was, she *did* know. It must be one of the reasons why she'd picked him. It made him easy to manipulate. Desperate people have few scruples about other folks' weaknesses. She had tapped into his private 3V fantasy even before coming down the Beanstalk—catching his attention at Carnival, making sure he'd come after her.

And whoever killed Gracchus had traced her contact through PROTEUS. No surprise there. Gracchus had been murdered *through* PROTEUS—using the Wyvyrn's control collar. Huge winged megafauna made nifty murder weapons. Pandora and her would-be killers had been conducting a silent duel in cyberspace, while Gracchus stalked his Wyvyrn, and the Noble Dog panted after Silvia Visconti.

Which was why Toni had to stay off the net—playing dead. Not using PROTEUS until he absolutely had to. Surprise was his best weapon. Whoever did all this was *not* infallible. They'd missed Pandora. And they'd missed him. If only by an angstrom.

His thoughts were still spinning in these circles when the ballistic transport's engines roared to life. G-forces slammed him into the cubicle cushioning. Like many stretches of real-time, the flight fast became a hideous bore. Interminable minutes of banging off padded walls. In-flight entertainment consisted of Toni tossing his cookies in free fall.

He emerged battered and dirty on a cargo pad over-looked by the Elysium rim wall. A far better place for his pur-poses than the usual entry ports atop the rim—less used, and watched over solely by security cams and a trusting crew of maintenance Chimps. Best of all, the cargo pad possessed a clean, vacant public toilet. Adept at bathing from a sink, while doing his laundry in the hand drier, Toni used the time to check on the search, tapping into Ali, Doc, and Harpo's con-trol channel. The search pattern had tightened. Large sections of the crater floor had been gone over, or ruled out. The remaining area continued to shrink.

It took time to crack the code on the Wyvyrn's control collar without alerting PROTEUS. But the code ended up being a simple binary transposition—any more encryption would have drawn unwanted attention to Dragon Hunt. The Wyvyrn also turned out to be in the prime search area.

Great. The more the merrier. Luckily the monster lay immobilized, paralyzed by its collar, pinned down now that it was no longer needed. Toni meant to do something about that—but not right now.

First, he had to find Pandora. Not a pleasing prospect. It meant going *in person* into Elysium—since he couldn't use his cyborg body without alerting PROTEUS. But he had no choice. Someone who had murdered the richest man in this part of the spiral arm would gladly invest a couple of mega-credits in making Toni go away. Pandora was his only protection. Come up with her alive, and he had half a chance. Without her, he would just be some homeless 3V addict with a weird story and an outrageous price on his head. An acutely terminal condition.

And he had to do it alone. The planetary authorities might be tough on drug addicts and tax cheats, but they were hardly up to interstellar conspiracies. Pair-a-Dice Security couldn't care less what happened on planet. And the Freeport Police were completely corrupt. Their idea of lending a hand would be to hold Toni for the highest bidder.

But the absolute worst of it was having to do it in *real-time*. In Verona, this would be no problem. Antonio the Noble Dog never failed at anything. But he was not Antonio. And this was not 3V. This was the *real* world—where everything could (and *did*) go wrong. Here, he could fail. Or *die*. God, how he hated real time! In Verona, none of this would even be *happening*.

Being the only human at the cargo pad, he had the run of the place. To take him into the crater, Toni selected a sky cycle, a hydrogen-filled parasail with a solar-assisted pedal propeller. He could not chance using his own credit, but he easily convinced the simple-minded rent-a-stand to charge the flight to a regular client's account.

Toni peddled the sky cycle straight off the cargo pad into an updraft along the windward side of the rimwall. Here hot surface air and prevailing winds blowing out of Nightside formed a great standing wave, rolling over Elysium rim. This was the easiest entrance to Elysium, and the air above the rim swarmed with fliers, orthopters, and sailplanes. He felt comfortably lost in the crowd. Beneath him, a green canopy of kilometer-tall trees filled the bottom of the crater, climbing up almost to the rim.

From his perch among the tourists and pleasure seekers,

Toni kept tabs on the search below—happily letting Ali, Doc, and Harpo do the leg work. He beat back and forth to windward, listening in on their calls. Hours on the exercise bike had kept his calves in shape, and soaring allowed him to save his strength for one frantic burst once they found Pandora.

Harpo hit the trail first. Chemosensors and a heat trace picked up Pandora's track, and Harpo's cyborg body went crashing after her, calling on Doc and Al to bring the hover car. Swooping down, Toni plunged through a break in the canopy. Getting ahead of Harpo, he dodged in among the tall trunks, keeping between the upper canopy and the tangle of ground cover, hopefully showing himself to Pandora.

Harpo signaled that he had an infrared contact, bearing ZERO-THREE-ZERO, just shy of a large clearing caused by the fall of a forest giant. Toni headed for the contact, spiraling down through slanting lanes of Prospero light filled with gaily colored day moths.

Pandora had picked a perfect spot for her pick-up. The fallen Goliath had taken out a dozen lesser trees, tearing a huge rent in the canopy. Clear sky showed through the ragged hole, and much of the tangle beneath had been flattened by falling timbers. Toni set down atop a mossy pile of toppled logs. Insects whirred up to greet him.

Pandora appeared, breaking cover to Toni's left, still wearing her synthetic leopard-skin. Her thigh-length boots were covered in mud, and her lacquered hair had drooping spikes—otherwise she seemed in decent shape. Scrambling atop the log pile, she leaped from timber to timber toward him.

Toni lifted an eyebrow as she hopped aboard the sky cycle behind him, landing on the back half of the banana seat. "Lady Silvia Lucetta Visconti?"

"Sorry about that, I was incredibly desperate." She sounded as if she meant it, particularly the last part. Her arms looped around his waist, pressing her hips against his back. "Let's go!"

"You almost got me killed," he pointed out.

"Might still happen," she assured him.

As if bent on proving her right, Harpo came crashing out of the undergrowth. Cyborg faces cannot register shock, but Harpo did come to a dead stop, sensors pointed forward. Not waiting for Harpo to recover, Toni kicked the emergency release on the sky cycle's hydrogen bottle.

The cycle's gas bag ballooned above them, lifting the sky cycle off the log pile. Toni backpedaled furiously, keeping them aimed at the hole in the canopy. Harpo dwindled until he looked like a plasti-metal toy abandoned in the clearing.

Pandora pulled them tighter together. Spiked hair tickled his neck. "Smashing. Absolutely smashing," she purred into his ear—her voice had a rich timbre to it, worthy of a Visconti heiress. Or a beautiful, wealthy young widow, with holdings in a dozen star systems. Obviously on top of the universe, she started giving orders, "Head for the Beanstalk. There's a gravity-drive yacht waiting on Pair-a-Dice. A Fornax Skylark—fast enough to get us comfortably lost."

Toni nodded, happy to have somewhere to run to. But at the moment, he had his hands full with the here-and-now, keeping the overloaded sky-cycle on an even keel while balancing his 3V deck on his lap. No easy task with Pandora holding tight to him, hips and breasts pressed against his spine, her hands clasped just above his groin. He eyed her over his shoulder. "Doing okay?"

"Sure, great. Can't you tell?" She plainly aimed to make the most of the moment. Passing through the canopy, Toni kept on going, meaning to get all the height he could out of the gas bag. For a laboring sky cycle trying to make a quick getaway, altitude is everything.

Trouble appeared almost at once. A silver gleam below them whipped into a quick climbing turn. The Dragon Hunt hover car. Doc and Ali must have picked up Harpo and were now coming for him.

He shouted to Pandora, "Hold tight." Releasing the gas

bag and the spent hydrogen bottle, Toni put the sky cycle into a screaming dive. He had no chance of outrunning a jet-powered hover car, but the dive would give him airspeed to work with—and the chance to make something happen.

Doc put in a call to him, "Toni, what in hell do you think you're doing?"

Having no good answer, Toni hung grimly into the dive. Treetops rushed up to greet him. The hover car did another fast turn and bored after him. "Give it up, Toni, we've got the speed to run you down." That was Harpo.

They had, the speed, but not the agility. Spotting a hole in the forest canopy, Toni side-slipped and angled in, dodging between kilometer-tall trunks. The hover car could not follow without risking hitting its rotors on the foliage or whacking into a tree. They had to throttle down just to draw even with him.

"Come on, Toni, we can make a deal." That was Doc again, ever the reasonable one.

"I doubt it." No deals. Toni had them right where he wanted them. He backpedaled, forcing them to come to a complete halt, hovering just above the canopy. Branches rattled in the prop wash.

"Nobody cares about you," Harpo assured him.

Toni smirked. "Tell me something I *don't* know."

"Give up the woman and we'll see you get away." Ali tried to sound like they had his interests at heart.

Toni was not even tempted. Without Pandora, he was just a loose end, waiting to be done away with. "They're going to kill her," he reminded them. "Just like they killed Gracchus."

"That's not our business," Harpo protested.

"Too bad, it should be." Toni hit the control key on his deck, sending out a coded signal.

The Wyvyrn roared out of its hiding place, saber-like mandibles flashing, wing segments beating, spine-tipped tail lashing. Given what had happened, the great segmented beast didn't need much encouragement from its control collar to fly into a blind frenzy. Toni merely gave its anger direction.

Doc managed to get off an anguished MAYDAY before the monster hit. Imagine a huge hundred-meter centipede, with wings instead of feet, slamming into the light plastic-aluminum hover car. The ship's lifting body hull crumpled, and the hover car flipped over, spinning out of control. It went whirling into the canopy, with the Wyvyrn still clinging to the hull, stabbing at it again and again with its giant stinging tail.

"*That* will teach you to trifle with the Noble Dog!" Toni couldn't hang around to enjoy the virtual deaths of Doc, Ali, and Harpo's cyborg bodies. Putting business ahead of pleasure, he pedaled off between the trees. Soon he was lost among the tourists swarming atop the standing wave at Elysium's windward rim.

Pandora sat comfortably safe in her yacht, a drink in her hand, her back to the Skylark's main view port, looking like she had swallowed the canary. A mobile auto-bar stood moored beside her couch, serving up a frothy blue liquor that misted like liquid oxygen.

Behind her, projected in the view port, lay Pair-a-Dice yacht harbor, backed by starlit void. Pair-a-Dice had grown in haphazard fashion from the original geosync station and Beanstalk terminus. Pleasure domes and gaming palaces came right up to the harbor edge, sticking out at odd angles amid the repair slips and taxi stands. The whole gleaming jumble ended abruptly in empty space. The "harbor" was merely a parking area around the geosync point. A couple of orbital yachts were clearly visible, and taxis going ship to shore showed up as tiny moving sparks. But most of the parked spacecraft were mere points of light, lost among the stars.

She told Toni, "Gracchus was damned good to me. We married for his money, but that didn't make me hate him.

Trouble was, too many folks stood to make trillions by his death. Like his bitch of a First Wife, and her little fuck mate Selene. You remember her? Came to the Wyvyrn hunt in a faerie gown?"

Toni nodded idly. Pandora had been doing all the talking, happy to be rich and alive.

"I mean, the guy was worth giga-credits. In Aesir system, he owned his own goddamn moon! My measly 2 percent was worth killing for a billion times over." Intersystem law made a small but immutable provision for secondary spouses.

She grinned at him. "Without a doubt, you saved my butt. And I'm gonna be grateful. Outrageously grateful. I'm fabulously rich, which is all I ever wanted to be. And I've seen way too many assholes stepping on people's faces to get somewhere, forgetting who gave them their start. Well, that ain't *me*." Pandora laughed provocatively, "Prepare to be rewarded beyond your wildest dreams!"

Toni stared at her. What he saw was Silvia Lucetta Visconti with her halo of golden hair, lounging on a day bed on the poop royal of her great lateen-rigged trading galley. A handsomely hung serving lad in blue and white Visconti livery stood ready to refill her wine goblet.

Behind her lay the sparkling waters of the Venice lagoon, backed by the tall Campanile and the sun-drenched colonnades of the Piazza San Marco, where the Grand Canal came sweeping out of the city, headed toward the sea. Toni could see the twin Columns of Execution marking the sea gate to Venice, and the Greek bell-and-onion domes of San Marco Basilica poking above the Doge's new Gothic palace. At the moment, Venice was besieged by high water. Wavelets lapped past the twin columns into the Piazzetta, flooding the "finest drawing room in Europe."

Silvia had had the effrontery to suggest that he sail away with her to the East—where she claimed to have inherited rich estates among the Isles. What presumption, even for a Visconti! He was Antonio Cansignorio della Scala, nephew to the prince, not some rich bitch's plaything. If the right people were poisoned, he would be heir to Verona!

And yet—Italy had gotten stale of late, with this obnoxious French Pope and no wars of note. Or at least none worth fighting in. Even Proteus had failed him, plunging Antonio into no end of trouble. And the East was said to be a real eye-opener—if you believed the Polos.

Besides, the Noble Dog had begun to feel he had somehow outgrown Verona . . .

Great Western

KIM NEWMAN

Kim Newman has emerged as one of the significant fantasy and horror writers in England in the last decade. His most recent book is a collection of linked stories, _Back in the USSA_, in collaboration with Eugene Byrne, and set in an alternate-universe twentieth century in which the Communist revolution happened in the USA, not Russia. His SF is usually some sort of hybrid (almost all of his fiction is some sort of hybrid of genres). As does Howard Waldrop or James P. Blaylock, Newman joyfully yokes pop culture images and historical figures and events in often unlikely but provocative juxtapositions. This piece is no exception, an alternate-present west-of-England western about the arrival of the railroads (in this case the Great Western Railway) and the social disruption of progress. It appeared in _New Worlds_, and a moment's comparison to the Gibson, above, and the Moorcock, below, will give some indication of the range of that impressive anthology. There is a tone and style in Newman's story perhaps reminiscent of the Pavane stories of Keith Roberts. It is also a retelling of a great Western genre novel and film.

Cleared paths were no good for Allie. She wasn't supposed to be after rabbits on Squire Maskell's land. Most of Alder Hill was wildwood, trees webbed together by a growth of bramble nastier than barbwire. Thorns jabbed into skin and stayed, like bee-stingers.

Just after dawn, the air had a chilly bite but the sunlight was pure and strong. Later, it would get warm; now, her hands and knees were frozen from dew-damp grass and iron-hard ground.

The Reeve was making a show of being tough on poaching, handing down short, sharp sentences. She'd already got a stripe across her palm for setting snares. Everyone west of Bristol knew Reeve Draper was Maskell's creature. Serfdom might have been abolished, but the old squires clung to their pre-War position, through habit as much as tenacity.

Since taking her lash, administered under the village oak by Constable Erskine with a razor-strop, she'd grown craftier. Wiry enough to tunnel through bramble, she made and travelled her own secret, thorny paths. She'd take Maskell's rabbits, even if the Reeve's Constable striped her like a tiger.

She set a few snares in obvious spots, where Stan Budge would find and destroy them. Maskell's gamekeeper wouldn't be happy if he thought no one was even trying to poach. The trick was to set snares invisibly, in places Budge was too grown-up, too far off the ground, to look.

Even so, none of her nooses had caught anything.

All spring, she'd been hearing gunfire from Alder Hill, resonating across the moors like thunder. Maskell had the Gilpin brothers out with Browning rifles. They were supposed to be ratting, but the object of the exercise was to end poaching by killing off all the game.

There were rabbit and pigeon carcasses about, some crackly bone bundles in packets of dry skin, some recent enough to seem shocked to death. It was a sinful waste, what with hungry people queueing up for parish hand-outs. Quite a few trees had yellow-orange badges, where Terry or Teddy Gilpin had shot wide of the mark. Squire Maskell would not be heartbroken if one of those wild shots finished up in her.

Susan told her over and over to be mindful of men with guns. She had a quite reasonable horror of firearms. Too many people on Sedgmoor died with their gumboots on and a bullet in them. Allie's Dad and Susan's husband, for two. Susan wouldn't have a gun in the house.

For poaching, Allie didn't like guns anyway. Too loud. She had a catapult made from a garden fork, double-strength rubber stretched between steel tines. She could put a nail through a half-inch of plywood from twenty-five feet.

She wriggled out of her tunnel, pushing aside a circle of bramble she'd fixed to hinge like a lid, and emerged in a clearing of loose earth and shale. During the Civil War, a bomb had fallen here and fizzled. Eventually, the woods would close over the scar.

When she stood up, she could see across the moors, as far as Achelzoy. At night, the infernal lights of Bridgwater pinked the horizon, clawing a ragged red edge in the curtain of dark. Now, she could make out the road winding through the wetlands. The sun, still low, glinted and glimmered in sodden fields, mirror-fragments strewn in a carpet of grass. There were dangerous marshes out there. Cows were sucked under if they set a hoof wrong.

Something moved near the edge of the clearing.

Allie had her catapult primed, her eye fixed on the rabbit. Crouching, still as a statue, she concentrated. Jack Coney nibbled on nothing, unconcerned. She pinched the nailhead, imagining a point between the ears where she would strike.

A noise sounded out on the moor road. The rabbit vanished, startled by the unfamiliar rasp of an engine.

"'S'blood," she swore.

She stood up, easing off on her catapult. She looked out towards Achelzoy. A fast-moving shape was coming across the moor.

The rabbit was lost. Maskell's men would soon be about, making the woods dangerous. She chanced a maintained path and ran swiftly downhill. At the edge of Maskell's property, she came to a stile and vaulted it—wrenching her shoulder, but no matter—landing like a cat on safe territory. Without a look back at the "TRESPASSERS WILL BE VENTILATED" sign, she traipsed between two rows of trees, toward the road.

The path came out half a mile beyond the village, at a sharp kink in the moor road. She squatted with her back to a signpost, running fingers through her hair to rid herself of tangles and snaps of thorn.

The engine noise was nearer and louder. She considered putting a nail in the nuisance-maker's petrol tank to pay him back for the rabbit. That was silly. Whoever it was didn't know what he'd done.

She saw the stranger was straddling a Norton. He had slowed to cope with the winds of the moor road. Every month, someone piled up in one of the ditches because he took a bend too fast.

To Allie's surprise, the motorcyclist stopped by her. He shifted goggles up to the brim of his hat. He looked as if he had an extra set of eyes in his forehead.

There were care-lines about his eyes and mouth. She judged him a little older than Susan. His hair needed cutting. He wore leather trews, a padded waistcoat over a dusty khaki shirt, and gauntlets. A brace of pistols was holstered at his hips, and he had a rifle slung on the Norton, within easy reach.

He reached into his waistcoat for a pouch and fixings.

Pulling the drawstring with his teeth, he tapped tobacco onto a paper and rolled himself a cigarette one-handed. It was a clever trick, and he knew it. He stuck the fag in his grin and fished for a box of Bryant and May.

"Alder," he said, reading from the signpost. "Is that a village?"

"Might be."

"Might it?"

He struck a light on his thumbnail and drew a lungful of smoke, held in for a moment like a hippie sucking a joint, and let it funnel out through his nostrils in dragon-plumes.

"Might it indeed?"

He didn't speak like a yokel. He sounded like a wireless announcer, maybe even more clipped and starched.

"If, hypothetically, Alder were a village, would there be a hostelry there where one might buy breakfast?"

"Valiant Soldier don't open till lunchtime."

The Valiant Soldier was Alder's pub, and another of Squire Maskell's businesses.

"Pity."

"How much you'm pay for breakfast?" she asked.

"That would depend on the breakfast."

"Ten bob?"

The stranger shrugged.

"Susan'll breakfast you for ten bob."

"Your mother."

"No."

"Where could one find this Susan?"

"Gosmore Farm. Other end of village."

"Why don't you get up behind me and show me where to go?"

She wasn't sure. The stranger shifted forward on his seat, making space.

"I'm Lytton," the stranger said.

"Allie," she replied, straddling the pillion.

"Hold on tight."

She took a grip on his waistcoat, wrists resting on the stocks of his guns.

Lytton pulled down his goggles and revved. The bike sped off. Allie's hair blew into her face and streamed behind her. She held tighter, pressing against his back to keep her face out of the wind.

When they arrived, Susan had finished milking. Allie saw her washing her hands under the pump by the back door.

Gosmore Farm was a tiny enclave circled by Maskell's land. He had once tried to get the farm by asking the newly widowed Susan to marry him. Allie couldn't believe he'd actually thought she might consent. Apparently, Maskell didn't consider Susan might hold a grudge after her husband's death. He now had a porcelain doll named Sue-Clare in the Manor House, and a pair of terrifying children.

Susan looked up when she heard the Norton. Her face was set hard. Strangers with guns were not her favorite type of folk.

Lytton halted the motorcycle. Allie, bones shaken, dismounted, showing herself.

"He'm pay for breakfast," she said. "Ten bob."

Susan looked the stranger over, starting at his boots, stopping at his hips.

"He'll have to get rid of those filthy things."

Lytton, who had his goggles off again, was puzzled.

"Guns, she means," Allie explained.

"I know you feel naked without them," Susan said sharply. "Unmanned, even. *Magna Carta* rules that no Englishman shall be restrained from bearing arms. It's that fundamental right which keeps us free."

"That's certainly an argument," Lytton said.

"If you want breakfast, yield your fundamental right before you step inside my house."

"That's a stronger one," he said.

Lytton pulled off his gauntlets and dropped them into the pannier of the Norton. His fingers were stiff on the buckle of his gunbelt, as if he had been wearing it for many years until it had grown into him like a wedding ring. He loosened the belt and held it up.

Allie stepped forward to take the guns.

"Allison, no," Susan insisted.

Lytton laid the guns in the pannier and latched the lid.

"You have me defenseless," he told Susan, spreading his arms.

Susan squelched a smile and opened the back door. Kitchen smells wafted.

A good thing about Lytton's appearance at Gosmore Farm was that he stopped Susan giving Allie a hard time about being up and about before dawn. Susan had no illusions about what she did in the woods.

Susan let Lytton past her into the kitchen. Allie trotted up.

"Let me see your hands," Susan said.

Allie showed them palms down. Susan noted dirt under nails and a few new scratches. When Allie showed her palms, Susan drew a fingernail across the red strop-mark.

"Take care, Allie."

"Yes'm."

Susan hugged Allie briefly, and pulled her into the kitchen.

Lytton had taken a seat at the kitchen table and was loosening his heavy boots. Susan had the wireless on, tuned to the Light Program. Mark Radcliffe introduced the new song from Jarvis Cocker and His Wurzels, "The Streets of Stogumber." A frying pan was heating on the cooker, tiny trails rising from the fat.

"Allie, cut our guest some bacon."

"The name's Lytton."

"I'm Susan Ames. This is Allison Conway. To answer your unasked question, I'm a widow, she's an orphan. We run this farm ourselves."

"A hard row to plough."

"We're still above ground."

Allie carved slices off a cured hock that hung by the cooker. Susan took eggs from a basket, cracked them into the pan.

"Earl Gray or Darjeeling?" Susan asked Lytton.

"The Earl."

"Get the kettle on, girl," Susan told her. "And stop staring."

Allie couldn't remember Susan cooking for a man since Mr. Ames was killed. It was jarring to have this big male, whiffy from the road and petrol, invading their kitchen. But also a little exciting.

Susan flipped bacon rashers, busying herself at the cooker. Allie filled the kettle from the tap at the big basin.

"Soldier, were you?" Susan asked Lytton, indicating his shoulder. There was a lighter patch on his shirtsleeve where rank insignia had been cut away. He'd worn several pips.

The stranger shrugged.

"Which brand of idiot?"

"I fought for the southeast."

"I'd keep quiet about that if you intend to drink in The Valiant Soldier."

"I'd imagined Wessex was mostly neutral."

"Feudal order worked perfectly well for a thousand years. It wasn't just landed gentry who resisted London Reforms. There are plenty of jobless ex-serfs around, nostalgic for their shackles and three hot meals a day."

"Just because it lasted a long time doesn't mean it was a good thing."

"No argument from me there."

"Mr. Ames was a Reformist too," Allie said.

"Mr. Ames?"

"My late husband. He opened his mouth too much. Some loyal retainers shut it for him."

"I'm sorry."

"Not your problem."

Susan wasn't comfortable talking about her husband. Mr. Ames had been as much lawyer as farmer, enthusiastically heading the Sedgmoor District Committee during the Reconstruction. He didn't realize it took more than a decision made in London Parliament to change things in the West. London was a long way off.

Allie brought Susan plates. Susan slid bacon and eggs from the pan.

"Fetch the tomato chutney from the preserves shelf," she said.

Outside, someone clanged the bell by the gate. Lytton's hand slipped quietly to his hip, closing where the handle of a revolver would have been.

Susan looked at the hot food on the table, and frowned at the door.

"Not a convenient time to come visiting," she said.

Hanging back behind Susan, Allie still saw who was in the drive. Constable Erskine was by the bell, vigorously hammering with the butt of his police revolver. His blue knob-end helmet gave him extra height. His gun-belt was in matching blue. Reeve Draper, arms folded, cringed at the racket his subordinate was making. Behind the officers stood Terry and Teddy Gilpin, Browning rifles casually in their hands, long coats brushing the ground.

"Goodwife Ames," shouted the Reeve. "This be a court order."

"Leave your guns."

"Come you now, Goodwife Ames. By right of law . . ."

Erskine was still clanging. The bell came off its hook and

thunked on the ground. The Constable shrugged a grin and didn't holster his pistol.

"I won't have guns on my property."

"Then come and be served. This here paper pertains to your cattle. The decision been telegraphed from Taunton Magistrates. You'm to surrender all livestock within thirty days, for slaughter. It be a safety measure."

Susan had been expecting something like this.

"There are no mad cows on Gosmore Farm."

"Susan, don't be difficult."

"It's Mrs. Ames, Mr. Reeve Draper."

The Reeve held up a fawn envelope.

"You'm know this has to be done."

"Will you be slaughtering Maskell's stock?"

"He took proper precautions, Susan. Can't be blamed. He'm been organic since 'fore the War."

Susan snorted a laugh. Everyone knew there'd been mad cow disease in the Squire's herd. He'd paid off the inspectors and rendered the affected animals into fertilizer. It was Susan who'd never used infected feed, never had a sick cow. This wasn't about British beef; this was about squeezing Gosmore Farm.

"Clear off," Allie shouted.

"Poacher girl," Erskine sneered. "Lookin' for a matchin' stripe on your left hand?"

Susan turned on the Constable.

"Don't you threaten Allison. She's not a serf."

"Once a serf, always a serf."

"What are they here for?" Susan nodded to the Gilpin brothers. "D'you need two extra guns to deliver a letter?"

Draper looked nervously at the brothers. Terry, heavier and nastier, curled his fingers about the trigger guard of his Browning.

"Why didn't Maskell come himself?"

Draper carefully put the letter on the ground, laying a stone on top of it.

"I'll leave this here, Goodwife. You'm been served with this notice."

Susan strode towards the letter.

Terry hawked a stream of spit, which hit the stone and splattered the envelope. He showed off his missing front teeth in an idiot leer.

Draper was embarrassed and angered, Erskine delighted and itchy.

"My sentiments exactly, Goodman Gilpin," said Susan. She kicked the stone and let the letter skip away in the breeze.

"Mustn't show disrespect for the law," Erskine snarled. He was holding his gun rightway round, thumb on the cock-lever, finger on the trigger.

From the kitchen doorway, close behind Allie, Lytton said, "Whose law?"

Allie stepped aside and Lytton strode into the yard. The four unwelcome visitors looked at him.

"Widow Ames got a stay-over guest," Erskine said, nastily.

"B'ain't no business of yourn, Goodman," said the Reeve to Lytton.

"And what if I make it my business?"

"You'm rue it."

Lytton kept his gaze steady on the Reeve, who flinched and blinked.

"He hasn't got a gun," Susan said, voice betraying annoyance with Lytton as much as with Maskell's men. "So you can't have a fair fight."

Mr. Ames had been carrying a Webley when he was shot. The magistrate, Sue-Clare Maskell's father, ruled it a fair fight, exonerating on the grounds of self-defense the Maskell retainer who'd killed Susan's husband.

"He'm interfering with due process, Mr. Reeve," Erskine told Draper. "We could detain him for questioning."

"I don't think that'll be necessary," Lytton said. "I just

stopped at Gosmore Farm for bacon and eggs. I take it there's no local ordinance against that."

"Goodwife Ames don't have no bed and breakfast license," Draper said.

"Specially *bed*," Erskine added, leering.

Lytton strolled casually toward his Norton. And his guns.

"Maybe I should press on. I'd like to be in Dorset by lunchtime."

Terry's rifle was fixed on Lytton's belly, and swung in an arc as Lytton walked. Erskine thumb-cocked his revolver, ineptly covering the sound with a cough.

"Tell Maurice Maskell you've delivered your damned message," Susan said, trying to get between Lytton and the visitors' guns. "And tell him he'll have to come personally next time."

"You'm stay away from thic rifle, Goodman," the Reeve said to Lytton.

"Just getting my gloves," Lytton replied, moving his hands away from the holstered rifle toward the pannier where his pistols were.

Allie backed away toward the house, stomach knotted.

"What's she afraid of?" Erskine asked, nodding at her.

"Don't touch thic fuckin' bike," Terry shouted.

Allie heard the guns going off, louder than rook-scarers. An applesized chunk of stone exploded on the wall nearby, spitting chips in her face. The fireflashes were faint in the morning sun, but the reports were thunderclaps.

Erskine had shot, and Terry. Lytton had slipped down behind his motorcycle, which had fallen on him. There was a bright red splash of blood on the ground. Teddy was bringing up his rifle.

She scooped a stone and drew back the rubber of her catapult.

Susan screamed for everyone to stop.

Allie loosed the stone and raised a bloody welt on Erskine's cheek.

Susan slapped Allie hard and hugged her. Erskine, arm trembling with rage, blood dribbling on his face, took aim at them. Draper put a hand on the Constable's arm, and forced him to holster his gun. At a nod from the Reeve, Teddy Gilpin took a look at Lytton's wound and reported that it wasn't serious.

"This be bad, Goodwife Ames. It'd not tell well for you if'n it came up at magistrate's court. We'm be back on Saturday, with the vet. Have your animals together so they can be destroyed."

He walked to his police car, his men loping after him like dogs. Terry laughed a comment to Erskine about Lytton.

Allie impotently twanged her catapult at them.

"Help me get this off him," Susan said.

The Norton was a heavy machine, but between them they hefted it up. The pannier was still latched down. Lytton had not got to his guns. He lay face-up, a bright splash of red on his left upper arm. He was gritting his teeth against the hurt, shaking as if soaked to the skin in ice-water.

Allie didn't think he was badly shot. Compared to some.

"You stupid man," Susan said, kicking Lytton in the ribs. "You stupid, stupid man!"

Lytton gulped in pain and cried out.

It wasn't as if they had much livestock. Allie looked round at the eight cows, all with names and personalities, all free of the madness. Gosmore Farm had a chicken coop, a vegetable garden, a copse of apple trees and a wedge of hillside given over to grazing. It was a struggle to eke a living; without the milk quota, it would be hopeless.

It was wrong to kill the cows.

Despair lodged like a stone in Allie's heart. This was not what the West should be. When younger, she'd read Thomas Hardy's Wessex novels, *The Sheriff of Casterbridge* and

Under the Hanging Tree, and she still followed *The Archers.*
In storybook Wessex, men like Squire Maskell always lost.
Alder needed Dan Archer, the wireless hero, to stride into The
Valiant Soldier, six-guns blazing, and lay the vermin in the
dirt.

There was no Dan Archer.

Susan held all her rage in, refusing to talk about the cows
and Maskell. She always concentrated on what she called
"the job at hand." Just now, she was nursing Lytton.
Erskine's shot had gone right through his arm. Allie had
looked for but not found the bullet, to give him as a souvenir.
He'd lost blood, but he would live.

Allie hugged Pansy, her favorite, and brushed flies away
from the cow's gummy eyes.

"I won't let them hurt you," she vowed.

But what could she do?

Depressed, she trudged down to the house.

Lytton was sitting up on the cot in the living room, with his shirt
off and a clean white bandage tight around his arm. Allie saw
he had older scars. This was not the first time he'd been shot.
He was sipping a mug of hot tea. Susan, bustling furiously,
tidied up around him. When he saw Allie, Lytton smiled.

"Susan's been telling me about this Maskell character.
He seems to like to have things his way."

The door opened and Squire Maskell stepped in.

"That I do, sir."

He was dressed for church, in a dark suit and kipper tie.
He knew enough not to wear a gunbelt on Gosmore Farm,
though Allie guessed he was carrying a small pistol in his
armpit. He had shot Allie's Dad with such a gun, in a dispute
over wages. Allie barely remembered her father, who had
been indentured on Maskell's farm before the War and an
NFU rep afterwards.

"I don't remember extending an invitation, Squire," Susan said evenly.

"Susan, Susan, things could be so much more pleasant between us. We are neighbors."

"In the same way a pack of dogs are neighbors to a fox gone to earth."

Maskell laughed without humor.

"I've come to extend an offer of help."

Susan snorted. Lytton said nothing but looked Maskell over with eyes that saw the gun under the hankie-pocket and the knife in the boot.

"I understand you have BSE problems? My condolences."

"There's no mad cow disease in my herd."

"It's hardly a herd, Susan. It's a gaggle. But without them, where would you be?"

Maskell spread empty hands.

"This place is hardly worth the upkeep, Susan. You're only sticking at it because you have a nasty case of Stubborn Fever. The land is worthless to anyone but me. Gosmore Farm is a wedge in my own holdings. It would be so convenient if I could take down your fences, if I could incorporate your few acres into the Maskell farm."

"Now tell me something I don't know."

"I can either buy from you now above the market value, or wait a while and buy from the bank at a knock-down price. I'm making an offer now purely out of neighborly charity. The old ways may have changed, but as Squire I still feel an obligation to all who live within my bailiwick."

"The only obligation your forefathers felt was to sweat the serfs into early graves and beget illegitimate cretins on terrorized girls. Have you noticed how the Maskell chin shows up on those Gilpin creatures?"

Maskell was angry now, but trying to keep calm. A vein throbbed by his eye.

"Susan, you're upset, I see that. But you must be realistic. Despite what you think, I don't want to see you on the mercy of the parish. Robert Ames was a good friend to me, and . . ."

"You can fuck off, Maskell," Susan spat. "Fuck *right* off."

The Squire's smile drained away. He was close to sputtering. His Maskell chin wobbled.

"Don't ever mention my husband again. And now leave."

"Susan," he pleaded.

"I think Goodwife Ames made herself understood," Lytton said.

Maskell looked at the wounded man. Lytton eased himself gingerly off the cot, expanding his chest, and stood. He was tall enough to have to bow his head under the beamed ceiling.

"I don't believe I've had . . ."

"Lytton," he introduced himself.

"And you would be . . . ?"

"I would be grateful if you left the house as Goodwife Ames wishes. And fasten the gate on your way out. There's a Country Code, you know."

"Good day," Maskell said, not meaning it, and left.

There was a moment of silence.

"That's the second time you've taken it on yourself to act for me," Susan said, angrily. "Have I asked your help?"

Lytton smiled. His hard look faded and he seemed almost mischievous.

"I beg pardon, Goodwife."

"Don't do it again, Lytton."

By the next day, Lytton was well enough to walk. But he couldn't ride: if he tried to grip the Norton's left handlebar, it was as if a redhot poker were pressed to his bicep. They were stuck with him.

"You can do odd jobs for your keep," Susan allowed. "Allie will show you how."

"Can he come feed the chickens?" Allie asked, excited despite herself. "I can get the eggs."

"That'll be a start."

Susan walked across to the stone sheds where the cows spent the night, to do the milking. Allie took Lytton by the hand and led him round to the chicken coop.

"Maskell keeps his chickens in a gurt prison," Allie told him. "Clips their beaks with pliers, packs them in alive like sardines. If one dies, t'others eat her. They'm *cannibal* chickens . . ."

They turned round the corner.

The chicken coop was silent. Tears pricked the backs of Allie's eyes. Lumps of feathery matter lay in the scarlet-stained straw.

Her first thought was that a fox had got in.

Lytton lifted up a flap of chicken wire. It had been cut cleanly.

The coop was a lean-to, a chickenwire frame built against the house. On the stone wall was daubed a sign in blood, an upside-down tricorn fork in a circle.

"Travelers," Allie spat.

There was a big Gypsy Site at Glastonbury. Since the War, Travelers were supposed to stay on the sites, living off the dole. But they were called Travelers because they didn't like to keep to one place. They were always escaping from sites and raiding farms and villages.

Lytton shook his head.

"Hippies are hungry. They'd never have killed and left the chickens. And smashed the eggs."

The eggs had been gathered and carefully stamped on.

"Some hippies be veggie."

The blood was still fresh. Allie didn't see how this could have been done while they were asleep. The killers must have struck fast, or the chickens would have squawked.

"Where's your vegetable garden?" Lytton asked.

Allie's heart pounded like a fist.

She showed him the path to the garden, which was separated from the orchard by a thick hedge. Beanpoles had been wrenched from the earth and used to batter and gouge the rest of the crops. Cabbages were squashed, young carrots pulped by boot heels, marrows exploded. The greenhouse was a skeleton, every pane of glass broken, tomato plants strewn and flattened inside. Even the tiny herb patch Allie had been given for herself was dug up and scattered.

Allie sobbed. Liquid squirted from her eyes and nose. Hundreds of hours of work destroyed.

There was a twist of cloth on the frame of the greenhouse. Lytton examined it: a tie-dyed poncho, dotted with emblem badges of marijuana leaves, multi-colored swirls and cartoon cats.

"Hippies," Allie yelled. "Fuckin' hippies."

Susan appeared at the gate. She swayed, almost in a swoon, and held the gate to stay standing.

"Hippies didn't do this," Lytton said.

He lifted a broken tomato plant from the paved area by the greenhouse door and pointed at a splashed yellow stain.

"Allie, where've you seen something like this recently?"

It came to her.

"Terry Gilpin. When he spat at thic letter."

"He has better aim with his mouth than his gun," Lytton commented, wincing. "Thankfully."

Lytton stood by his Norton, lifting his gauntlets out of the pannier.

"Are you leaving?" Allie asked.

"No," Lytton said, taking his gunbelt, "I'm going down to the pub."

He settled the guns on his hips and fastened the buckle. The belt seemed to give him strength, to make him stand straighter.

Susan, still shocked, didn't protest.

"Are you'm going to shoot Squire Maskell?" Allie asked.

That snapped Susan out of it. She took Allie and shook her by the shoulders, keening wordlessly.

"I'm just going to have a lunchtime drink."

Allie hugged Susan fiercely. They were on the point of losing everything, but gave each other the last of their strength. There was something Maskell couldn't touch.

Lytton strolled towards the front gate.

Allie pulled away from Susan. For a moment, Susan wouldn't let her go. Then, without words, she gave her blessing. Allie knew she was to look after Lytton.

He was halfway down the street, passing the bus shelter, disused since the service was cut, when Allie caught up with him. At the fork in the road where the village oak stood was The Valiant Soldier.

They walked on.

"I hope you do shoot him," she said.

"I just want to find out why he's so obsessed with Gosmore Farm, Allie. Men like Maskell always have reasons. That's why they're pathetic. You should only be afraid of men without reasons."

Lytton pushed open the door, and stepped into the public bar. This early, there were few drinkers. Danny Keogh sat in his usual seat, wooden leg unslung on the floor beside him. Teddy Gilpin was swearing at the Trivial Pursuit machine, and his brother was nursing a half of scrumpy and a packet of crisps, ogling the Tiller Girl in UI.

Behind the bar, Janet Speke admired her piled-up hair in the long mirror. She saw Lytton and displayed immediate interest, squirming tightly in an odd way Allie almost understood.

Terry's mouth sagged open, giving an unprepossessing view of streaky-bacon-flavor mulch. The Triv machine fell silent, and Teddy's hands twitched away from the buttons to his gun-handle. Allie enjoyed the moment, knowing everyone in the pub was knotted inside, wondering what the stranger—her friend, she realized—would do next. Gary Chilcot, a weaselly little Maskell hand, slipped away, into the back bar where the Squire usually drank.

"How d'ye do, Goodman," said Janet, stretching thin red lips around dazzling teeth in a fox smile. "What can I do you for?"

"Bells. And Tizer for Allie here."

"She'm underage."

"Maskell won't mind. We're old friends."

Janet fetched the whisky and the soft drink. Lytton looked at the exposed nape of her neck, where wisps of hair escaped, and caught the barmaid smiling in the mirror, eyes fixed on his even though he was standing behind her.

Lytton sipped his whisky, registering the sting in his eyes.

Janet went to the jukebox and put on Portishead. She walked back to the bar, almost dancing, hips in exaggerated motion. Music insinuated into the spaces between them all, blotting out their silent messages.

The door opened and Reeve Draper came in, out of breath. He had obviously been summoned.

"I've been meaning to call again on Goodwife Ames," he said to Lytton, not mentioning that when last he had seen Lytton the newcomer was on the ground with a bullethole in his shoulder put there by the Reeve's Constable. "Tony Jago, the Traveler Chieftain, has escaped from Glastonbury with a band of sheep-shaggin', drug-takin' gyppos. We'm expecting raids on farms. Susan should watch out for them. Bad lot, gyppos. No respect for property. They'm so stoned on dope they'm don't know what they'm doin'."

Lytton took a marijuana leaf badge from his pocket. One of the emblems pinned to the poncho left in the ravaged garden. He tossed it into Terry Gilpin's scrumpy.

"Oops, sorry," he said.

This time, Terry went for his gun and fumbled. Lytton kicked the stool from under him. Terry sprawled, choking on crisps, on the floor. With a boot-toe, Lytton pinned Terry's wrist. He nodded to Allie, and she took the gun away. Terry swore, brow dotted with ciderstinking sweat bullets.

Allie had held guns before, but not since Susan took her in. She had forgotten how heavy they were. The barrel drooped even though she held the gun two-handed, and accidentally happened to point at Terry's gut.

"If I made a complaint against this man, I don't suppose much would happen."

Draper said nothing. His face was as red as strawberry jam.

"I thought not."

Terry squirmed. Teddy gawped down at his brother.

Lytton took out his gun, pointed it at Teddy, said "pop," and put it back in its holster, all in one movement, between one heartbeat and the next. Teddy goggled, hand hovering inches away from his own gun.

"That was a fair fight," Lytton said. "Do you want to try it again?"

He let Terry go. Rubbing his reddened wrist, the Maskell man scurried away and stood up.

"If'n you gents got an argument, take it outside," Janet said. "I've got regulars who don't take to ruckus."

Lytton strolled across the room, toward the back bar. He pushed a door with frosted glass panels, and disclosed a small room with heavily-upholstered settees, horse-brasses on beams and faded hunt scenes on the wallpaper.

The Squire sat at a table with papers and maps spread out on it. A man Allie didn't know, who wore a collar and tie, sat with him. Erskine was there too, listening to Gary Chilcot, who had been talking since he left the bar.

The Squire was too annoyed to fake congeniality.

"We'd like privacy, if you please."

Lytton looked over the table. There was a large-scale survey map of the area, with red lines dotted across it. The corners were held down by ashtrays and empty glasses. The Squire had been illustrating some point by tapping the map, and his well-dressed guest was frozen in mid-nod.

Lytton, stepping back from the back bar, let the door swing closed in the face of Erskine, who was rushing out. A panel cracked and the Constable went down on his knees.

Allie felt excitement in her water.

Terry charged but Lytton stepped aside and lifted the Maskell man by the seat of his britches, heaving him up over the bar and barreling him into the long mirror. Glass shattered.

Janet Speke, incandescent with proprietary fury, brought out a shotgun, which Lytton pinned to the bar with his arm.

"My apologies, Goodwife. He'll make up the damage."

There was nothing in the barmaid's pale blue eyes but hate. Impulsively, Lytton craned across and kissed her full on the lips. Hot angry spots appeared on her cheeks as he let her go. He detached her from the shotgun.

"You should be careful with these things," he said. "They're apt to discharge inconveniently if mishandled."

He fired both barrels at a framed photograph of Alder's victorious skittles team of '66. The noise was an astounding crash. Lytton broke the gun and dropped it. Erskine, nose bloody in his handkerchief, came out of the back bar with his Webley out and cocked.

This time, it was different. Lytton was armed.

Despite the hurt in his left shoulder, Lytton drew both his pistols in an instant and, at close range, shot off Erskine's ears. The Constable stood, appalled, blood pouring from fleshy nubs that would no longer hold his helmet up.

Erskine's shot went wild.

Lytton took cool aim and told the Constable to drop his Webley.

Erskine saw sense. The revolver clumped on the floor.

In an instant, Lytton holstered his pistols. The music came back, filling the quiet that followed the crashes and shots. Terry moaned in a heap behind the bar. Janet kicked him out. Erskine looked for his ears.

Lytton took another sip of Bells.

"Very fine," he commented.

Janet, lipstick smeared, touched her hair, deprived of her mirror, not knowing where free strands hung.

Lytton slipped a copper-colored ten shilling note onto the bar.

"A round of drinks, I think," he said.

Danny Keough smiled and shook an empty glass.

Outside, in the car park of The Valiant Soldier, Allie bubbled over. It was the most thrilling thing. To see Terry hit the mirror, Teddy staring at a draw he'd never beat, the Reeve helpless, Janet Speke and the Squire in impotent rage and, best of all, Barry Erskine with his helmet-brim on his nose and blood gushing onto his shoulders. For a moment, Alder was like *The Archers,* and the villains were seen off.

Lytton was somber, cold, bravado gone.

"It was just a moment, Allie. An early fluke goal for our side. They still have the referee in their back pocket and fifteen extra players."

He looked around the car park.

"Any of these vehicles unfamiliar?"

Maskell's ostentatious Range Rover was parked by Janet's pink Vauxhall Mustang. The Morris pick-up was the Gilpins'. The Reeve's panda car was on the street. That left an

Austin Maverick Allie had never seen before. She pointed it out.

"Company car," he said, tapping the windshield.

The front passenger seat was piled with glossy folders that had "GREAT WESTERN RAILWAYS" embossed on their jackets.

"The clouds of mystery clear," he mused. "Do you have one of your nails?"

Puzzled, she took a nail from her purse and handed it over.

"Perfect," he said, crouching by the car door, working the nail into the lock. "This is a neat trick you shouldn't learn, Allie. There, my old sapper sergeant would be proud of me."

He got the door open, snatched one of the folders, and had the door shut again.

They left in a hurry, but slowed by the bus stop. The rusting shelter was fly-posted with car-boot sale announcements. Lytton sagged. His shirt-shoulder spotted where his wound had opened again. Still, he was better off than Earless Erskine.

"It's choo-choos, I'll be bound," he said. "The track they run on is always blooded."

There was activity at the pub as Maskell's party loped past the village oak into the car park. Maskell was in the center, paying embarrassed attention to his guest, who presumably hadn't expected a bar brawl and an ear-shooting to go with his ploughman's lunch and a lecture on local geography.

The outsider got into his Maverick and Maskell waved him off. Then, he started shouting at his men. Allie smiled to hear him so angry, but Lytton looked grim.

That evening, after they had eaten, Lytton explained to Susan, showing her the maps and figures. Allie struggled to keep up.

"It's to do with Railway Privatization," he said. "The measures that came in after the War, that centralized and nationalized so many industries, are being dismantled by the Tories. And private companies are stepping in. With many a kickback and inside deal."

"There's not been a railway near Alder for fifty years," Susan said.

"When British Rail is broken up, the companies that have bits of the old network will be set against each other like fighting dogs. They'll shut down some lines and open up others, not because they need to but to get one over on the next fellow. GWR, who are chummying up with the Squire, would like it if all trains from Wessex to London went through Bristol. They can up the fares, and cut off the Southeastern company. To do that, they need to put a branch line here, across the Southern edge of Maskell's farm, right through your orchard."

Susan understood, and was furious.

"I don't want a railway through my farm."

"But Maskell sees how much money he'd make. Not just from selling land at inflated prices. There'd be a watering halt. Maybe even a station."

"He can't do the deal without Gosmore Farm?"

"No."

"Well, he can whistle 'Lillibulero.'"

"It may not be that easy."

The lights flickered and failed. The kitchen was lit only by the red glow of the wood fire.

"Allie, I told you to check the generator," Susan snapped.

Allie protested. She was careful about maintaining the generator. They'd once lost the refrigerator and had a week's milk quota spoil overnight.

Lytton signaled for quiet. He drew a gun from inside his waistcoat.

Allie listened for sounds outside.

"Are the upstairs windows shuttered?" Lytton asked.

"I asked you not to bring those things indoors," Susan said, evenly. "I won't have guns in the house."

"You soon won't have a choice. There'll be unwelcome visitors."

Susan caught on and went quiet. Allie saw fearful shadows. There was a shot and the window over the basin exploded inward. A fireball flew in and plopped onto the table, oily rags in flames. With determination, Susan took a flat breadboard and pressed out the fire.

Noise began. Loudspeakers were set up outside. Music hammered their ears. The Beatles' "Helter Skelter."

"Maskell's idea of hippie music," Lytton said.

In the din, gunshots spanged against stones, smashed through windows and shutters.

Lytton bundled Susan under the heavy kitchen table, and pushed Allie in after her.

"Stay here," he said, and was gone upstairs.

Allie tried putting her fingers in her ears and screwing her eyes shut. She was still in the middle of the attack.

"Is Maskell going to kill us?" she asked.

Susan was rigid. Allie hugged her.

There was a shot from upstairs. Lytton was returning fire.

"I'm going to help him," Allie said.

"No," shouted Susan, as Allie slipped out of her grasp. "Don't . . ."

She knew the house well enough to dart around in the dark without bumping into anything. Like Lytton, she headed upstairs.

From her bedroom window, which had already been shot out, she could see as far as the treeline. There was no moon. The Beatles still screamed. In the orchard, fires were set. Hooded figures danced between the trees, wearing ponchos and beads. She wasn't fooled. These weren't Jago's Travelers but Maskell's men.

Allie had to draw the line here. She and Susan had been pushed too far. They'd lost men to Maskell, they wouldn't lose land.

A man carrying a fireball dashed toward the house, aiming to throw it through a window. Allie drew a bead with her catapult and put a nail in his knee. She heard him shriek above the music. He tumbled over, fire thumping onto his chest and spreading to his poncho. He twisted, yelling like a stuck pig, and wrestled his way out of the burning hood.

It was Teddy Gilpin.

He scrambled back, limping and smoldering. She could have put another nail in his skull.

But didn't.

Lytton was in the hallway, switching between windows, using bullets to keep the attackers back. One lay still, face-down, on the lawn. Allie hoped it was Maskell.

She scrambled out of her window, clung to the drainpipe, and squeezed into shadows under the eaves. Like a bat, she hung, catapult dangling from her mouth. She monkeyed up onto the roof, and crawled behind the chimney.

If she kept them off the roof, they couldn't get close enough to fire the house. She didn't waste nails, but was ready to put a spike into the head of anyone who trespassed. But someone had thought of that first. She saw the ladder-top protruding over the far edge of the roof.

An arm went around her neck, and the catapult was twisted from her hand. She smelled his strong cider-and-shit stink.

"It be the little poacher," a voice cooed.

It was Stan Budge, Maskell's gamekeeper.

"Who'm trespassin' now?" she said, and fixed her teeth into his wrist.

Though she knew this was not a game, she was surprised when Budge punched her in the head, rattling her teeth, blurring her vision. She let him go. And he hit her again. She lost her footing, thumped against tiles and slid toward the gutter, slates loosening under her.

Budge grabbed her hair.

The hard yank on her scalp was hot agony. Budge pulled her away from the edge. She screamed.

"Wouldn't want nothing to happen to you," he said. "Not yet."

Budge forced her to go down the ladder, and a couple of men gripped her. She struggled, trying to kick shins.

Shots came from house and hillside.

"Take her round to the Squire," Budge ordered.

Allie was glad it was dark. No one could see the shamed tears on her cheeks. She felt so stupid. She had let Susan down. And Lytton.

Budge took off his hood and shook his head.

"No more bleddy fancy dress," he said.

She had to be dragged to where Maskell sat, smoking a cigar, in a deckchair between the loudspeakers.

"Allison, dear," he said. "Think, if it weren't for the Civil War, I'd *own* you. Then again, at this point in time, I might as well own you."

He shut off the cassette player.

Terry Gilpin and Barry Erskine—out of uniform, with white lumps of bandage on his head—held her between them. The Squire drew a long thin knife from his boot and let it catch the firelight.

Maskell plugged a karaoke microphone into the speaker.

"Susan," he said, booming. "You should come out now. We've driven off the gyppos. But we have someone you'll want to see."

He pointed the microphone at her and Terry wrenched her hair. Despite herself, she screamed.

"It's dear little Allison."

There was a muffled oath from inside.

"And your protector, Captain Lytton. He should come out too. Yes, we know a bit about him. Impressive war record, if hardly calculated to make him popular in these parts. Or anywhere."

Allie had no idea what that meant.

"Throw your gun out, if you would, Captain. We don't want any more accidents."

The back door opened, and firelight spilled out. A dark figure stepped onto the verandah.

"The gun, Lytton."

A gun was tossed down.

Erskine fairly slobbered with excitement. Allie felt him pressing close to her, writhing. Once he let her go, he would kill Lytton, she knew.

Lytton stood beside the door. Another figure joined him, shivering in a white shawl that was a streak in the dark.

"Ah, Susan," Maskell said, as if she had just arrived at his Christmas Feast. "Delighted you could join us."

Maskell's knifepoint played around Allie's throat, dimpling the skin, pricking tinily.

In a rush, it came to her that this had very little to do with railways and land and money. When it came down to it, the hurt Maskell fancied he was avenging that he couldn't have Susan. Or Allie.

Knowing why didn't make things better.

Hand in hand, Lytton and Susan came across the lawn. Maskell's men gathered, jeering.

"Are you all right, Allison?" Susan asked.

"I'm sorry."

"It's not your fault, dear."

"I have papers with me," Maskell said, "if you'd care to sign. The terms are surprisingly generous, considering."

Lytton and Susan were close enough to see the knife.

"You sheep-shagging bastard," Susan said.

Lytton's other gun appeared from under her shawl. She

raised her arm and fired. Allie felt wind as the bullet whistled past. Maskell's jaw came away in a gush of red-black. Susan shot him again, in the eye. He was thumped backward, knife ripped away from Allie's throat, and laid on the grass, heels kicking.

"I said I didn't like guns," Susan announced. "I never said I couldn't use one."

Lytton took hold of Susan's shoulders and pulled her out of the way of the fusillade unleashed in their direction by Budge and Terry Gilpin.

Allie twisted in Erskine's grasp and rammed a bony knee between his legs. Erskine yelped, and she clawed his ear-bandages, ripping the wounds open.

The Constable staggered away, and was peppered by his comrades' fire. He took one in the lungs and knelt over the Squire, coughing up thick pink foam.

In a flash of gunfire, Allie saw Lytton sitting up, shielding Susan with his body, arm outstretched. He had picked up a pistol. The flashes stopped. Budge lay flat dead, and Gilpin gurgled, incapacitated by several wounds. Lytton was shot again too, in the leg.

He had fired his gun dry, and was reloading, taking rounds from his belt.

Car-lights froze the scene. The blood on the grass was deepest black. Faces were white as skulls. Lytton still carefully shoved new bullets into chambers. Susan struggled to sit up.

Reeve Draper got out of the panda car and assessed the situation. He stood over Maskell's body. The Squire's face was gone.

"Looks like you'm had a bad gyppo attack," he said.

Lytton snapped his revolver shut and held it loosely, not aiming. The Reeve turned away from him.

"But it be over now."

Erskine coughed himself quiet.

Allie wasn't sorry any of them were dead. If she was crying, it was for her father, for the chickens, for the vegetable garden.

"I assume Goodwife Ames no longer has to worry about her cows being destroyed?" Lytton asked.

The Reeve nodded, tightly.

"I thought so."

Draper ordered Gary Chilcot to gather the wounded and get them off Gosmore Farm.

"Take the rubbish too," Susan insisted, meaning the dead.

Chilcot, face painted with purple butterflies, was about to protest but Lytton still had the gun.

"Squire Maskell bain't givin' out no more pay packets, Gary," the Reeve reminded him.

Chilcot thought about it and ordered the able-bodied to clear the farm of corpses.

Allie woke up well after dawn. It was a glorious spring day. The blood on the grass had soaked in and was invisible. But there were windows that needed mending.

She went outside and saw Lytton and Susan by the generator. It was humming into life. Lytton had oil on his hands.

In the daylight, Susan seemed ghost-like.

Allie understood what it must be like. To kill a man. Even a man like Squire Maskell. It was as if Susan had killed a part of herself. Allie would have to be careful with Susan, try to coax her back.

"There," Lytton said. "Humming nicely."

"Thank you, Captain," said Susan.

Lytton's eyes narrowed minutely. Maskell had called him Captain.

"Thank you, Susan."

He touched her cheek.

"Thank you for everything."

Allie ran up and hugged Lytton. He held her too, not ferociously. She broke the embrace. Allie didn't want him to leave. But he would.

The Norton was propped in the driveway, wheeled out beyond the open gate. He walked stiffly away from them and straddled the motorcycle. His leg wound was just a scratch.

Allie and Susan followed him to the gate. Allie felt Susan's arm around her shoulders.

Lytton pulled on his gauntlets and curled his fingers around the handlebars. He didn't wince.

"You're Captain UI Lytton, aren't you?" Susan said.

There was a little hurt in his eyes. His frown-lines crinkled.

"You've heard of me."

"Most people have. Most people don't know how you could do what you did in the War."

"Sometimes you have a choice. Sometimes you don't."

Susan left Allie and slipped around the gate. She kissed Lytton. Not the way Lytton had kissed Janet Speke, like a slap, but slowly, awkwardly.

Allie was half-embarrassed, half-heartbroken.

"Thank you, Captain Lytton," Susan said. "There will always be a breakfast for you at Gosmore Farm."

"I never did give you the ten shillings," he smiled.

Allie was crying again and didn't know why. Susan let her fingers trail through Lytton's hair and across his shoulder. She stood back.

He pulled down his goggles, then kicked the Norton into life and drove off.

Allie scrambled through the gate and ran after him. She kept up with him, lungs protesting, until the village oak, then sank, exhausted, by the curb. Lytton turned on his saddle and waved, then was gone from her sight, headed out across the moors. She stayed, curled up under the oak, until she could no longer hear his engine.

Turnover

GEOFFREY A. LANDIS

Geoff Landis is characteristically a hard SF writer, widely published in the magazines and often seen on award nomination ballots, and that's where this story is coming from. It appeared in *Interzone,* where a significant amount of the best humorous SF is published these days. One of the traditional hallmarks of satire is the world turned upside down, a clever way to expose the absurdity of conventional behavior, and in this case some clunky and old fashioned SF storytelling. The third word in the story is a suspicious intrusion from conventional fantasy and by the end of the first sentence we know we are in the world of deadpan. This story goes to show that a heavy hand sometimes delivers the strongest blow.

The scientist's guild had a requirement that each accredited scientist must have a beautiful assistant to ask questions. Doctor Piffelheimer's beautiful assistant was a young man named Percival Kensington. She looked him over. The cool-suit he was wearing, a necessary accoutrement against the Venusian temperature, had the advantage of being a skin-tight, form-fitting garment, padding and revealing every curve of his perfectly shaped body, down to and including the almost indecent bulge between his thighs.

The surface of Venus was almost hot enough for the rocks to glow. It was a good thing that the perfect thermal insulator had been invented, or it would have been completely impossible to send a team to Venus to answer important scientific questions.

Except for her assistant Percy, the surface of Venus held very little to see. One spot on the barren rock looked very much like another. Dr. Piffelheimer picked one at random and pointed. "This looks like a good spot."

Percy obediently lugged the equipment over to the spot. Fortunately the ultradrill floated on a carpet of electrostatic repulsion, and lugging the five-ton mass of the drill to the indicated spot required little more than guiding it with a finger in the right direction. "Explain to me what we're trying to find out from this core," he said, and cocked his head in a charming tilt to listen. They must have trained him perfectly in scientists' assistant school; this was exactly the type of obvious question that a beautiful assistant was supposed to ask.

Piffelheimer motioned him to start the ultradrill while she expounded. The ultradrill would bore downward at a rate of 200 meters a minute. It made a racket like a herd of mating elephants while doing so, but fortunately the helmets of the coolsuits were perfect acoustic insulators as well as perfect thermal insulation, so she knew that her voice over the intercom was flawlessly clear.

"The surface of Venus is very anomalous," Piffelheimer expounded carefully. "This was first really understood back in the last years of the twentieth century, when the primitive space probes discovered that the crater distribution was uniform across the surface."

"What's anomalous about that?" Percy asked, completely on cue.

"Crater count indicates the age of the surface," Piffelheimer said. "Since meteor bombardment occurs randomly at every point on the surface, a uniform crater distribution means that the surface of Venus is all precisely the same age. But, as every geologist knows, a geological surface is periodically resurfaced, by tectonic forces, by vulcanism, and the like. Vulcanism is necessary to get the heat out of the interior of the planet. So a planet cannot possibly have a surface of uniform age."

"But you just said it does."

"That's right. This is the scientific mystery, and we're about to find the answer to it."

"Oh. How are we going to do that?"

"By drilling and inserting heat-flow probes," she said. "The mystery is, how does the planet Venus release heat from the interior, if it doesn't resurface the planet through vulcanism?"

"Aren't there any theories?"

"Well, there is one." Piffelheimer made a face. "One wacko from the twentieth century, a scientist named Turcotte, proposed periodic, catastrophic resurfacing. Every 500 million years or so, the entire surface of Venus resurfaces all at once. The whole surface of the planet becomes one single magma ocean, and all the heat of the interior is released at once. Then, of course, it cools down, and since the whole thing was molten at the same time, every part of the surface is the same age."

"Well, that makes sense." Percy looked down at the drill controls. "One kilometer, and drilling steady. So, why don't we like that theory?"

"Because it's a catastrophic theory."

Percy looked blank. Charming, but blank.

"Catastrophism is anathema to geologists," Piffelheimer explained. "It smacks of religion—the hand of God wiping the planet clean. Noah's flood and such. Real geologists are uniformitarians. It's our job to show that the processes of geology are gradual and continuous."

"But if this Turbot theory—"

"Turcotte."

"Turcotte theory was right—"

"But it's not."

"But if it was right, what causes this resurfacing?"

Piffelheimer shrugged. The heat builds up. Eventually something triggers it."

"Two kilometers deep, running steady," Percy said. "How often does it resurface?"

"I told you. It doesn't." She was getting a little annoyed with the conversation, although she couldn't really blame Percy. After all, his job was to ask innocent questions. Time to change the subject. She looked around. Nothing but gray, blasted rock under them, uniform gray clouds above them. Between the gray and the gray was the clear air of the surface. "Have you looked at the horizon?" she asked. "Notice the way it seems to curve up around us, as if we were at the bottom of a shallow bowl."

"Yes, due to the refraction effect from the density gradient of the thick atmosphere," Percy said. "If the air were clear enough, we would be able to see ourselves on the other side of the planet. We can't of course, due to Rayleigh scattering. You didn't answer my question. How often, according to Turcotte, does this resurfacing event on Venus occur?"

"Every 500 million years, give or take," Piffelheimer said, annoyed. She really shouldn't have answered the question at all, since Percy was going way beyond his job description in pressing it in the first place, but she was so used to expounding automatically that it didn't occur to her to not answer until after she already had.

"And how long ago was the last time it happened?"

"Five hundred million years," she said.

"Then there must be a lot of interior heat waiting to get out," Percy said. "What, exactly, triggers the catastrophic release?"

Piffelheimer shrugged, annoyed. "Anything. An asteroid impact, I suppose might trigger it."

"Or maybe a drill?"

There was no need for Piffelheimer to answer him. The rock surface had suddenly split open at the site of the drilling, separating into three lines that radiated away from the drill point and streaked for the horizon. Each of the crevasses split into a network of sidecracks, which instantly fragmented still further. No doubt there was an ominous thunder accompanying the whole process as well, but of course the insulation muffled that. An orange glow from below lit up the clouds, and the cracks widened until the magma, welling up from below, washed over them.

Later, as they bobbed in the magma in their coolsuits, Piffelheimer had a perfect opportunity to expound on the value of perfect thermal insulation, but she decided to stay silent. Kensington probably knew it all anyway, damn him.

"If you think I'm gonna set my nice clean spaceship down in that," came the voice in her headset, "you got another thing coming."

She looked up. The expedition transport ship was hovering over them. As she watched, a rope (woven of refractory fibers, no doubt, since it didn't melt in the heat) fell toward them and ploiked down in the lava next to her. The correct procedure, Piffelheimer knew, is for scientist to carry beautiful assistant to safety. She glanced over at Percy, floating cheerfully on his back a few meters away, and decided, screw that. She pulled herself up the rope. Let him pull himself up.

Oh, well. After all, it had been a good day for science, and the scientists' guild ought to be justifiably proud, she reflected. She had verified beyond any possible scientific objections a theory that had been hithertofore only a conjecture.

With the help of her beautiful but scatterbrained assistant, of course.

The Mendelian
Lamp Case

PAUL LEVINSON

Paul Levinson runs an online classroom system, and combines the skills of communications with a philosophical rigor. He edits the *Journal of Social and Evolutionary Systems* and in 1997 he published a science nonfiction book, *The Soft Edge*. He has been publishing short fiction for several years now, and is proud to be a member of the *Analog* Mafia, an aggregation of writers most identified with Stanley Schmidt's magazine—this story is from *Analog*. Last year Levinson cut loose with several fine stories, including tales in the continuing saga of Phil D'Amato, of which this is one. "The Mendelian Lamp Case" is filled with the kind of surprises I use to find and value in the stories of Robert A. Heinlein, wonders that make me rethink what I thought were solved problems or conventional solutions. At its best, this story is outrageously inventive. Years ago, the Seminoles went to ground in the Everglades with their sewing machines and came out years later with Seminole Patchwork, a previously unknown mathematical tiling. This story is about what is happening in rural Pennsylvania.

Most people think of California, or the midwest, when they think of farm country. I'll take Pennsylvania, and the deep greens on its red earth, any time. Small patches of tomatoes and corn, clothes snapping brightly on a line, and a farmhouse always attached to some corner. The scale is human . . .

Jenna was in England for a conference, my weekend calendar was clear, so I took Mo up on a visit to Lancaster. Over the GW Bridge, coughing down the Turnpike, over another bridge, down yet another highway stained and pitted then off on a side road where I can roll down my windows and breathe.

Mo and his wife and two girls were good people. He was a rarity for a forensic scientist. Maybe it was the pace of criminal science in this part of the country—lots of the people around here were Amish, and Amish are non-violent—or maybe it was his steady diet of those deep greens that quieted his soul. But Mo had none of the grit, none of the cynicism, that comes to most of us who traverse the territory of the dead and the maimed. No, Mo had an innocence, a delight, in the lights of science and people and their possibilities.

"Phil." He clapped me on the back with one hand and took my bag with another. "Phil, how are you?" his wife Corinne yoo-hooed from inside. "Hi Phil!" his elder daughter Laurie, probably sixteen already, chimed in from the window, a quick splash of strawberry blond in a crystal frame.

"Hi—" I started to say, but Mo put my bag on the porch and ushered me toward his car.

"You got here early, good," he said, in that schoolboy conspiratorial whisper I'd heard him go into every time he came across some inviting new avenue of science. ESP, UFOs, Mayan ruins in unexpected places—these were all catnip to Mo. But the power of quiet nature, the hidden wisdom of the farmer, this was his special domain. "A little present I want to pick up for Laurie," he whispered even more, though she was well out of earshot. "And something I want to show you. You too tired for a quick drive?"

"Ah, no, I'm okay—"

"Great, let's go then," he said. "I came across some Amish techniques—well, you'll see for yourself, you're gonna love it."

Strasburg is fifteen minutes down Rt. 30 from Lancaster. All Dairy Queens and 7-Elevens till you get there, but when you turn off and travel a half a mile in any direction you're back a hundred years or more in time. The air itself says it all. High mixture of pollen and horse manure that smells so surprisingly good, so real, it makes your eyes tear with pleasure. You don't even mind a few flies flitting around.

We turned down Northstar Road. "Jacob Stoltzfus's farm is down there on the right," Mo said.

I nodded. "Beautiful." The sun looked about five minutes to setting. The sky was the color of a robin's belly against the browns and greens of the farm. "He won't mind that we're coming here by, uh—"

"By car? Nah, of course not," Mo said. "The Amish have no problem with non-Amish driving. And Jacob, as you'll see, is more open-minded than most."

I thought I could see him now, off to the right at the end of the road that had turned to dirt, gray-white head of hair and beard bending over the gnarled bark of a fruit tree. He wore plain black overalls and a deep purple shirt.

"That Jacob?" I asked.

"I think so," Mo replied. "I'm not sure."

We pulled the car over near the tree, and got out. A soft autumn rain suddenly started falling.

"You have business here?" The man by the tree turned to address us. His tone was far from friendly.

"Uh, yes," Mo said, clearly taken aback. "I'm sorry to intrude. Jacob—Jacob Stoltzfus—said it would be okay if we came by—"

"You had business with Jacob?" the man demanded again. His eyes looked red and watery—though that could've been from the rain.

"Well, yes," Mo said. "But if this isn't a good time—"

"My brother is dead," the man said. "My name is Isaac. This is a bad time for our family."

"Dead?" Mo nearly shouted. "I mean . . . what happened? I just saw your brother yesterday."

"We're not sure," Isaac said. "Heart attack, maybe. I think you should leave now. Family are coming soon."

"Yes, yes, of course," Mo said. He looked beyond Isaac at a barn that I noticed for the first time. Its doors were slightly open, and weak light flickered inside.

Mo took a step in the direction of the barn. Isaac put up a restraining arm. "Please," he said. "It's better if you go."

"Yes, of course," Mo said again, and I led him to the car.

"You all right?" I said when we were both in the car, and Mo had started the engine.

He shook his head. "Couldn't be a heart attack. Not at a time like this."

"Heart attacks don't usually ask for appointments," I said.

Mo was still shaking his head, turning back on to Northstar Road. "I think someone killed him."

Now forensic scientists are prone to see murder in a ninety-year old woman dying peacefully in her sleep, but this was unusual from Mo.

"Tell me about it," I said, reluctantly. Just what I needed—death turning my visit into a busman's holiday.

"Never mind," he muttered. "I babbled too much already."

"Babbled? You haven't told me a thing."

Mo drove on in brooding silence. He looked like a different person, wearing a mask that used to be him.

"You're trying to protect me from something, is that it?" I ventured. "You know better than that."

Mo said nothing.

"What's the point?" I prodded. "We'll be back with Corinne and the girls in five minutes. They'll take one look at you, and know something happened. What are you going to tell *them*?"

Mo swerved suddenly onto a side road, bringing my kidney into sticking contact with the inside door handle. "Well, I guess you're right about that," he said. He punched in a code in his car phone—I hadn't noticed it before.

"Hello?" Corinne answered.

"Bad news, honey," Mo said matter of factly, though it sounded put on to me. No doubt his wife would see through it too. "Something came up in the project, and we're going to have to go to Philadelphia tonight."

"You and Phil? Everything okay?"

"Yeah, the two of us," Mo said. "Not to worry. I'll call you again when we get there."

"I love you," Corinne said.

"Me too," Mo said. "Kiss the girls good night for me."

He hung up and turned to me.

"Philadelphia?" I asked.

"Better that I don't give them too many details," he said. "I never do in my cases. Only would worry them."

"She's worried anyway," I said. "Sure sign she's worried when she didn't even scream at you for missing dinner. Now that you bring it up, I'm a little worried now too. What's going on?"

Mo said nothing. Then he turned the car again—mercifully more gently this time—onto a road with a sign that advised that the Pennsylvania Turnpike was up ahead.

I rolled up the window as our speed increased. The night had suddenly gone damp and cold.

"You going to give me a clue as to where we're going, or just kidnap me to Philadelphia?" I asked.

"I'll let you off at the Thirtieth Street Station," Mo said. "You can get a bite to eat on the train and be back in New York in an hour."

"You left my bag on your porch, remember?" I said. "Not to mention my car."

Mo just scowled and drove on.

"I wonder if Amos knows?" he said more to himself than me a few moments later.

"Amos is a friend of Jacob's?" I asked.

"His son," Mo said.

"Well I guess you can't very well call him on your car phone," I said.

Mo shook his head, frowned. "Most people misunderstand the Amish—think they're some sort of Luddites, against all technology. But that's not really it at all. They struggle with technology, agonize over whether to reject or accept it, and if they accept it, in what ways, so as not to compromise their independence and self-sufficiency. They're not completely against phones—just against phones in their homes—because the phone intrudes on everything you're doing."

I snorted. "Yeah, many's the time a call from the Captain pulled me out of the sack."

Mo flashed his smile, for the first time since we'd left Jacob Stoltzfus's farm. It was good to see.

"So where do Amish keep their phones?" I might as well press my advantage, and the chance it would get Mo to talk.

"Well, that's another misconception," Mo said. "There's not one monolithic Amish viewpoint. There are many Amish groups, many different ways of dealing with technology. Some allow phone shacks on the edges of their property, so they can make calls when they want to, but not be disturbed by them in the sanctity of their homes."

"Does Amos have a phone shack?" I asked.

"Dunno," Mo said, like he was beginning to think about something else.

"But you said his family was more open than most," I said.

Mo swiveled his head to stare at me for a second, then turned his eyes back on the road. "Open-minded, yes. But not really about communications."

"About what, then?"

"Medicine," Mo said.

"Medicine?" I asked.

"What do you know about allergies?"

My nose itched—maybe it was the remnants of the sweet pollen near Strasburg.

"I have hay fever," I said. "Cantaloupe sometimes makes my mouth burn. I've seen a few strange deaths in my time due to allergic reactions. You think Jacob Stoltzfus died from something like that?"

"No," Mo said. "I think he was killed because he was trying to prevent people from dying from things like that."

"Okay," I said. "Last time you said that and I asked you to explain you said never mind. Should I ask again or let it slide?"

Mo sighed. "You know, genetic engineering goes back well before the double helix."

"Come again?"

"Breeding plants to make new combinations probably dates almost to the origins of our species," Mo said. "Darwin understood that—he called it 'artificial selection.' Mendel doped out the first laws of genetics breeding peas. Luther

Burbank developed way many more new varieties of fruit and vegetables than have yet to come out of our gene-splicing labs."

"And the connection to the Amish is what—they breed new vegetables now too?" I asked.

"More than that," Mo said. "They have whole insides of houses lit by special kinds of fireflies, altruistic manure permeated by slugs that seek out the roots of plants to die there and give them nourishment—all deliberately bred to be that way, and the public knows nothing about it. It's biotechnology of the highest order, without the technology."

"And your friend Jacob was working on this?"

Mo nodded. "Techno-allergists—our conventional researchers—have recently been investigating how some foods act as catalysts to other allergies. Cantaloupe tingles in your mouth in hay fever season, right?—because it's really exacerbating the hay fever allergy. Watermelon does the same, and so does the pollen of mums. Jacob and his people have known this for fifty years—and they've gone much further. They're trying to breed a new kind of food, some kind of tomato thing, which would act as an anti-catalyst for allergies—would reduce their histamic effect to nothing."

"Like an organic Hismanol?" I asked.

"Better than that," Mo said. "This would trump any pharmaceutical."

"You okay?" I noticed Mo's face was bearing big beads of sweat.

"Sure," he said, and cleared his throat. "I don't know. Jacob—" he started coughing in hacking waves.

I reached over to steady him, and straighten the steering wheel. His shirt was soaked with sweat and he was breathing in angry rasps.

"Mo, hold on," I said, keeping one hand on Mo and the wheel, fumbling with the other in my inside coat pocket. I finally got my fingers on the epinephrine pen I always kept there, and angled it out. Mo was limp and wet and barely conscious over the wheel. I pushed him over as gently as I could and went with my foot for the brake. Cars were speeding by us, screaming at me in the mirror with their lights. Thankfully Mo had been driving on the right, so I only had one stream of lights to blind me. My sole finally made contact with the brake, and I pressed down as gradually as possible. Miraculously, the car came to a reasonably slow halt on the shoulder of the road, and we both seemed in one piece.

I looked at Mo. I yanked up his shirt, and plunged the pen into his arm. I wasn't sure how long he'd not been breathing, but it wasn't good.

I dialed 911 on the car phone. "Get someone over here fast," I yelled. "I'm on the Turnpike, eastbound, just before the Philadelphia turnoff. I'm Dr. Phil D'Amato, NYPD Forensics, and this is a medical emergency."

I wasn't positive that anaphylactic shock was what was wrong with him, but the adrenaline couldn't do much harm. I leaned over his chest and felt no heartbeat. Jeez, please.

I gave Mo mouth-to-mouth, pounded his chest, pleading for life. "Hang on, damn you!" But I knew already. I could tell. After a while you get this sort of sickening sixth sense about these things. Some kind of allergic reaction from hell had just killed my friend. Right in my arms. Just like that.

EMS got to us eight minutes later. Better than some of the New York City times I'd been seeing lately. But it didn't matter. Mo was gone.

I looked at the car phone as they worked on him, cursing and trying to jolt him back into life. I'd have to call Corinne and tell her this now. But all I could see in the plastic phone display was Laurie's strawberry blond hair.

"You okay, Dr. D'Amato?" one of the orderlies called.

"Yeah," I said. I guess I was shaking.

"These allergic reactions can be lethal all right," he said, looking over at Mo.

Right, tell me about it.

"You'll call the family?" the orderly asked. They'd be taking Mo to a local hospital, DOA.

"Yeah," I said, brushing a burning tear from my eye. I felt like I was suffocating. I had to slow down, stay in control, separate the psychological from the physical so I could begin to understand what was going on here. I breathed out and in. Again. Okay. I was all right. I wasn't really suffocating.

The ambulance sped off, carrying Mo. He *had* been suffocating, and it killed him. What had he been starting to tell me?

I looked again at the phone. The right thing for me to do was to drive back to Mo's home, be there for Corinne when I told her—calling her on the phone with news like this was monstrous. But I had to find out what had happened to Mo— and that would likely not be from Corinne. Mo didn't want to worry her, didn't confide in her. No, the best chance of finding out what Mo had been up to seemed to be in Philadelphia, in the place Mo had been going. But where was that?

I focused on the phone display—pressed a couple of keys, and got a directory up on the little screen. The only 215 area code listed there was for a Sarah Fischer, with an address that I knew to be near Temple University.

I pressed the code next to the number, then the Send command.

Crackle, crackle, then a distant tinny cellular ring.

"Hello?" a female voice answered, sounding closer than I'd expected.

"Hi. Is this Sarah Fischer?"

"Yes," she said. "Do I know you?"

"Well, I'm a friend of Mo Buhler's, and I think we, he, may have been on his way to see you tonight—"

"Who are you? Is Mo okay?"

"Well—" I started.

"Look, who the hell are you? I'm going to hang up if you don't give me a straight answer," she said.

"I'm Dr. Phil D'Amato. I'm a forensic scientist—with the New York City Police Department."

She was quiet for a moment. "Your name sounds familiar for some reason," she said.

"Well, I've written a few articles—"

"Hold on," I heard her put the phone down, rustle through some papers.

"You had an article in *Discover*, about antibiotic-resistant bacteria, right?" she asked about half a minute later.

"Yes, I did," I said. In other circumstances, my ego would have jumped at finding such an observant reader.

"Okay, what date was it published?" she asked.

Jeez. "Uh, late last year," I said.

"I see there's a pen and ink sketch of you. What do you look like?"

"Straight dark hair—not enough of it," I said—who could remember what that lame sketch actually looked like?

"Go on," she said.

"And a moustache, reasonably thick, and steel-rimmed glasses." I'd grown the moustache at Jenna's behest, and had on my specs for the sketch.

A few beats of silence, then a sigh. "Okay," she said. "So now you get to tell me why you're calling—and what happened to Mo."

Sarah's apartment was less than half an hour away. I'd filled her in on the phone. She'd seemed more saddened than surprised, and asked me to come over.

I'd spoken to Corinne, and told her as best I could. Mo had been a cop before he'd become a forensic scientist, and I guess wives of police are supposed to be ready for this sort of thing, but how can a person ever really be ready for it after twenty years of good marriage? She'd cried, I'd cried, the kids cried in the background. I'd said I was coming over—and I know I should have—but I was hoping she'd say "no, I'm okay, Phil, really, you'll want to find out why this happened to Mo" . . . and that's exactly what she did say. They don't make people like Corinne Rodriguez Buhler any more.

There was a parking spot right across the street from Sarah's building—in New York this would have been a gift from on high. I tucked in my shirt, tightened my belt, and composed myself as best I could before ringing her bell.

She buzzed me in, and was standing inside her apartment, second floor walk-up, door open, to greet me as I sprinted and puffed up the flight of stairs. She had flaxen blond hair, a distracted look in her eyes, but an easy, open smile that I didn't expect after the grilling she'd given me on the phone. She looked about thirty.

The apartment had soft, recessed lighting—like a Paris-by-gaslight exhibit I'd once seen—and smelled faintly of lavender. My nose crinkled. "I use it to help me sleep," Sarah said, and directed me to an old, overstuffed Morris chair. "I was getting ready to go to sleep when you called."

"I'm sorry—"

"No, I'm the one who's sorry," she said. "About giving you a hard time, about what happened to Mo," her voice caught on Mo's name. "You must be hungry," she said, "I'll get you something." She turned around and walked toward another room, which I assumed was the kitchen.

Her pants were white, and the light showed the contours of her body to good advantage as she walked away.

"Here, try some of these to start," she returned with a bowl of grapes. Concord grapes. One of my favorites. Put one in your mouth, puncture the purple skin, jiggle the flesh around on your tongue, it's the taste of Fall. But I didn't move.

"I know," she said. "You're leery of touching any strange food after what happened to Mo. I don't blame you. But these are okay. Here, let me show you," and she reached and took a dusty grape and put it in her mouth. "Mmm," she smacked her lips, took out the pits with her finger. "Look— why don't *you* pick a grape and give it to me. Okay?"

My stomach was growling and I was feeling light-headed already, and I realized I would have to make a decision. Either leave right now, if I didn't trust this woman, and go somewhere to get something to eat—or eat what she gave me. I was too hungry to sit here and talk to her and resist her food right now.

"All right, up to you," she said. "I have some Black Forest ham, and can make you a sandwich, if you like, or just coffee or tea."

"All three." I decided. "I mean, I'd love the sandwich, and some tea please, and I'll try the grapes." I put one in my mouth. I'd learned a long time ago that paranoia can be almost as debilitating as the dangers it supposes.

She was back a few minutes later with the sandwich and the tea. I'd squished at least three more grapes in my mouth, and felt fine.

"There's a war going on," she said, and put the food tray on the end table next to me. The sandwich was made with some sort of black bread, and smelled wonderful.

"War?" I asked and bit into the sandwich. "You think what happened to Mo is the work of some terrorist?"

"Not exactly." Sarah sat down on a chair next to me, a cup of tea in her hand. "This war's been going on a very long time. It's a bio-war—much deeper rooted, literally, than anything we currently regard as terrorism."

"I don't get it," I said, and swallowed what I'd been chewing of my sandwich. It felt good going down, and in my stomach.

"No, you wouldn't," Sarah said. "Few people do. You think epidemics, sudden widespread allergic reactions, diseases that wipe out crops or livestock just happen. Sometimes they do. Sometimes it's more than that." She sipped her cup of tea. Something about the lighting, her hair, her face, maybe the taste of the food, made me feel like I was a kid back in the sixties. I half expected to smell incense burning.

"Who are you?" I asked. "I mean, what was your connection to Mo?"

"I'm working on my doctorate over at Temple," she said. "My area's ethno/botanical pharmacology—Mo was one of my resources. He was a very nice man." I thought I saw a tear glisten in the corner of her eye.

"Yes he was," I said. "And he was helping you with your dissertation about what—the germ warfare you were talking about?"

"Not exactly," Sarah said. "I mean, you know the academic world, no one would ever let me do a thesis on something that outrageous—it'd never get by the proposal committee. So you have to finesse it, do it on something more innocuous, get the good stuff in under the table, you know, smuggle it in. So, yeah, the *subtext* of my work was what we—I—call the bio-wars, which are actually more than just germ warfare, and yeah, Mo was one of the people who were helping me research that."

Sounded like Mo, all right. "And the Amish have something to do with this?"

"Yes and no," Sarah said. "The Amish aren't a single, unified group—they actually have quite a range of styles and values—"

"I know," I said. "And some of them—maybe one of the splinter groups—are involved in this bio-war?"

"The main bio-war group isn't really Amish—though they're situated near Lancaster, have been for at least 150 years in this country. Some people think they're Amish, though, since they live close to the land, in a low-tech mode. But they're not Amish. Real Amish would never do that. But some of the Amish know what's going on."

"You know a lot about the Amish," I said.

She blushed slightly. "I'm former Amish. I pursued my interests as far as a woman could in my Church. I pleaded with my bishop to let me go to college—he knew what the stakes were, the importance of what I was studying—but he said no. He said a woman's place was in the home. I guess he was trying to protect me, but I couldn't stay."

"You know Jacob Stoltzfus?" I asked.

Sarah nodded, lips tight. "He was my uncle," she finally said, "my mother's brother."

"I'm sorry," I said. I could see that she knew he was dead. "Who told you?" I asked softly.

"Amos—my cousin—Jacob's son. He has a phone shack," she said.

"I see," I said. What an evening. "I think Mo thought that those people—those others, like the Amish, but not Amish—somehow killed Jacob."

Sarah's face shuddered, seemed to unravel into sobs and tears. "They did," she managed to say. "Mo was right. And they killed Mo too."

I put down my plate, and reached over to comfort her. It wasn't enough. I got up and walked to her and put my arm around her. She got up shakily off her chair, then collapsed in my arms, heaving, crying. I felt her body, her heartbeat, through her crinoline shirt.

"It's okay," I said. "Don't worry. I deal with bastards like that all the time in my business. We'll get these people, I promise you."

She shook her head against my chest. "Not like these," she said.

"We'll get them," I said again.

She held on to me, then pulled away. "I'm sorry," she said. "I didn't mean to fall apart like that." She looked over at my empty teacup. "How about a glass of wine?"

I looked at my watch. It was 9:45 already, and I was exhausted. But there was more I needed to learn. "Okay," I said. "Sure. But just one glass."

She offered a tremulous smile, and went back into the kitchen. She returned with two glasses of a deep red wine. I sat down, and sipped. The wine tasted good—slightly Portuguese, perhaps, with just a hint of some fruit and a nice woody undertone.

"Local," she said. "You like it?"

"Yes, I do," I said.

She sipped some, then closed her eyes and tilted her head back. The bottoms of her blue eyes glinted like semi-precious gems out of half-closed lids.

I needed to focus on the problem at hand. "How exactly do these bio-war people kill—what'd they do to Jacob and Mo?" I asked.

Her eyes stayed closed a moment longer than I'd expected—like she'd been daydreaming, or drifting off to sleep. Then she opened them and looked at me, shaking her head slowly. "They've got all sorts of ways. The latest is some kind of catalyst—in food, we think it's a special kind of Crenshaw melon—that vastly magnifies the effect of any of a number of allergies." She got up, looked distracted. "I'm going to have another glass—sure you don't want some more?"

"I'm sure, thanks," I said, and looked at my glass as she walked back into the kitchen. For all I knew, catalyst from that damn melon was in this very glass—

I heard a glass or something crash in the kitchen.

I rushed in.

Sarah was standing over what looked like a little hurricane lamp, glowing white but not burning on the inside, broken on the floor. A few little house bugs of some sort took wing and flew away.

"I'm sorry," she said. She was crying again. "I knocked it over. I'm really not myself tonight."

"No one would be in your situation," I said.

She put her arms around me again, pressing close. I instinctively kissed her cheek, just barely—in what I instantly hoped, after the fact, was a brotherly gesture.

"Stay with me tonight," she whispered. "I mean, the

couch out there opens up for you, and you'll have your privacy. I'll sleep in the bedroom. I'm afraid . . ."

I was afraid too, because a part of me suddenly wanted to
pick her up and carry her over to her bedroom, the couch,
anywhere, and lay her down, softly unwrap her clothes, run
my fingers through her sweet-smelling hair and—

But I also cared very much for Jenna. And though we'd
made no formal lifetime commitments to each other—

"I don't feel very good," Sarah said, and pulled away
slightly. "I guess I had some wine before you came and—" her
head lolled and her body suddenly sagged and her eyes rolled
back in her skull.

"Here, let me help you." I first tried to buoy her up, then
picked her up entirely and carried her into her bedroom. I put
her down on the bed, gently as I could, then felt the pulse in
her wrist. It may have been a bit rapid, but seemed basically
all right. "You're okay," I said. "Just a little shock and
exhaustion."

She moaned softly, then reached out and took my hand.
I held it for a long time, till its grip weakened and she was definitely asleep, and then I walked quietly into the other room.
I was too tired myself to go anywhere, too tired to even figure
out how to open her couch, so I just stretched out on it and
managed to take off my shoes before I fell soundly asleep. My
last thoughts were that I needed to have another look at the
Stoltzfus farm, the lamp on her floor was beautiful, I hoped I
wasn't drugged or anything, but it was too late to do anything
about it if I was . . .

I awoke with a start the next morning, propped my head up
on a shaky arm and leaned over just in time to see Sarah's
sleek wet backside receding into her bedroom. Likely from
her shower. I could think of worse things to wake up to.

"I think I'm gonna head back to Jacob's farm," I told her

over breakfast of whole wheat toast, poached eggs, and Darjeeling tea that tasted like a fine liqueur.

"Why?"

"Closest thing we have to a crime scene," I said.

"I'll come with you," Sarah said.

"Look, you were pretty upset last night—" I started to object.

"Right, so were you, but I'm okay now," Sarah said. "Besides, you'll need me to decode the Amish for you, to tell you what you're looking for."

She had a point. "All right," I said.

"Good," she said. "By the way, what *are* you looking for there?"

"I don't really know," I admitted. "Mo was eager to show me something at Jacob's."

Sarah considered, frowned. "Jacob was working on an organic antidote to the allergen catalyst—but all that stuff is very slow acting, the catalyst takes years to build up to dangerous levels in the human body—so I don't see what Jacob could've shown you on a quick drive-by visit."

If she had told me that last night, I would have enjoyed the grapes and ham sandwich even more. "Well, we've got nowhere else to look at this point," I said, and speared the last of my egg.

But what did that mean about what killed Mo? Someone had been giving him a slow-acting poison too, which had been building up inside both of them for x number of years, with the result of both of them dying on the same day?

Not very likely. There seemed to be more than one catalyst at work here. I wondered if Mo had told Jacob anything about me and my visit. I certainly hoped not—the last thing I wanted was that decisive second catalyst to in some way have been me.

▲   ▲   ▲

We were on the Turnpike heading west an hour later. The sun was strong and the breeze was fresh—a splendid day to be out for a ride, except that we were going to investigate the death of one of the nicest damn people I had known. I'd called Corinne to make sure she and the girls were all right. I told her I'd try to drop by in the afternoon if I could.

"So tell me more about your doctoral work," I asked Sarah. "I mean your real work, not the cover for your advisors."

"You know, too many people equate science with its high-tech trappings—if it doesn't come in computers, god-knows-what-power microscopes, the latest DNA dyes, it must be magic, superstition, old-wives-tale nonsense. But science is at core a method, a rational mode of investigating the world, and the gadgetry is secondary. Sure, the equipment is great—it opens up more of the world to our cognitive digestion, makes it amenable to our analysis—but if aspects of the world are already amenable to analysis and experiment, with just our naked eyes and hands, then the equipment isn't all that necessary, is it?"

"And your point is that agriculture, plant and animal breeding, that kind of manipulation of nature has been practiced by humans for millennia with no sophisticated equipment," I said.

"Right," Sarah said. "But that's hardly controversial, or reason to kill someone. What I'm saying is that some people have been doing this for purposes other than to grow better food—have been doing this right under everyone's noses for a very long time—and they use this to make money, maintain their power, eliminate anyone who gets in their way."

"Sort of organized biological crime," I mused.

"Yeah, you could put it that way," Sarah said.

"And you have any examples—any evidence—other than your allergen theory?" I asked.

"It's fact, not a theory, I assure you," Sarah said. "But

here's an example: Ever wonder why people got so rude to each other, here in the US, after World War II?"

"I'm not following you," I said.

"Well, it's been written about in lots of the sociological literature," Sarah said. "There was a civility, a courtesy, in interpersonal relations—the way people dealt with each other in public, in business, in friendship—through at least the first half of the twentieth century, in the US. And then it started disintegrating. Everyone recognizes this. Some people blame it on the pressures of the atomic age, on the replacement of the classroom by the television screen—which you can fall asleep or walk out on—as the prime source of education for kids. There are lots of possible culprits. But I have my own ideas."

"Which are?"

"Everyone was in the atomic age after World War II," Sarah said. "England and the Western World had television, cars, all the usual stimuli. What was different about America was its vast farmland—room to quietly grow a crop of something that most people have a low-level allergy to. I think the cause of the widespread irritation, the loss of courtesy, was quite literally something that got under everyone's skin—an allergen designed for just that purpose."

Jeez, I could see why this woman would have trouble with her doctoral committee. But I might as well play along—I'd learned the hard way that crazy ideas like this were pooh-poohed at one's peril. "Well, the Japanese did have some plans in mind for balloons carrying biological agents—deadly diseases—over here near the end of the war."

Sarah nodded. "The Japanese are one of the most advanced peoples on Earth in terms of expertise in agriculture. I don't know if they were involved in this, but—"

The phone rang.

McLuhan had once pointed out that the car was the only place you could be, in this technological world of ours, away from the demanding, interrupting ring of the phone. But that of course was before car phones.

"Hello," I answered.

"Hello?" a voice said back to me. It sounded male, odd accent, youngish but deep.

"Yes?" I said.

"Mr. Buhler, is that you?" the voice said.

"Ahm, no, it isn't, can I take a message for him?" I said.

Silence. Then, "I don't understand. Isn't this the number for the phone in Mr. Buhler's car?"

"That's right," I said, "but—"

"Where's Mo Buhler?" the voice insisted.

"Well, he's—" I started.

I heard a strange clicking, then a dial tone.

"Is there a call-back feature on this?" I asked Sarah and myself. I pressed *69, as I would on regular phones, and pressed Send. "Welcome to AT&T Wireless Services," a different deep voice said. "The cellular customer you have called is unavailable, or has traveled outside of the coverage area—"

"That was Amos," Sarah said.

"The kid on the phone?" I asked, stupidly.

Sarah nodded.

"Must still be in shock over his father," I said.

"I think he killed his father," Sarah said.

We drove deep into Pennsylvania, the blacks and grays and unreal colors of the billboards gradually supplanted by the greens and browns and earth-tones I'd communed with just yesterday. But the natural colors held no joy for me now. I realized that's the way nature always had been—we romanticize its beauty, and that's real, but it's also the source of drought, famine, earthquake, disease, and death in many guises . . . The question was whether Sarah could possibly be right in her theory about how some people were helping this dark side of nature along.

She filled me in on Amos. He was sixteen, had only a formal primary school education, in a one-room schoolhouse, like other Amish—but also like some splinter groups of the Amish, unknown to outsiders, he was self-educated in the science and art of biological alchemy. He was apprentice to his father.

"So why would he kill him?" I asked.

"Amos is not only a budding scientist, Amish-style, he's also a typically headstrong Amish kid. Lots of wild oats to sow. He got drunk, drove cars, along with the best of them in the Amish gangs."

"Gangs?"

"Oh, yeah," Sarah said. "The Groffies, the Ammies, and the Trailers—those are the three main ones—Hostetler writes about them in his books. But there are others, smaller ones. Jacob didn't like his son being involved in them. They argued about that constantly."

"And you think that led to Amos killing his father?" I asked, still incredulous.

"Well, Jacob's dead, isn't he? And I'm pretty sure that one of the gangs Amos belongs to has connections to the bio-war Mafia people I've been telling you about—the ones that killed Mo too."

We drove the rest of the way in silence. I wasn't sure what to think about this woman and her ideas.

We finally reached Northstar Road, and the path that led to the Stoltzfus farm. "It's probably better that we park the car here, and you walk the path yourself," Sarah said. "Cars and strange women are more likely to arouse Amish attention than a single man on foot—even if he is English. I mean, that's what they call—"

"I know," I said. "I've seen *Witness*. But Mo told me that Jacob didn't mind cars—"

"Jacob's dead now," Sarah said. "What he liked and what his family like may be two very different things."

I recalled the hostility of Jacob's brother, another of

Sarah's uncles, yesterday. "All right," I said. "I guess you know what you're talking about. I should be back in thirty to forty minutes."

"Okay," Sarah squeezed my hand and smiled.

I trudged down the dirt road, not really knowing what I hoped to find at the other end.

Certainly not what I did find.

I smelled the smoke, the burnt quality in the air, before I came upon the house and the barn. Both had been burned to the ground. God, I hoped no one had been in there when these wooden structures went.

"Hello?" I shouted.

My voice echoed across an empty field. I looked around and listened. No animals, no cattle. Even a dog's rasping bark would have been welcome.

I walked over to the barn's remains, and poked at some charred wood with my foot. An ember or two winked into life, then back out. It was close to noon. My guess was this had happened—and quickly—about six hours earlier. But I was no arson expert.

I brushed away the stinking smoke fumes with my hand. I pulled out my flashlight, a powerful little halogen daylight simulation thing Jenna had given me, and looked around the inside of the barn. Whatever had been going on here, there wasn't much left of it now . . .

Something green caught my eye—greener than grass. It was the front cover, partially burned, of an old book. All that was left was this piece of the cover—the pages in the book, the back cover, were totally gone. I could see some letters, embossed in gold, in the old way. I touched it with the tip of my finger. It was warm, but not too hot. I picked it up and examined it.

"of Nat" one line said, and the next line said "bank."

Bank, I thought, Nat Bank. What was this, some kind of Amish bankbook, for some local First Yokel's National Bank?

No, it didn't look like a bankbook cover. And the "b" in this bank was a small letter, not a capital. Bank, bank, hmm . . . wait, hadn't Mo said something to me about a bank yesterday? A bank . . . Yes, a Burbank. Darwin and Burbank! Luther Burbank!

Partner of Nature by Luther Burbank—that was the name of the book whose charred remains I held in my hand. I'd taken out a copy of it years ago from the Allerton library, and loved it.

Well, Mo and Sarah were right about at least one thing— the reading level of at least some Amish was a lot higher than grade school—

"You again!"

I nearly jumped out of my skin.

I turned around. "Oh, Mr.—" it was the man we'd seen here yesterday—Jacob's brother.

"Isaac Stoltzfus," he said. "What are you doing here?"

His tone was so unsettling, his eyes so angry, that I thought for a second he thought that I was responsible for the fire. "Isaac. Mr. Stoltzfus," I said. "I just got here. I'm sorry for your loss. What happened?"

"My brother's family, thank the Deity, left to stay with some relatives in Ohio very early this morning, well before dawn. So no one was hurt. I went with them to the train station in Lancaster. When I returned here, a few hours later, I found this." He gestured hopelessly, but with an odd air of resignation, to the ruined house and barn.

"May I ask you if you know what your brother was doing here?" I hazarded a question.

Isaac either didn't hear or pretended not to. He just continued on his earlier theme. "Material things, even animals and plants, we can always afford to lose. People are what are truly of value in this world."

"Yes," I said, "but getting back to what—"

"You should check on your family too—to make sure they are not in danger."

"My family?" I asked.

Isaac nodded. "I've work to do here," he pointed out to the field. "My brother had four fine horses, and I can find no sign of them. I think it best that you go now." And he turned and walked away.

"Wait . . ." I started, but I could see it was no use.

I looked at the front cover of Burbank's book. This farm, Sarah's bizarre theories, the book—there still wasn't really enough of any of them at hand to make much sense of this.

But what the hell did Isaac mean about my family?

Jenna was overseas, and not really family—yet. My folks lived in Teaneck, my sister was married to an Israeli guy in Brookline . . . what connection did they have to what was happening here?

Jeez—none! Isaac hadn't been referring to them at all.

I was slow on the uptake today. He'd likely mistaken me for Mo—he'd seen both of us for the first time here yesterday.

He was talking about Mo's family—Corinne and the kids.

I raced back to the car, the smoky air cutting my throat with a different jagged edge each time my foot hit the ground.

"What's going on?" Sarah said.

I waved her off, jumped in the car, and put a call through to Corinne. Ring, ring, ring. No answer.

"What's the matter?" she asked again.

I quickly told her. "Let's get over there," I said, and turned the car, screeching, back on to Northstar.

"All right, take it easy," Sarah said. "It's Saturday— Corinne could just be out shopping with the kids."

"Right, the day after their father died—in my arms," I said.

"All right," she said again, "but you still don't want to get into an accident now. We'll be there in ten minutes."

I nodded, tried Corinne's number again, same ring, ring, ringing.

"Fireflies likely caused the fire," Sarah said.

"What?"

"Fireflies—a few of the Amish use them for interior lighting," Sarah said.

"Yah, Mo mentioned that," I said. "But fireflies give cool light—bioluminescence—no heat."

"Not the ones I've seen around here," Sarah said. "They're infected with certain heat-producing bacteria—symbionts, really, not an infection—and the result gives both light and heat. At least, that's the species some of these people use around here when winter starts setting in. I had a little Mendelian lamp myself—that's what they're called—you know, the one that broke on the floor in my place last night."

"So you think one of those . . . lamps went out of control and started the fire?" I asked. Suddenly I had a vision of burning up as I slept on her couch.

Sarah chewed her lip. "Maybe worse—maybe someone set it to go out of control. Or bred it that way—a bioluminescent, bio-thermic time-bomb."

"Your bio-mob covers a lot of territory," I said. "Allergens that cause low-level irritation in millions of people, catalysts that amplify other allergens to kill at least two people, anti-catalytic tomato sauce, and now pyrotechnic fireflies."

"Not that much distance at all when you're dealing with co-evolution and symbiosis," Sarah said. "Hell, we've got acidophilous bacteria living in us right now that help us digest our food. Lots more difference between them and us than between thermal bacteria and fireflies."

I put my foot on the gas pedal and prayed we wouldn't get stopped by some eager-beaver Pennsylvania trooper.

"That's the problem," Sarah continued. "Co-evolution, bio-mixing-and-matching, is a blessing and a curse. When everything's organic, and you cross-breed, you can get marvelous things. But you can also get flies that burn down buildings."

We finally got to Mo's house.

"Damn." At least it was still standing, but there was no car in the driveway. And the door was half open.

"You wait in the car," I said to Sarah.

She started to protest.

"Look," I said. "We may be dealing with killers here—you've been saying that yourself. You'll only make it harder for me if you come along and I have to worry about protecting you."

"Okay," she nodded.

I got out of the car.

Unfortunately, I didn't have my gun—truth is, I never used it anyway. I didn't like guns. Department had issued one to me when I'd first come to work for them, and I'd promptly put it away in my closet. Not the most brilliant move I'd ever made, given what was going on here now.

I walked into the house, as quietly as I could. I thought it better that I not announce myself—if Corinne and the kids were home, and I offended or frightened them by just barging in, there'd be time to apologize later.

I walked through the foyer and then the dining room that I'd never made it into to taste Corinne's great cooking yesterday. Then the kitchen and a hallway, and—

I saw a head, strawberry blond on the floor, poking out of a bedroom.

Someone was on top of her.

"Laurie!" I shouted and dove in the room, shoving off the boy who was astride her.

"Wha—" he started to say, and I picked him up, bodily, and threw him across the room. I didn't know whether to turn to Laurie or him—but I figured I couldn't do anything for

Laurie with this kid at my back. I grabbed a sheet off the bed, rolled it tight, and went over to tie him up.

"Mr., I—" He sounded groggy, I guess from hitting the wall.

"Shut up," I said, "and be glad I don't shoot you."

"But I—"

"I said shut up." I tied him as tightly as I could. Then I dragged him over to the same side of the room as Laurie, so I could keep an eye on him while I tended to her.

"Laurie," I said softly, and touched her face with my hand. She gave no response. She was out cold on something— I peeled back her eyelid, and saw a light blue eye floating, dilated, drugged out on who knew what.

"What the hell did you do to her? Where's her mother and sister?" I bellowed.

"I don't know—I mean, I don't know where they are," the kid said. "I didn't do anything to her. But I can help her."

"Sure you can," I said. "You'll excuse me if I go call an ambulance."

"No, please, Mr., don't do that!" the kid said. His voice sounded familiar. Amos Stoltzfus!

"She'll die before she gets to the hospital," he said. "But I have something here that can save her."

"Like you saved your father?" I asked.

There were tears in the kid's eyes. "I got there too late for my father. How did you know my—Oh, I see, you're the friend of Mo Buhler's I was talking to this morning."

I ignored him and started walking out of the room.

"Please. I care about Laurie too. We're—we've been seeing each other—"

I turned around and picked him up off the floor. "Yeah? That's so? And how do I know you didn't somehow do this to her?"

"There's a medicine in my pocket. It's a tomato variant. Please—I'll drink half of it down to show you it's okay, then you give the rest to Laurie—we don't have much time."

I considered for a moment. I looked at Laurie. I guess I didn't have anything to lose having the kid drink half of whatever he was talking about. "Okay," I said. "Which pocket?"

He gestured to his left front jeans.

I pulled out a small vial—likely contained only five or six ounces.

"You sure you want to do this?" I asked. I suddenly had a queasy feeling—I didn't want to be the vehicle of some sick patricidal kid's suicide.

"I don't care whether you give it to me or not," Amos said. "Just give some to Laurie already! Please!"

I have to make gut decisions all the time in my line of work. Only usually not about families I deeply care about. I thought for another second, and decided.

I bypassed his taking the sample, and went over to Laurie. I hated to give her any liquid when she was still unconscious—

"It's absorbed on the back of the tongue," Amos said. "It works quick."

God, I hoped this kid was right—I'd kill him with my bare hands if this wasn't right for Laurie. I put an ounce or two on her tongue. A few seconds went by. More. Maybe thirty seconds, forty . . . "Goddamnit, how exactly long does this—"

She moaned, as if on cue. "Laurie?" I asked, and patted her face.

"Mmm . . ." She opened her eyes. And smiled! "Phil?"

"Yeah, honey, everything's okay," I said.

"Laurie!" Amos called out from across the room.

Laurie got up. "Amos? What are you doing here? Why are you tied up like that?"

She looked at him and then me like we were both crazy.

"Long story, never mind," I said, and went over to untie Amos. I found myself grinning at him. "Good on you, you were right, kid," I said.

He smiled back.

"Where are your Mom and Emma?" I asked.

"Oh," Laurie suddenly looked sadder than I'd ever seen her. "They went over to the funeral home this morning, that's where Dad is, to make arrangements. They took your car, Mom found the keys for it in your bag." And she started crying.

Amos put his arms around her, comforting her.

"You have any idea what happened to you? I mean, after your Mom and sister left?" I asked gently.

"Well," she said, "some nice lady was coming around selling stuff—you know, soaps, perfumes, and little household things—like Avon, but some company I never heard of. And she asked me if I wanted to smell some new perfume—and it smelled wonderful, like a combination of lilacs and the ocean, and then . . . I don't know, I guess you were calling me, and I saw Amos tied up and . . . what happened? Did I pass out?"

"Well—" I started.

"Uhm, Mr., ahm, Phil—" Amos interrupted.

"It's Dr. D'Amato, but my friends call me Phil, and you've earned that right," I said.

"Okay, thanks, Dr. D'Amato—sorry, I mean Phil—but I don't think we should hang around here. These people—"

"What do you mean?" I said.

"I'm saying I don't like what the light looks like in this house. They killed my father, they tried to poison Laurie, who knows what they might have planted—"

"Okay, I see your point," I said, and saw again the Stoltzfus farm—Amos's farm—ashes in the dirt.

I looked at Laurie. "I'm fine," she said. "But why do we have to leave?"

"Let's just go," I said, and Amos and I ushered her out. The first thing I noticed when we were out of the house was that Sarah and my car—Mo's car—were gone.

The second thing I noticed was a searing heat on the back

of my neck. I rushed Laurie and Amos across the street, and turned back to squint at the house.

Intense blue-white flames were sticking their searing tongues out of every window, licking the roof and the walls and now the garden with colors I'd never seen before.

Laurie cried out in horror. Amos held her close. "Fireflies," he muttered.

The house burned to the ground in minutes.

We stood mute, in hot/cold shivering shock, for what felt like a long, long time.

I finally realized I was breathing hard. I thought about allergic reactions. I thought about Sarah.

"They must've taken Sarah," I said.

"Sarah?" Amos asked, holding Laurie tight in a clearly loving way. She was sobbing.

"Sarah Fischer," I said.

Laurie and Amos both nodded.

"She was a friend of my father's," Laurie said.

"She's my sister," Amos said.

"What?" I turned to Amos. Laurie pulled away and looked at him too. He had a peculiar, almost tortured sneer on his face, mixture of hatred and heartbreak.

"She left our home more than ten years ago," Amos said. "I was still just a little boy. She said she could no longer be bound by the ways of our *Ordnung*—she said it was like agreeing to be mentally retarded for the rest of your life. So she left to go to some school. And I think she's been working with those people—those people who killed my father and burned Laurie's house."

I suddenly tasted the grapes in my mouth from last night, sweet taste with choking smoke, and I felt sick to my stomach. I swallowed, took a deliberate deep breath.

"Look," I said. "I'm still not clear what's really going on

here. I find Laurie unconscious—you, someone, could've put a drug in her orange juice for all I know. The house just burned down—could've been arson with rags and lighter fluid, just like we have back in New York, New York." Though I knew I'd never seen a fire quite like that.

Laurie stared at me like I was nuts.

"They were fireflies, Mr. D'A— Phil," Amos said. "Fireflies caused the fire."

"How could they do that so quickly?"

"They can be bred that way," Amos said. "So that an hour or a day or week after they start flying around, they suddenly heat up to cause the fire. It's what you *scientists*," he said with ill-concealed derision, "call setting a genetical switch. Mendelian lamps set to go off like clockwork and burn—Mendel bombs."

"Mendel bombs?"

"Wasn't he a genetical scientist? Worked with peas? Insects are simple like that too—easy to breed."

"Yeah, Gregor Mendel," I said. "You're saying Sarah— your sister—was involved in this?"

He nodded.

I thought about the lamp on Sarah's floor.

"Look, Amos, I'm sorry about before—I don't really think you did anything to Laurie. It's just—can you show me any actual *evidence* of this stuff? I mean, like, the fireflies *before* they burn down a house?"

Amos considered. "Yeah, I can take you to a barn—it's about five miles from here."

I looked at Laurie.

"The Lapp farm?" she asked.

Amos nodded.

"It's okay," she said to me. "It's safe. I've been there."

"All right, then," I said. But Mo's car—and my car— were still gone. "How are we going to get there?"

"I parked my buggy at my friend's—about a quarter of a mile from here," Amos said.

▲   ▲   ▲

Clop, clop, clop, looking at a horse's behind, feeling like one—based on what I was able to make sense of in this case. Horses, flames, mysterious deaths—all the ingredients of a Jack Finney novel in the nineteenth century. Except this was the end of the twentieth. And so far all I'd done is manage to get dragged along to every awful event. Well, at least I'd managed to save Laurie—or let Amos save her. But I had to do more—I had to stop just witnessing and reacting, and instead get on top of things. I represented twentieth century science, for godsake. Okay, it wasn't perfect, it wasn't all powerful. But surely it had taught me enough to enable me to do *something* to counter these bombs and allergens, these . . . Mendelian things.

I'd also managed to get through to Corinne at the funeral home from a pay phone on a corner before we'd gotten into Amos's buggy. I'd half expected his horse and buggy to come with a car phone—a horse phone?—that was how crazy this "genetical" stuff was getting me. On the other hand, I guess the Amish could have rigged up a buggy with a cellular phone running on battery at that . . . Well, at least I was learning . . .

"We should be there in a few minutes." Amos leaned back from the driver's seat, where he held the reins and clucked the lone horse along. He—Amos had told me the horse was a he—was a dark brown beautiful animal, at least to my innocent city eyes. The whole scene, riding along in a horse and buggy on a bright crisp autumn day, was astonishing—because it wasn't a buggy ride for a tourist's five dollar bill, it was real life.

"You know, I ate some of your sister's food," I blurted out the qualm that occurred to me again. "You don't think, I mean, that maybe it had a slow-acting allergen—"

"We'll give you a swig of an antidote—it's pretty universal—when we get to John Lapp's, don't worry," Amos leaned back and advised.

"Sarah—your sister—was telling me something about some low-grade allergen let loose on our population after World War II. Didn't kill anyone, but made most people more irritable than they'd been before. Come to think of it, I suppose it indeed could have been responsible for lots of deaths, when you take into account the manslaughters that result from people on edge, arguments gone out of control."

"You're talking the way Poppa used to," Laurie said.

"Your dad talked about those allergens?" I asked.

"No," Laurie said. "I mean he was always going on about manslaughter, and how it had just one or two little differences in spelling from man's laughter, and how those differences made all the difference."

"Yeah, that was Mo all right," I said.

"That's John Lapp's farm up ahead," Amos said.

The meadow was green, still lush in this autumn. It was bounded by fences that looked both old, and, implausibly, in very good condition. Like we'd been literally traveling back in time.

"So, Amos, your opinion on your sister's idea about the allergens?" I prompted.

"I don't know," he said. "That was my sister's area of study."

A barn, a big barn, but no different on the outside than hundreds of other barns in the countrysides of Pennsylvania and Ohio. How many of them had what this one had inside?

Variations of Sarah's words played in my ears. Why do we expect science to always come in high-tech wrappings? Darwin was a great scientist, wasn't he, and just the plain outside world was his laboratory. Mendel came upon the workings of genetics by cultivating purple and white flowering peas in his garden. Was a garden so different from a barn? If anything, it was even lower-tech.

A soft pervasive light embraced us as we walked inside—keener than fluorescent, more diffuse than incandescent, a cross between sepiatone and starlight maybe, but impossible to describe with any real precision if you hadn't actually seen it, felt its photons slide through your pupils like pieces of a breeze.

"Fireflight," Amos whispered, though I had realized that already. I'd seen fireflies before, loved them as a boy, poured over Audubon guides to insects with pictures of their light, but never anything like this.

"We have lots of uses for insects, more than just light," Amos said, and he guided me over, Laurie on his arm, to a series of wooden contraptions all entwined with nets. I looked closer, and saw swarms of insects—bees mostly, maybe other kinds—each in its own gauzed compartment. There were several sections with spiders too.

"These are our nets, Phil," Amos said. "The nets and webs of our information highway. Our insects are of course far slower and smaller in numbers than your electrons, but far more intelligent and motivated than those non-living things that convey information on yours. True, our communicators can't possibly match the pace and reach of the broadcast towers, the telephone lines, the computers all over your world. But we don't want that. We don't need the speed, the high blood pressure, the invasion of privacy, that your electrons breed. We don't want the numbers, the repetition, all the clutter. Our carriers get it right, for the jobs that we think are important, the first time."

"Well they certainly get it just as deadly," I said, "at least when it comes to burning down houses. Nature strikes back." And I marveled again at the wisdom of these people, this boy—which, though I disagreed about the advantages of bug-tech over electricity, bespoke a grasp of information theory that would do any telecom specialist proud—

"Nature was never really gone, Dr. D'Amato," a deep voice that sounded familiar said.

I turned around. "Isaac . . ."

"I apologize for the deception, but my name is John Lapp. I pretended to be Jacob's brother at his farm because I couldn't be sure that you weren't videotaping me with some kind of concealed camera. Jacob and I are roughly the same height and weight, so I took the chance. You'll forgive me, but we have great distrust for your instruments." His face and voice were "Isaac Stoltzfus"'s, all right, but his delivery was vastly more commanding and urbane.

I noticed in the corner of my eye that Laurie's were wide with awe. "Mr. Lapp," she stammered, "I'm very honored to meet you. I mean, I've been here before with Amos," she squeezed his hand, "but I never expected to actually meet you—"

"Well, I'm honored too, young lady," Lapp said, "and I'm very very sorry about your father. I only met him once— when I was first pretending to be 'Isaac' the other day—but I know from Jacob that your father was a good man."

"Thank you," Laurie said, softly.

"I have something for you, Laurie Buhler," Lapp reached into his long, dark coat and pulled out what looked like a lady's handbag, constructed of a very attractive moss-green woven cloth. "Jacob Stoltzfus designed this. We call it a lamp-case. It's a weave of special plant fibers dyed in an extract from the glow-worm, with certain chemicals from lumines-cent mushrooms mixed into the dye to give the light staying power. It glows in the dark. It should last for several months, as long as the weather doesn't get too hot. Then you can get a new one. From now on, if you're out shopping after the sun sets, you'll be able to see what you have in your case, how much money you have left, wherever you are. From what I know of young lady's purses—I have three teenaged daugh-ters—this can be very helpful. Some of you seem to be lugging half the world around with you in there!"

Laurie took the case, and beamed. "Thank you so much," she said. She looked at me. "This is what Poppa was going to get for me the other night. He thought I didn't know—he wanted to pick this purse up, at Jacob Stoltzfus's farm, and surprise me for my birthday tomorrow. But I knew." And her voice cracked and tears welled in her eyes.

Amos put his arms around her again, and I patted her hair.

"Mo would've wanted to get to the bottom of this," I said to Lapp. "What can you tell me about who killed him—and Amos's father?"

He regarded me, without much emotion. "The world is changing before your very eyes, Dr. D'Amato. Twelve-hundred pound moose walk down the mainstreet in Brattleboro, Vermont. People shoot 400-lb bears in the suburbs of New Hampshire—"

"New Hampshire is hardly a suburb, and Mo wasn't killed by a bear—he died right next to me in my car," I said.

"Same difference, Doctor. Animals are getting brazen, bacteria are going wild, allergies are rampant—it's all part of the same picture. It's no accident."

"Your people are doing this, deliberately?" I asked.

"My people?—No, I assure you, we don't believe in aggression. These things you see here"—he waved his hand around the barn, at all sorts of plants and small animals and insects I wanted to get a closer look at—"are only to make our lives better, in quiet ways. Like Laurie's handbag."

"Like the fireflies that burn down buildings?" I asked.

"Ah, we come full circle—this is where I came in. Alas, we unfortunately are not the only people on this Earth who understand more of the power of nature than is admitted by your technological world. You have plastics, used for good. You also have plastic used for evil—you have semtex, that blew up your airplane over Scotland. We have bred fireflies for good purposes, for light and moderate heat, as you see right here," he pointed to a corner of the barn, near where we were standing. A fountain of the sepiatone and starlight seemed to emanate from it. I looked more carefully, and saw the fountain was really a myriad of tiny fireflies—a large Mendelian lamp. "We mix slightly different species in the swarm," Lapp continued, "carefully chosen so that their flashings overlap to give a continuous, long-lasting light. The mesh is so smooth that you can't see the insects themselves, unless you examine the light very closely. But there are those who have furthered this breeding for bad purposes, as you found out in both the Stoltzfus and Buhler homes."

"Well, if you know who these people are, tell me, and I'll see to it that they're put out of business," I said.

For the first time, I noticed a smear of contempt on John Lapp's face. "Your police will put them out of business? How? In the same way you've put your industrial Mafia out of business? In the same way you've stopped the drug trade from South America? In the same way your United Nations, your NATO, all of your wonderful political organizations have ended wars in the Middle East, in Europe, in Southeast Asia all these years? No thank you, Doctor. These people who misuse the power of nature are *our* problem—they're not our people any longer but they come originally from our people— and we'll handle them in our own way."

"But two people are dead—" I protested.

"You perhaps will be too," Amos said. He proffered a bottle with some kind of reddish, tomatoey-looking liquid.

"Here, drink this, just in case my sister gave you some slow-acting poison."

"A brother and a sister," I said. "Each tells me the other's the bad guy. Classic dilemma—for all I know this is the poison."

Lapp shook his head. "Sarah Stoltzfus Fischer is definitely bad," he said solemnly. "I once thought I saw some good that could be rekindled in her, but now . . . Jacob told Mo Buhler about her—"

"Her name was on Mo's car phone list," I said.

"Yes, as someone Mo was likely investigating," Lapp said.

"I told Jacob he was wrong to tell Mo so much. But Jacob was stubborn—and he was an optimist. A dangerous combination. I'm sorry to say this," he looked with hurt eyes at Laurie, "but Mo Buhler may have brought this upon Jacob and himself because of his contacts with Sarah."

"If Poppa believed in her, then that's because he still saw some good in her," Laurie insisted.

John Lapp shook his head, sadly.

"And I guess I made things worse by contacting her, spending the night with her—" I started saying.

All three gave me a look.

"—alone, on the couch," I finished.

"Yes, perhaps you did make things worse," Lapp said. "Your style of investigation—Mo Buhler's—can't do any good here. These people will have you running around chasing your own tail. They'll taunt you with vague suggestions of possibilities of what they're up to—what they've been doing. They'll give you just enough taste of truth to keep you interested. But when you look for proof, you'll find you won't know which end is up."

Which was a pretty good capsule summary of what I'd being feeling like.

"They introduced long-term allergen catalysts into our bloodstreams, our biosphere, years ago," Lapp went on. "Everyone in this area has it. And once you do, you're a sitting duck. When they want to kill you, they give you another catalyst, short-term, any one of a number of handy biological agents, and you're dead within hours of a massive allergic attack to some innocent thing in your environment. So the two catalysts work together to kill you. Of course, neither one on its own is dangerous, shows up as suspicious on your blood tests, so that's how they get away with it. And no one even notices the final innocent insult—no one is ordinarily allergic to an autumn leaf from a particular type of tree against your skin, or a certain kind of beetle on your finger. That's why we developed the antidote to the first catalyst—it's the only way we know of breaking the allergic cycle."

"Please, Phil, drink this." Amos pushed the bottle on me again.

"Any side effects I should know about? Like I'll be dead of an allergic attack in a few hours?"

"You'll probably feel a little more irritable than usual for the next week," Lapp said.

I sighed. "What else is new."

Decisions . . . Even if I had the first catalyst, I could live the rest of my life without ever encountering the second.

No, I couldn't go on being so vulnerable like that. I liked autumn leaves. But how did I know for sure that what Amos was offering me was the antidote, and not the second catalyst? I didn't—not for sure—but wouldn't Amos have tried to leave me in Mo's house to burn if he'd wanted me dead? Decisions . . .

I drank it down, and looked around the barn. Incredible scene of high Victorian science, like a nineteenth century trade card I'd once seen for an apothecary. Enough to make my head spin. Then I realized it *was* spinning—was this some sort of reaction to the antidote? Jeez, or was the antidote the poison after all? No—the room wasn't so much spinning, as the light, the fireflight, was flickering . . . in an oddly familiar way.

Lapp was suddenly talking, fast, arguing with someone. Sarah!

"There's a Mendel bomb here," she was shouting. "Please. You all have to leave."

Lapp looked desperately around the room, back at Sarah, and finally nodded. "She's right," he said and caught my eye. "We all have to leave now." He grabbed on to Sarah's shoulder, and beckoned me to follow.

Amos had his arm around Laurie, and was already walking quickly with her towards the door. Everyone else was scurrying around, grabbing what netted cages they could.

"No," I said. "Wait." An insight was just nibbling its way into my mind.

"Doctor, please," Lapp said. "We have to leave now."

"No, you don't," I said. "I know how to stop the bomb."

Lapp shook his head firmly. "I assure you, we know of no remedy to stop this. We have perhaps seven, maybe eight minutes at most. We can rebuild the barn. Human lives we cannot rebuild."

Sarah looked at me with pleading eyes.

"No," I insisted, looking past Sarah at Lapp. "You can't just keep running like this from your enemies, letting them burn you out. You have incredible work going on here. I can stop the bomb."

Lapp stared at me.

"Okay, how's this," I said. "You clear out of here with your friends. No problem. I'll take care of this with *my* science and then we'll talk about it, all right? But let me get on with it already."

Lapp signaled the last of his people to leave. "Take her," he said, and passed custody of Sarah along to a big burly man with a gray-flecked beard. She tried to resist but was no match for him.

Lapp squinted at the flickering fireflies. They were much more distinct now, as if the metamorphosis into bomb mode had coarsened the nature of the mesh.

He turned to me. "I'll stay here with you. I'll give you two minutes and then I'm yanking you out of here. What does your science have to offer?"

"Nothing all that advanced," I said, and pulled my little halogen flashlight out of my pocket. "Those are fireflies, right? If they've retained anything of the characteristics of the family *Lampyridae* I know about, then they make their light only in the absence of daylight, when the day has waned—they're nocturnal. During the day, bathed in daylight, they're just like any other damn beetle. Well, this should make the necessary adjustment." I turned up the flashlight to its fullest daylight setting, and shone it straight at the center of the swirling starlight fountain, which now had a much harsher tone, like an ugly light over an autopsy table. I focused my halogen on the souped-up fireflies for a minute and longer. Nothing happened. The swirling continued. The harsh part of their light got stronger.

"Doctor, we can't stay here any longer," Lapp said.

I sighed, closed my eyes, and opened them. The halogen flashlight should have worked—it should have put out the light of at least some of the fireflies, then more, disrupting their syncopated overlapping pattern of flashing. I stared hard at the fountain. My eyes were tired. I couldn't see the flies as clearly as I could a few moments ago . . .

No . . . of course!

I couldn't see as clearly because the light was getting dimmer!

There was no doubt about it now. The whole barn seemed to be flickering in and out, the continuous light effect had broken down, and each time the light came back, it did so a little more weakly . . . I kept my halogen trained on the flies. It was soon the only light in the barn.

Lapp's hand was on my shoulder. "We're in your debt, Doctor. I almost made the fool's mistake of closing my mind to a source of knowledge I didn't understand—a fool's mistake, as I say, because if I don't understand it, then how can I know it's not valuable?"

"Plato's Meno Paradox strikes again," I said.

"What?"

"You need some knowledge to recognize knowledge, so where does the first knowledge come from?" I smiled. "Wisdom from an old Western-style philosopher—I frequently consult him—though actually he probably had more in common with you."

Lapp nodded. "Thank you for giving us this knowledge of the firefly, that we knew all along ourselves but didn't realize. From now on, the Mendel bombs won't be such a threat to us—once we notice their special flicker, all we'll need to do is flood the area with daylight. Plain daylight. Sometimes we won't even need your flashlight to do it—daylight is after all just out there, naturally for the asking, a good deal of the time."

"And in the evenings, you can use the flashlight—it's battery operated, no strings attached to central electric companies," I said. "See, I've picked up a few things about your culture after all."

Lapp smiled. "I believe you have, Doctor. And I believe we'll be all right now."

"Yeah, but it was a good thing you had Sarah Fischer to warn you this time, anyway," I said.

Of course, the enemies of John Lapp and Amos Stoltzfus would no doubt come up with other diabolical breedings of weapons. No one ever gets a clear-cut complete victory in these things. But at least the scourge of Mendel bombs would be reduced. I guess I'd given them an SDI for these pyro-fireflies—imperfect, no doubt, but certainly a lot better than nothing.

I was glad, too, about how Sarah Fischer had turned around. She'd come back to the barn to warn us. Said she couldn't take the killing anymore. She said she had nothing directly to do with Mo's or Jacob's—her father's—deaths, but she could no longer be part of a community that did such things. She had started telling me about the allergens—the irritation ones—because she wanted the world to know. I wanted to believe her.

I'd thought of calling the Pennsylvania police, having them take her into custody, but what was the point? I had no evidence on her whatsoever. Even if she had set the Mendel bomb in John Lapp's barn—which I didn't believe—what could I do about that anyway? Have her arrested for setting a bomb made of incendiary flies I'd been able to defuse by shining my flashlight—a bomb that Lapp's people were unwilling in any way to even acknowledge to the outside world, let alone testify about in court? No thank you—I've been laughed out of court enough times as it is already.

And Lapp said his people had some sort of humane program for people like Sarah—help her find her own people and roots again. She needed that. She was a woman without community now. Shunned by all parties. The worst thing that could happen to someone of Sarah's upbringing. It was good that John Lapp and Amos Stoltzfus were willing to give her a second chance—offer her a lamp of hope, maybe the real meaning of the Mendelian lamp, as it Lapp had aptly put it.

I rolled my window down to pay the George Washington Bridge toll. It felt good to finally be back in my own beat-up car again, I had to admit. Corinne was off with the girls to resettle in California. I'd said a few words about Mo at his funeral, and now his little family was safely on a plane out West. I couldn't say I'd brought his murderers to justice, but at least I'd put a little crimp in their operation. Laurie had kissed Amos goodbye, and promised she'd come back and see him, certainly for Christmas . . .

"Thanks, Chief." I took the receipt and the change. I felt so good to be back I almost told him to keep the change. I left the window rolled down. The air had its customary musky aroma—the belches of industry, the exhaust fumes of even EPA-clean cars still leaving their olfactory mark. Damn, and didn't it feel good to breathe it in. Better than the sweet air of Pennsylvania, and all the hidden allergens and catalysts it might be carrying. It had killed both Jacob and Mo. They'd been primed with a slow-acting catalyst years ago. Then the second catalyst had been introduced, and whoosh . . . some inconsequential something in their surroundings had set the last short fuse. Just as likely a stray firefly of a certain type that buzzed at their ankles, or landed on their arm, as anything else. Jacob's barn had been lit by them. The lamp was likely the other thing Mo had wanted to show me. There were likely one or two fireflies that had gotten into our car on the farm, and danced unseen around our feet as we drove to Philadelphia that evening . . . A beetle for me, an assassin for Mo.

The virtue of New York, some pundit on the police force once had said, is that you can usually see your killers coming. Give me the soot and pollution, the crush of too many people and cars in a hurry, even the mugger on the street. I'll take my chances.

I unconsciously slipped my wallet out of my pocket. This thinking about muggers must have made me nervous about my money. It was a fine wallet—made from that same special lamp-weave as Laurie's handbag. John Lapp had given it to me as a little present—to remember Jacob's work by. For a few months, at least, I'd be able to better see how much money I was spending.

Well, it was good to have a bit more light in the world— even if it, like the contents it illuminated, was ever-fleeting . . .

Kiss Me

KATHERINE MacLEAN

Katherine MacLean entered the science fiction field in 1949 and produced some of the fine hard SF short stories of the 1950s. Like Judith Merril and Virginia Kidd, she was one of the bright, tough-minded young women who entered the SF scene in the late 1940s and helped change the face of SF in the next decade. She was at her best and most influential in short fiction. Her collections, *The Diploids* and *The Trouble with You Earth People,* are filled with gems but now hard to find. She took a break and then produced some fine work in the 1970s, including her best novel, *The Missing Man.* By the end of that decade, she had left again, moved to Portland, Maine, and only returns to writing SF sporadically, for fun. This story is from *Analog* and shows the lighthearted side of hard SF. It's an interesting contrast to the Landis story.

Denny's new girlfriend, Laury, was not interested in science; she was busy studying computer applications to business, but she was pretty and she hung around his laboratory most of her free time and happily listened to him explain what he was doing.

This time his laboratory was full of frogs.

"This bunch is from South Africa, and this bunch in the plastic crate," he pointed, "they are from Kenya." He moved his skinny self over to a big damp glass box. "These are from a lake in Georgia, where they fell into a fishing boat. Usually people only send in frog falls when they come down in dry territory or on city sidewalks, come down like rain. Maybe they come down over lakes too, but on a lake, they could have jumped into the boat from the water. So I don't trust this batch."

Laury stared solemnly at each one, trying to see some exciting difference. All the frogs were dark brown, or green with spots, or a pinkish tan, and they all had big yellow-gold eyes. "Beebeeb," said a big one.

"But they all look normal!" she was disappointed. "They don't look strange at all." She picked the biggest tan one from his glass box and kissed it, but nothing about it changed. It stared at her and puffed its throat in and out, "Reebeeb."

She put it back. "Reebeeb," she said back.

Denny was eager to explain. "That's what's strange about them, there aren't any tree frogs or desert toads or poison frogs or any of the interesting ones, the frogs people send in from frog falls are always the same three kinds, no matter where they are from."

"Where did you get all these frogs?" She tapped on the

side of the glass box. Most of them jumped away from her finger into the water, and some jumped toward her finger and bumped their noses on the glass.

"Ouch," she said sympathetically to the ones who had bumped their noses. "That must have hurt."

Denny was pleased by her interest. "The whole collection—" he waved at the room full of glass-faced boxes full of frogs, "was turned over to me by the Charles Fort Foundation. People are always sending them frogs from sidewalks and city roofs. They are funding me for a research project on the frogs that come down in frog falls."

"Funding you?" She looked at him with admiration. Scientists seemed to have a talent for generating money for their most kooky projects. "What do they want you to do?"

"Just study their genes. I put it to the university gene fingerprinter machine. So far just normal *Rana pippens* and such. No lead there." He leaned warmly against her shoulder to point. "That bunch is from a desert in Arizona. Look at the date on the label. They were just sent in this week."

Laury was baffled. "Arizona? Frogs don't grow in deserts, do they? They grow in water."

Denny was excited. "They didn't grow in the desert. They rained out of the sky. A rain of frogs. The bible has something about rains of frogs in Egypt. But when it happens in a desert, ten or twenty miles from the nearest puddle, people really notice it and save some frogs to look at. Then I have a chance to get samples."

She was indignant. "You think I'll believe frogs fall out of the sky? You're putting me on. How did they get into the sky?"

"Here, read this," He shoved a big book into her hands. "It's a collection of reports about frogs raining from the sky." Dennis pointed at a photograph of a wrinkled-looking toad. "Ask me where that toad came from."

Obediently she asked, "Where did it come from?" She

calculated the chances of making a tourist business about frog falls. Could Denny predict them?

"It was found inside a lump of coal. That means it's a billion years old or so. Maybe all frogs and toads came from rains of frogs. Maybe rains of frogs started life on land, instead of lungfish. Frogs are a billion years old."

She looked at the big one she had kissed. "They don't look that old." She thought of putting a million-year-old frog on display. Would anyone pay admission?

He took a deep breath to control his temper and looked at her figure for consolation. "I don't mean these frogs. I mean the ancestors of all frogs. And maybe we are descended from them too. My theory is that some alien space satellite was set in orbit to seed Earth with life, and it has been cloning frog eggs and raising pollywogs, and launching frogs down on us ever since Earth cooled and the oceans condensed. I'm sure that when I map all the frog falls and their dates they're going to show an orbit line around the Earth. With that for a clue I can get an observatory to locate the alien satellite in orbit around Earth and get it on camera launching frogs." He spun around in glee. "Ha! On CNN and the cover of *Science!*"

"Why would aliens launch frogs at us?" Laury asked. "Is it an invasion?"

"Calm down, Laury. Frogs aren't going to hurt us. They never have. They're too small. All they do is hop around, swim, lay eggs and eat bugs. They don't live long enough to become civilized and start wars." Denny started a round of throwing little white worms into the glass boxes. The frogs' tongues shot out and yanked the worms into their mouths so suddenly the insects seemed to vanish.

"Some of these are adult males. The green ones that say Peeeep and the big ones that say Reebeeb and Beebeeb are singing to attract females. They mature to be adults in one year."

Laury nodded, "That's their real problem, too much sex at an early age, retards growth, distracts from learning."

The big tan one in the glass case said, "Reebeeb reebeeb," in a deep musical voice, still staring at her.

"You shouldn't have kissed him," Denny said, "Kiss me instead."

"You never know about superstitions until you try them. He didn't turn into a prince," said Laury. "But if he's only a year old he'd make a pretty small prince anyhow, still in diapers, so it's a good thing it didn't work."

"But he's an adult." Denny moved closer. "I'm an adult too. I'm a consenting adult. Kiss me. Maybe I'll turn into a prince."

"Maybe you'll turn into a frog." She kissed him but his green baseball cap got in the way. He spun the visor to the back, crossed his legs, and tried again.

The big frog sang "Reeebeeb reeebeeb!" and hopped at them, butting his nose against the glass.

"He's not very smart," said Laury. "No kind of invader from a spaceship can conquer anything being so small and dumb. Maybe they were sent down to be invaders from outer space, but Earth is too sexy for them and they become adults instead of growing up."

"If you put thyroid into the water of the pollywogs they turn to their adult shape when they are really tiny. The tiny females can even lay eggs." Denny said absently, watching Laury.

"That's not the kind of growing up I meant. That's the opposite. I mean—what can you give them to keep them from getting sexy so they can keep on growing and get bigger?"

"Oh." Denny looked at the big pink one. He went to medical reference on his computer and let it search Retarded Growth, Premature Maturity, and Dwarfism, and sat down to read it on screen. "It says it's pituitary hormone, low pituitary hormone," he said. "I can expose some of them to pituitary hormone to increase growth and retard maturity. I'll write it up as another project and they'll grant me more money. Grantsmanship. Do you know that frogs have more

DNA than humans? I could claim it means that they have more shapes available, not just tadpole and frog."

He stayed up reading and typing and did not take Laury on a date that night, or the next night, or any time the next two weeks. She grew angry and when she graduated with her MBA she volunteered for the Peace Corps and went off to balance books for a community improvement incorporation in Mexico. It was easy. She had free time to find a beach and let the students try to teach her wind surfing.

In a hotel bar on a beautiful beach she met a handsome man who owned the hotel. She moved into the hotel for a few years, remaining after the Peace Corps job was over, balancing his books and enjoying water sports in the day, and dancing and lovemaking with the handsome man at night. Her hair sunbleached a brighter blonde and her tan grew darker.

When the handsome man married a girl who had been chosen by his mother, Laury accepted his apology with an inscrutable smile, packed, wiped out all the hotel's financial records from the computer and shredded all the paper records, and caught a plane back to California.

She found out that Denny had been given another doctorate on his frog research and now had a bigger laboratory and some employees, and best of all he was still unmarried. She arrived at Denny's laboratory sure she looked more beautiful than ever.

"Honey, I'm back from Mexico," she called out to the back of a man in a green cap wearing Denny's favorite T-shirt.

The man turned and stood up tall. His face was shiny tan and very wide, his eyes were bright gold and very big, and his mouth stretched almost from ear to ear.

He was surprisingly attractive.

"I've never forgotten you," he said in a deep musical voice. "Kiss me again."

London Bone

MICHAEL MOORCOCK

Michael Moorcock is one of the great writers, editors, public figures in SF of the latter half of this century. He can write, he can sing, he can play guitar (he was in the band Hawkwind for a while), and is at present the greatest English writer living in Bastrop, Texas. He was the force behind the New Wave of the 1960s in England, the prophet of change in SF in that decade, and the influential editor of the great magazine, *New Worlds,* that was the home of the avant garde in SF. There is of course a direct descent from that magazine to the anthology edited by David Garnett titled *New Worlds,* from which this story is reprinted. Moorcock, more than any other figure, broke in two the history of SF in the second half of this century. SF since Moorcock's advent in 1964 is contemporary, before him it is mostly literary history. This, it seems to me is one great significance of the New Wave, that it divides history, the way John W. Campbell divided history. Nothing was the same after *New Worlds* magazine. Even the continuing production of familiar SF existed forever after in a new context. Last year he was the guest of honor at the World SF Convention in San Antonio, Texas, so there is no doubt he remains a strong presence in SF today, though no longer the fiery nexus of the 60s. Still, the best original anthology of 1997 wouldn't have existed without him. "London Bone" is mature Moorcock, rich, complex, socially textured, morally engaged SF.

For Ronnie Scott

ONE

My name is Raymond Gold and I'm a well-known dealer. I was born too many years ago in Upper Street, Islington. Everybody reckons me in the London markets and I have a good reputation in Manchester and the provinces. I have bought and sold, been the middleman, an agent, an art representative, a professional mentor, a tour guide, a spiritual bridge-builder. These days I call myself a cultural speculator.

But, you won't like it, the more familiar word for my profession, as I practiced it until recently, is *scalper*. This kind of language is just another way of isolating the small businessman and making what he does seem sleazy while the stockbroker dealing in millions is supposed to be legitimate. But I don't need to convince anyone today that there's no sodding justice.

"Scalping" is risky. What you do is invest in tickets on spec and hope to make a timely sale when the market for them hits zenith. Any kind of ticket, really, but mostly shows. I've never seen anything offensive about getting the maximum possible profit out of an American matron with more money than sense who's anxious to report home with the right items ticked off the *beento* list. We've all seen them rushing about in their overpriced limos and mini-buses, pretending to be individuals: **Thursday: Changing-of-the-Guard, Harrods, Planet Hollywood, Royal Academy, Tea-At-the-Ritz, *Cats*.** It's a sort of tribal dance they are all compelled to perform. If they don't perform it, they feel inadequate. **Saturday: Tower of London, Bucket of Blood, Jack-the-Ripper talk, Sherlock Holmes Pub, Sherlock Holmes tour, Madame Tussaud's, Covent Garden Cream Tea, *Dogs*.** These are people so traumatized by contact with strangers that their only security lies in these rituals, these well-blazed trails and familiar chants. It's my job to smooth their paths, to make them exclaim how pretty and wonderful and elegant and *magical* it all is. The street people aren't a problem. They're just so many charming Dick Van Dykes.

Americans need bullshit the way koala bears need eucalyptus leaves. They've become totally addicted to it. They get so much of it back home that they can't survive without it. It's your duty to help them get their regular fixes while they travel. And when they make it back after three weeks on alien shores, their friends, of course, are always glad of some foreign bullshit for a change.

Even if you sell a show ticket to a real enthusiast, who has already been forty-nine times and is so familiar to the cast they see him in the street and think he's a relative, who are you hurting? Andros Loud Website, Lady Hatchet's loyal laureate, who achieved rank and wealth by celebrating the lighter side of the moral vacuum? He would surely applaud my enterprise in the buccaneering spirit of the free market. Venture capitalism at its bravest. Well, he'd applaud me if he had time these days from his railings against fate, his horrible understanding of the true nature of his coming obscurity. But that's partly what my story's about.

I have to say in my own favor that I'm not merely a speculator or, if you like, exploiter. I'm also a patron. For many years, not just recently, a niagara of dosh has flowed out of my pocket and into the real arts faster than a cat up a Frenchman. Whole orchestras and famous soloists have been brought to the Wigmore Hall on the money they get from me. But I couldn't have afforded this if it wasn't for the definitely iffy *Miss Saigon* (a triumph of well-oiled machinery over

dodgy morality) or the unbelievably decrepit *Good Rockin'
Tonite* (in which the living dead jive in the aisles), nor, of
course, that first great theatrical triumph of the new millennium. *Schindler: The Musical.* Make' em weep, Uncle Walt!

So who is helping most to support the arts? You, me, the
lottery?

I had another reputation, of course, which some saw as a
second profession. I was one of the last great London characters. I was always on late-night telly lit from below and Iain
Sinclair couldn't write a paragraph without dropping my
name at least once. I'm a quintessential Londoner, I am. I'm a
Cockney gentleman.

I read Israel Zangwill and Gerald Kersh and Alexander
Barron. I can tell you the best books of Pett Ridge and Arthur
Morrison. I know Pratface Charlie, Driff and Martin Stone,
Bernie Michaud and the even more legendary Gerry and Pat
Goldstein. They're all historians, archeologists, revenants.
There isn't another culture-dealer in London, oldster or child,
who doesn't at some time come to me for an opinion. Even
now, when I'm as popular as a pig at a Putney wedding and
people hold their noses and dive into traffic rather than have
to say hello to me, they still need me for that.

I've known all the famous Londoners or known someone
else who did. I can tell stories of long-dead gangsters who
made the Krays seem like Amnesty International. Bare-
knuckle boxing. Fighting the fascists in the East End. Gun-
battles with the police all over Stepney in the 1900s. The
terrifying girl gangsters of Whitechapel. Barricading the Old
Bill in his own barracks down in Notting Dale.

I can tell you where all the music halls were and what was
sung in them. And why. I can tell Marie Lloyd stories and
Max Miller stories that are fresh and sharp and bawdy as they
day they happened, because their wit and experience came out
of the market streets of London. The same streets. The same
markets. The same family names. London is markets. Markets
are London.

I'm a Londoner through and through. I know Mr. Gog personally. I know Ma Gog even more personally. During the day I can walk anywhere from Bow to Bayswater faster than any taxi. I love the markets. Brick Lane. Church Street. Portobello. You won't find me on a bike with my bum in the air on a winter's afternoon. I walk or drive. Nothing in between. I wear a camel-hair in winter and a Barraclough's in summer. You know what would happen to a coat like that on a bike.

I love the theater. I like modern dance, very good movies and ambitious international contemporary music. I like poetry, prose, painting and the decorative arts. I like the lot, the very best that London's got, the whole bloody casserole. I gobble it all up and bang on my bowl for more. Let timid greenbelters creep in at weekends and sink themselves in the West End's familiar deodorized shit if they want to. That's not my city. That's a tourist set. It's what I live off. What all of us show-people live off. It's the old, familiar circus. The big rotate.

We're selling what everybody recognizes. What makes them feel safe and certain and sure of every single moment in the city. Nothing to worry about in jolly old London. We sell charm and color by the yard. Whole word factories turn out new rhyming slang and saucy street characters are trained on council grants. Don't frighten the horses. Licensed pearlies pause for a photo-opportunity in the dockside Secure Zones. Without all that cheap scenery, without our myths and magical skills, without our whorish good cheer and instincts for trade—any kind of trade—we probably wouldn't have a living city.

As it is, the real city I live in has per square inch more creative energy at work at any given moment than anywhere else on the planet. But you'd never know it from a stroll up the Strand. It's almost all in those lively little sidestreets the English-speaking tourists can't help feeling a bit nervous about and which the French adore.

If you use music for comfortable escape you'd probably find more satisfying and cheaper relief in a massage parlor than at the umpteenth revival of *The Sound of Music*. I'd tell that to any hesitant punter who's not too sure. Check out the phone boxes for the ladies, I'd say, or you can go to the half-price ticket-booth in Leicester Square and pick up a ticket that'll deliver real value—Ibsen or Shakespeare, Shaw or Greenbank. Certainly you can fork out three hundred sheets for a fifty-sheet ticket that in a justly ordered world wouldn't be worth two pee and have your ears salved and your cradle rocked for two hours. Don't worry, I'd tell them, I make no judgments. Some hardworking whore profits, whatever you decide. So who's the cynic?

I went on one of those tours when my friends Dave and Di from Bury came up for the Festival of London in 2001 and it's amazing the crap they tell people. They put sex, violence and money into every story. They know fuck-all. They soup everything up. It's *Sun*-reader history. Even the Beefeaters at the Tower. Poppinsland. All that old English duff.

It makes you glad to get back to Soho.

Not so long ago you would usually find me in the Princess Louise, Berwick Street, at lunch time, a few doors down from the Chinese chippy and just across from Mrs. White's trim stall in Berwick Market. It's only a narrow door and is fairly easy to miss. It has one bottle-glass window onto the street. This is a public house which has not altered since the 1940s when it was very popular with Dylan Thomas, Mervyn Peake, Ruthven Todd, Henry Treece and a miscellaneous bunch of other Welsh adventurers who threatened for a while to take over English poetry from the Irish.

It's a shit pub, so dark and smoky you can hardly find your glass in front of your face, but the look of it keeps the tourists out. It's used by all the culture pros—from arty types with backpacks, who do specialized walking tours, to famous gallery owners and top museum management—and by the heavy metal bikers. We all get on a treat. We are mutually dependent in our continuing resistance to invasion or change, to the preservation of the best and most vital aspects of our culture. We leave them alone because they protect us from the tourists, who might recognize us and make us put on our masks in a hurry. They leave us alone because the police won't want to bother a bunch of well-connected middle-class wankers like us. It is a wonderful example of mutuality. In the back rooms, thanks to some freaky acoustics, you can talk easily above the music and hardly know it's there.

Over the years there have been some famous friendships and unions struck between the two groups. My own lady wife was known as Karla the She Goat in an earlier incarnation and had the most exquisite and elaborate tattoos I ever saw. She was a wonderful wife and would have made a perfect mother. She died on the A1, on the other side of Watford Gap. She had just found out she was pregnant and was making her last sentimental run. It did me in for marriage after that. And urban romance.

I first heard about London Bone in the Princess Lou when Claire Rood, that elegant old dyke from the Barbican, who'd tipped me off about my new tailor, pulled my ear to her mouth and asked me in words of solid gin and garlic to look out for some for her, darling. None of the usual faces seemed to know about it. A couple of top-level museum people knew a bit, but it was soon obvious they were hoping I'd fill them in on the details. I showed them a confident length of cuff. I told them to keep in touch.

I did my Friday walk, starting in the horrible pre-dawn chill of the Portobello Road where some youth tried to sell me a bit of scrimshawed reconstitute as "the real old Bone." I warmed myself in the showrooms of elegant Kensington and Chelsea dealers telling outrageous stories of deals, profits and crashes until they grew uncomfortable and wanted to talk about me and I got the message and left.

I wound up that evening in the urinal of The Dragoons in Meard Alley, swapping long-time-no-sees with my boyhood friend Bernie Michaud who begins immediately by telling me he's got a bit of business I might be interested in. And since it's Bernie Michaud telling me about it I listen. We settled down in a quiet corner of the pub. Bernie never deliberately spread a rumor in his life but he's always known how to make the best of one. This is kosher, he thinks. It has a bit of a glow. It smells like a winner. A long-distance runner. He is telling me out of friendship, but I'm not really interested. I'm trying to find out about London Bone.

"I'm not talking drugs, Ray, you know that. And it's not bent." Bernie's little pale face is serious. He takes a thoughtful sip of his whisky. "It is, admittedly, a commodity."

I wasn't interested. I hadn't dealt in goods for years. "Services only, Bernie," I said. "Remember. It's my rule. Who wants to get stuck paying rent on a warehouse full of yesterday's faves? I'm still trying to move those *Glenda Sings Michael Jackson* sides Pratface talked me into."

"What about investment?" he says. "This is the real business, Ray, believe me."

So I heard him out. It wouldn't be the first time Bernie had brought me back a nice profit on some deal I'd helped him bankroll and I was all right at the time. I'd just made the better part of a month's turnover on a package of theaterland's most profitable stinkers brokered for a party of filthy-rich New Muscovites who thought Chekhov was something you did with your lottery numbers.

As they absorbed the quintessence of Euro-ersatz, guaranteed to offer, as its high emotional moment, a long, relentless bowel movement, I would be converting their hard roubles back into beluga.

It's a turning world, the world of the international free market and everything's wonderful and cute and pretty and *magical* so long as you keep your place on the carousel. It's not good if it stops. And it's worse if you get thrown off altogether. Pray to Mammon that you never have to seek the help of an organization that calls you a "client." That puts you outside the fairground forever. No more rides. No more fun. No more life.

Bernie only did quality art, so I knew I could trust that side of his judgment, but what was it? A new batch of Raphaels turned up in a Willsden attic? Andy Warhol's lost landscapes found at the Pheasantry?

"There's American collectors frenzied for this stuff," murmurs Bernie through a haze of Sons of the Wind, Motorchair and Montecristo fumes. "And if it's decorated they go through the roof. All the big Swiss guys are looking for it. Freddy K in Cairo has a Saudi buyer who tops any price. Rose Sarkissian in Agadir represents three French collectors. It's never catalogued. It's all word of mouth. And it's already turning over millions. There's one inferior piece in New York and none at all in Paris. The pieces in Zurich are probably all fakes."

This made me feel that I was losing touch. I still didn't know what he was getting at.

"Listen," I say, "before we go any further, let's talk about this London Bone."

"You're a fly one, Ray," he says. "How did you suss it?"

"Tell me what you know," I say. "And then I'll fill you in."

We went out of the pub, bought some fish-and-chips at the Chinese and then walked up Berwick Street and round to his little club in D'Arblay Street where we sat down in his office and closed the door. The place stank of cat pee. He doted on his Persians. They were all out in the club at the moment, being petted by the patrons.

"First," he says, "I don't have to tell you, Ray, that this is strictly double-schtum and I will kill you if a syllable gets out."

"Naturally," I said.

"Have you ever seen any of this Bone?" he asked. He went to his cupboard and found some vinegar and salt. "Or better still, handled it?"

"No," I said. "Not unless it's fake scrimshaw."

"This stuff's got a depth to it you've never dreamed about. A luster. You can tell it's the real thing as soon as you see it. Not just the shapes or the decoration, but the quality of it. It's like it's got a soul. You could come close, but you could never fake it. Like amber, for instance. That's why the big collectors are after it. It's authentic, it's newly discovered, and it's rare."

"What bone is it?"

"Mastodon. Some people still call it mammoth ivory, but I haven't seen any actual ivory. It could be dinosaur. I don't know. Anyway, this bone is *better* than ivory. It's in weird shapes, probably fragments off some really big animal."

"And where's it coming from?"

"The heavy clay of good old London," says Bernie. "A fortune at our feet, Ray. And my people know where to dig."

TWO

I had to be straight with Bernie. Until I saw a piece of the stuff in my own hand and got an idea about it for myself, I couldn't do anything. The only time in my life I'd gone for a gold brick I'd bought it out of respect for the genius running the scam. He deserved what I gave him. Which was a bit less than he was hoping for. Rather than be conned, I would throw the money away. I'm like that with everything.

I had my instincts, I told Bernie. I had to go with them. He understood completely and we parted on good terms.

If the famous Lloyd Webber meltdown of '03 had happened a few months earlier or later I would never have thought again about going into the Bone business, but I was done in by one of those sudden changes of public taste which made the George M. Cohan crash of '31 seem like a run of *The Mousetrap*.

Sentimental fascism went out the window. Liberal-humanist contemporary relevance, artistic aspiration, intellectual and moral substance and all that stuff was somehow in demand. It was *better* than the sixties. It was one of those splendid moments when the public pulls itself together and tries to grow up. Jones's *Rhyme of the Flying Bomb* song cycle made a glorious comeback. *American Angels* returned with even more punch. And Sondheim made an incredible comeback.

He became a quality brand-name. If it wasn't by Sondheim or based on a tune Sondheim used to hum in the shower, the punters didn't want to know. Overnight, the public's product loyalty had changed. And I must admit it had changed for the better. But my investments were in *Cats,* and *Dogs* (Lord Webber's last desperate attempt to squeeze from Thurber what he sucked from Eliot), *Duce!* and *Starlight Excess,* all of which were now taking a walk down *Sunset Boulevard.* I couldn't even get a regular price ticket for myself at *Sunday in the Park, Assassins* or *Follies. Into the Woods* was solid for eighteen months ahead. I saw *Passion* from the wings and *Sweeney Todd* from the gods. *Five Guys Named Mo* crumbled to dust. *Phantom* closed. Its author claimed sabotage.

"Quality will out, Ray," says Bernie next time I see him at the Lou. "You've got to grant the public that. You just have to give it time."

"Fuck the public," I said, with some feeling. "They're just nostalgic for quality at the moment. Next year it'll be something else. Meanwhile I'm bloody ruined. You couldn't drum a couple of oncers on my entire stock. Even my ENO side-bets have died. Covent Garden's a disaster. The weather in Milan didn't help. That's where Cecilia Bartoli caught her cold. I was lucky to be offered half-price for the Rossinis without her. And I know what I'd do if I could get a varda at bloody Simon Rattle."

"So you won't be able to come in on the Bone deal?" said Bernie, returning to his own main point of interest.

"I said I was ruined," I told him, "not wiped out."

"Well, I got something to show you now, anyway," says Bernie.

We went back to his place.

He put it in my hand as if it were a nugget of plutonium, a knuckle of dark, golden Bone, split off from a larger piece, covered with tiny pictures.

"The engravings are always on that kind of Bone," he said. "There are other kinds that don't have drawings, maybe from a later date. It's the work of the first Londoners, I suppose, when it was still a swamp. About the time your Phoenician ancestors started getting into the upriver woad-trade. I don't know the significance, of course."

The Bone itself was hard to analyze because of the mixture of chemicals which has created it, and some of it had fused, suggesting prehistoric upheavals of some kind. The drawings were extremely primitive. Any bored person with a sharp object and minimum talent could have done them at any time in history. The larger, weirder-looking Bones, had no engravings.

Stick people pursued other stick people endlessly across the fragment. The work was unremarkable. The beauty really was in the tawny ivory color of the Bone alone. It glowed with a wealth of shades and drew you hypnotically into its depths. I imagined the huge animal of which this fragment had once been an active part. I saw the bellowing trunk, the vast ears, the glinting tusks succumbing suddenly to whatever had engulfed her. I saw her body swaying, her tail lashing as she trumpeted her defiance of her inevitable death. And now men sought her remains as treasure. It was a very romantic image and of course it would become my most sincere sales pitch.

"That's six million dollars you're holding there," said Bernie. "Minimum."

Bernie had caught me at the right time and I had to admit I was convinced. Back in his office he sketched out the agreement. We would go in on a fifty-fifty basis, funding the guys who would do the actual digging, who knew where the Bonefields were and who would tell us as soon as we showed serious interest. We would finance all the work, pay them an upfront earnest and then load by load in agreed increments. Bernie and I would split the net profit fifty-fifty. There were all kinds of clauses and provisions covering the various problems we foresaw, and then we had a deal.

The archeologists came round to my little place in Dolphin Square. They were a scruffy bunch of students from the University of Norbury who had discovered the Bone deposits on a run-of-the-mill field trip in a demolished Southwark housing estate and knew only that there might be a market for them. Recent cuts to their grants had made them desperate. Some lefty had come up with a law out of the Magna Carta, or whatever, saying public land couldn't be sold to private developers. Now there was a court case disputing the council's right to sell the estate to Livingstone International. This also put a stop to the planned rebuilding, so we had indefinite time to work.

The stoodies were grateful for our expertise, as well as our cash. I was happy enough with the situation. It was one I felt we could easily control. Middle-class burbnerds get greedy the same as anyone else, but they respond well to reason. I told them for a start-off that all the Bone had to come in to us. If any of it leaked onto the market by other means, we'd risk losing our prices and that would mean the scheme was over. Terminated, I said significantly. Since we had reputations as well as investments to protect there would also be recriminations. That's all I had to say. Since those V-serials kids think we're Krays and Mad Frankie Frasers just because we like to look smart and talk properly.

We were fairly sure we weren't doing anything obviously criminal. The stuff wasn't treasure trove. It had to be cleared before proper foundations could be poured. Quite evidently LI didn't think it was worth paying security staff to shut the site. We didn't know if digging shafts and tunnels was even trespass, but we knew we had a few weeks before someone started asking about us and by then we hoped to have the whole bloody mastodon out of the deep clay and nicely earning for us. The selling would take the real skill and that was my job. It was going to have to be played sharper than South African diamonds.

After that neither Bernie nor I had anything to do with the dig. We rented a guarded lockup in Clapham and paid the kids every time they brought in a substantial load of Bone. It was incredible stuff. Bernie thought that chemical action, some of it relatively recent, had caused the phenomenon. "Like chalk, you know. You hardly find it anywhere. Just a few places in England, France, China and Texas." The kids reported that there was more than one kind of animal down there, but that all the Bone had the same rich appearance. They had constructed a new tunnel, with a hidden entrance, so that even if the building site was blocked to them, they could still get at the Bone. It seemed to be a huge field, but most of the Bone was at roughly the same depth. Much of it had fused and had to be chipped out. They had found no end to it so far and they had tunneled through more than half an acre of the dense, dark clay.

Meanwhile I was in Amsterdam and Rio, Paris and Vienna and New York and Sydney. I was in Tokyo and Seoul and Hong Kong. I was in Riyadh, Cairo and Baghdad. I was in Kampala and New Benin, everywhere there were major punters. I racked up so many free airmiles in a couple of months that they were automatically jumping me to first class. But I achieved what I wanted. Nobody bought London Bone without checking with me. I was the acknowledged expert. The prime source, the best in the business. If you want Bone, said the art world, you want Gold.

The Serious Fraud Squad became interested in Bone for a

while, but they had been assuming we were faking it and gave up when it was obviously not rubbish.

Neither Bernie nor I expected it to last any longer than it did. By the time we drew a line under our first phase of selling, we were turning over so much dough it was silly and the kids were getting tired and were worrying about exploring some of their wildest dreams. There was almost nothing left, they said. So we closed down the operation, moved our warehouses a couple of times and then let the Bone sit there to make us some money while everyone wondered why it had dried up.

And at that moment, inevitably, and late as ever, the newspapers caught on to the story. There was a brief late-night TV piece. A few supplements talked about it in their arts pages. This led to some news stories and eventually it went to the tabloids and became anything you liked from the remains of Martians to a new kind of nuclear waste. Anyone who saw the real stuff was convinced but everyone had a theory about it. The real exclusive market was finished. We kept schtum. We were gearing up for the second phase. We got as far away from our stash as possible.

Of course a few faces tracked me down, but I denied any knowledge of the Bone. I was a middle-man, I said. I just had good contacts. Half-a-dozen people claimed to know where the Bone came from. Of course they talked to the papers. I sat back in satisfied security, watching the mud swirl over our tracks. Another couple of months and we'd be even safer than the house I'd bought in Hampstead overlooking the Heath. It had a rather forlorn garden the size of Kilburn which needed a lot of nurturing. That suited me. I was ready to retire to the country and a big indoor swimming pool.

By the time a close version of the true story came out, from one of the stoodies who'd lost all his share in a lottery syndicate, it was just one of many. It sounded too dull. I told newspaper reporters that while I would love to have been involved in such a lucrative scheme, my money came from theater tickets. Meanwhile, Bernie and I thought of our warehouse and said nothing.

Now the stuff was getting into the culture. It was chic. *Puncher* used it in their ads. It was called Mammoth Bone by the media. There was a common story about how a herd had wandered into the swampy river and drowned in the mud. Lots of pictures dusted off from the Natural History Museum. Experts explained the color, the depths, the markings, the beauty. Models sported a Bone motif.

Our second phase was to put a fair number of inferior fragments on the market and see how the public responded. That would help us find our popular price—the most a customer would pay. We were looking for a few good millionaires.

Frankly, as I told my partner, I was more than ready to get rid of the lot. But Bernie counseled me to patience. We had a plan and it made sense to stick to it.

The trade continued to run well for a while. As the sole source of the stuff, we could pretty much control everything. Then one Sunday lunchtime I met Bernie at The Six Jolly Dragoons in Meard Alley, Soho. He had something to show me, he said. He didn't even glance around. He put it on the bar in plain daylight. A small piece of Bone with the remains of decorations still on it.

"What about it?" I said.

"It's not ours," he said.

My first thought was that the stoodies had opened up the field again. That they had lied to us when they said it had run out.

"No," said Bernie, "it's not even the same color. It's the same stuff—but different shades. Gerry Goldstein lent it to me."

"Where did he get it?"

"He was offered it," he said.

We didn't bother to speculate where it had come from. But we did have rather a lot of our Bone to shift quickly. Against my will, I made another world tour and sold mostly to other dealers this time. It was a standard second-wave operation but run rather faster than was wise. We definitely missed the crest.

However, before deliveries were in and checks were cashed, Jack Merrywidow, the fighting MP for Brookgate and E. Holborn, gets up in the House of Commons during telly-time one afternoon and asks if Prime Minister Bland or any of his dope-dazed cabinet understand that human remains, taken from the hallowed burial grounds of London, are being sold by the piece in the international marketplace? Mr. Bland makes a plummy joke enjoyed at Mr. Merrywidow's expense and sits down. But Jack won't give up. Next week he's back on telly for the *Struggle of Parliament* interview. Jack's had the Bone examined by experts. It's human. Undoubtedly human. The strange shapes are caused by limbs melting together in soil heavy with lime. Chemical reactions, he says. We have—he raises his eyes to the camera—been mining mass graves.

A shock to all those who still long for the years of common decency. Someone, says Jack, is mining more than our heritage. Hasn't free market capitalism got a little bit out of touch when we start selling the arms, legs and skulls of our forebears? The torsos and shoulder-blades of our honorable dead? What did we use to call people who did that? When was the government going to stop this trade in corpses?

It's denied.

It's proved.

It looks like trade is about to slump.

I think of framing the checks as a reminder of the vagaries of fate and give up any idea of popping the question to my old muse Little Trudi, who is back on the market, having been dumped by her corporate suit in a fit, he's told her, of self-disgust after seeing *The Tolstoy Investment* with Eddie Izzard. Bernie, I tell my partner, the Bone business is down the drain. We might as well bin the stuff we've stockpiled.

Then two days later the TV news reports a vast public interest in London Bone. Some lordly old queen with four names comes on the evening news to say how by owning a piece of Bone, you own London's true history. You become a curator of some ancient ancestor. He's clearly got a vested interest in the stuff. It's the hottest tourist item since Jack the Ripper razors and OJ gloves. More people want to buy it than ever.

The only trouble is, I don't deal in dead people. It is, in fact, where I have always drawn the line. Even Pratface Charlie wouldn't sell his great-great-grandmother's elbow to some overweight Jap in a deerstalker and a kilt. I'm faced with a genuine moral dilemma.

I make a decision. I make a promise to myself. I can't go back on that. I go down to the Italian chippy in Fortess Road, stoke up on nourishing ritual grease (cod, roe, chips and mushy peas, bread and butter and tea, syrup pudding), then heave my out-of-shape, but mentally prepared, body up onto Parliament Hill to roll myself a big wacky-baccy fag and let my subconscious think the problem through.

When I emerge from my reverie, I have looked out over the whole misty London panorama and considered the city's complex history. I have thought about the number of dead buried there since, say, the time of Boadicea, and what they mean to the soil we build on, the food we still grow here and the air we breathe. We are recycling our ancestors all the time, one way or another. We are sucking them in and shitting them out. We're eating them. We're drinking them. We're coughing them up. The dead don't rest. Bits of them are permanently at work. So what am I doing wrong?

This thought is comforting until my moral sense, sharpening itself up after a long rest, kicks in with—but what's different here is you're flogging the stuff to people who take it home with them. Back to Wisconsin and California and Peking. You take it out of circulation. You're dissipating the deep fabric of the city. You're unraveling something. Like, the real infrastructure, the spiritual and physical bones of an ancient settlement . . .

On Kite Hill I suddenly realize that those bones are in some way the deep lifestuff of London.

It grows dark over the towers and roofs of the metropolis. I sit on my bench and roll myself up a further joint. I watch the silver rising from the river, the deep golden glow of the distant lights, the plush of the foliage, and as I watch it seems to shred before my eyes, like a rotten curtain. Even the traffic noise grows fainter. Is the city sick? Is she expiring? Somehow it seems there's a little less breath in the old girl. I blame myself. And Bernie. And those kids.

There and then, on the spot, I renounce all further interest in the Bone trade. If nobody else will take the relics back, then I will.

There's no resolve purer than that which you draw from a really good reefer.

THREE

So now there isn't a tourist in any London market or antique arcade who isn't searching out Bone. They know it isn't cheap. They know they have to pay. And pay they do. Through the nose. And half of what they buy is crap or fakes. This is a question of status, not authenticity. As long as we say it's good, they can say it's good. We give it a provenance, a story, something to color the tale to the folks back home. We're honest dealers. We sell only the authentic stuff. Still they get conned. But still they look. Still they buy.

Jealous Mancunians and Brummies long for a history old enough to provide them with Bone. A few of the early settlements, like Chester and York, start turning up something like it, but it's not the same. Jim Morrison's remains disappear from Pére La Chaise. They might be someone else's bones, anyway. Rumor is they were KFC bones. The revolutionary death-pits fail to deliver the goods. The French are furious. They accuse the British of gross materialism and poor taste. Oscar Wilde disappears. George Eliot. Winston Churchill. You name them. For a few months there is a grotesque trade in the remains of the famous. But the fashion has no intrinsic substance and fizzles out. Anyone could have seen it wouldn't run.

Bone has the image, because Bone really is beautiful.

Too many people are yearning for that Bone. The real stuff. It genuinely hurts me to disappoint them. Circumstances alter cases. Against my better judgment I continue in the business. I bend my principles, just for the duration. We have as much turnover as we had selling to the Swiss gnomes. It's the latest item on the *beento* list. "You *have* to bring me back some London Bone, Ethel, or I'll never forgive you!" It starts to appear in the American luxury catalogs.

But by now there are ratsniffers everywhere—from Trade and Industry, from the National Trust, from the Heritage Corp, from half-a-dozen South London councils, from the Special Branch, from the CID, the Inland Revenue and both the Funny and the Serious Fraud Squads.

Any busybody who ever wanted to put his head under someone else's bed is having a wonderful time. Having failed dramatically with the STOP THIS DISGUSTING TRADE approach, the tabloids switch to offering bits of Bone as prizes in circulation boosters. I sell a newspaper consortium a Tesco's plastic bagfull for two-and-a-half mill via a go-between. Bernie and I are getting almost frighteningly rich. I open some bank accounts offshore and I become an important anonymous shareholder in the Queen Elizabeth Hall when it's privatized.

It doesn't take long for the experts to come up with an analysis. Most of the Bone has been down there since the seventeenth century and earlier. They are the sites of the old plague pits where legend had it still-living bodies were thrown in with the dead. For a while it must have seemed like

Auschwitz-on-Thames. The chemical action of lime, partial burning, London clay and decaying flesh, together with the broadening spread of the London water-table, thanks to various engineering works over the last century, letting untreated sewage into the mix, had created our unique London Bone. As for the decorations, that, it was opined, was the work of the pit guards, working on earlier bones found on the same site.

"Blood, shit and bone," says Bernie. "It's what makes the world go round. That and money, of course."

"And love," I add. I'm doing all right these days. It's true what they say about a Roller. Little Trudi has enthusiastically rediscovered my attractions. She has her eye on a ring. I raise my glass. "And love, Bernie."

"Fuck that," says Bernie. "Not in my experience." He's buying Paul McCartney's old place in Wamering and having it converted for Persians. He has, it is true, also bought his wife her dream house. She doesn't seem to mind it's on the island of Las Cascadas about six miles off the coast of Morocco. She's at last agreed to divorce him. Apart from his mother, she's the only woman he ever had anything to do with and he isn't, he says, planning to try another. The only females he wants in his house in future come with a pedigree a mile long, have all their shots and can be bought at Harrods.

FOUR

I expect you heard what happened. The private Bonefields, which contractors were discovering all over South and West London, actually contained public bones. They were part of our national inheritance. They had living relatives. And stones, some of them. So it became a political and a moral issue. The Church got involved. The airwaves were crowded with concerned clergy. There was the problem of the self-named bone-miners. Kids, inspired by our leaders' rhetoric, and aspiring to imitate those great captains of free enterprise they had been taught to admire, were turning over ordinary graveyards, which they'd already stripped of their salable masonry, and digging up somewhat fresher stiffs than was seemly.

A bit too fresh. It was pointless. The Bone took centuries to get seasoned and so far nobody had been able to fake the process. A few of the older graveyards had small deposits of Bone in them. Brompton Cemetery had a surprising amount, for instance, and so did Highgate. This attracted prospectors. They used shovels mainly, but sometimes low explosives. The area around Karl Marx's monument looked like they'd refought the Russian Civil War over it. The barbed wire put in after the event hadn't helped. And as usual the public paid to clean up after private enterprise. Nobody in their right mind got buried any more. Cremation became very popular. The borough councils and their financial managers were happy because more valuable real estate wasn't being occupied by a non-consumer.

It didn't matter how many security guards were posted or, by one extreme Authority, land-mines: the teenies left no grave unturned. Bone was still a profitable item, even though the market had settled down since we started. They dug up Bernie's mother. They dug up my cousin Leonard. There wasn't a Londoner who didn't have some intimate unexpectedly back above ground. Every night you saw it on telly.

It had caught the public imagination. The media had never made much of the desecrated graveyards, the chiseled-off angels' heads and the uprooted headstones on sale in King's Road and the Boulevard St. Michel since the 1970s. These had been the targets of first-generation grave-robbers. Then there had seemed nothing left to steal. Even they had balked at doing the corpses. Besides, there wasn't a market. This second generation was making up for lost time, turning over the soil faster than an earthworm on E.

The news shots became clichés. The heaped earth, the

headstone, the smashed coffin, the hint of the contents, the leader of the Opposition coming on to say how all this has happened since his mirror image got elected. The councils argued that they should be given the authority to deal with the problem. They owned the graveyards. And also, they reasoned, the Bonefields. The profits from those fields should rightly go into the public purse. They could help pay for the Health Service. "Let the dead," went their favorite slogan, "pay for the living for a change."

What the local politicians actually meant was that they hoped to claim the land in the name of the public and then make the usual profits privatizing it. There was a principle at stake. They had to ensure their friends and not outsiders got the benefit.

The High Court eventually gave the judgment to the public, which really meant turning it over to some of the most rapacious borough councils in our history. In the 1980s, that Charlie Peace of elected bodies, the Westminster City Council, had tried to sell their old graveyards to new developers. This current judgment allowed all councils at last to maximize their assets from what was, after all, dead land, completely unable to pay for itself, and therefore a natural target for privatization. The feeding frenzy began. It was the closest thing to mass cannibalism I've ever seen.

We had opened a fronter in Old Sweden Street and had a couple of halfway presentable slags from Bernie's club taking the calls and answering inquiries. We were straight up about it. We called it *The City Bone Exchange*. The bloke who decorated it and did the sign specialized in giving offices that long-established look. He'd created most of those old-fashioned West End Hotels you'd never heard of until 1999. "If it's got a Scottish name," he used to say, "it's one of mine. Americans love the skirl of the pipes, but they trust a bit of brass and varnish best."

Our place was almost all brass and varnish. And it worked a treat. The Ritz and the Savoy sent us their best potential buyers. Incredibly exclusive private hotels gave us taxi-loads of bland-faced American boy-men, reeking of health and beauty products and bellowing their credentials to the wind, rich matrons eager for anyone's approval, massive Germans with aggressive cackles, stern orientals glaring at us, daring us to cheat them. They bought. And they bought. And they bought.

The snoopers kept on snooping but there wasn't really much to find out. Livingstone International took an aggressive interest in us for a while, but what could they do? We weren't up to anything illegal just selling the stuff and nobody could identify what if anything had been nicked anyway. I still had my misgivings. They weren't anything but superstitions, really. It did seem sometimes that for every layer of false antiquity, for every act of disneyfication, an inch or two of our real foundations crumbled. You knew what happened when you did that to a house. Sooner or later you got trouble. Sooner or later you had no house.

We had more than our share of private detectives for a while. They always pretended to be customers and they always looked wrong, even to our girls. Livingstone International had definitely made a connection. I think they'd found our mine and guessed what a windfall they'd lost. They didn't seem at one with themselves over the matter. They even made veiled threats. There was some swagger came in to talk about violence but they were spotties who'd got all their language off old nineties TV shows. So we sweated it out and the girls took most of the heat. Those girls really didn't know anything. They were magnificently ignorant. They had tellies with chips which switch channels as soon as they detect a news or information program.

I've always had a rule. If you're caught by the same wave twice, get out of the water.

While I didn't blame myself for not anticipating the Great Andrew Lloyd Webber Slump, I think I should have guessed what would happen next. The tolerance of the public for bullshit had become decidedly and aggressively negative. It was like the Bone had set new standards of public aspiration as well as beauty. My dad used to say that about the Blitz. Classical music enjoyed a huge success during the Second World War. Everybody grew up at once. The Bone made it happen again. It was a bit frightening to those of us who had always relied on a nice, passive, gullible, greedy punter for an income.

The bitter fights which had developed over graveyard and Bonefield rights and boundaries, the eagerness with which some borough councils exploited their new resource, the unseemly trade in what was, after all, human remains, the corporate involvement, the incredible profits, the hypocrisies and politics around the Bone brought us the outspoken disgust of Europe. We were used to that. In fact, we tended to cultivate it. But that wasn't the problem.

The problem was that our *own* public had had enough.

When the elections came round, the voters systematically booted out anyone who had supported the Bone trade. It was like the sudden rise of the anti-slavery vote in Lincoln's America. They demanded an end to the commerce in London Bone. They got the Boneshops closed down. They got work on the Bonefields stopped. They got their graveyards and monuments protected and cleaned up. They got a city which started cultivating peace and security as if it was a cash crop. Which maybe it was. But it hurt me.

It was the end of my easy money, of course. I'll admit I was glad it was stopping. It felt like they were slowing entropy, restoring the past. The quality of life improved. I began to think about letting a few rooms for company.

The mood of the country swung so far into disapproval of the Bone trade that I almost began to fear for my life. Road and anti-abortion activists switched their attention to Bone merchants. Hampstead was full of screaming lefties convinced they owned the moral highground just because they'd paid off their enormous mortgages. Trudi, after three months, applied for a divorce, arguing that she had not known my business when she married me. She said she was disgusted. She said I'd been living on blood-money. The courts awarded her more than half of what I'd made, but it didn't matter any more. My investments were such that I couldn't stop earning. Economically, I was a small oil-producing nation. I had my own international dialing code. It was horrible in a way. Unless I tried very hard, it looked like I could never be ruined again. There was no justice.

I met Bernie in *The King Lyar* in Old Sweden Street, a few doors down from our burned-out office. I told him what I planned to do and he shrugged.

"We both knew it was dodgy," he told me. "It was dodgy all along, even when we thought it was mastodons. What it feels like to me, Ray, is—it feels like a sort of a massive transformation of the *zeitgeist*—you know, like Virginia Woolf said about the day human nature changed—something happens slowly and you're not aware of it. Everything seems normal. Then you wake up one morning and—bingo!—it's Nazi Germany or Bolshevik Russia or Thatcherite England or the Golden Age—and all the rules have changed."

"Maybe it was the Bone that did it," I said. "Maybe it was a symbol everyone needed to rally round. You know. A focus."

"Maybe," he said. "Let me know when you're doing it. I'll give you a hand."

About a week later we got the van backed up to the warehouse loading bay. It was three o'clock in the morning and I was chilled to the marrow. Working in silence we transferred every scrap of Bone to the van. Then we drove back to Hampstead through a freezing rain.

I don't know why we did it the way we did it. There would have been easier solutions, I suppose. But behind the high walls of my big back garden, under the old trees and etiolated rhododendrons, we dug a pit and filled it with the glowing remains of the ancient dead.

The stuff was almost phosphorescent as we chucked the big lumps of clay back on to it. It glowed a rich amber and that faint, rosemary smell came off it. I can still smell it when I go in there to this day. My soft fruit is out of this world. The whole garden's doing wonderfully now.

In fact London's doing wonderfully. We seem to be back on form. There's still a bit of a bone trade, of course, but it's marginal.

Every so often I'm tempted to take a spade and turn over the earth again, to look at the fortune I'm hiding there. To look at the beauty of it. The strange amber glow never fades and sometimes I think the decoration on the Bone is an important message I should perhaps try to decipher.

I'm still a very rich man. Not justly so, but there it is. And, of course, I'm about as popular with the public as Percy the Pedophile. Gold the Bone King? I might as well be Gold the Grave Robber. I don't go down to Soho much. When I do make it to a show or something I try to disguise myself a bit. I don't see anything of Bernie any more and I heard two of the stoodies topped themselves.

I do my best to make amends. I'm circulating my profits as fast as I can. Talent's flooding into London from everywhere, making a powerful mix. They say they haven't known a buzz like it since 1967. I'm a reliable investor in great new shows. Every year I back the Iggy Pop Awards, the most prestigious in the business. But not everybody will take my money. I am regularly reviled. That's why some organizations receive anonymous donations. They would refuse them if they knew they were from me.

I've had the extremes of good and bad luck riding this particular switch in the zeitgeist and the only time I'm happy is when I wake up in the morning and I've forgotten who I am. It seems I share a common disgust for myself.

A few dubious customers, however, think I owe them something.

Another bloke, who used to be very rich before he made

some frenetic investments after his career went down the drain, called me the other day. He knew of my interest in the theater, that I had invested in several West End hits. He thought I'd be interested in his idea. He wanted to revive his first success, *Rebecca's Incredibly Far Out Well* or something, which he described as a powerful religious rock opera guaranteed to capture the new nostalgia market. The times, he told me, they were a-changin'. His show, he continued, was full of raw old-fashioned R&B energy. Just the sort of authentic sound to attract the new no-nonsense youngsters. Wasn't it cool that Madonna wanted to do the title role? And Bob Geldof would play the Spirit of the Well. *Rock and roll, man! It's all in the staging, man! Remember the boat in Phantom? I can make it look better than real. On stage, man, that well is W.E.T. WET! Rock and roll!* I could see that little wizened first punching the air in a parody of the vitality he craved and whose source had always eluded him.

I had to tell him it was a non-starter. I'd turned over a new leaf, I said. I was taking my ethics seriously.

These days I only deal in living talent.

Story Copyrights